Tales of the Fantastic and the Phantasmagoric

JOHN URBANCIK

This is a work of fiction. Similarities to persons, living or dead, are neither intended nor should be inferred.

ACKNOWLEDGMENTS

Tons of people have assisted me in some way over the years, and there's no way I could include or remember everyone who contributed to these particular stories. So here's a list of people likely to have been involved in some way: Mery-et Lescher, India Turner, Mom (Judy Urbancik); the other Five Horsemen (Brian Keene, Mike Oliveri, Michael T. Hyuck, Jr., and Geoff Cooper); Bad Moon Books (especially Roy Robbins and Liz Scott); Francesca (for the Portuguese); John Pierro (for the art originally with *House of Shadow and Ash*); Sabine and the Rose Fairy. I know I left people out. I apologize.

For Imaginarians Everywhere

CONTENTS

INTRODUCTION

Who is John Urbancik?

That's the purpose of an introduction, right? Introduce you to the author and the tales. Answer the oft-poised question: is that even a real word? (It is.) Explain why these particular stories.

Let's start with the easy question. Who is John Urbancik? I can say with some authority (because I'm writing this as if he's not me, when most certainly I am him) he is all the things it says on his business card: *Writer. Photographer. Adventurer. Man.*

The most important, obviously (no, not the last) is *Writer.* Otherwise, this wouldn't be a collection of his stories, but of his photographs, his travelogues, and manly accomplishments. First and foremost, before all other things, he is a word slinger, a phraseologist, a storyteller, a metaphorist, a wordsmith, a fantasist, a dreamer, an imaginarian, a tale master, a black belt in the stylographic arts, and an able liar. Then he can be all those other things, and maybe one or two others besides.

The nine novellas (stories too long to be considered short and too short to be considered novels) include five previously published but rare tales from the past decade. The other four are new, never before seen, the results of a novella-writing project he took in 2012. *(Note: the electronic version of this collection only has eight novellas.)*

In front of each is a vignette (which may be a misnomer; let's just say short shorts), a mix of previously seen and unseen. A break between the longer pieces, they are not always meant to be complete stories but to be ideas, hints, and suggestions of something more than they are.

There's a selection from two sets of *6 Nights of Midnight*, tiny things set in the City of Night (also the setting for novellas *Beneath Midnight* and *Madmen, Poets & Thieves*, both of which are included herein, and the novel *Once Upon a Time in Midnight*, which is not).

There's also a profile of the author. That's different from an introduction like this.

Each novella has its own afterword to tell you something about the piece (maybe its history, publication or otherwise; maybe how it came to be written; maybe something heretofore secret and unknown and hidden).

Tales of the Fantastic and the Phantasmagoric is meant to highlight the genres in which the author plays: fantasy, dark fantasy, and horror— or, as he sometimes likes to put it, fairy tales and ghost stories. The title is unique, but its form was borrowed from Edgar Allan Poe's *Tales of the Grotesque and Arabesque*, and also meant to tap into the ideas of classic pulp magazines (*Amazing Stories, Weird Tales, Astonishing Stories, Fantastic Adventures*, etc.).

I hope you enjoy this collection of the Fantastic and the Phantasmagoric. And then I hope you go on-line, find the author (tell him I sent you), and tell him something secret, unknown, and hidden.

THE
STORY

THE
STORY

It begins with blood and screaming. It ends with death. All the stuff in the middle is filler.

Madmen

Poets

&

Thieves

Madame & Thieves

Ah, but of course I remember the sun. I wasn't born in this horrible dark place, and believe me, I'll be elsewhere when I die. So yes, I remember the sun, and I remember sunrise over the ocean, so when a woman such as she walks into a room, wearing a dress the color of an ocean sunrise, with eyes like a twilight sky and hair like spider webs in moonlight—believe me, I know a mystery when I see one, and she, whoever she may be, whatever else she may claim, is one hundred percent mystery. I immediately know I must see her again, speak with her without restraint, unlock her passions and lose myself in her poisons. I'd known other women, a great many, I daresay, but the moment this mystery entered the room wearing an ocean sunrise, I forgot the names of all of them.

In fact, I can think of nothing and no one else, and can't recall why I'd been in the room in the first place, nor who else might be here. It could as easily have been a prison or a dancehall, though of course it's something bland, a restaurant, filled with a wait staff dressed quite casually. I should be surrounded by tuxedoes and capes and men with pocket watches, and certainly the woman wrapped in an ocean sunrise deserves nothing less. I gather my courage and wits from the darkest crevices within my very soul and, quite daringly, I stride across the big room and sit in the chair opposite her.

She sits alone. Such are the depths of her mystery, that she should ever be forced to dine alone except by choice. She looks at me with eyes like weapons and asks, "Do I know you?"

"Absolutely, I wish that was true," I say. "Would you allow me the chance to change the answer to an unambivalent yes?"

She does a great many things in response. She taps a perfectly painted fingernail on the edge of the table one time. Twice, she blinks, once perhaps to find meaning in my words and once more to find words to fit her meaning. She glances away, fleetingly, searching for some hidden camera or jokester or thief, but she cannot keep her eyes away.

I know it will be up to me to get this conversation started, so I say, "My name is Derek Smith, which may perhaps not sound like the most descriptive of names, except that I am, indeed, a smithy of a type. What would you prefer I call you?"

She graces me, then, with a smile, and says, "Angeline."

"Wonderful," I say. "I love a name with multiple syllables. You can change the meaning merely by adjusting your inflection and emphasis. Your mother, I believe, did you the greatest service by giving you such a wondrous name."

"You're trying my patience," she says.

Until that moment, I'd forgotten where we were. This is not my living room, or the concourse outside an opera house; this is a restaurant, and two waiters have arrived to take her order. More precisely, one has arrived to inquire if there was anything he could get her, and the other has come to be on hand should the thing she require be my removal.

"My apologies, then," I say, standing, still overcome by the ocean sunrise. "I must have mistaken you for a lover I lost in a dream." I do not, cannot, wait for a response. I flee. I go back to my table, where I take my coat and leave some coins, finish my whiskey in a single shot, and then, only after all that, I flee the restaurant.

Of course, I cannot go far. The gravity of the woman wrapped in an ocean sunrise is far too great a force to resist. I find a place to stand, where I can support my shoulders against bricks older than my bones, and think about the great poems I will write as I uncover each layer of mystery. I look up to the moon and implore her, the goddess within her or the very rock in the sky, I know not. I beg for the right words. I fear I may have already blundered, or at least put myself at a great disadvantage. I must learn to pace myself, or to think before I act, but then I wouldn't be who I am and what would be the fun in that?

Time means nothing to me. It flows and ebbs and turns back upon itself at its whim, not mine. In this City of Night, it is always nighttime, even when it is noon, so you cannot convince me to trust in a clock or a watch or a timekeeper of any sort. When the appointed hour arrives, you might say, the mystery wrapped in an ocean sunrise emerges from the restaurant, sees me in my spot across the street, and strides straight toward me. She smiles, but not in some grandiose way; it's without promise or conviction. When she's still several paces away but has captured my gaze, she says, "You waited for me." It isn't a question, so I give no answer. "You're mad."

"I might be," I admit, "but I blame you."

"You don't know the first thing about me," she says.

"I know your mother named you Angeline," I says. "I know you dined alone, though I cannot fathom why. I could have sat across from you and admired you from close up, rather than from afar."

She looks over her shoulder. "You can't see inside the restaurant from here," she says.

"But I see the memory of you perfectly fine," I say, tapping my head beside my eye. "Isn't that worth something?"

"No," she says.

"It's worth something to me," I tell her.

"You're wrong," she says. "It's nothing. It's less than nothing. It's *sad*, is what it is."

"Sad, then," I say, "is still more than nothing."

"Have you got any money?" she asks.

"As much as I need."

"Excellent," she says. "Buy me a drink."

* * *

Never let anyone buy you a drink. You make that kind of deal, you want to be sure of the terms. You have to get what's best for you. When you allow someone to buy your drink, you're admitting they own you, or a piece of you, even if only for a little while. It could be the last little while you've got.

But when someone offers to let you buy them a drink, that's something different. That's something deeper and far more meaningful. This is no quick exchange, no tit for tat, no shallow affair. This isn't the end of the negotiations. You're in for the long haul and the hard sell and, believe me, one hell of a runaround. You're about to have your world twisted, distorted, and deranged.

So when she commands it, when she states it like you've got no choice, and it's absolutely true that you don't, there's no room for negotiation. There's only one question: in or out? This is the point in the game where the rules have already been defined, but maybe not yet revealed; this is where you put yourself, with full intention and purpose and desire and not necessarily an ounce of wisdom; this is how you suffer. And trust me, you will suffer.

I'm in. Of course I'm in. I started this, I'm going to finish it. I'm no longer sure of the playing field. This isn't the game I thought it was. Suddenly, I'm in danger, and I've always had a problem understanding danger. Always seems so shallow, don't you think?

There's one thing about bars; they are all the same. You rotate the bartenders and the staff, change out the cheap black and white flyers advertising one kind of atonal band for another, you end up with the same cheap bourbon and a fleshy crowd of lust-addled kids desperate to shred their childhoods. They hide under neon lights and mirrors and fancy names. I tell Angeline I know a place without pretense, where the sign only says *The Bar*, at the end of Whiskey Road. It's a short road, but it lives up to its name. It provides only one bar, but it is probably the dirtiest, grittiest, most realistic bar in this or any other city. They've changed it. New ownership, apparently. I don't remember the bartender, but they're interchangeable, so what does that matter? I order two double shots of bourbon with whiskey chasers. Angeline smiles, raises her glass in a toast, and throws it back like a pro.

"Two more," she tells the bartender.

I give her my best smile. I don't give that away very often. I say, "I like you."

She says, "I know."

We take our second set of drinks to a dark booth near the window. I ignore my reflection. Never liked the way he mocks me. All white teeth and glittering eyes, and always, always one day further from his last shave than me.

"You haven't got a lot of time," she tells me.

"Time," I say, "is meaningless here. We're in Midnight." The city's named for a time, and it's always nighttime, except when the sky goes blood red for dawn and dusk. I don't bother to tell her these things; she knows.

But she says, "I decide when and if and where."

Before she gets too far, I say, "I decide how and why."

She flashes her teeth at me. "Fair enough." She finishes another drink and asks, "What do you want to know?"

"Anything," I tell her. "Everything. I want to know what makes you sing in the shower. I want to know when you stole your first lollipop. I want to know where you're from and where you're going and why. More than anything else, I want to know why." I run away with it. I'm not restricting my answer to the things I want to know about her. Life's too short for limitations. "I want to know where to catch the bus in Bermuda, and where it will take us."

"We'll never get to Bermuda," she tells me.

I laugh. "I don't care."

"And if I lie to you?" she asks.

"Then I'll be encouraged."

"And if I tell you only truths?"

"I'll be encouraged," I say.

She leans closer and narrows her eyes to deliver a line that hurts. "And if I turn you away?"

I don't answer immediately, but I am at least honest. "Then I go away."

"That's all it would take?"

"I might ask you to reconsider," I say.

"And why should I do such a thing?"

I lean back. There is no question like *why*. Answers need not be complete, nor straight, nor comprehensible. In real life, the best answer, the only answer, is *why not?* But you have to weigh the situation. This is not the time for such an answer. She wants me to work, and she wants to work herself, but she doesn't want some pop psych response anyone can parrot. I say, "I'll write you a poem."

"I don't need another poem."

"It's not strictly about need," I tell her.

She licks her lips. She's the predator here. I never had a chance. "Show me."

* * *

We make love like fireworks, vibrantly, raucously, with a full orchestra and a drunken, cheering crowd on both sides of the river. There's no river in Midnight, and no crowd in my living room, and no sounds we don't make. She's delicious and energetic and insatiable and completely unleashed. By the time it's over, I'm out of breath, we're coated with sweat, and we need whiskey to calm ourselves. I always have a bottle or five in the kitchen.

She thumbs through the books on my shelves. She learns everything about me. She whispers promises we both know she'll never keep.

"The moon and the stars," she tells me.

But I don't want the moon.

* * *

We sleep late on the living room floor. When I wake, I leave her sleeping, naked and beautiful, to get my notepad. I scribble words that make no sense. I find it hard to compose. I craft something short but inexpressive. I find expression and sensation, but it's verbose and unfocused. In total, I find maybe two good words, two excellent and pliable words, but they're useless on their own so I rip out all of this morning's pages and crumple them into a ball.

From the floor, Angeline says, "No."

I shake my head. "It's a failed attempt," I tell her.

"What, can I not know your failures?"

I hand over the paper. She unrolls the pages, reads them thoroughly and thoughtfully. She flips through them, rearranges in her own head the things I've failed to write, plays with my words and phrases and emotions, and finally nods. "You're right. This is crap." She crushes it and tosses it aside. The street light through the window hits her just right, highlighting the arc of her neck, her jawline, her cheekbone. I want to make poetry. Or love.

This doesn't happen to me every day.

* * *

There's a place for poets and wordsmiths and rhymers and tale tellers. It's always smoky, and it's always dark, except on stage in the spotlight. It never closes, and the floor is always open, so you can bring your tambourine and sing anytime you want. I listen a lot. I'm always looking for a word to steal. There's got to be one perfect word. I've never run across it. I've used fantastic words. I've bent phrases into useful and implausible shapes. But I've never found perfection. I know why. It's not just the voice in which you write, but the voice by which you read, recite, serenade. The real problem is, you can only discover perfection through failure.

I sit in my corner with a line of empty shot glasses in front of me. They can't all be mine. A girl with long, thin hair and hollow eyes, speaking softly into the microphone, tries to tell me about lost loves and lost souls and lost ways. She hasn't ever lost her way. She's all of nineteen and thinks she's seen the world. She's never even seen the sun.

No one in Midnight will ever see the sun.

She's dull, but patient, which cannot possibly be a good combination. She wants to cry up there, but she doesn't dare ruin her makeup. Her words haven't got the depth. I know when she's finished because there's a quick round of lackluster applause.

The waitress brings me another shot glass. God, I love that woman. She keeps me in line, and in fluidity. She throws me a wink when she thinks she can get away with it. She thinks she's safe with me. She's not. She's just smarter than me, is all. I say thanks, and she calls me something condescending like hon or slick or pal. I know she doesn't mean it.

The girl sits across from me. I feel like I might fall into those hollow eyes. I try to lean back without being offensive. I'm not afraid of being offensive. I'm afraid of losing my balance. She says, "You didn't like it."

"What's not to like?" I ask.

"Everyone else, they tell me how beautiful my poems are."

"They lie."

"I know."

I smile. "Buy me a drink?"

She does. She buys for the two of us. She says, "I need you."

"No, you don't," I tell her.

"My poems need you."

"Your poems need life," I tell her. "Live."

"I can't."

"Why not?"

"I'm afraid."

"Good. Be afraid," I say. "There's lots to fear. Life can suck sometimes. It's okay. It gives you strength. Be afraid, but do it anyway."

"I've never seen you up there," she tells me.

I smile. I shrug. I say, "I have nothing to say."

"I don't believe you."

"You shouldn't," I tell her. "I lie."

"You're playing with me," she says.

"You tell me you need me, and then say I'm playing with you? What makes you think I've got anything to give you. What makes you think I know what I'm talking about?"

"You don't know a thing," she says. She's not mean about it. "I just need you to tell me when I'm going in the wrong direction."

"Fine," I say. "You're going in the wrong direction."

"And to point me in the right."

"Ah." I nod. I drink my drink. "That's the trick, isn't it?"

"I need to know if I'm real," she tells me. She's pleading. She's begging. She's reaching across the table and gripping both my wrists tightly enough to leave bruises. I don't remember losing my hands to her. I'll have to give her extra points for that.

"What's your name?" I ask.

"Ivy."

"Given, or chosen?" I ask.

She doesn't know how to smile. She's sad, but she's bored with sad. She says, "Given and chosen."

I say, "It's a good name."

* * *

Later, in my living room, entangled with Angeline the way we should be entangled, blissfully happy, I say, "She wants me to teach her."

"About poetry?"

"About life."

Angeline grins at me in the dark. She traces her perfectly red fingernail down my chest, forging a new rivulet in a map to nowhere. "I don't think you know the difference."

"I did," I admit. "Once."

"You think that matters?"

I shake my head. It's hard to concentrate when Angeline's lips are so close. I feel the breath of every word on my neck. I'm intoxicated by her. I ask, "Are you jealous?"

"I don't own jealousy, "she says. "I own you."

* * *

I don't hear voices. I don't read secret messages off the sides of cereal boxes. I don't believe in gypsy magic any more than you do. So if an omen presents itself to me all wrapped in frilly ribbons and bows, I'll rip apart the paper like an eager, greedy Christmas child. But I might not see past the shiny bells. I might hear nothing but whistles. If there's some mystical talent for foresight, I do not have it. I sometimes have trouble with hindsight, which is less remarkable by far yet equally as impressive. It all comes down to patterns, doesn't it? And some patterns, let's face it, make your eyes hurt.

I've been owned before, in a variety of ways. There are numerous meanings to the word. I've been beaten, defeated, bought, sold, bartered, lied to, and on both the giving and receiving end of confessions. I have faults. I have failings. I have perfect recall of the present, and I remember names better than most. Names are, after all, extremely important. Ask any magician, even the ones who lie. Especially the ones who lie; I dare you to find any other type.

So when Ivy says, "I didn't see it coming," I have to admit, neither did I.

It, in this case, is the kid on the stage, the one who's got words pouring out of his mouth like showers of emeralds and diamonds. I like sharp words. I should use more. I scribble some of his into my notepad. I say nothing to Ivy. She sits too close to me, on the same side of the table, close enough to press her right arm to my left, which I don't need it except to hold down the notepad. And she's buying the drinks.

The words in my notepad are meaningless jumbles of mismatched syllables, broken phrases, crooked thoughts, and empty revelations. The kid talks fast. I can't keep up. More than once, he steals entire lines from other languages. I'm crying. My hand aches from the ferocity. Ivy lays her head on my shoulder; I don't know who she's trying to comfort. I can't shrug her off. Everyone thinks she's mine and I'm hers. It might be true, in a way. But no one, not even Ivy, knows about my secret love.

The kid's got short hair and wide eyes. He's got a glass of whiskey in his hand, but I haven't seen him lift it. He's reciting his words from memory, or he's making them up on the spot. If he's that good, I should book the Suicide Penthouse at the Midnight Towers and take a dive. He's got his eyes closed, and his lips are like angel's lips, so I've got several layers of jealousy crashing around inside. I've never looked as delectable as he must. I can't see him in that way, but I can see how he can be seen. I'm not blind.

"I had no idea," Ivy says.

"Shut up and listen." Maybe I'm a little harsh, but that's what she wants from me—what she needs from me. That's why she's hanging on me like the last leaf on a winter oak. She won't let go, but one strong wind might knock her away.

The kid is one mighty strong wind.

"What's his name?" I ask.

Ivy says, "Evan."

Evan. Damn. That's a nice name. No hard consonants like Derek. It flows off the tongue. Another reason to hate him.

Ivy sighs next to my ear. Her hand clutches my thigh. When did that happen? I never noticed before. She likes what she hears. It's exciting.

She's taking it out on me. There's no way this will end well.

Eventually, the kid leaves the stage, as all prodigies must. He disappears into the dark, probably kidnapped by groupies or cultists or gypsies or freaks. I keep wasting ink in my notepad. I keep wasting words and pages and ideas. I have good ideas. I have horrible execution.

What's the deciding factor? What makes the kid such a force on that stage? Is it his damn lips? His throat? The words he extracts from his intestines?

"I want to write a poem," Ivy whispers. I look into her brown, beseeching eyes. I slide my notepad across the table and offer my pen. She takes it, she kisses the side of my mouth as a thank you, and she does a bit of scribbling of her own.

She bites the side of her lip as she writes, sucks it into her mouth like she's drawing words from flesh. She concentrates so hard on the paper, there should be lasers. There should be tiny black smoking holes on the paper. She twirls her fragile, thin hair with the hand that doesn't write, a nervous gesture that accomplishes nothing, a repetitive motion to keep her occupied. It's unconscious, constant movement like that that keeps her so skinny.

She doesn't scribble, doesn't spew ink like vomit onto the page. She writes tiny and tight, and when she crosses something out it's with a single, elegant line through the middle. She wields the pen like a dagger, like a weapon sprung in the dark, in close range, slid beneath the ribs when your victim thought it was all posturing and empty threats. I see a word or two that I like, and say so. She smiles but otherwise ignores me, as she should. I can't teach her anything. I don't know what she expects.

No one's on the stage. It's quiet, except for the drinking and the smoking and the under-the-breath chatter that always fills this place. Ivy adjusts the microphone to the right height, then calmly, shyly, reads the words she's written. They're good words, but they're not great, and she doesn't know enough about inflection to embolden what she's written. There's some random clapping when she's done. I smile. I always smile. I like smiling almost as much as grinning; but they're not the same thing.

"Nice," I say.

"You lie."

"No. But I don't tell the complete truth."

"What was I missing?"

"Tone," I say. "Inflection. Meaning. It wasn't about you."

"Should it be?"

"Even when it's not, yes."

She crowds in next to me, asks my goddess of a waitress for another round of whiskey, and says, "What would I do without you?" She overvalues me. I've given her nothing. I have nothing to give.

* * *

I visit my father's grave. I can't see the actual burial plot. It's in another city. You can't get there from here. But there's a big cemetery next to the Mirage, that big green park, all those trees growing without the aid of sunlight. I'll never understand. My father's grave, back home, is an anonymous, nearly blank piece of granite, a hole in which his bones slowly become ash and dust. So in this Mirage cemetery, I long ago chose an anonymous, nearly blank slate and named it my father's. He either hears me or he doesn't, wherever I go.

I talk to my father a lot. Makes up for the times we didn't talk when he was alive. I start the way I always start. "I wish I had something to say."

He speaks to me through a crow that alights upon the tomb. "You've never had something to say."

The crow is black and small. It looks at me with one eye at a time. It preens. It listens.

"Why do you always have to use a crow?" The crow, my father, doesn't answer. Why should he? It's too obvious. "I met a girl." Silence. "She's like me. Adventurous."

"Self destructive?" the crow asks.

"No."

"Then not like you."

"I didn't have to be this way," I tell the crow, my father. "I'm actually quite happy."

"You've never been happy."

"You're not happy unless I'm not happy."

The crow bristles, adjusts its wings, looks at me with the other eye. My shadow doesn't fall across my father's stand-in grave. There are no shadows in a City of Night. It's all shadows here.

I tell my father, "We weren't done. You didn't have to die."

The crow flies away. Damn crow. I cross myself, mutter some prayer

I don't really remember from Catholic school, then leave. I wipe my
eyes with the back of my fist. I never learn anything from my father. I
never learn.

* * *

"Roses?" Angeline asks.

We're walking. The park is cold and silent and empty. The paved
path winds aimlessly and randomly. There's a cart selling caramel
apples, candied apples, oversized pretzels. There's another cart selling
roses. Red, pink, white, yellow, orange. A whole range, all in bloom, all
challenging me to make a move.

It's a precarious situation. I can't read Angeline's tone. She's
surprised. Anxious. Anxious that I'll buy her a rose, or that I won't? I buy
two, one red, one white. I give the red one to Angeline.

"This is dangerous," she tells me.

"What isn't?"

"What do you want?" she asks.

It's another open ended question. She might have a specific answer
in mind. I don't know it. I say, "I want the moon to shine more brightly
at night. I want the sun to crest over the top of that mountain and laugh
at us. I want sand and coconuts."

"Don't go predictable on me," she says.

"I want world peace," I tell her. "I want all the reins to all the horses
of all the kings. I want wooden puppets and chocolate drops and vivid,
sweet oranges that drip their juices down my hand and wrist and
forearm when I tear them open. I want poetic armaments with which I
can vanquish my enemies."

"You have no enemies," she tells me.

I look her in the eye. I challenge her to hold my gaze. I say, with my
eyes, which can say a great many things at once, that I love her and need
her and want her, that I fear her and will reject her, that I cannot give
her what she wants, that she doesn't know what she wants at all, that the
city is only as stale as its residents who are its lifeblood and its cancer
both. I tell her, with my eyes, that she knows nothing about me. With
my voice, with my softest whisper, I admit, "I have enemies."

Then I ask, more loudly, to prove what's been said is now behind us,
"Would you like to know a secret?"

"I know many secrets," she tells me.

"Would you like one of mine?"

She blinks. She's met my gaze, she's met my challenge, she's won my game. She says, "Yes."

"I know where there's a window that can take us away from here. It's a high window, a tall window, narrow and fragile and frightening, but it's not a window, precisely, in that it's a doorway. And it's not a doorway, precisely, in that it's a mirror. And it's not a mirror, not at all, though it is in every way that matters and many ways that don't. This mirror, this window, this doorway, can lead us home again."

She reveals another secret. "You can always go home."

That's when my father, the crow, laughs. I didn't even see him until then. He takes off, leaves his lamppost, leaves me there on the dark, dirty streets, abandons me once again to wolves and tigers and myself.

* * *

I give the white rose to Ivy. It might take her a while to understand. I may be part of her past by then, or she part of mine. Smoke curls around the poets trudging to the stage, one at a time, a line of them drunk on whiskey or relaxed by scarlet. I tried one of those little red pills alone in my living room. I woke up in an office with a day job, a retirement plan, a boss who liked me, a co-worker who despised me, and a coffee mug. It was the strangest thing. I found myself surrounded by blue tinted cubicle walls with a spreadsheet and less than half a clue. They gave me a paycheck. I lost three months. Never trust a drug that puts you out of your head for three months.

They recite or read or rearrange words they found or borrowed or stole. Ivy takes notes. She still sits too close. She likes me. She thinks I can offer insight and critical analysis and profundity.

I scribble in my notepad. It's tactile. The scratch of pen on paper, the sweet aroma of creative ambition wafting amid the cigarette smoke and cloves and vanilla perfumes and various spices combine to lead me down well-trodden paths. But there's a turnoff, there, maybe, or here, or right beside me.

Ivy lights a cigarette. She has a Zippo lighter she got from a pawn shop near Whiskey Road. She wrote a poem about it. I don't know why. She started smoking a week or a month ago because she thinks the ash will help her concentrate. She thinks it makes her look good. Rings of smoke rise from her fingers, and tendrils seep through her nostrils and eyes. She squints now. Did she always squint? She asks, "Have you ever written a perfect poem?"

"No one can write a perfect poem," I tell her.

"That's not true."

"Of course it's true. It's the truest thing I've ever said."

She's shaking her head. "I can't believe that."

"There's no such thing."

I'm shattering the walls of her foundation. She refuses to listen, so I sneak in more deeply. "You can write a poem that's perfect for you, and perfect for the moment, and perfect for the image, but how can it possibly be perfect for someone else who's never experienced that moment, who's not been inside your flesh and mind? You can make me know, but you can't make me change. A perfect poem would do that. A perfect poem would be perfect for everyone all the time in every way."

"That's too much," she says.

"Aiming for perfection is a madman's game," I tell her.

"You have to help me."

"You have to help you."

"I can't."

"Then I can't."

"You can't?" she asks. "Or you won't?"

The waitress saves me. She's a godsend. She's an angel. She brings fresh glasses. The line in front of me seems thin. I frown. I frown in an exaggerated way. The waitress touches my shoulder as she walks away, whispers a promise most fluid. I think she owns the place. I think she's a failed wordsmith. I think she knows the things Ivy thinks I know. I think her name is Ann, but it's not.

Ivy's still looking at me. She actually expects an answer. She's got that cigarette in one hand, the white rose in the other, squeezing both so tightly she's dropping ash on the table and the thorns bite the insides of her closed fist. Blooddrops run down her wrist, her arm, hit the leg of my jeans one at a time.

Her eyes reveal nothing and everything. She hasn't found herself yet. She thinks she will turn a corner and discover the self she's always known lived inside her. But you don't find yourself; you build yourself. And her foundation, we already know, is fragile and hollow as her eyes. She searches for answers in mine.

"We have to get out of here," I tell her.

Air is a wonderful thing. From the rooftops, we look down like gods on a throbbing city in constant upheaval. The mountains still rise above, but the buildings plunge deep into the earth, deeper than we can see, and their tendrils, their alleys and lanes and apartments and courtyards, stretch outward and inward, into the hearts of the mountains, to the very edge of the forest.

Outside, beyond the walls and the edges, even the forests are constant activity, signs of motion ebbing this way and that, the self-proclaimed gypsies and sinners and thieves, the righteous and the exiled, moving in and out of the city as if boundaries don't exist.

I lean over the edge and look down. Ivy pulls me back. "I can't lose you," she says. "I have too much to learn."

I grin. "You can't lose me," I say. Gravity will never have her way with me. Nor light. I'm on the edge of shadow, and I cannot fall. She hasn't learned anything.

"I'm afraid," she says.

"Fear inhibits," I say. "Or it emboldens. Which does it do to you?"

Meekly, she admits, "It inhibits."

"Don't let it."

"How do I not?"

I tell her stories about the Monkey Man, living on the rooftops, hopping from here to there, never touching the ground, feeding off the birds, drinking the rain. I tell her about the Bird Man, living on the rooftops, flitting from there to here, never going inside, scavenging for food, drinking the rain. I tell her about the spiders and the snakes and the whippoorwill I've never seen but hear all the time. The crow, my father, perches on an antennae; I don't tell her about him.

I'm telling her about the Shadow Man, living under the streets, sneaking from here to there, never surfacing, scavenging and killing and thieving and hiding, tapping into the underground pipes so he can drink our water, when it becomes apparent she's not my only audience. There's also the crow, my father, silently judging and finding me failing. But there's another, a shape, a shadow, not the Shadow Man because we're too high above the ground, yet someone I recognize. Someone I should recognize. Someone I should, perhaps, fear.

I've been the Monkey Man and the Bird Man and the Shadow Man. I've soared above the city where the clouds go red at the change between night and day. I've prowled the alleys. I've breathed stagnant air in underground tunnels no man has seen in a hundred years or more. I've saved and slain. I've prayed. I've listened at the feet of the Wandering Reverend and discerned the truths from the lies. I've practiced the blackest of magic. I've told the worst of lies, and also the greatest. I've killed a man with the pen in my pocket. He deserved it. I'd do it again. But I've never known fear, never understood the dark or the heights. I've winked at death because everyone winks at death, you can't get away from winking at death, it's a thing death requires and demands, and though I may be a great many things I'm not so foolish as to ignore death's wishes.

I stare at the man in the shadows, the man on the rooftop. I stare until Ivy stares.

He steps out of the darker shadow and into the lighter shadow. This City of Night provides nothing but shadows. The crow, my father, positions himself for a better view.

"Your words," the man says, holding out a hand, asking for more.

"I gave them to her, not to you."

He grins. "I admit, I stole the gist of them. I'm sorry."

"You're apologizing?"

"I am."

"No one apologizes," I say. "That can't be sincere." Yet it seems like it is.

"My name's Robin," the man says. He's not moving anymore. I don't think he's looked at Ivy even once. "Rob, if you prefer."

"What do you prefer?" I ask.

He grins. He grins like I grin. I like that. Now I understand fear. He says, "I don't."

"Derek," I admit. "Derek Smith."

He tilts his head. "Ah," he says. "The poet," he says. "The poet's son," he says.

He knows me. In the space of two minutes, he knows me more completely and thoroughly than Ivy will ever know me. His eyes aren't hollow at all. His eyes are wicked. His eyes are mischief.

* * *

She's wrapped in ocean sunset the next time I see her. She's let her hair down and her eyes gleam. The dress is cut low, the heels are high.

She's dressed for a funeral, but without the black. "It's time," Angeline says.

I protest.

"I've got another life to live," she tells me. We all do.

"I'm not who I was," she tells me. Who ever is?

"This isn't the end," she tells me.

"Of course it is."

"It's not," she says. Now who's protesting? She says, "It's time, is all. To move forward or move on."

"There's a difference?"

"Of course there is. Decisions must be made."

"No," I say. "Decisions are misguided far too often."

"Remember, *when* is my purview." Yes, I ceded *when;* but I held onto *why* and I held onto *how.* Apparently, that doesn't matter. "It was the rose, of course."

"The red rose?" I ask.

"The white." Like a dagger, of course. I knew it then. I know it now. The colors make flowers mean something different, but can't change the fact of the rose. I haven't learned any of these woman's mysteries. I haven't resolved my own paradoxes. I'm irredeemable. I'm out of step.

"You're bound in too many ways," she says.

"You've become serious," I tell her.

"I've always been serious," she says. Even when she wasn't, she was serious about it. I know this now. I don't understand it. I can't focus that sharply.

We're in the bar again, on Whiskey Road, double shots and chasers set on the table between us like an alcoholic wall. Smoke obscures her features. Dark lights cast her in chiaroscurist color.

I say, "Okay." I've always been willing to risk the things no one else will risk. I tempt the shadows. I dare the shadows to expose themselves to me. I have faith in my own skills, my own weaknesses. I crawl amid the dark every day and night. I am the shade in the dance. I am the blade in the ribs. I am not afraid. "Okay," I say again. "I'm in. I'm all in."

I see the surprise on her face. The shadows hide it quickly. "You are?" The words spill out like ink.

"Isn't that what you want?"

"It's not what I expected."

"You should know me better," I say.

"I thought I did."

I shake my head. I throw back my drink. I take her hand and kiss it gently and lean over the table. I whisper. Whisper trumps shadow every time. It's like that children's game. Shadow covers secret—or shadow covers knife, I never quite remember. Knife cuts whisper. It must be a knife. Secrets can only cut when they fail to remain secrets. Knife cuts whisper. Whisper trumps shadow. When you scream, you lose all the subtlety and all the strength of the whisper. When you holler, you give up control, you put yourself in a bad place. When you whisper, you shatter secrets. You leave your mark. I lean close enough to whisper, so that my lips brush her ear, my breath warms her flesh. It means more when I whisper it. "I'm all in."

She grabs me by the back of the head, holds me close, kisses me softly, kisses me roughly, and whispers, "I'll need a ring."

I have no diamonds. But I know someone who does. In a whisper, I promise.

* * *

The band's signer is a pixie-like blonde from some beach city in another world. She hasn't seen the sun in ages—there's no sun to be seen in Midnight, and the moon does nothing for your tan—so she's brilliantly pale. Dressed all in black, the only color is around her eyes. The eyes themselves, they're as hollow as Ivy's eyes, and as dark in the center, but she paints red between her eyes and her brows, or blue, or yellow, depending on the night. Tonight it's red. Tonight, her eyes match her lips, and otherwise she's all stark shadow. She can't pull it off. Her words, her tone don't have the sorrow. She's a sun worshipper without a god, but she doesn't know melancholia the way she wants to know it. So her songs sound trite and pretty and vacuous.

"I think she's wonderful," Angeline says.

The band's drummer knows what he's doing. He's been around. He can play rock and jazz, hard and soft, quick and slow. He can pound out a melody. His eyes are cracked, like his skin. He's older than he is, and he'll die much sooner than he should. It's the drugs, the miles, the music. How he ended up backing the waif, I can't imagine. It's not up to me to imagine. He's a percussive god. I say so.

Angeline agrees.

The bass is so powerful, it swallows the player. He or she makes it do things it should never do, and makes it do these things beautifully. I once dreamt of music like that in New Orleans or Memphis, but those places are a long way from this place. Anyhow, it's the instrument playing the player. I can't recall the musician's face even as I look straight at it.

The violin is sad but shallow, broken, uncertain. He's got some skills, he does, but he doesn't believe it. That's his problem. He plays it like a guitar, like a fresh lover, like a blind man who can suddenly see. He's almost got it. He almost pulls the discordant sounds together, almost makes the song live.

"He keeps missing a note," Angeline says, but she doesn't know which.

I don't remember where we are, or what time it is. I know it's nighttime. It's always nighttime. I know the band has been playing all night, will play deep into the morning so long as there's someone here to hear them, and I'm sure we're not alone in the club. But there are mirrors, smoke and shadows, and spotlights that pick out all but one of the players. The violinist skips a note. The singer fumbles over her words, frowns, picks up where she left off. Someone—see, I told you we weren't alone here—someone cheers her on. She doesn't acknowledge him. She looks, instead, at me, as though she's only just seen me.

Angeline snakes her hand over my shoulder, up the nape of my neck, so she can turn my head to hers. She demands that kind of control. She says, "Do you love me?"

I try to be honest. "I've never known any greater love."

After the band has packed its instruments and the bar has spewed us out onto the streets, Angeline asks, "Do you love me?"

I try to be honest. "I've never known any greater love."

Submerged in my apartment again, jazz on the stereo, whiskey on the rocks, sweat on our bodies, streetlight spilling in through the windows, Angeline asks, "Do you love me?"

I try to be honest. I say, "Yes."

* * *

I go to my mother.

She sits on a plain wooden chair in the center of the room. A spotlight falls on her from above. She's the star of her own cabaret show, except that she doesn't sing and she doesn't dance. She sits, arms draped over the plain wood, eyes sullen and lonely and unfocused. Ink stains her cheeks. She's been crying. Her eyes are red and puffy. So are her ankles. Her lips are red. She kissed my forehead with that mouth, when I was a kid, when I fell from a fence, when another boy on the playground pushed me down in the rocks.

My mother brought me here after my father died. I don't blame her. She didn't know. A missed road sign, a wrong turn, suddenly you're in Midnight instead of Cincinnati. That's how it happens. You blink one time too many, you find yourself in another land.

I can't leave this place while she's here. I can't take her with me when I go. I will die on the streets of another, faraway city, but she will die here, in this room, in this facility, in this asylum. They keep her sedated. They keep her quiet and soft. They keep her, because I cannot.

They give me an identical chair so I can sit across from my mother, so I can keep her eyes at a level, so she doesn't have to strain herself. I say, "Mom."

She doesn't always know I'm here. She glances toward the window, the one with the iron bars. The crow, my father, looks in on us. I can't tell if he approves. There's light, like sunlight, pushing through the window, falling on the floor in a grid, but it's tinted sodium yellow, it's harsh and unrelenting.

I say, "Mom."

She doesn't move. She doesn't look at me. She doesn't try to get up. She never speaks anymore, but sometimes she whispers. With her honey velvet drawl, she says my name. "Derek."

"I'm here, mom."

She's already not listening. So I tell her anyway. I tell her I've met a girl, a living poem, flesh fashioned from my dreams. She's smart and strong, all the things a mom likes to hear. The crow, my father, laughs. Fresh ink spills from the corners of my mother's eyes. They stain her cheeks blue, just like her fingertips, her dull and cracked nails, just like the veins crawling down the length of her arms.

I tell her I'm teaching another girl. This one hasn't lost her way, she's never known her way, she may never find a way, but she's eager and anxious and I might as well teach someone.

My mother whispers. "Another girl." It's a question, without the strength of a question. She raises her eyes just enough to meet mine, just enough to focus for a fraction of a second. She sees me. She smiles. My mother has the loveliest smile. She says, "You want something."

I'm losing her already. I say, "Yes." She doesn't ask what. She drifts

30

back to her world. Maybe it's Cincinnati. I wouldn't know. I've never been there. Neither has she. I ask, because I have to ask. I doubt she'll hear me. "I want to give her a ring."

My mother doesn't respond. The crow, my father, squawks his disapproval. "I've seen this girl," he says. "I've followed her when you weren't with her. I've seen the things she does. You're making a mistake."

I glare at the crow, my father, who cannot hear me through the window. "She's my mistake to make."

The crow, my father, shakes his head. "You never learn."

My mother whispers, "My ring."

She's slipped it off her finger. It's diamond. It's not large. It's not overpowering. It's the last thing my father gave her, the only thing my father gave her. He never gave either of us anything. My mother was always the voice. My mother was always the heart. My mother cries tears of ink and, long ago, set down my path before me. My mother slips the ring off her finger and lets it drop to the floor. It crashes like a brick. It scratches the fake tile.

I kneel before my mother to retrieve the ring. I kiss her forehead. I say, "Thank you, mom." But she no longer looks at me, or at anything. She's looking inside. The gears of her mind have been kicked again into action. She's composing poetry no one will ever hear or read.

* * *

Evan's poeticizing again. He must spend hours memorizing the words, the rhymes, and the metaphors, because he's not reading them. He's making eye contact. He's connecting. He's speaking to every individual soul in the place. His contact is brief, but the words are melodious and fucking deep. I'm awed. I'm captivated. I'm enthralled. And I hate him, with everything I am, because he seems to know something I only pretend to know. Ivy feels it. She must. She's neither stupid nor untalented. Her ears force the connections her mind can't make on its own.

We're not alone. There's a dozen other poets, two dozen hangers-on besides, and the waitress who smiles for me her secret smile. I think she owns me. I think she knows it. I think she knows better.

But we're really not alone. In the opposite corner, the yang to my yin, the white to my black, the disruption to my sweet and pleasant

31

garden, Robin sits, Rob if you prefer, listening and passing judgment and pretending I'm not here. He smokes the same brand of cigarette as Ivy. Her pack floats on the table, on our side of the line of empty whiskey glasses. The fortification stands weakly tonight. The deluge of words, the hint of danger, put me on edge.

Ivy's Zippo sits on the table, too, next to my notepad. It gives me ideas. The chrome reflects some hidden side of me, but shoots it in another direction so I, the me on this side of the lighter, cannot see it. The chrome works like a mirror. My reflection is fortunate. It exists on the other side of Midnight.

The city closes in on us. I feel the weight of the mountains. I feel the cracks in the foundations, artificial tunnels and highway and apartments and malls, all underground waiting for the mountains to collapse. The ceiling crushes me. The waitress brings another drink. She knows I need it, but it's not enough.

I tell Ivy I need air. She waves me away. Have I already become merely that? I escape the poets and the liars, the vultures and the wolves. I reach the surface. Under the open night sky, under the constellations and a sickle moon, I swallow huge gulps of breath. Cars pass. People. Poets come and go. Around me, the prostitutes solicit their business, the cops patrol their streets, the card readers tell their futures. One of these is an old man, a blind man, though of course the blindness is a lie. It's part of the act. I play my part, pay my fee, and beg for a sign.

He pulls cards. He touches the faces of them, as if reading Braille. He mutters under his breath, he shakes his head, he touches the back of my hand. "There's a woman," he tells me.

I'm not impressed. "There's always a woman."

"I see you dancing," he says. "Or swinging in the wind. Hanging? That can't be right. Dancing, I'm sure of it. Twirling and...and..." He tapers off. He searches for the right word. He knows he's got me hooked, but he also knows I'll leave in thirty seconds if he doesn't find the word he needs. I have enough words. They bounce around in my head, a pinball machine gone amok and awry. He settles on, "Dancing."

"You said dancing."

He leans forward, gripping my wrist now. "I meant *dancing.* The kind with bullets."

I tell him I don't like guns.

"I know," he says.

"That doesn't prove anything," I remind him.

"I know that, too," he says. Then he spits out a title for me, something meant to prove himself: "*Poet.*" He says it with venom. With teeth.

I like the way he says it. "Say that again."

"*Poet,*" he whispers, but he's lost the vehemence and the weight. It's just a word now, meaning nothing it never meant before. "Dancer."

* * *

I'm no dancer. I know a waltz from a tango, if I'm watching, because one has a rose and the other's set in Vienna. But I don't know a pirouette from an arabesque. I have no sense of balance. I like jazz when I don't have to think about it. Jazz should be felt. I don't have a dancer's body, either. I'm not lean or lithe, I'm not athletic, I'm not going to break or slide or twist.

Angeline wants to dance.

There's a place, she says, so we go. There's a lot of light, but it's inconsistent and frenetic. The numerous mirrors make me feel safe and exposed. The music is electric, heavy with bass, rhythmic but constant. It never eases up. It never breathes. One song flows into the next without any indication, as though the musicians cannot say anything unless other musicians say the same thing. As poetry, it fails. As jazz, it fails, except it steals liberally from jazz, and after a while I begin to think this is music I can like, this is music I can dance to.

I'm no dancer, except with Angeline. On the floor, pressed between other gyrating dancers, we express desire. We seek union. We tease and tempt. We touch and fade away. But every time I'm about to understand, every instance in which I start to think the moves make sense, that the fluidity transcends mere motion and emotion, the parameters change. Maybe it's the rhythm. Maybe it's the atmosphere. Maybe it's because I'm never any closer to breaking the mystery of dance than I ever was before.

"You dance like a madman," she tells me. So does she. We're soaked with sweat. We ache. We've unlocked things and hidden things. We have much to learn about each other.

I tell her, "I have a ring."

"That's not how you do it."

"I'm not doing it," I tell her. "I'm just giving you fair warning."

"I'll consider myself warned," she says.

We dance till dawn, and dance again in my living room, and bring the ways of dance to our lovemaking. I sleep for three days after.

* * *

Ivy fails to perform. Up on that stage, she reads with all the authority of a middle school boy caught masturbating in the girl's locker room. She makes eye contact with our feet. She sometimes looks up at me, but if she's seeking permission or adulation, I don't know and I don't offer either. They're not mine to give. She stumbles through the words, but the phraseology is there, the images striking. Only the lyricism is lacking, and that's entirely in her delivery.

Reluctantly, after arriving safely but uninspiringly at the end, she abandons the stage and takes the seat next to me. The waitress brings more whiskey. My notepad quivers in my hand.

She asks, "Where have you been?"

"Sleeping."

"You never tell me anything real," she says.

I shake my head. I throw out an "On the contrary" because I can. "Everything I've said has been real."

"But not what I want to hear."

Something's changed. I'm not yet sure what. "I thought you sought enlightenment."

She says, "Then enlighten me." Then she adds, "Or I'll find someone else who can."

I haven't really looked at her in a long time. She's always been a ghost to me, the misty remnants of something I and others like me have always feared we'd become. She's aimless, but not without destination. She looks sad, truly sad, in a way I've never seen before, and I wonder how long she's been this way.

"I can give you a lot more," I tell her.

"You can," she says. "But you don't."

Though our whiskey is empty, the waitress smartly avoids our little booth. Some kid is up there reading, or pretending to read. He's shier than Ivy ever was. He's got no potential.

"You want to know if you have potential," I say.

"We all *have* potential," she says.

"Ah." I shake my head. "Are you fulfilling yours?"

"Am I?"

I'm still shaking my head. "A question like that, the answer changes every day, every minute. On the stage just now, you strove for your potential with your words, but not with your voice."

"I see."

"You don't," I tell her. "You don't unleash yourself."

She leans closer to me, and I smell the perfume of her, perhaps the perfume she's always worn. She's so young. So eager. So very sad. Through gritted teeth, she says, "Unleash me."

* * *

I unleash her.

She's wild, uninhibited, risky and risqué, unafraid, uncontrollable. Ivy sheds more than her clothes when she undresses.

Her apartment is small. The bed, a chair, a table functioning as a desk, and a small shelf of books crowd the rooms. There's only one window, a sliver, that lets in no light. The walls absorb the lamp's feeble attempts at illumination. There's nothing here, real or not, except the poetess herself, and a bottle of bourbon-infused wine that, to me, tastes bitter, but I drink it when she offers.

"You don't know how long I've wanted to do that," she says.

"You're right," I say. "I don't."

She stares at me in the dark. I wonder what she sees. My scars? Ink tears slipping from the corner of my eye? She says nothing. She lies. She has much to say. It's up to me to breathe life into the conversation. Without it, we will wither. We will scatter. We will die.

I say, "You don't need me."

That's not what she expects.

I lay my palm on her chest, between her breasts. I apply only enough pressure. "You're fully armed. You're ready. All you need, you have within. Let it out."

"It's not that easy," she says.

"It can be."

She shakes her head. She unleashes me, rips open my scars, carves her name into my flesh with her fingernails, sucks the breath out of my mouth, gives me her own in exchange. It's urgent, and continues well past the time when we both should stop. Maybe outside it's dawn, or past dawn, or past dusk. There's no knowing. There's no caring.

After it's over, again, I whisper, "Write me a poem."

35

"I can't."

"Only one."

"I can't."

"I've already been writing one for you," I tell her.

"I've never seen it."

I shake my head. "You never will. It's not good. It's not deep poetry."

"Is it a love poem?"

I laugh. "No, of course not."

"Is it almost done?" she asks.

"I'm afraid so," I tell her, "but not yet. But this isn't about me. It's you. It's all you. Put pencil to paper. Tell the paper what you've been telling me all night."

"I've been lying to you."

"I don't care."

She gets her notepad, and her pen; and, in the dark, with full ferocity, she scrapes the paper. She's furious. She's intense. She's everything a poet should be. I leave her to it. I don't want to interfere. She's flipping pages and going at it even as I shut the door behind me.

* * *

The band plays.

I'm alone in a corner in the dark with my whiskey, my thoughts, and my notepad. I've got my own furious words to disgorge. It's a mess on the page, but I have light here, and music, and some semblance of solitude.

The singer recognizes me now. I've come one, two dozen times before, always with my notepad, sometimes with Ivy and sometimes with Angeline. Between sets, I almost see the face of the bassist, but even in silence the instrument overwhelms the player. The drummer plays with his sticks, pounding out a solo on the brick walls in the back corner. I can't hear it. The singer, the pixie blonde with vacuous words, buys me a shot of whiskey and sits across from me uninvited. In this world, especially in this city, we've transcended the need for invitations. We move in without regard to protocol or sensibility. It's not the world my mother fled when she took me here.

"You come, you listen, you scribble," she says. She smiles. She's pretty, with baby-soft cheeks and baby-fine blonde hair that probably shouldn't be as straight as she wants it. It curves, but doesn't curl. It wants to curl. She's inhibiting herself. "Have you nothing to say?"

"Often, I speak far too much," I tell her.

"You like the music?"

"Your drummer, he's got talent."

"The rest of us?"

I shrug. "I'm not a music critic."

"You must come back for a reason. Is it my voice?" She's smiling, flirting, but I don't know if I can lie to her.

"It's your eyes," I say.

"You can't see my eyes from here."

"Oh, but I can." I lean forward. I reach across the table and take her hands in mine. "Your eyes are hollow, just like your words. You may be pretending at depth, but you're swimming in the shallow end of the pool."

She doesn't pull her hands away. "That's cruel."

"I'm often cruel."

"I don't think that's true."

I'll give her a point for that. I give her a smile. "I'm often honest," I admit, "and that's usually the same thing."

"I have the feeling you know something I need to know," she tells me.

I have the same feeling, but I don't admit it.

"What's your name?" she asks.

"Smith," I say, pretending at suave. "Derek Smith."

"Call me Sage."

"That's not your name."

She squeezes my hands, releases them, stands. "I don't think you care about that."

After the break, the band plays again, the drummer keeping everyone in tempo, Sage making a sad attempt at guiding the audience through a forest of sorrow. She touches a real leaf here or there. She gives it more than I've seen her give before. She watches me from the stage. I don't ignore her, but I'm more involved with the pages in my notepad. I'm burning through them. I'm scratching out as much as I'm scribbling. The bass's rhythm overwrites my own. I'm taken by it, so the words I write are crap.

I tear out pages. I want to go back to the waitress. Sometimes, in the deep night, she'll bring me that extra shot of whiskey that keeps me going. I don't know how I've survived this long. I don't remember eating anything but Midnight's finest.

Since Sage is focused on me, she sings more coherently, more correctly, more evocatively. The man on the violin picks up on this. I don't think he misses a single note in the entire set. The drummer is their glue. The bass threatens to swallow the stage. Before it's over, I have to argue for another drink. The bar closes. I hate when a bar closes.

"Let's go for a walk," Sage tells me.

"Through the streets?"

"Through the park."

We're not far from the Mirage. It's all impossible trees and ravens and winding paths and madmen proclaiming the end times. We walk, we hold hands, we trade stories about orange juice and wild cherries and surfboards.

"What is it you think I know?" I ask her.

She giggles. She giggles a lot. She doesn't trust herself to form the words, doesn't trust her mouth to say them, doesn't trust me or anyone else to hear what she means. I can't help her work through her issues. Instead of answering, she lies. "I don't know."

Later, sitting by a fountain, she asks me to tell her a poem, to read something from my notepad. It contains nothing complete, nothing near ready. She convinces me anyhow. I read broken fragments, orphans, miserable rhymes. For the first time since I've ever known her, she doesn't look sad.

I should be frightened. I'm not smart enough for that.

When I'm done, she kisses me. Embarrassed, she apologizes, then runs off into the forest like a pixie.

A crow, my father, laughs at me.

* * *

She wears a shade of indigo reminiscent of the middle of the night, and since it's always the middle of the night here I'm certain it's meant to be camouflage. It doesn't work, though, when you have a face that demands attention, when your hair cascades over your shoulders like thousand-foot tall waterfalls in China. She sits at a table, alone again, in a restaurant, and I'm sure I've seen her there before.

I take the seat across from her before the wait staff can arrive with water. She looks at me with eyes like weapons and says, "Do I know you?"

"nambivalently, yes." She's still a mystery. I've learned nothing of her.

When she smiles, it's like the world's cracking open and I'm only just learning to take my first step. I teeter over precipices filled with pools of acidic ink. I reach down, hold my hands close to the liquid surface, feel the bubbling, boiling, roiling power.

She pulls her hand away.

I don't think I ever saw her before this place, but it wasn't tonight. It runs together. She's an ocean sunrise in disguise.

"You've asked me questions," I tell her.

"I have."

"You've challenged me," I tell her.

"I have."

"I like to be challenged."

She doesn't respond to this. She should say, "I know," but she's skipped, and it throws off my rhythm. I have to catch my breath to regain my equilibrium.

"I like to be challenged," I say again. "I do." There, that's better. "You've also threatened me."

She raises her eyebrows. "Have I?"

"Everything about me has changed. I see things I've never seen before. I hear what's always gone unheard. I'm learning things."

"What are you learning?"

I shake my head. She's throwing my rhythm again. "Now is not the time for questions. This is my soliloquy."

"You get one of those?" she asks.

"Of course I do. We all get at least one. Two, if we're fortunate. For the greatest of us, people like Shakespeare, like Poe, an unlimited abundance of them await at arm's length, free and ready for the plucking." I lower my voice, confiding. "Many among these great, however, are unnamed and anonymous, devoured by history so that no trace remains."

"That's awful."

"Yes," I admit. "It is."

Men who are not as well dressed as they should be considering their positions arrive to inquire about our wants and desires. They bring glasses of water and folded menus and listen to every requested nuance—no tomatoes, for instance.

"Go on," Angeline says. "Your soliloquy."

"Ah, that." I smile, because it's all I can do. I see the ocean sunrise underneath, I see the lines of her lips and the dimples at the small of her back. I see the wasted words and crumpled papers wherein I tried to create something that matched the beauty of her, the elegance of her, the grace and the perfection. Sometimes, I must eventually realize but have yet to admit, there simply are no words. "I'm learning things. I'm growing. I'm dying inside, and being rebirthed, and running around in circles. I'm catching all the things I've never caught before, and throwing back all the things I've always grasped. I'm turning things over. I'm exploring."

"I think," she says, interrupting again, "you've always been something of an explorer." I'm glad of the interruption. I have no idea what I'm saying. I'm rambling.

Food arrives. A violinist strolls between tables. It's not the guy from the band. This one is skilled, albeit somewhat stilted. He's played these songs so often, he's lost the passion for them. When he comes near, I wave him over, I can wave a person over these days, and I tell him, "Play me something you've never played before."

He's confused, so I ease his suffering with generous, surreptitious compensation, and tell him as plainly as I can, "Invent something."

"Something romantic?" he asks.

I shrug. "If that's how you feel."

He does an admirable job of it. He plays notes he hasn't heard in years, puts them together nicely. There's nothing perfect about the tune; it strays, it hiccups, it meanders. But it's emotive. It's provocative. Though it's a sad song, it makes me happy. And it makes Angeline happy.

"Is this my song?" she asks.

"I can't imagine why not."

"I think it's wonderful," she says.

"You think a great many things are wonderful," I remind her.

Then I throw the questions at her, easy first, until I can get through to the most difficult question ever asked. "Am I wonderful?"

"Yes," she says, with enthusiasm.

"How long has it been?"

"Three months, a year, perhaps a decade," she says. She shrugs. "I don't think I care."

"Neither do I. How much longer can it possibly be?"

She narrows her eyes and throws a question back at me. "What makes you think it will go beyond this table, this night, this sonata?"

I waste a moment's thought on the violinist. How much time did I buy?

I show Angeline my mother's ring, the one with the diamond. I'm on one knee. I'm doing everything traditionally. The whole restaurant seems to notice. Except for the violin, all other sounds and noises fade away. "Ah, but I think we might very well have a long, long time ahead of us."

She smiles. She takes the ring, slips it on precisely the right finger, per tradition, and says, "I think you're right."

* * *

The man from the shadows, Robin, Rob if you prefer, waits again in the shadows. He finds me at random on a street under the eternal night. He steps out nonchalantly, marveling at the faux-coincidence of our meeting at precisely the spot where he's been waiting for me. I've never had a stalker before, not one who wanted me dead.

He does, too. I'm sure of it. There's a knife tucked into his jeans, a butterfly knife; he can make it spin and sing and dance, he can dazzle, he can cut and carve and lunge and slice.

I start. I don't need to begin with his lies. "I've been expecting you."

"You have?"

"Since you started your thievery, I've been conscious of every word. I expect hands to lunge out of the walls and steal the letters, the phrases, the thoughts and ideas. I share my notepad out of desperation, to ascertain the current existence of ugly things I've written before. I expect the pages to be blank, but thus far they haven't been. That can only mean one thing."

He tilts his head. He grins. He doesn't mind being caught; he wants the challenge. He expects nothing less of me. He asks, "What's that?"

"You haven't gotten to me yet."

"Wouldn't you know?"

My initial impression proves unfounded. "I thought you might be a bit sneakier."

"There's no need for stealth," he says. "I can come out and say everything I want to say."

"To this point," I remind him, "you haven't."

He shoves his hands in his coat pockets. He's fingering that knife, stroking it, exciting it. The weapon wants to play. It practically pulses in his coat. I'm surprised he can stand it.

On a nearby mailbox, the crow, my father, alights. Curiously, he merely watches. And preens. Damn crows.

"Okay, you've got me there," Rob says. "I haven't said anything. But I've been meaning to. Building up the nerve, you might say."

"Please," I say, "get it over with."

"You stole my girl."

It's laughable, so I laugh. What else should I do? I consider my options. He's got a knife, but so do I. I've also got a pen, a notepad, an extensive knowledge of words like *conundrum* and *palindrome* and *conflagration*, none of which are presently useful. I can run, or walk, or turn my back, with the ease of a panther.

He says, "It's not funny."

"Actually," I admit, "I have no idea what you're talking about. I've never stolen anything in my life, and I have no girls to speak of."

"Oh, I've been watching you."

I nod. I know this.

"You've got at least a dozen, maybe two, hanging on your every word. You trade on your past."

"I don't remember my past."

"Shall I remind you?"

I consider it, but it's tangential. "No," I say. "Go on. Who's your *girl?*" I don't like the way he uses the word, so I spit it back with some venom, but thus far I'm not following him. I need a name. Any name. Give me a name, and maybe I can put it together with one of the half-sketched poems in my notepad. Maybe I can recall a face, the words we shared, the touch of her lips.

He gives me a name.

I don't hear him. Maybe it's a bit of thunder, distant, rolling through at precisely the moment he speaks. Maybe a subway rumbled to a halt beneath the street. Maybe I simply don't want to hear it. But I feel I owe him something, an answer to the accusation if nothing else, and I cannot properly respond without knowing. "I'm sorry," I say, "I did not hear that."

He enunciates carefully, exaggeratedly, letting every syllable slide from his tongue as if a whole word in itself. It's condescending. I have to concentrate to put the syllables together. He says it with an unusual, imperfect accent, another thing he's stolen. He says, "Anne. Jeh. Lean."

I smile. I call him a liar.

* * *

There are two kinds of people in the world. There are always two. No one who describes kinds of people can break it down more cleanly than that, but they're always wrong. There's no such thing as black and white anymore. This twenty-first century doesn't allow it. Different shades, hues, tones, tints, and dyes paint uncertainty over any imaginable two-kinds system. In fact, there are people who know what's going on, and people who don't know. In the middle, there are the people who know only a particular thing, or know that thing from a particular vantage point. I don't know what I mean, precisely, except to say that I completely and utterly understand Robin, Rob if you prefer, despite that he makes no sense.

"Theft," I tell Angeline, "has certain requirements. I fail to see how I've met any of those requirements."

She smiles. She shrugs. She doesn't care. She says, "You didn't steal me." My mother's ring shines on her finger like it belongs there.

I can't shake the feeling that, perhaps, I did steal. "I swept you away from somewhere."

"Oh, yes, absolutely," she admits. "Monotony. Boredom. Listlessness."

"Are you describing this man Robin?" I ask.

"Not intentionally," she says, "but yes."

"The restaurant?"

"It's a special place for us," she says. "He wasn't there."

"Was he supposed to be?"

She thinks on this. There are multiple answers. On some level, any of them could be correct. She says, "No. You were supposed to be."

"*I was.*"

"He wasn't."

"Thievery implies conditions," I tell her again. "A right to ownership."

"No one has ever owned me."

I'm puzzled. "Have I not staked my own claim?"

She holds up her hand, putting my mother's ring between us. She asks, "This?" She answers, "This is no claim, Derek, but a promise. Are you telling me you don't understand?"

"Oh, no, I understand," I say.

"What have you promised?"

"To obey," I say, "and be obeyed."

"There is no past," she says. "There is no shadow in the dark, unless we ourselves are the shadows. You told me that, I believe."

"I may have said something to that effect."

"Obey me now," she says. "Make me scream."

* * *

Some weapons do more damage than others. I don't like guns. Too loud, too messy, too uncontrollable. Sure, I've got a friend who can hit the eraser on a pencil in your hands from three hundred yards away with a 9mm, but that's a special talent and I won't be putting that to the test again anytime soon. Knives are also messy, but personal. You have to get close, breathe the same air, feel the knots of your opponent's muscles. Poison has a certain elegance, but the waitress bringing me my poison cannot be bought. She knows the heart and soul of me. She could kill me more easily with her eyes.

I killed a man once. I used the right weapon. I can't trust Robin, Rob if you prefer, to be so meticulous.

Evan poeticizes on stage. Ivy rests her head in her hands and sighs. I scribble in my notepad, but all my words are violent. I loathe them. I go through several pages, but I cannot completely tune Evan out. His words leak onto my paper. The juxtaposition of his perfect inflections and my vicious meanderings could, potentially, with a little finesse, result in unheralded beauty. Instead, I get babies and strained peas.

At some point, I lay down my pen, I close my eyes, I simply listen. I hear Evan's words as he finishes. I hear Ivy's breath. I hear the waitress bring more whiskey. She touches my shoulder as she walks away, whispers in my ear, implores me to take care of myself.

Silence follows Evan because no one's brave enough to climb that stage. The stool sits empty, no longer inviting but challenging would-be poets to rise to the occasion. The spotlight falls flatly against the wall, a metaphor of something I can no longer recall.

Ivy says, "I found a new teacher."

"You're finally done with me?" I ask.

"You finished first." In fact, I didn't, but that's not what she means. "You promised to teach me the things I need."

"I promised nothing," I remind her.

"You implied it."

"I've always answered your questions," I tell her. "I've given you all the things you've asked for. What is it you want?"

"He's taught me things about meter I didn't think I could know. He's revealed rhymes I never imagined. He's connected disparate concepts in ways that, frankly, would make you jealous."

"I'm not the jealous type," I tell her.

"I know."

"Then why are you here?"

"Can I not have two teachers?"

"No."

"Why not? I need more than you can give me."

"Then you've taken all you can take from me. There's nothing left."

"That's not true."

"Of course it's true," I say. "That's why you're telling me."

"He admires you."

"A lot of people have claimed to," I admit.

"He says I shouldn't leave you."

"Then don't."

"He says you still have lessons to be taught."

Her phrasing is wrong. I can't ignore that. I open my eyes, hold her head with one hand behind her neck, draw her close enough that we can share a secret. I touch her ear with my lips as I ask in a whisper, "What does he intend to teach me?" I don't let go. I wait. I wait a long time. I can feel her lips trembling against the side of my throat. She cries silently. The cold tears slide down her cheek and fall onto my neck. I let go of the tension and hold her, simply hold her, and allow her the luxury of crying for me in secret.

* * *

When the band plays, they play for me. The players don't know this. The faceless nameless bass player slips inside the instrument and gives everything away except identity. That's all that's lacking: that one thing that separates you from all the others like you. I cross my fingers in some sign of unity, respect, and hopefulness. A day may come where the player steps out of that shadow.

The drummer, as always, holds them together. He guides them and sets them off in random directions. They're more jazz today, more impromptu, more enlivened. He doesn't just permit this, he encourages

45

it. He follows along, pushing and prompting, leading from behind, providing context and purpose.

The violinist misses his notes, but he catches the tone, so it's okay.

And Sage, singing there, wonderful and beautiful and haunting, is slipping further into the hollowness that's followed her here. She doesn't belong in Midnight. This City of Night will consume her. This City of Night will eviscerate her. This City of Night will disintegrate her by degrees, first making fine dust and sand of her insides, then fusing them into smooth, fragile glass. When her heart succumbs, when it's solid and dangerous to herself and to others, it will shatter. The shards will protrude from her chest and her back, and will fill the hollowness of her eyes with sharp, icy death.

I feel responsible.

The more she feels, the deeper she gets into anything whatsoever, the closer she comes to this end.

Between sets she sits with me, she tells me stories about her childhood, the beaches, the sands, the gothic tendencies, the exotic dancing that paid her way through college.

"You were a dancer?" I ask.

She narrows her eyes. "I don't dance like that anymore."

"But you do dance." It's not a question.

"Not when I sing."

"Of course not."

"That would be foolish," she says. "And arrogant."

I ask if she's ever been to the rooftops, if she's ever danced under the light of the full moon, to the beats of only our hearts.

She says, "Tonight."

But she means in the morning, in the darkest hours before dawn. Even in this Midnight, even where the sun never shows its skin, darkness comes in degrees. The music never ends. You hold it inside yourself. You bring it with you. So we dance, slow and close, two bodies melded together, under the soft light of the moon.

"I'm broken," she tells me.

"All of us are."

"Me more than others."

"You're not broken," I tell her. "You're lost." Her eyes reflect this, but she looks away. "You're away from home."

"I have my music."

I shake my head. "You restrain yourself."

"Are you saying I shouldn't?"

"I'm saying you shouldn't."

She smiles, lays her pixie head against my chest. "You think you know so much. Why haven't you fixed yourself?"

"I'm not imperfectly broken," I tell her.

"And you think I am?"

"You think you're not?"

"You're right," Sage says. "I've lost myself here. But sometimes I think, and only sometimes, maybe I can find where I belong."

"This is Midnight," I say. "Nobody leaves."

"Maybe where I belong," Sage says, "isn't a place, but a person."

I warn her, "That's excessively romantic."

She kisses me, gingerly, on the lips. She uses one of those weighty, meaningful whispers, and says, "Maybe it's you."

This is one of those moments that can reverberate through the history of you. When you're old and feeble and looking back, this is a moment, no matter what happens next, that will always leave you wondering. What if it went some other way? What if the things that happened didn't?

The crow, my father, shakes his head and flies away.

"You've got the soul of a poet," Sage tells me. "You belong here, this City of Night. It suits you. You and the city breathe together. You can help me, I'm sure of it."

"You're desperate," I tell her.

"Damn right, I am."

I close my eyes. We've stopped dancing; we stand there, in each other's arms, trembling, inhaling and exhaling in opposition to the other. She kisses me again, all softness and tenderness. She holds back her desperation. She holds back her desire. She's willing to let her audience take, but she's not yet able to give.

I have her face in my hands. I hold her away from me. If she casts her hollow eyes upon mine, if she looks at me straightly and steadily, I might forget the things I've forgotten. I tell her I think I know a way to help her. Sage moves gently, and so do I. All urgency is held back. There's no rush. We slip in and out of each other quietly, like the whisperings of ghosts, like the barest traces of shadow.

Before I leave her, there on the rooftops with only my father and his kind to watch over her, I whisper a heavy promise.

* * *

She says she loves me. I believe her.

* * *

The sign says Midnight Psychiatric Institution. Most people just call it The Asylum. Some who know better call it Midnight Tears. There's a rumor the place has been closed for years, but I know better. The chains outside have rusted over the gate, but they're no less strong. I sneak in the same way I always do. I slip through the glassless window, I climb the stairs, I smile at the nurses and orderlies and doctors in their white coats. Sometimes, I think they think I live here.

My mother's chamber is large and empty. I can imagine myself chained to the cement floor, half naked, sweaty and crying, staring into the faces of anonymous visitors.

The crack where my mother's ring had fallen has spread its tendrils throughout the asylum. There are cracks in the walls, outside and in, wood or stone. There are cracks in the mirrors, all save one, but one is all I will need.

I whisper, "Mom?" No one answers. No one comes to tell me where she's gone. The floor in her chamber is a network of webbed cracks; if I walk too heavily, it will break and I will fall. Who knows what madness awaits beneath?

One of the nurses looks familiar. I ask her, "Where's my mom?"

She checks a chart. She almost ignores me entirely. "You'll have to ask the doctors."

"I can't talk to the doctors again."

"Afraid they'll commit you?" she asks.

"What did you do to my mother?"

The nurse lowers her chart and meets my stare. "What did *I* do?" she asks. "You drove her mad, Mr. Smith. You drove her here. You *took* her here, told the doctors to keep her until she died, and then you visited and visited and visited until you got everything you wanted from her."

"I only wanted her to be my mom."

"You took her applause and her love, her talent, and her words. You took her *ring*."

"She gave it."

The nurse sneers. "She gave you everything, didn't she?"

"You're wasting your time," the crow, my father says from the windowsill.

The nurse takes her charts and goes away. She leaves me with that sneer. It hurts. I sit on the floor, where I would've been chained, where I would've cried, and I wipe tears from my eyes before they can form.

"You've accomplished nothing," the crow, my father says.

"I've found..." But I cannot find the words.

"You're not a poet. You're not even alive."

"Ah, but I am alive." I stand up to the crow, my father. I raise my head and I raise my voice. "Why must you haunt me?"

"We *are* connected by blood, Derek."

"We're divided by our cities."

"You're pathetic," the crow, my father tells me. "You think your fate is tied to the fate of this city. It's not. This city will be grand, and it will be terrible. It will save millions and destroy millions. Five hundred years from now, this city will persist, but there'll be no memory of you, there'll be nothing of you at all but your mother's work. You were the least of her accomplishments."

"You're wrong."

"You keep saying so. Prove it."

I yell. I swing at my father though I cannot possibly reach the crow on the windowsill. Isn't that the way a boy becomes a man: challenge your father? Have I been nothing but a boy all these decades? I rage at the sill. I ignore the nurses and the orderlies, the patients and the doctors. They leave me alone in this chamber, my mother's chamber, where nothing remains of her but the cracks in the floor.

I hurl words at the sill. I sling the best and the worst I've got. I unleash. It takes a long while to spend myself. I collapse to my knees again, I hold out my arms as if chained, and sob.

The nurse brings me water and a cookie. She holds me from behind and says soothing nonsensical things. She tells me, "You couldn't leave while she was here. You're free now, Mr. Smith. You're free."

"I need sedation," I tell her.

She shakes her head. "Not without talking to the doctors."

"I won't talk to the doctors again."

The nurse is evil. "Then find your own sedation."

Evan says things. His words vibrate and resonate and leave impressions. The waitress brings fresh whiskey. Ivy sighs. Ivy sighs again.

"You want me to say something," I say, which might count as something but not here, not now.

"You've been crying."

"Of course I've been crying."

"Talk to me."

"What would you have me say?"

"Tell me something truthful."

I shake my head. "I'll tell you something honest."

"You've always been honest with me."

"Mostly," I admit.

"It's my turn."

"Is it?"

"It's time for a lesson."

I glance at the stage. Evan's words bounce off the walls. They can crush, or they can be severed. He doesn't care which. That's his secret.

But Ivy shakes her head. "I wish it was him," she says. "I would learn anything from him."

"Have you not been listening?" I ask.

"Outside," Ivy says. "Upstairs. On the rooftops."

Again on the rooftops. The different roofs are all the same. There's gravel, or paved, industrial sized air conditioning units, pipes and vents and wires and antennae. A cold wind whips through us. Ivy lights a cigarette with her Zippo lighter, inhales deeply, then throws the cigarette aside. "I've had enough," she says.

"It was never more than a crutch."

"I'm no longer hobbled."

I raise an eyebrow. I can do that. "No?"

She hands me her chrome Zippo, pulls out a piece of paper, and reads me her newest poem. It's gorgeous, but it's sentimental. It's raw and rough and honest, and it's about me. It's about love and hatred and fear. It's only about three minutes long, but it's piercing. She reads it better than she's read anything before. She asks, "What do you think?"

"I think it's beautiful."

"I think it's awful," she says, "that I don't feel that way anymore."

"No?"

"You don't touch me," she says. "Not like you did."

"You've grown."

"I've outgrown you," she says.

"Oh." I have no response.

"She'll learn much more from me," he says.

He appears out of nowhere, as though formed of wind and ice and shadow. He reaches for Ivy's hand, but his eyes are on me and only me. Robin, Rob if you prefer, grins at me and says, "You're nothing."

"I've heard that before," I tell him. Indeed, the crow, my father, watches us now from the very edge of the rooftop. We're a dozen stories high.

"You've lost," he says. "You'll lose everything."

"I didn't realize it was a contest."

"It's always been a contest," Ivy tells me, but I don't look at her. She's not the one here to kill me.

"I expected worse," I admit.

"We're not done," he says. He turns to Ivy, drops to a knee. "I'm yours, Ivy. Will you be mine? Will you marry me? Will you stay with me forever, fight alongside me in my wars as I fight alongside you in yours?"

"You think poetry is war?" I ask.

"Yes," Ivy says, to both of us. "Yes, yes, a thousand times yes."

My mother's ring is already on her finger. He puts his hand over it. He looks at me through the corner of his eyes. "We'll always be tied together," he says. Then to me, and only me, he says, "I have stolen everything from you, don't you see? You can die now." He nods toward the edge, toward the crow, my father. "You're free to jump now."

I look at my father. He says nothing. He flies away. He abandons me. I walk to the edge of the rooftop and look down at the pulsing, brilliantly lit City of Night, at the streets and the mouths of tunnels and the windows in the mountainside, at the gardens and the monuments, buildings old and new, at this twisting metaphor of my own inaccessible life.

Rob whispers encouragement. When I look back, Ivy has turned away. The wind catches her hair. She's never been so beautiful, or so poisonous. Rob has a gun, a black steel Oliveri. He holds it at his hip like a crime noir gangster. It's pointed at me. "This only ends one way," he tells me.

"I expected better from you," I say, and I jump.

* * *

You expect the last flight of your life to end quickly and sharply. But it doesn't end that way at all. The crow, my father, had flown away over a line of fire escapes. It rocks and rings when I hit it, and it bites into my ankles and calves and back, but nothing breaks—nothing except the window when I kick it. I glance up before going inside, and there's Robin, Rob if you prefer, staring over the edge, his mouth an O, the gun hanging limply in his hand. I give him a little grin and a wave.

It's not a goodbye wave. It's one of beckoning.

He's committed now. He has to follow.

The woman's apartment is messy. I come in through the kitchen. She sits in the living room watching something bland on the television box. She glances at me with some degree of fear and a bit of hope. Maybe I'm here to relieve the monotony? Maybe I can save her?

I'll save someone, maybe, but not her.

I say, "Thank you," though she knows not why, and burst into a dim, dank hall. There are other apartment doors, perhaps a closet, a set of stairs going down, and a frightening elevator. Once, I dreamt of elevators crashing, and I've never boarded one since. I'm not about to change that.

There are other stairs. It takes half a minute, way too long, to find them, despite that I've been here before, and climb them again. When I break out into the open air, Ivy sways at the edge, staring down, quivering, crying, looking beautiful and, in her head, composing what she thinks will be the poetry of her life.

She turns as I grab her arm. "Oh, God," she says. She falls into me, violently shaking her head.

Rob explodes onto the rooftop with his finger on the trigger. He shoots. I'll never forget the echo of the gunshot. The force of the bullet nearly knocks me off my feet; but it's not me that it hits. It's all I can do to keep Ivy from plummeting over the edge. Her blood burns me like acid.

Rob's face is an expressionist painting of fury. He raises the gun again.

A murder of crows rise up from all sides. The flurry of black wings, of angry caws, of beaks that pick at dead flesh, confuses and disorients everyone but me. I knew my father would never abandon me. He never has.

Rob rushes blindly forward. I'm not so blind. I let Ivy drop to the rooftop, not over the edge, and rise to meet him. For a moment, it seems we'll both fall over the edge. The gun escapes. The wind gales. Rob screams. I scream. We all scream as the world rages. We struggle like wrestlers, like bears, right there at the edge, neither strong enough to throw over the other. I want to be that strong. I want to be that swift, that courageous, that skilled. I'm none of these things. I'm merely fighting for my life. Again.

In the end, I cannot save myself.

A gunshot settles it. Rob looks surprised. I'm surprised. His expressionist painting of a face has distorted into something more closely resembling pain. His grip on me slackens. He slips to the side, closer to the edge, and teeters. He won't fall without my help. Ivy, on her back, bleeding, crying, had only strength enough for one shot.

I extricate myself from Rob's grasp. I let go. I think about giving the tiniest little shove. I can watch Rob tumble over the side of the building, turning end over end until crashing into the ground. Though I may be a thief, I am no murderer. I step back and let him drop to his knees. I recognize the position.

Ivy says, "He lied to me."

I look at her. I cannot quite smile, but I give her something. "I know."

* * *

I sleep and dream for days. My dreams are chaotic messes of flying and running and splintered glass. I finish all the whiskey in the apartment and stare out the window as the storm encroaches. When storm comes to Midnight, it comes to stay. It crackles and releases deluge after deluge. Waterfalls form off the sides of buildings. There's one outside my window. I could descend it in a canoe. Maybe it will take me elsewhere.

I have no phone. It doesn't ring. I don't miss it. I don't need the contact. I need to work through the visions, the images, and the words. Yes, when I wake, I scribble in my notepad, I cross out whole lines and tear out pages. I burn through an entire pad and several pens. I have plenty.

The words I write aren't worthy of poetry; the notepad serves as a scratchpad, a sketchbook, a collection of raw and rough and honest ideas rather than fully formed verse. I whisper secrets to my mother; she must, somewhere, be listening, lying beneath the surface of a pool of ink, eyes open but clouded, lips parted and cold. The crow, my father, makes no appearance.

When I use up this pad, I scratch out words on the walls, into the coffee table, the posts of my bed.

When I use up the pens, I cry and collect the ink tears in an antique perfume bottle. Indigo swims inside the glass like eels. I remember swimming in the ocean. I remember ocean sunrises and the middle of the night and a dress once worn by a woman I will never forget.

She comes at dawn or dusk—I cannot be sure. She makes me drink water, but she's also brought whiskey. She feeds me bread and cheese and chocolate. She holds me like a baby. She wears my mother's ring on precisely the right finger. I touch the back of her hand, her fingernails, her lips. She smiles and repeats promises already made.

"You decide when," I remind her.

She smiles. She brushes back my hair and wipes my brow with a washrag. She says, "Now. Today. Today would be perfect."

She wants a preacher, a priest, a rabbi, anyone with authority. A captain would be good, but there's no shore at Midnight and therefore no ships, no pirates, no mates, and no captains. There's a man called the Admiral, but I don't believe he ever served. He's old and, quite honestly, a bit off the tune. When he roams the Midnight Tears, he does so with pride and honor. But he doesn't see who he's talking to anymore.

"Not the court," Angeline says. "Not the court alone."

"Of course not."

"That would be...less than what we should have."

On the streets, there's a reverend who wanders, a man dressed all in black who will tell you he is no priest. He has a daughter. He sees things I cannot. He points them out to me, sometimes, when he's on the corner, on his milk crate, spouting words like poetry in every language imaginable. He's a madman, if ever there's been one, but he's outside, on the streets, and today, at my corner.

"Yes," Angeline says, giving the Wandering Reverend her biggest smile, "he would do nicely."

"Would I?" he asks.

"We want to be wedded," I tell him. "We want to be wedded now, today, in the eyes of a god."

"Don't you care which god?" he asks.

I don't. Angeline doesn't, either, so we don't answer.

"That's a beautiful ring," he says of my mother's ring on Angeline's finger.

"It's old," I tell him.

"It's a real promise," he says. "It's binding, more so than anything I can say or hold you to. Do you understand that?"

"I do."

"Save the *I do* for the proper moment," he says, turning to Angeline. "You know what you're getting into?"

"It's up to me, is it not?" she asks.

"You know who he is and what he is and all the things he'll give you, now and forever?" the Wandering Reverend asks.

"I do."

"Now's not the moment," the Wandering Reverend says, "but I suppose it's done, then, is it not? You do, you both do, so hold each other's hands, here before me, and answer me these questions." He asks. They're quite traditional, and quite natural in his voice. He could be a power. He is a power. I hadn't feared him before today. "Do you, Derek Smith?" he asks, and "Do you, Angeline?" We both respond with the proper words. We have witnesses there on the street, salespeople and executives and bakers and bankers, taxi drivers, prostitutes, beggars and thieves, and poets. Yes, the poets pour onto the streets for our impromptu wedding, even Ivy, who silently cries.

When the Wandering Reverend says, "You may kiss the bride," I do so enthusiastically, and the crowd roars its approval.

* * *

"I suppose I have other lessons to learn," Ivy says. She pushes the whiskey away from her. "I cannot believe you still sit with me."

"You still have lessons," I say.

"You're not who you were."

"Neither are you."

"I've grown."

"So you said. But still, you're here."

"Other lessons," she admits.

"Then we should begin."

The waitress brings fresh whiskey, but we've barely touched what she's already brought. The line of empty glasses is not so impenetrable as it's been. "Is everything okay?" she asks me.

"Everything will be," I tell her.

"I've always known that," the waitress tells me, patting my shoulder as she goes. I catch her hand and pull her, gently, closer.

I whisper so that no one, not even Ivy, can hear. "You lie."

"So what if I do?"

"You were concerned."

"I was always concerned," she tells me.

I smile. "I like that."

"Don't get used to it." She walks away. I won't see her again tonight.

Evan's up on the stage, screaming words now, scratchy and rough words that aren't near as clever as I once believed. Even Ivy ignores him. She scribbles in her notepad. I scribble in mine. She bites her lower lip as she writes, just as I do. She picked it up from me. She's never been more beautiful.

I set down my pen. I look into Ivy's eyes. I ask, "*Is* everything alright?"

She smiles at me but doesn't slow down her scribbling. She says, "It will be."

* * *

Sage sings with fragile melancholy, but it's lost all its edge. She sways like a pixie, not like a dancer. She thinks she sings for me, but she doesn't sing for anyone anymore.

"She's still wonderful," Angeline tells me. I agree.

The violinist hits his notes. It's nice to hear. He hits most of his notes, anyhow, and that's probably good enough, at least for the moment. He's exploring. He's expanding. He's learning his limitations but also breaking through them.

"He hasn't found himself yet," Angeline suggests. "He hasn't got the emotion." I agree. Sage has got the emotion, but she masks it. She battles it.

The bass absorbs its player. For some, there's no hope. Perhaps the player should turn to photography, or the culinary arts. We can always use another good chef. This city is in painfully short supply. The player may have talent with oils or with knives, but there's no coming out from behind that instrument.

Angeline agrees.

There's no drummer tonight. Maybe he's sick. Maybe he's dead. Maybe he's just not strong enough to hold together a broken band.

Angeline doesn't mention the drummer. As the band reaches the end of its last set, she leans over and kisses my neck and says into my ear, "I'll be waiting for you."

She's gone before Sage reaches the table. Sage sits. Sage pouts. "I saw you," she says.

"I heard you," I tell her.

"We're doomed," Sage says.

I take her hand. "No," I tell her. "The band is doomed. For you, though, I believe we may find salvation."

"I cannot have the things I want."

"No one can have all the things they want."

"You're cold to me now," she says.

"On the contrary," I say, "I've never felt more deeply, more passionately, about anything."

"Not even her?"

"Forget her. This isn't about her. It's about you."

"Me and you?"

I shake my head. "I have something to show you."

The Midnight Tears lays hidden in a rundown, abandoned, industrial area, where there are crows and shadows and people in the shadows whom you do not want to meet. They stir in the presence of a blonde little pixie like Sage, but I don't let her linger. I bring her to the gate where the rusted chains hold it closed.

"My mother died in there," I tell her.

"No."

"Yes."

"Why bring me here, then?" she asks.

"There's still hope," I tell her.

I lead her through the iron fence and in through a glassless window. We avoid the orderlies and the doctors, though the nurse that sees us acknowledges me with a sad smile and a weak nod. The cracks have grown worse. They're out of control. They've infected the nurse's flesh. Everything here is so fragile, I'm afraid.

We climb the stairs, we pass other patients. The place has never been so quiet or hollow. I lead Sage by the hand; her grip is tight. She trembles.

"I don't believe in hope," she says. "Not in a place like this. A place like this, there's never been hope, there's never been comfort or justice. Why would you bring me here?"

"I'm not bringing you *here*," I tell her.

She stops walking. She makes me stop. I hope she knows I'm doing this for her. "You love me," she says.

"Of course I do."

"Are you lying to me?"

"Of course not," I say. "You don't understand love, if you think that I can. But I will tell you this, if it helps. You *will* understand, one day, perhaps when you're older or, perhaps, when you find that place you're looking for."

"You think you know things," she says. "I think you make things up."

"I think you're right," I say. "But you're also wrong."

The one mirror is still intact. The cracks have circled it without penetrating. It's full length, in my mother's chamber, where I can still see her sitting on her wooden stool and I can still see me chained to the concrete floor. Now, it's desolate and stark.

We look at ourselves in the mirror. It's smudged and dirty and very, very old, so the image is glossy and distorted. Except for Sage's blonde hair, the mirror knows nothing of vibrancy. It's a long mirror. It looks deeply into us, just as we look deeply into it. There are greater and lesser paths, perhaps, and maybe I have no idea where it really leads. Maybe I only think I know.

"You're willing to lose me?" Sage asks.

"You were never mine to lose."

"I'm not ready," she says.

"You'll wither here," I tell her. "You'll die. You need the sun, but you also need the loss."

"The loss of you?" she asks.

I nod. "And the loss of who you've been."

"Who, exactly, have I been?" she asks.

I admit I don't know. "But you'll find out."

The mirror shimmers. The cracks have thickened, and the mirror shifts.

"Come with me," Sage says.

I let go of her hand. I've already found my place, here in this dismal City of Night; I belong with an ocean sunrise and the indigo of midnight.

Sage steps across the mirror's threshold.

She shimmers on the other side. She turns, puts her hand up to the glass. She's wearing my mother's ring on precisely the right finger. She says, "I love you."

I touch the glass, but cannot take her hand, not anymore. I whisper, because whispers carry strength no shout can ever know. "I love you."

She turns and walks through the gloom into something else. I can only imagine what else.

* * *

Evan recites his mediocre poetry. He looks to me for approval, but I cannot give it. Half the poets have disappeared or wandered off or simply never returned. I don't recognize the place.

The waitress brings me whiskey. I sip. It tastes bitter, like it's lost all its vibrancy and all its depth. I have my notepad. I look to it for my own salvation. Finally, finally, after all of this and everything, I write a poem worth writing. I reread it. I cry. I take out Ivy's Zippo and set fire to the page. It burns perfectly. Beautifully. Completely.

AFTERWORD

While *Beneath Midnight* gave me a chance to explore the city for the first time, *Madmen, Poets & Thieves* gave me an opportunity to explore what might happen to a person there. A great many people probably lead normal, even productive lives. It's a city, a real and regular city, with economic tides and interdependent social spheres, the shiny and good as well as the tarnished and forgotten.

Here, we get a view of the city, and its asylum, from a protagonist who may or may not be entirely reliable. His perception is not the same as mine or yours. He's focused, but narrowly; he's dishonest with himself; he hallucinates, or at least blurs the line between reality and imagination. He may be mad. He may be poetic. He may be a thief. He may also be a liar. He may also be a victim of his own lies. Still, he gives us some hints about life in the City of Night. You can glean important facts from the things he says.

I'll let you in on a secret: Derek has a sister. He never says this, never suggests this, but in my mind it was always true, so I tell you now: you've met her.

I'll let you in on another secret: like in any other place, everyone living in Midnight is going to have their own take on the city, their own beliefs and fears and hopes that will color what they see and what they know—or what they think they know.

Another secret: a lot of stories about Midnight's history and lore circulate within the city itself, some of which have been mentioned in various Midnight stories past and present. Some contradict others. That's because they can't all be true.

Truth, ultimately, is a matter of perception. Have you given much thought to what colors your perceptions?

dry
seas

Seven seas: one night reflecting the sickle moon, but dry by dawn.

The seabed overflowed with suffocating fish still flopping about, the skeletons of lost sailors, a forest of orange and yellow and red coral. Octopus, ready to be fried. Sharks.

A boy, Peter, ventured into the labyrinthine new world with all his courage and imagination, and found a stranded mermaid.

Her scales, though glistening like emeralds, shed flakes of dry, green dust. Her breasts were bare and beautiful, unlike anything Peter had seen except in his most secret dreams. Her hair was yellow, not golden, her eyes the color of sky.

"Please," she pleaded.

"But what can I do?" Peter asked.

"The Leviathan," she said, "that most fearsome creature from the old stories, yet exists."

But Peter had never heard of such a thing.

"It can be killed by neither sword nor fire," she said, "and lives alone in the deep."

"Then how?"

"It must be drowned." Which, of course, befuddled Peter. Still, he went deeper into the sea, passing wrecked ships and bulbous squid. Crabs and lobsters scattered from his path. The sandy floor felt hard, tough, and he wondered what could have taken all the water so suddenly and completely.

He met the ghost of a pirate, whose hand was a hook, whose eye was an empty socket. Colorful anemone swam within his gnarled, translucent beard. "No further, landlubber."

"But something strange has happened."

"Aye, something strange indeed," the pirate ghost said, "and it has freed me from this shadowy grave."

"Then go," Peter said, "walk the earth. I seek the Leviathan to bring water back to the seas."

"Then, child, I wish you luck."

Deeper, he passed whales that could swallow him whole, had they not been beached. And there, ahead, the massive Leviathan waited.

With only his courage and imagination, Peter approached. "You are stranded."

63

"I have drunk the seas dry," it answered, "so as not to drown within its depths."

Peter smiled, moved by pity. "How long have you lived under the surface of the sea?"

"Many an age."

"And how many times have you drowned?"

"Many a time," the Leviathan said, its answer a surprise.

"But have you died?"

"Again and again, yes."

"Yet still you breathe."

The Leviathan nodded.

"But you merely breathe," Peter said. "You cannot swim, nor drink, nor see your friends."

"I am Leviathan. I have no friends."

Peter considered this. "I will be your friend."

Overcome with sorrow or joy or both, the Leviathan wept. From its ducts, the waters of all the seas spilled forth. The sands drunk deeply. The mantas sailed again, and also the barracudas, and the sea dragons.

But Peter could not swim, and could not breathe under water; and the Leviathan died once more beneath the swell of its own tears.

Peter never again walked on dry land, no, but he did not die; he had rescued the mermaid with all the creatures of the sea, and she returned to rescue him with her kiss.

NECROPOLIS

ΛΕΣΒΟΓΝΣ

Shed no tear
for these dry bones
—The Book of Lost Fates

I. Suffer the Illusion

1.

    In the great city of the dead, gravestones and mausoleums seem to go on forever in every direction. Statues of angels and virgins and cherubs and even Jesus himself stand watch over the dead, as ravens (an unkindness of ravens) watch over the marble and granite and stone.

    In the great city of the dead, the breeze is always chilled and the grass never seems either overgrown or recently mowed. The clouds, even when fluffy and white, appear somewhat grayer and slightly trembling. The shadows feel thick and soundless.

    In the great city of the dead, there is life, there is movement, and there is song. Ravensong.

2.

    "Suffer the illusion."

    Kevin looked up at his wife. "I'm sorry?"

    "The inscription on this tombstone," Jill said. "Suffer the illusion. No name, no date, nothing else."

    Kevin grunted, and looked again at the unfolded paper in his hand. It was supposed to be a map of the cemetery. They were lost.

    "Don't you think that's a little...*odd?*"

    "Very," Kevin said, pointing at the center of the photocopied map. It wasn't entirely illegible. "I think we're here."

    Jill leaned over the paper, saw the letters *STI* under Kevin's finger, and asked, "Does that help?"

    Kevin frowned. "It should."

    Truth was, Kevin could never handle a map. He couldn't find China on a map of Asia, couldn't find Starbucks at the mall, and failed miserably when trying to refold a street atlas.

    Jill shielded her eyes from the sun as they looked toward it. "That way's definitely west." She looked at the map again. "Up the map, then. North." She pointed, but Kevin hesitated. She was making an assumption, that west and the left side of the paper were the same. He wasn't so sure.

They weren't looking for a particular grave. They sought a well. There were three, according to the map; they wanted the one labeled *Sabine's Wishing*. Why, exactly, Kevin couldn't remember, but he and Jill both had a dollar coin in their pockets, meant to be tossed and wished upon, and they might already be on their way home if they hadn't gotten lost in the woods.

Not every cemetery was large enough to have woodland. Trees and bushes and underbrush had overrun one of the older sections of the cemetery. The headstones were cracked and mostly unreadable; the dates they could make out were primarily in the 1800s, with one as early as 1783. Stones marked rectangular plots—once magnificent, now neglected and in disrepair. Trees had pushed some out of the way in their growth.

And now, having escaped the woods (not on the map), and having entered a newer old section (late 1800s and early 1900s), there was really no telling if they'd made any progress.

The map was useless. It had colored sections indicating Catholic and Anglican and Jewish and Muslim and Chinese, and pointers specifying various monuments (including Sabine's Wishing), but nothing that matched anything they could see.

Jill led the way. Kevin folded the map into quarters and stuffed it into his pocket.

3.

The soft sounds of flute carried on the cool breeze. It was distant, lonely but lovely, and mournful. The remnants of someone's fractured dreams.

Kelli paused to listen. The song wove through the trees and around the monuments. It beckoned, and Kelli was sure anyone who heard would feel its pull.

She was equally sure no one heard it but her.

She looked in the direction of its source—west, into the sun, so she really couldn't see much of anything. She pointed her camera but didn't take a picture; it wouldn't come out.

She was in an old part of the cemetery. She hadn't seen anyone else for at least an hour. Her digital camera counted 118 shots. She suspected 10 might be good. Sunset approached; in the meantime, she could take a moment to discover the flutist. And perhaps photograph him or her.

(She'd gotten one shot, earlier, of a Vietnamese girl sitting next to a plot so fresh no stone had yet been placed there; instead, there was a wooden cross with Vietnamese calligraphy and the girl sitting next to it, Indian-style, her hands on her knees and palms facing the sky, her eyes closed. She didn't cry but, as Kelli watched, she gently rocked back and forth, and seemed oblivious to the sun's glare.)

She had never heard of someone mourning their loved ones with a flute serenade, but Kelli had never heard of a lot of things which must be true and even common. Somewhere. Just outside her realm of experience.

In this part of the cemetery, weeds had overtaken the grass and grew undeterred; but unlike sections that were even older, the stones were still in mostly straight lines. Every few dozen yards, there were circles, with trees or fountains or statues at the center, where paths cut through the rows of stones intersected.

At one of these circles, in which a plain stone cross had long ago been overrun by ivy, she paused. A raven perched atop the tall cross. It watched, silent, its feathers so black they were blue.

Kelli paused to take a photograph. Even with the sun behind them, the bird and cross would stand out in silhouette. When the camera clicked, the flute fell silent.

She almost cursed. She never cursed—well, not often—but this was one of those times. She felt she had missed something remarkable.

But the song hadn't ended; it had merely taken a breath. Kelli rounded the cross, following the musical lure, as the raven cawed and took flight—in the direction of the flutist.

4.

"One million souls," Anna said. "A whole city."

"A lot of people," Darren said. "What are we doing here again?"

"Testing a legend."

"Do we have to say somebody's name backwards in a mirror after dark?"

She shot him a look that was as much amusement as exasperation. "Do you really think people do things like that?"

"Some people, sure," Darren said. "Not the smart ones."

Anna shrugged. It caused her hair to swirl, and therefore Darren's gut, but he didn't betray it. "That's not how magic works," she said.

"You didn't bring a book of spells, did you?"

"Where would I get something like that?"

"There are shops."

"Real spellbooks," Anna said, "you can't get at shops."

They were so deep in the cemetery, Darren could look in any direction and see only gravestones to the horizon, and a few scattered people saying prayers and leaving flowers. As they moved into an older section, fewer people were visible.

He followed Anna. He always followed Anna. Only partly because she always had interesting places to lead him. She had the wisdom of mountaintop gurus and the excitement of a child, and she knew a little about everything.

"The legend," she said, "since you weren't listening last night..."

"We finished three bottles of wine last night," Darren reminded her. "You weren't listening any more than I was."

She stopped, faced him, and met his eyes with a steady, frightening gaze. "I'm always listening."

After a moment, he looked away, and read an inscription on the stone nearest him (*fallen asleep with Jesus*).

"The legend," she said again, "is that the houses are open."

"The mausoleums?" Darren asked.

"*Houses*," Anna said. "Specifically, St. John's Chapel and all the rest houses."

"I suppose there's a ghost in the chapel?" Darren asked. He didn't believe in ghosts. He didn't believe in aliens or telepathy or anything the president said, either; but if Anna said phantoms gave midnight mass in St. John's, then the phantoms were real.

"Not that I know of," Anna said. "But this is a cemetery. One million souls."

"So you said."

"I'm sure one or two of them might be...restless."

"So we're not going to the chapel, then?" Darren asked.

As they'd walked, the grass became thicker and more tangled, overrunning more of the burial plots. Here, all the graves were completely outlined, either with stones or iron, though some of the stones had been cracked or broken and all of the iron had rusted to the core. With every step, the dates on the epitaphs stretched farther back in time.

70

Anna laughed ahead of him, one of those heart-stopping siren sounds, and tapped her bag. "I brought wine. But we'll have to be civilized and drink politely from the bottle."

5.

In the great city of the dead, at any given hour, even after the gates have closed, someone mourns. Someone cries, and someone sits quietly by a mother's grave. Or a child's. As dusk approaches, however, the regular visitors, those who have recently lost loved ones or who blithely follow routine, tend to depart, and those who remain are more vigilant and more serious about their mourning.

The great city of the dead isn't home to merely the dead. It houses shattered hopes and unrealized dreams.

6.

Despite Kevin's misgivings, they finally found the well. He was forced to admit it was more impressive than he'd expected (and this whole thing had been his idea). It was roofed, with four thin columns, two steps up from each direction. The wood structure around it was sun bleached but still strong. A huge, perfect spider's web blocked one of the entrances, so they used another. There, holding hands, he and Jill stared down the stone well.

With the sun so low, shadows hid the bottom. He saw only darkness.

"Okay," Jill said, squeezing his hand and holding up a dollar coin. "Here goes nothing." She clamped her eyes shut, muttered, took a deep breath, and held the air as she tossed the coin. It dropped down the center of the well, and made a small splash when it reached the water.

Kevin reached into his pocket...and found no coin.

"Your turn," Jill said.

"Did I give you my dollar?" he asked.

"Of course not. It's in your pocket."

He checked the other pocket. "No, nothing."

"Then I guess you don't get your wish." She grinned.

He checked both pockets again. He felt the frown growing on his face. He almost asked Jill if she had another coin, but instead returned her grin and said, "But I've already gotten my wish."

She stepped back, down one step then the second, and said, with just a touch of bitterness threatening to spoil it, "Can you keep her?"

She ran.

Kevin hesitated, looked left (toward the setting sun), right, and then took off after Jill.

The paths were narrow, crowded with overgrown brush and weeds, and time (or vandals) had shattered a few of the headstones. Others were tilted. One or two threatened to fall. The stones were taller now, and more tightly packed, as if they'd moved to another section, topped with cherubs and crosses and ivy.

Jill glanced back once or twice. He had cut her lead in half before he tripped.

7.

Rounding the row's corner, Jill aimed for the mausoleums. There were several groupings in this cemetery, as well as the occasional vault in the midst of a field of modest granite. These were mostly brown or gray stone, old but not entirely neglected, and she reached them much more quickly than she expected.

Looking back, she saw Kevin scrambling to his feet. Jill laughed, and turned onto the path that cut between these two rows of mausoleums.

Another path bisected this street. She rounded the corner. A man was there. He thumped her in the chest. She fell backwards, directed by his hand, and crashed into the wall—and then beyond it. Nothing shifted or moved, nothing shattered or broke or opened; she simply passed through stone and into the mausoleum.

When she tried to push forward, the stone was solid and unforgiving. She screamed.

8.

"Music," the first boy said.

Two boys and a girl sat atop a slab of marble covering a grave. The words etched on the gravestone were still distinct, and proclaimed a date of death of 1902.

"Soothes the savage beast," said the second boy.

"Good one."

After a brief pause, the second boy said, "is the language of love."

"I thought that was French," the girl said.

"Italian," said the first boy.

"No, music," said the second boy. "How many love songs do you know?"

"Lots," the girl said. "So?"

"How many songs do you know that aren't love songs?"

Behind them, still unnoticed, Kelli took a picture. Despite that it was digital, there was still a muted click. The three children turned as one, and stared. The flute, Kelli noticed, had softened, but was not gone.

"Maybe she won't see us," the second boy said.

The girl slapped his arm. "Shush."

"She's looking right at us," the first boy said.

"Music," Kelli said, quietly, "is the food of love."

"Shakespeare," the girl said, clapping her hands.

"No," the first boy said. "Shakespeare said *if music be the food of love, play on.*"

"Shush," the second boy said, looking at the two of them.

"It's too late," the girl said. "She already sees us."

"No," Kelli said, "I didn't see anything. I'm just wandering around aimlessly with my camera."

"You're not wandering around aimlessly," the first boy said. "You're following the piper."

"Maybe," the second boy said, lowering his voice, "she's seen the Ringmaster."

"No, sorry," Kelli said, meaning to walk past. "But you're right, I'm following the piper." As if on cue, the flute's volume rose, the tune weaving around the children and tickling Kelli's ears.

The first boy shook his head and the girl let out an exaggerated gasp and covered her mouth with both hands. The second boy hopped off the grave and stepped into the path. He was more than a foot shorter than Kelli, but he set his hands on his hips and said, "No."

9.

The rest house was small, square, and brick. Simple. Empty doorways faced north and south, windows east and west, two benches inside that could each carry two, maybe three people. The wood benches had been painted white. The bricks, inside and out, had faded, and many looked to be crumbly; red and brown dust coated the stone floor.

They sat on one of the benches, their backs to the setting sun.

"Now what?" Darren asked.

"Now," Anna said, pulling the wine out of her bag with a flourish, "we *rest*." She found a corkscrew in the bag. Half a minute later, she tilted the bottle over her lips, then passed it to Darren.

It was red wine, of course; when she had a choice, and she often did, Anna never drank anything else. A *good* red, too, that was a given, though Darren found the first swallow a little harsh on his throat.

Returning the bottle, he said, "If we're planning to be here all night, I hope you brought another bottle."

She shook her head. "Will have to make do with the one. You're supposed to be a man, you should've had two, three bottles of wine in your bag."

"I'm a man," Darren said. "I don't have a bag."

"That's just stupid." She took another drink. "The sun'll be setting soon."

"That mean something?"

"It's a thin time," Anna said. "Colors are richer. Air thicker. Spirits more restless. Green looks yellow and blue looks black, and if we're lucky, we'll see a will o' the wisp."

"Sometimes, you're crazy."

"Isn't that why you love me?"

Something caught in Darren's throat. And stomach. She said it so playfully, so casually, as though it were a given and all was right in the world. And it was true, completely and entirely, he would follow Anna to any dark corner this earth offered—or any other earth, should it be necessary. Despite this, he wasn't likely to get any more than a peck on the cheek, probably only a hug, and certainly not any sign that she, in fact, might one day eventually decide she felt even the smallest amount of love for him. So when she said things like that, *that's why you love me*, she never seemed to actually believe it.

Oh, she accepted, and maybe even relied on it, but she would never believe.

"Cemetery's a thin place, too," Anna continued, all unaware of what she'd said. "Look, you can see the ravens out there, and the clouds are virgin white and yet somehow still menacing."

Darren glanced outside; long, thin clouds streaked the sky like razor slashes.

"Aren't will o' the wisps some strange glowing fungus?" Darren asked.

Anna took another gulp of wine and thrust the bottle at him. "You need this more than I do."

Darren accepted the bottle. "You just want something to happen to you? Anything at all."

"Not just something," Anna said, much more quietly than usual. "Something interesting."

He could never quite gather the courage to suggest that he, in fact, might be something interesting, so instead he took a long swallow of red and looked out the window behind them. The sun hid behind the tree line, though he still had to squint.

Anna remained silent for a while, perhaps allowing the sun to settle further, or simply waiting for the wine. Darren drank a bit more, was about to give the bottle back, and hesitated.

At first, he thought it was a trick of the shadows. A reflection of something beyond his field of vision. He wouldn't go so far as to call it a delusion. After a moment, he decided it was definitely real. "Anna," he said. "Look."

She did. He heard her gasp.

In the middle of the field, where before there had been only a wide expanse of grass separating two of the oldest sections of the cemetery, a series of tents had popped up. If there had been a fair before Anna and Darren reached the rest house, he was sure they would've seen it.

But that's what it looked like. A miniature fairgrounds. Instead of typical fair crowds, there were one or two dozen ravens perched in pairs on top of the tents.

A sweet smell, like candied apples, reached them, and a single raven's caw, and a sudden breeze.

"Shangri La?" Anna said, standing.

Darren was shaking his head. "How did we not see that? It's not a carnival, is it? No." He was certain of that now. "A camp?"

Anna moved to the window and leaned out over the bricks. Definitively, in a tone that left no room for argument, she said, "Fairies."

Though he couldn't argue, Darren knew, without question or reservation, she was wrong.

10.

Twilight struck.

Death is but one path
by which we exit this life.
—The Book of Lost Fates

II. Twilight

1.

The sky: a stark, yellowish white, not bright but disconcerting, streaked with bleak clouds like gashes in its face, sick with them, and lending every granite and marble stone a flat but wicked tint, sharpening the shadows, with neither moon nor sun, and not a single visible star.

In the great city of the dead, twilight lingers.

2.

When she gave up screaming, Jill started searching for a doorknob. A latch. A window. Anything. She ran her hands along the cold stone wall, afraid to move too far, unable to see through the deepest, most penetrating darkness imaginable. Whoever had first said *dark as the grave* must've known what they were talking about.

She tried not to think about it. If she focused on the fact that she was actually inside a mausoleum...she shivered, and wiped sweat from her forehead, and struggled to control her breathing.

"Jill!" It was Kevin, muted but not distant, just on the other side of the stone.

"Get me out of here!"

"How...how'd you get in?"

"I..." She didn't know. "I just did. Get me out!"

"It's locked." She didn't hear him doing anything, just his voice, but he must've been right outside pulling on latches and knobs Jill couldn't see. "I'll...I'll go find someone. A caretaker. They've got to have a key."

"Hurry."

Silence. Jill continued running her hands along the wall, surprised at its smoothness, not at all shocked at its chill.

"He won't be fast enough," someone said in the darkness behind her.

Jill closed her eyes, as if that mattered, took as deep a breath as she could manage—presently, quite a feat—and spoke with very deliberate words. "You put me in here."

"Yes."

"Why?" He offered no immediate answer, so she added, "Who are you?"

He smiled. She could sense it, and hear it in his response. "I'm the man you wished for."

3.

It didn't take Kevin very long to get thoroughly lost.

4.

Kelli stepped back, staring at the kid who had put himself in her path. "No?" The flute sounded more distant. Her trigger finger—the one she used to take pictures—itched. She wanted a shot of the flutist, whoever it was, weaving through the grave markers.

"No," the boy said again, expanding his chest and pointing his chin.

"He's right," the first boy said, jumping off the marble slab. "The music will lead you astray."

"She's already astray," the girl said.

"So are we," the boy reminded her. "And Ronnie's right, she shouldn't go after him. Haven't you ever heard of Hamelin?"

"The place with the rats?" Kelli asked.

"I thought it was snakes," the second boy, Ronnie, said.

"Children," the girl said.

"Wasn't St. Patrick the Pied Piper?" Ronnie asked.

"Shush," the girl said.

"Didn't the children just run away and settle somewhere else?" Ronnie asked.

"Don't mind him," the girl said. "He doesn't know anything."

"I know lots of things."

"Name one."

"I know she shouldn't follow the flute."

The first boy stepped between Ronnie and Kelli. "Ronnie's right," he said again. "Pay the piper and all that."

"I'm just out taking pictures," Kelli said, showing them the camera. "I promise, I won't say a word to him." She couldn't hear the flute anymore. It had drifted out of range, and the sun had dipped under the horizon, and this was exactly the moment she needed to be using her itching trigger finger. "I'm not looking for trouble."

"Did Poe write about the piper?" Ronnie asked.

"Grimm," the first boy said.

"And Browning," the girl added.

The first boy stepped close enough to grab Kelli, but she stayed her ground. "Tell us," he said, "when did you last go to the circus?"

"What?"

"Clowns," the boy said. "Elephants. Trapezes."

"Gray always says the trapeze," Ronnie said.

"That's because he was a flier," the girl said.

Ronnie came around Gray's side. "He always forgets the magicians. I want to be a magician when I get bigger."

"You can't," the girl said. "You're a juggler."

"I don't want to be a juggler."

"You're a juggler," the girl said again.

"Anyway," Gray said, raising his voice over the others, "when were you there?"

Kelli couldn't remember the last time she'd been to the circus. She didn't think they meant Cirque du Soleil, though she'd seen one of their traveling shows not too long ago. "I went to the carnival last autumn."

Gray made a face. "Ugly people, carnies. What about the circus?"

Kelli shook her head. "Years."

Gray frowned. Ronnie turned away and kicked a rock off the path.

"They left without us," the girl said. "I'm sure they noticed by now. The Ringmaster. He'll come back for us."

"He can't. He's got to press on," Gray said. "No going backwards. I hate to say it, but he'll have to replace us along the way. He can't come back."

"But...we're irreplaceable."

"No," Ronnie said sadly, "we're not." He stepped off the path and climbed back onto the marble slab. Gray, too, stepped aside.

"Godspeed," Gray said. "And good luck."

Kelli, thoroughly weirded out and barely able to comprehend what had just happened, walked past them. She almost didn't glance back, but she did. The girl, whose name she never heard, hopped off the grave and ran to her.

"Take this," the girl said, holding out a huge, colorful ring, bright glass beads designed to look like a red, purple, and green flower on a brass setting.

"Why?" Kelli asked.

The girl shrugged. "Because I can." Then she lowered her voice to confide, "In the circus, I twirled the baton."

Rather than accept the wine, Anna, whose eyes never strayed from his, stepped away.

6.

He should recognize something. A landmark. A street. A path. There ought to be signposts and labels, and the damned map should be a lot more helpful than it was. But none of this was true. Kevin finally sighed and, out of breath, leaned against a crooked headstone and closed his eyes.

He tried not to cry.

Here, wherever that was, all the graves were crooked, and many had toppled over or broken apart. Wild grass and weeds had overtaken the entire area, even growing through cracks in the stone rectangles marking the individual plots. He was already leaning on the stone before he realized his weight might be enough to knock it over.

He snapped away, as if he'd just touched something mysterious and gooey.

He'd run after Jill and lost his wife. (He couldn't admit she was inside one of those things, how could she be?) He'd run looking for a caretaker and lost himself. He wouldn't be able to find the mausoleums again even if he'd gotten someone with a full set of keys. He never saw Sabine's Wishing again, or the tomb marked *Suffer the Illusion,* or anything else even remotely familiar.

He had to remind himself this had been his idea.

He wiped away a tear that had managed to squeeze out from under his lids and opened his eyes again. The strange, stark twilight sky looked like someone had turned up the contrast too high. A raven, on a nearby cross (on the one arm still remaining; the other arm had fallen off and lay in pieces around the stone), stared down at him.

"What are *you* looking at?" he demanded.

The raven said nothing.

Another bird, closer but behind him, cawed. This one sat atop a weeping statue of Mary. He thought he saw actual tears, but realized it was one of his again. The stone said *Lenore. Lost, 1845.* Behind that, another read *Annabel Lee, with the angels now, 1849.*

"You're mad," Kevin told the graves.

With a soft flutter, the raven flew away.

What if Jill never got out? What if she was trapped forever, or if she'd already run out of air? Would they think he'd done it? There'd be inquiries. Police would necessarily uncover all their secrets. His secrets. They'd search for motives, and opportunity, and find plenty of both.

"Real men," said a woman's voice, a juxtaposition of girlishness and seduction, "are not afraid to cry." Barely a whisper, her breath chilly under his ear, but when he turned he was alone.

He peered around the headstone and said, just loud enough to hear it himself, "I'm not afraid."

At the top of the hill, a woman looked down at him, her raven-black dress and hair fluttering in the breeze. Green eyes: he saw those from here and felt their pressure. She didn't move or wave or speak, didn't so much as shift her weight; if the wind hadn't played around her, Kevin might've mistaken the woman for another statue. There were so many, and she stood stone-still.

For a long, long moment, he forgot about his wife. It wasn't a sudden lust for this woman, who was too thin to be his type anyway, but an oblivion that filled his chest. A vast, endless nothingness in which his heart beat out a crisp, lonely staccato.

The moment passed, Kevin regained all his sense and memory, and he waved to the woman. "I need help!" he called, hurrying up the hill toward her. "My wife..."

The woman wasn't there.

7.

Kelli, taking pictures as she walked, was marveling at the stretch of time this strange twilight had taken when she reached the mausoleums.

Two rows of vaults faced each other, all topped with crosses, adorned with cherubs and angels. On one, a crucifix was set upon a round mirror, so the bronze Jesus was backed by four seemingly separate reflections, three being abstract and stark as the sky, one being a cross until Kelli moved closer and all the images shifted.

She positioned herself right, with the cross visible again, and took another picture.

There were no dates here, only family names, flowers, chains on one iron gate, marble doors with engravings showing the countenance of saints, rosary beads and candles and snapshots hanging by any means present. It almost felt like a city, except no one sat on the stoop and, to be perfectly honest, no one would answer if she knocked.

Just to be sure, of course, she didn't knock.

It would be dark soon. She had a flashlight in her camera bag; she'd come prepared. She wasn't too far from the main road cutting through the cemetery; it would lead her back to the gates. She had put some thought into this before setting out. She didn't mean to get caught alone in the dark with only the fireflies to guide her home.

After all, she didn't trust the fireflies.

She didn't think most of tonight's pictures would work. The light was too bleached and bleak, the contrast too high. She expected she'd have something to work with when she got home, but not what she'd been seeking. The streaked clouds should've been wonderful at picking up the reds of sunset, and her camera was exceptionally well-suited for capturing such colors. Instead, it was...strange. Eerie. Which must've been why she'd started thinking about the people not living inside these vaults.

Camera still in hand, she decided to call it a night and head home.

8.

"You're mistaken," Jill told the ghostly voice. "I wished for no man."

"You cannot lie to me," he told her.

"I..." She hesitated. "My wish was for someone *with* me."

"You wished for a perfect man."

"I wished for my man to be perfect."

"You're going to argue semantics with me?"

"It was my wish." She pounded on the cold, stone wall. "Let me out."

"Is that a wish, as well?"

"Damn you."

"Another wish?" the voice asked. He sounded closer now. She felt his presence behind her, in the absolute darkness. She spun, swinging an open hand, slapping only air, though perhaps a black smoke shifted in the murk.

"My husband," Jill said, "will be back. With people."

"A caretaker, yes," the voice said. "I heard."

Silence. Jill held her breath to hear any hint of the man locked in with her, but she heard no sound of movement and no breath. "What do you want?"

"This and that," the man said. "What do you want?"

"I already told you."

"You've contradicted yourself," the man said. "Wishing for one thing, wishing for another. There was a king once, in some medieval land, a boy king who ascended at far too early an age. He built his kingdom upon wishes. Whims. Fancy. He erected palaces unsurpassed in the history of imagination. He amassed treasures and wonders from every corner of the earth. There are more than four, you know. From every corner, he gathered jewels and sculptures and musical instruments some say were enchanted. An entire kingdom, built upon the wishes of a boy king."

The man paused. Jill wanted nothing more than to get out, back into the open air, away from this stranger who was obviously mad, but her curiosity bested her. "What happened?"

"Like all things of cloud and mist, he lost his kingdom to the breeze."

"Sad," Jill admitted. "Is there a point?"

"Stop wishing."

Jill laughed, because otherwise she'd have to scream and she didn't think her throat could take too much of that and she might never stop.

"What's your name?" the man asked.

"You don't know?"

"Do I look like a god to you?"

He looked like nothing, as that was all she could see, so she didn't respond.

"My name's Auguste."

"It's not."

"It is. And I'm pleased to meet you." He paused. "You are?"

"Not so pleased," she said, and then, finally, "Jill."

"Such a plain name."

"I'm a plain girl."

"Oh no, Jill," he said. "You're something extraordinary. I can't call you Jill. Have you any other name?"

"My mom used to call me Star Flower when I was a baby."

"You're trying to hurt me," Auguste said.

"Then it'll have to be Jill."

Somehow, ludicrous as it was if she gave it too much thought, conversing with Auguste about trivial things and in such a lighthearted way kept her from falling fully into panic. She'd had a moment of it, at the start, but her control was slight at best.

"I'll help you out, Jill," Auguste said, "though I rather wish you'd stay. You've already come so far."

"So far?"

"There are layers," he said, "between life and death. You cross one just by being at the cemetery. You're one step closer already. Twilight, another step."

"How many steps are there?"

"For some, only one."

"I'm not dead," Jill said. Just to be sure, she held a hand in front of her face. She wasn't just breathing, she was practically panting.

"Not yet."

9.

Five years.

That's how long Anna had known Darren. He'd known her longer, perhaps, but she wasn't sure of it. Depends on whose version of how they met you believed. She thought they were both right, which made it difficult to place a date on their first meeting. No less than five years, of that she was certain.

Anna was certain of other things, too, many things, but at the moment, none of those seemed very important.

Five years, she'd known him, but now his eyes had a glint she'd never seen, a mischievousness that did not well suit a man holding a knife. A sword. Whatever the hell it was.

She'd thought it might be enchanted. Now, she feared it was cursed.

She took another step back, away from this man who alternatively loved and frustrated her, her closest ever friend, the one person she'd always thought she could trust.

It was the harshness of the freaky twilight air reflecting in his eyes, surely this and nothing more.

"Aren't you going to drink?" he asked, thrusting the bottle toward her—the bottle, not the weapon, Darren was still Darren no matter how the coming night lit him.

She took the bottle, but kept her eyes on him as she drank from it. He didn't seem to notice, and turned to look back toward the rest house. "Suppose we'll have to keep on resting," he said.

"They're out," Anna told him. "All about us, we just can't see them."

"Then they're not really about us, are they?" Darren asked, whirling back on her. "They're about mysteries and secrets, they're about themselves, but they're certainly not about *us*."

"Darren," Anna said, putting into her voice all the playfulness she could muster, "are you drunk?"

He grinned. "Not yet."

"Am I safe with you?"

He narrowed his eyes. "What kind of question is that? Of course you're safe with me. You've always been safe with me." He sighed deeply, melodramatically, and said, "Too safe, actually, but I'm not about to change that."

She'd never felt the need to ask before.

"You realize I love you, don't you?" Darren asked. "I might've said it, you might've heard it, but you've never really known it."

"I've always known." Not a lie.

"Ah," he said, nodding. Then, with an exaggerated flourish, he turned away from her and stared into the cemetery. Away from the rest house. She watched, aware that a moment had passed and she'd allowed it to pass, had hoped never to actually face the moment head on, and because of that glint in his eye and the cursed blade in his hand, Anna suddenly felt nervous.

It wasn't like her.

It didn't suit her.

She didn't like it.

And it wasn't like Darren, either, to make her nervous.

"It should be dark," he said. "But I can still see amazingly well."

She stepped forward, put a hand on his shoulder. "What do you see?"

His voice hitched. "Ravens."

They were everywhere, she suddenly realized. Atop the tents, in the trees, evenly spaced on the headstones and vaults near them. If the birds had all been looking at them, she would've freaked. But still, there were so many.

He turned again, his eyes filled with tears, the malicious glint nearly completely gone. An overwhelming wave of pity struck Anna, capped with happiness and joy and love, all the possibilities and impossibilities their pairing would've represented. Sadness. Elation. She felt lightheaded, wavering, unsteady.

He embraced her. Tight. Enveloping. Arms clear around her back, head on her shoulder, as much to support himself. She hugged him back, a familiar and comfortable expression...

He slid the blade between the ribs just beside her spine. It didn't hurt as much as she would've imagined, but it was hot, and wet, and the hot was only in her back because the rest of her quickly chilled. She tried to breathe, but couldn't draw in any air.

"I love you," Darren whispered.

Anna moved her mouth, but no sound came out. The barren white of twilight faded quite suddenly to night.

10.

Inside the mausoleum, Jill couldn't see night fall, but she felt it. Even in the burial chamber, she thought—or imagined—she could see her breath. And Auguste, with her, sighed with pleasure, as if relieved of a great and terrible burden.

11.

Only birds. Kevin looked left and right, sure there had been a woman here, but the sudden shift to moonlight made it hard to see much of anything. If not for the ravens, he would've been utterly alone.

Trust not thine eyes
under the tricksy light of the moon
—The Book of Lost Fates

III. Nevermore

1.

In the great city of the dead, corpses are interred almost daily. A million bodies reside under its grass, though perhaps not so many souls.

In the great city of the dead, there are sections devoted to Catholics, Protestants, Jews, Muslims, and Asians. There's an area for Greek Orthodox, another for Russian Orthodox. The least elaborately decorated section belongs to dead Quakers.

In the great city of the dead, there are crypts beneath chapels, there are walls holding ashes behind plaques and roses, there are vaults and mausoleums and headstones and footstones and memorials and shrines. There are local and national heroes, some of whom have been forgotten in the two or three centuries since their passing, others who will be forgotten after the news ink dries.

In the great city of the dead, there are mice and rabbits and birds and insects, and a number of these die or become prey within its gates.

The great city of the dead holds a place for you.

2.

Kevin didn't like being alone.

He wished Jill was with him. But it was on account of Jill that he'd gotten so lost. He couldn't blame her, not exactly; there had been enough blame already.

But the past had passed. Those sins were mere memories.

If he had a flashlight, Kevin would have no idea where to go. He could sit, hope for a watchman to come along, perhaps bearing a lantern and listening for the bells that indicated a living person underground.

Like Jill, inside that mausoleum.

If he couldn't find a caretaker, Kevin could at least find his way back to his wife. The woman he loved. The woman who, as a girl, had answered all of his dreams. He should have the strength, the fortitude, to dig his way through solid marble to release her. Damn it, why did he always have to be so *weak*?

"Real men," the woman's voice said, again a whisper, "do not fear fear."

He looked around, unable to see anything but the silhouettes of gravestones and the ragged limbs of trees and the innumerable black-feathered birds. "Who are you?"

She answered with a question: "Are you a real man?"

Kevin swallowed, peering deep into the darkness. "I am."

"Real men do not hesitate."

Then he saw her, accented by the light of the moon but barely visible at the far end of the next row of granite and stone. Hair flowing gently. Dress fluttering. Eyes so green, the color reached through the night and across the cemetery and ripped away a chunk of his chest. His mouth dried, and an involuntary shudder ran to his fingertips.

He managed to say, "Wait." Getting his feet to move took a little more effort. But this time, he did not let his eyes stray. He did not look away when a nearby raven called out. He stumbled over a twig in the path, but did not fall. She became more difficult to discern as he got closer, swallowed by the dark, but her siren-eyes were beacons and he would absolutely not lose his way.

When he was close enough to speak like normal people, still walking closer, he said, "Who are you?"

She smiled. Held out a hand to him. Black cloth from the dress dripped gypsy-like from her arm. Her lips were red, and she wore bright eyeshadow of blue and yellow and purple slashes that must've doubled the size of her eyes. She was beautiful, not in a typical or conventional way, not in any way Kevin could describe. Her face, her whole body, was made up of flowing arcs, curves, arches, and waves. Her hand didn't simply reach out to him, it cascaded, and he would've reached back even if he hadn't felt obligated to do so.

Her grip was tight, her fingers warm, her nails some red that department stores probably called wild cherry dream or bloodmuse.

Kevin realized, quite suddenly, that he was more thoroughly lost than he could've imagined.

3.

Unsure of what else to do, Darren cried. Good, long, and hard. He let the tears fly, and rocked with the sobs, and rubbed his hands on his jeans in an attempt to clear the blood. And then he'd lift Anna's head again, stroke her cheek or brush a strand of hair from her face. She was cooling already, and after losing a small pond the blood had finally stopped gushing.

And Darren still clutched the knife, holding onto it in case the world ended and he had to face the minions of Hell, gripping it as if it was the only tether to his fractured sanity. He told her again and again how much he'd loved her, how he'd always loved her, how all the world ought to end with her, but she let loose her last breath without a response, and her eyes glazed over and no longer focused on anything.

Not even Darren.

He dropped some curses between the tears, though they were poorly aimed and ultimately pointless. At one point, he rocked Anna like a baby, shushing her, telling her everything would be alright.

And everything would be. He was sure of it. Whatever came his way, he was ready. Prepared. He'd never been so strong. He'd made the kind of sacrifice demanded by wicked gods throughout the ages. The pain hurt worse than if he'd stabbed himself.

Eventually, the tears dried, the rocking subsided. And a lady put a comforting hand on his shoulder and whispered, "Everything will be alright."

4.

Despite that Kelli had her flashlight, or maybe because of it, the lightning bugs seemed drawn to her. They were everywhere, now that she was walking down the road. The strip of asphalt was lined by gravestones, and there wasn't a single streetlamp to be seen. Even the offices, in which someone surely must still be working, were dark; it was as if there was a blackout.

No cars, either, but that was to be expected. Gates closed at dusk. Who wanted to be trapped inside the cemetery overnight?

The fireflies made no sound, at least none that Kelli heard, but there was the occasional call of a raven or rustling of field mice. She wasn't concerned. Not worried. Not the least bit intimidated.

She wondered if those kids still sat on the tombstone playing word games.

She even wondered if she'd really seen them.

She pointed the light back, toward the mausoleums. They were just on the other side of those vaults. A ten minute walk, if she didn't stop to take pictures. Go back? No, she couldn't do that, shouldn't. Why?

And again, the wind carried the sounds of a flute.

"Okay," she said, mostly to herself; only an agent of Fate might've heard. But she didn't move. A magpie stared at her from its perch on a nearby headstone, the white feathers of its chest illuminated by the fireflies. Its black beak bobbed, and it sang a full measure of notes, its usual song, perhaps in answer to the flute.

The flutist played on, standing behind the mausoleums, his back to Kelli, no more visible than a ghost in the moonlight.

She took several pictures, no flash; the musician silhouetted against the sky, houses of death on one side, woods on the other. Not likely to come out, but her camera was good. She approached the magpie. It flew off. Kelli perched her camera on top of the stone (she carried no tripod), pointed it up toward the flutist, and took a few more shots.

The flutist continued. Kelli knew she should be happy, but she wanted more. She wanted closer.

She started up the hill.

5.

"Houdini would've escaped by now," Auguste said.

Jill was exhausted. Not just physically. She kept back her emotions, lest they overwhelm, but the effort was monumental. She wanted to scream and cry and beat this Auguste to death with her fists. And Kevin, too, this had been his idea.

(No, the running had been hers, but she felt better focusing her anger outward.)

She wanted to tear apart the mausoleum walls. Burrow out. Escape. Yes, Houdini would've done it, but she was no Houdini.

Maintaining an even voice, Jill said, "You're not going to help me, are you?"

"Is that what you want, then? My help?"

"Damn you, yes," Jill said.

He left.

She couldn't see, didn't hear any footstep, didn't feel any sudden movement in the air. She couldn't say how she knew, but she was alone.

Mostly alone.

There were the corpses.

She turned back to the wall, reached for where a knob might be— and snatched her hand back when it touched something soft. Something that moved.

"Oh, God," she said, stepping back, deeper into the dark. She bumped another wall, this one also smooth and cold. She tried not to think about what she'd touched, what it might've been. Not a body, no. Not something dead.

Now she heard them. Or imagined it. Sets of legs, eight apiece, scurrying up and down the walls, across the floor. Dropping from the ceiling on threads.

One landed on her head. She felt each of its eight legs, a span as large as her hairdresser's hand, lighter than a deck of playing cards.

Still backing away, she swiped it off. It hit the ground with a thud.

Jill bumped the wall behind her. Or something not quite a wall, perhaps a sarcophagus, stone and heavy but only as high as her chest. She pushed away from it. Her hands came back sticky with web.

A spider jumped on her arm. She didn't understand how they could see her, as she couldn't see a damned thing and she'd been in here long enough for her eyes to adjust to any light, had it been there.

She threw it off. Another landed in her hair, and then she felt one climbing her leg. Under her pants. When it bit her, she pounded the butt of her fist into her calf and squashed the spider, leaving a wet spot on her leg even as another bit her in the back of the neck.

They were crawling all over her now. A dozen spiders or more. She brushed off what she could, reached behind her back and scraped her hand on stone, and they continued biting.

6.

The fireflies followed her.

As a child, she remembered catching them in plastic milk cartons. She remembered thinking she should have mason jars for the job, but it wasn't until much later that she even knew what a mason jar looked like.

Now, they seemed intent on catching her. They crisscrossed in front of her, an entire sprinkle of fireflies (like a clutter of spiders or an unkindness of ravens. Some hit her, though they had no sting, no bite, no talon, and no weight.

As she got closer to the flutist, as his wonderful lullaby (for that's what it had become) grew clearer, the lightning bugs seemed to double in number. And then, quite suddenly, they scattered.

The song stopped. Slowly, casually, the flutist turned, looked down the hill at Kelli with a hard, harsh gaze. "Who are you?" he asked.

The question surprised her. "Kelli."

"Kelli," he said. "Well?"

She looked around her but found no answers, so she made up her own. "That was beautiful."

He hefted the flute in one hand. "This?"

"That," Kelli said. "You." She couldn't see him, not entirely, but the sound of his voice was as soothing, as irresistible, as his music. She had to consciously tell her feet to stop, and even then wasn't entirely sure they obeyed.

"You interrupted," he said. "I'll have to go again from the start. Do you know the song?"

"Never heard it before."

"I'm not surprised." He lifted the instrument to his lips—which effectively hid his glare—inhaled, and blew. Notes floated seamlessly from the flute (which surely must be silver, if not magic), but he stopped after a single bar, lowered the instrument, and asked, "Are you a soprano?"

"I can't sing."

"Pity." Then he resumed, from the beginning again, and Kelli melted. After a very short while, she barely noticed anymore the ravens sitting atop the nearby vaults; if one called out, she did not hear it—nor what might've been screaming from within one of the mausoleums, as the sound drowned in the lullaby. Kelli herself drowned. She forgot about the camera, the flashlight, the fireflies. She forgot where she was. Before the song ended, she nearly forgot *who* she was. She managed, somehow, to maintain that piece of knowledge.

The flutist lowered his instrument, glared again at her, and asked, "Aren't you at least going to give me a dollar for my efforts?"

7.

When a door opened, it didn't matter which door it was, or where it led, or who had opened it. Didn't matter if it had been locked. Could've been her husband on the other side, Kevin, hopeless and helpless as he was. Or Auguste, the ghost, or whatever he was. She might've found herself on the streets of Budapest. Prague. Milwaukee. Jill would've bet money against emerging in the cemetery.

She would've lost.

But she was more concerned with the spiders.

Stumbling into the grass beside the mausoleum, she crushed two under her knees. She flung them off her arms, shook her head wildly to dislodge more. Then stared in horror at the burgeoning welts across her arms, swelling red marks where they had bitten her. She had trouble breathing through her throat. Her eyes itched, her blood burned. Jill whimpered and fell over. Felt more spiders crawling over her, but couldn't care anymore, couldn't do anything about it, could barely open her eyes.

And when she did, in the dark, in the cemetery, she saw the feet of a man decked out in full white tie regalia: silk tailcoat, white waistcoat beneath it, gleaming shoes with diamond buckles, diamond cufflinks. So amazingly out of place, she saw him through the pain, through the blindness that erased all else. "Poisoned..." she gasped.

He shook his head and bent at the knees to be closer to her. "Venom," he corrected. "Five or six different kinds, it would seem. A shock, to see so many species of spider living harmoniously within the confines of King's Vault, don't you agree?"

Jill was foaming at the mouth now, and could no longer focus on the overdressed Auguste. Even closing her eyes hurt, but at least then she could be reasonably sure it would be a short-lived pain.

"Look, they're all going away," Auguste said. "I think you scared them." He put a warm—no, hot—hand on her shoulder. "I should tell you, they can't hurt you. It's all in your mind. How you think you should react. They weren't venomous, none of them, merely a nest of wolf spiders, nasty though they may be, but certainly harmless."

He continued speaking, but the words jumbled and slipped and, try as she might, Jill could concentrate on nothing past the agony. She might've thrown up, or imagined it, or merely wished for any form of relief.

August removed his hand, stood, and stepped away. "When you're done," he said, "I'll be over here."

Jill managed one last breath, and then nothing. No more. Her heart stopped pumping, the blood stilled in her veins. All at once, the pain vanished. All pain. Every ache, every twist, every discomfort she'd been feeling, the scratch on her hand and the bites and the venom, gone.

Jill waited.

She opened her eyes.

Still on the ground. She saw the last few spiders scuttling off. Heard their ever-so-light footsteps on the grass. Noticed the glint of diamonds just beyond the edge of the mausoleum and just in front of the woods. She heard a lullaby, carried on the wind, so wonderful a song she could never let herself fall asleep to it, yet could never resist. She focused on that music, the certainty that there was someone else near, someone other than Auguste, who had not only released her from the tomb but had imprisoned her there.

She wasn't one to forget or forgive so easily—as Kevin had learned.

Jill wiped her mouth. She felt lighter, freer, unbound. Looking down at her fingers, she saw through them, but only slightly, grass beneath her hand, and the remains of a crushed spider the size of her fist.

Slowly, deliberately, she rose to her feet, pushing off the ground and even using the mausoleum's wall for support. The stone's texture was visible through her hand. She inhaled deeply, the first since she had stopped, but it went nowhere so she let it loose.

The distant flute paused.

Jill turned to Auguste. "You killed me."

"You're not dead."

"I'm not alive."

He shrugged, one shouldered, and said, "Such narrow definitions."

"Whatever it is," Jill said, "you did it."

He shook his head. "I must plead not guilty, though you may choose not to believe it. I merely…helped. You were already on the path."

"There is no path," Jill said. "You're a murderer."

"Well, there is that," Auguste said. "But you are not my victim."

Tears dropped from her eyes. She hadn't realized she'd been crying, the water was so light and ethereal. Where the tears landed—only four or five, for now—little white flowers sprouted. She wiped her eyes, refusing to give in to sobs.

"Thus, your husband was already too late," Auguste said. "You had slipped from life."

"What do you want from me?"

"Ah, finally, a direct and specific question, and one deserving of an answer." He grinned. From the ground, she hadn't noticed the cape, the cane, the white gloves and scarf. She had never seen anyone so fancily dressed, not even Kevin at their wedding, not even the priest.

A minute passed, and another, and Jill realized Auguste had no intention of giving an answer.

8.

"How can you know that?" Darren asked, not looking at the lady behind him. He couldn't see anything but Anna on the ground before him, and the knife he still gripped, and all the blood, and the future he'd erased.

He didn't look at this lady who claimed everything would be alright, because in his heart, he knew she was right. As right as any woman—or man—who ever existed. Her voice carried wisdom, ageless and timeless and limitless. Though he'd asked how she could know, he didn't need an answer, and none was offered.

"Take her," the lady said.

Darren nodded. He shoved the knife into his belt, maybe slicing his jeans and cutting his leg, but he felt nothing. He slipped his arms under Anna, one beneath her legs, the other at the top of her back. She weighed nothing. He rose, careful not to let Anna's head tilt back, and said, "Where are we going?"

"Someplace safe."

Darren smiled. It was a sad, defeated smile, but honest and true. *Someplace safe*, she'd said, and that sounded wonderful.

9.

Kevin held her hand for a long while, standing at the crest of the hill, caressed by the breeze and witnessed by the ravens. He didn't know who she was, only that she owned a part of him now, some deep and hidden corner of his heart and soul he had never before known existed.

"Real men," she said, "do not fear love."

Kevin stared at her red lips. They hadn't seemed to move, but he couldn't be sure, not with the shadows and his unnatural intoxication. His knees trembled. What strength he had fled, taking with it his hopes and dreams and...

"Help me," he said, again remembering the mausoleum, but his voice was small and pathetic. "My wife."

The birds all around him rustled. Several took flight, others landed, they cawed and screeched and cackled. A raven landed on the woman's shoulder. With one black eye, it looked directly at Kevin and said, in a deep, gravel voice, "Nevermore."

Kevin shook his head, slowly at first, growing more vehement. "No." He said it again, as if repetition gave the word weight. "*No*."

"Nevermore," said the raven.

The woman stepped closer, so those gorgeous red lips came next to his ear, and she whispered delicately, "Not afraid to cry." The raven took off; the darkness swallowed it.

Kevin cried. The tears rolled freely down his cheek, splashing on the ground at his feet. Where they fell, little white flowers sprouted, flowers that for no reason whatsoever reminded Kevin of Jill. His wife. The woman he'd loved, the woman he'd failed.

"Drink," the woman said. With her free hand, she offered a cup. It was small, the clouded liquid inside swirling. Kevin accepted it, sniffed, detected a hint of poppy, maybe sugar, even cocoa.

"Nepenthe," the woman said, to answer his unvoiced question. "Real men are not afraid to forget."

When she takes your hand,
walk comfortably with Nyx.
The night is hers.
So, too, are you.
—The Book of Lost Fates

IIII. Covenant

1.

In the great city of the dead, the dark is deep and thick and rich and never barren. There are stories and songs and poems and lies.

In the great city of the dead, night is relentless. Bare tree limbs are indeed skeletons. Vines entwine. Statues breathe. Creatures speak, both hideously and wondrously. Rats are rabid. Spiders venomous. Birds ravenous. Wind is the breath of demons.

In the great city of the dead, even atheists steal a moment for prayer.

2.

Carrying Anna (he couldn't say her body, or her corpse), Darren let the lady lead him away from the tents, away from the rest house, between rows of old, crooked headstones. To *someplace safe,* wherever and whatever that may be. He hadn't even looked at this lady, couldn't describe her face or her skin color or what she wore. His eyes were, primarily, on Anna, and whatever else was necessary to make sure he didn't drop her.

She was so cold. He never remembered her being cold. She might've needed a jacket more often than not, might've frozen solid through her mittens in the snow, but this was early autumn; most leaves hadn't started to change, and summer's heat lingered during the day.

He only noticed the change of season at night, when the temperature dropped some, but it wasn't mitten and snow weather, it wasn't cause enough for Anna's skin to be so frigid and her lips so blue.

Darren tried to get a better idea of where they were. The wine was gone, the knife still in his belt. There were woods to one side, and mausoleums ahead preceded by a chapel.

Which, of course, must be the lady's *someplace safe.* At the moment, he didn't remember safe.

"What happens now?" Darren asked, as the lady passed the path to the chapel door.

She paused, turned to look at him, but said nothing. With the moon behind her, Darren only saw her silhouette. It distressed him that he couldn't see her face. Was she smiling? Glaring? Sizing him up like a slab of roast?

Finally, the lady asked, "How far would you go for her?"

"How far is there?"

3.

Kelli gave the flutist a dollar. It was the least she could do.

Accepting it without touching her, he stuffed it into a pants pocket. "Do you have a request?" he asked.

"Request?"

He half-sighed, half-snarled. "Anything in particular you want to hear?"

"Nothing in particular, no," Kelli said, her voice taking on a dreamy quality she'd never before known. "Anything is good. Whatever."

"I'm already tired of you." He turned.

Shocked, Kelli didn't know how to respond. She ran after him, put a hand on his shoulder, mumbled something like, "Wait."

He swatted her hand away with enough force to sting, and whirled on her, raising the flute as a weapon. He paused, long enough for Kelli to recover from flinching, and then he struck her on the side of the head.

She nearly toppled. Dropped her camera in the grass. She touched her head where he'd hit her; her hand came away sticky and wet. She opened her mouth, sure she wanted to say something, but when no words came she closed it again.

"You get nothing," the flutist said.

"But...I gave you a dollar."

"And I asked for a request."

She averted her eyes. "I don't know any songs for flute."

The flute whistled, briefly, as it moved, and he hit her again. Kelli's head rung. She staggered. "Stop that."

He hit her again.

This time, she nearly fell, not because it was an overwhelmingly hard blow (it wasn't), but because the succession dazed and bewildered her. She managed to stay on her feet, but stepped back and aside, out of the flute's reach.

"Please," Kelli said. "A song. Any song."

He sneered, stroking the end of his flute where it had hit her. "You got blood on my instrument. And hair."

"I'm..." It was his fault, but she couldn't say that. "I'm sorry."

He withdrew a handkerchief from a pocket and used it to clean his flute. Kelli stared, dumfounded and dizzy, finally understanding what she was doing. Confronting a stranger. Challenging him. Allowing herself to be abused. Standing there and simply taking it.

The smart thing to do was turn around and leave.

She bent to pick up her camera first. Couldn't leave that. She watched the flutist over her shoulder as she returned to her feet, and kept her eyes on him as she descended the hillside. He took his time, wiping the flute, and didn't once look at her. He wasn't very handsome, rather disheveled and unkempt. Now that his song was just a memory, Kelli saw the blemishes, the scars, the chaotic tangle of his hair and the wild, mad intensity in his eyes. He, on the other hand, riveted all his attention on his instrument.

Satisfied, he lifted it to his lips, didn't even glance in her direction, and started to play.

Something in Kelli's stomach lurched. She would've described it as her heart, but she knew it was too low and far grittier. It was the tune; in her last moment of absolute clarity, she recognized this. She tried not to listen. But ears didn't close as eyes might; when she touched the side of her head in an effort to cover them, it hurt.

The pain kept her sane, but only for a moment.

The flute was silver. It must've been, the way it reflected the moonlight. His fingers danced over the keys, his lips were parted ever so slightly. Kelli stopped walking. Listened. Enjoyed. Eventually, she came closer, and this time she could see the flutist's grin. It couldn't rightly be called a smile, not behind that embouchure, but it reached the corners of his closed eyes and sent a shiver through Kelli's insides.

4.

"I'm done, then," Jill said, walking into the little street running between the two rows of mausoleums. She felt exposed—by the moonlight, by a mirror behind a cross on a door, by the watchful cherub eyes that seemed to adorn every vault. She looked back twice, but Auguste seemed content to remain where he was. He held the cane in front of him, both hands resting on it, his whole body tilted slightly to one side—and also his head. He looked cocky enough to expect Jill to come back.

No chance of that.

She wanted to call out for Kevin. But that would've involved taking a deep breath, which in turn would've reminded her she wasn't breathing at all. What if her voice had no more substance than the wind?

She stepped closer to one of the vaults, where a crucified Jesus averted his eyes. Behind the sculpture, in the mirror, she didn't see much more than darkness, and just a hint of her own eyes. As if it was confirmation.

"I'm not dead," she whispered.

The cemetery looked entirely different, as if the paths had shifted at nightfall. Kevin might've run in any direction seeking help, and was probably out there now, lost amongst the tombstones, waiting for some watchman to rescue him.

"And me," she reminded him in a whisper.

Behind her, Auguste laughed. Not loudly. Sounded as if he tried desperately *not* to laugh, in fact. A ruse. This whole thing was a charade. Where were the hidden cameras? The jokers? Kevin was probably in on it, too, the lynchpin.

She tried to ignore the fact that no one could've arranged for her breathing to stop; after all, it must've been psychosomatic. Maybe she'd been hypnotized to believe she wasn't breathing when, in fact, she was panting and gasping.

Maybe it was a final delusion, and she was still inside King's Vault with the spiders and their venoms.

Up ahead, the music sounded louder. Not some phantom sound, but an actual man standing on the hill with a flute pressed to his lips. The song was nice, and it tugged at her, but she didn't care.

With long, confident strides, she left the mausoleums, reached the street, picked a direction, and went.

She only stopped when she saw a girl staring open-mouthed at the flutist.

"He's just a man," Jill told her. "Not worth the effort."

The girl blinked at her. "Can I walk with you?"

Jill glanced back. No sign of Auguste. "Sure. I'm Jill."

"Kelli."

"Pleased to meet you."

"Do you know you're not breathing?" Kelli asked.

"I think I know."

"It's disconcerting. I can't believe I can even see it, but it's obvious."

"I'm not dead."

Kelli nodded. "That's good."

"You're bleeding," Jill said, reaching for—but not touching—the side of the girl's head.

"It's nothing. A scratch."

"We're both pretty fucked up, aren't we?" Jill asked.

Kelli laughed, or cried, or both, and the duo walked away from the musician.

5.

Even in the great city of the dead, you cannot simply walk away from your problems.

6.

For a long while, Kevin stared, the cup and its milky drink blurred by tears.

The surface reflected a ghostly image of Jill, barely an echo. She was insubstantial, walking alongside another woman. The other bled. His wife didn't breathe. There were spiders in her hair, and welts all over her skin where they'd bitten her. Her eyes were veiled by cobwebs and did not focus.

He couldn't hear them, but he saw the lines on Jill's cheek marking the path of her tears.

"Nepenthe," the woman said again. "To forget."

Kevin's voice was barely a whisper. "I failed her."

"Yes. You failed her *again*."

"I can't," Kevin said, meeting the woman's eyes. "No."

7.

Kelli walked beside Jill all the way to the iron fence that marked the edge of the cemetery. The gates in the road were closed to prevent cars from entering, but beside those, lit by a streetlamp, was an opening for pedestrians.

Jill had shaken her from the flutist's spell. She wasn't sure how or why; she hadn't fully realized she'd been entrapped in the first place. Entrapped was *not* the same as enraptured. Listening to the flute, she'd been mistaken.

(She still heard its lullaby from somewhere in the back of her mind. It would stay with her the rest of her life.)

On the inside of the fence, Kelli paused, took Jill's hand in hers, and said, "Thanks."

"Thank you," Jill said. "I think I was lost."

"We were."

Jill shook her head. "Not any more." They smiled, awkwardly, two strangers who had together faced something, neither of them sure of exactly what that something had been, and released each other's hands.

"You're still not breathing," Kelli said, taking one step back.

"On the other side of that fence," Jill nodded toward the gate, "I will."

Kelli waited for the other woman to go first. She held her breath. She didn't expect this to work. Where was the mad flutist? Would he step in front of her, just at the last moment, and start beating her again? Would she stand for it?

She was ashamed. And scared. Scared, not because of the musician or what he did, but because of what she'd done—or more precisely, that she'd done nothing.

The flute started a new song as Jill stepped through the gate.

8.

The dead, on their own, cannot easily leave the great city of the dead.

9.

A two lane road ran alongside the cemetery. Across from that, there was a small field. During the day, children played ball there, and tag, and any other games that involved a lot of running. There were a few little shops, houses that had converted over time, mostly selling fresh gravestones, a mortuary house and two florists. Garbage cans lined the road tonight, expecting to be emptied in the morning.

There was no parking on the side of the road nearest the cemetery, and only a few cars in the spots on the other side of the street. Nothing drove up or down, but the streetlamps were evenly spaced and bright enough.

The moon wasn't full, but it reflected plenty of sunlight.

A warmer breeze blew in the street than in the cemetery. At the threshold, Jill felt the difference, and it soothed her. She inhaled deeply, more out of habit than need, and stepped through.

A wave of dizziness struck. She felt lightheaded. Weak in the knees. Nauseous. She dropped to the ground and threw up venom. A spider danced on a thread from her head like any other stray hair.

She hadn't made it out. She'd gone through the gate, but the step had taken her someplace else. There was no street before her, no iron at her side, no bleeding girl behind her. There was only the grass, and the stone vaults, and a brisk wind. Her fingers were numb, her whole hands, even her toes. She wiped her mouth, lifted her head, and stared again at King's Vault.

Offering a hand to help Jill to her feet, Auguste said, "We simply cannot continue to call you Jill."

10.

Kelli stepped forward, reaching for Jill, but the other woman was gone. Whisked away, blurred as if caught in motion by her camera, thrown back into the cemetery the moment she escaped it.

Kelli snatched her hand back lest it pass through the gate.

The flute sounded closer now, not a lullaby anymore, not even soothing. Sinister. Oily. Not the sound of a flute at all. She turned. The musician strolled alongside the road, staying in the grass, as nonchalant as ever. He might not have seen her, except he came straight for her. His eyes were half closed, she could see that even from the gate.

She knew she had to resist. She even succeeded, at first; and she felt when she started slipping. Failure first became possible, then probable, then a fact. Her arms hung limply at her sides, her eyes glazed over, and she ambled toward the approaching musician in some bizarre, surreal caricature of the classic lovers running toward each other in a field. Except in this case, they were in a cemetery; and instead of running, he pranced; and instead of running, she hobbled. And when they should've thrown their arms around each other and spun around in the sunlight, the flute fell silent.

11.

The lady didn't lead Darren far, though it seemed to take forever. They passed the chapel (St. John's) and climbed the hill to the mausoleums. Most had family names engraved into them, and religious sculptures and passages of scripture, but Darren didn't care. Anna was shockingly light in his arms, her body so cold it froze his chest where she was pressed against him.

At one time, she had been everything. But never cold. Not like this.

The lady paused in front of one of the mausoleums, turned, and extended an arm to say *Go right in.* The door stood open. Inviting. Threatening to swallow him whole. The darkness of the tomb was palpable. He was afraid of what may wait on the other side. He didn't look at the name etched above the door; he didn't want to know anything more.

"How far will you go?" the lady asked again.

He looked down at Anna's quiet, beautiful face, and said, "All the way." He held her close, careful not to bang her head on the marble doorjamb, and entered.

The darkness was not complete. Stone sarcophagi stood on either side. Plaques alongside open slabs cut into both walls named the corpses that hid within the coffins. Three spots on both sides, only the bottom right still empty.

Another woman stood at the rear of the mausoleum. She appeared less ethereal than his guide; he would've said she was human, except for the cobweb eyes and the red sores that covered her skin. Beside her, a man in fancy black and white, complete with cape and top hat and cane. He was smaller than the woman, but more regal.

He was important.

But it would be the woman who spoke. He knew.

Darren looked again into Anna's soft, unfocused eyes. The irises had completely lost their color. Or maybe it was a trick of the shadows.

The woman seemed anxious. She looked to the man beside her. "I'm not ready for this," she told him.

"Who ever is?"

"Something's wrong," Darren told her. "With Anna. She's stopped breathing. She's stopped bleeding." The woman looked confused, so he added, "I love her."

The woman looked at Anna, then again at Darren, really looked this time, as if seeing them for the first time. "So?"

Darren didn't know what to do. He didn't know why he was here. He looked to the man for help, a sign, anything, but the man's eyes never left the woman. There were spiders in her hair. And hanging from her fingertips. He saw more as his eyes adjusted. "Help me."

12.

Kevin studied the woman with him. Her green eyes, the colors around them. Red lips that should've tempted him. Her hair and clothes, drifting lazily in the wind, were like feathers. She seemed insubstantial, or indistinct, like she wasn't really there.

Or not *only* there. Moonlight glimmered in her hair and eyes. The breeze seemed to originate from within her. He had the impression that, were he to slip a hand under her clothes, he would find no skin.

He lowered the cup. The nepenthe. "I don't want to forget."

The woman, who was as much night as anything else, released his hand. She reached into an unseen pocket and withdrew a coin.

A dollar.

"You lost this," she said. "Use it well."

When he took the coin, she shimmered. Her body exploded into a hundred ravens and scattered. One perched upon a headstone as the others disappeared in the night. It looked at him, cawed, and flitted to the next stone.

Holding the cup and the coin, Kevin followed his guide.

13.

The flutist drove his instrument like a saber between Kelli's breasts. He sneered. The silver broke skin and cracked bone and pierced her heart; she could do nothing but watch and know that she should've protected herself. She'd taken self defense classes. She had the lungs for screaming. The legs for running.

Instead, she stood there. And touched the wonderful, bright instrument, even as her blood stained the silver.

"Damn you," the musician said, snarling at her. "Now I'll need a new instrument."

"It was..." Kelli sought an appropriate word, but there were none to be found. It was difficult enough standing; speaking took the last of her energy. The song had anesthetized her, so she felt almost nothing except the chill creeping into her chest. She found one, overly simple word: "Beautiful."

But the musician was gone. Only the memory of the song remained. That echo kept Kelli comfortable until, lying on the ground, she finally closed her eyes.

14.

The raven led Kevin straight to Sabine's Wishing, the well at which Jill had made her wish, where Kevin realized he'd lost his coin. He lost a lot of things. Losing himself was the worst of it, and he did it all the time.

Not after tonight. Nevermore.

He looked into the cup, saw his wife—wondrous, sensational Jill— but she was no longer the same woman. Something else. Someone else. Her eyes were clouded and gray, her face longer, the man at her side a servant—but not hers. She was cloaked by darkness, as if by night itself.

The raven, perched on the far edge of the well, cawed, (did it say "Nevermore"?) and flew away.

"Real men," she whispered, and perhaps this time told the truth, "don't surrender to fear."

Looking away from the nepenthe, Kevin made his wish and tossed the coin. And then he dumped the nepenthe, every drop of it, into the well.

The promise of dawn
is merely another promise
broken.
—The Book of Lost Fates

V. Wishes

1.

In the great city of the dead, the ravens pick at the girl's body and she tries to stop them, but she cannot move, so she tries to stop them in her mind. Where she still hears a lullaby.

In the great city of the dead, a man with only one chance tosses everything into a hole.

In the great city of the dead, a corpse hangs in the arms of a man who was never her lover.

In the great city of the dead, a woman believes she has the power to do something. She belongs to the spiders, and she is wrong.

2.

Jill clutched her throat, gasping, choking, desperate to draw a breath. At first, she didn't think she'd succeed, that she'd suffocate on spider silk.

She dropped to her hands and knees, retching, gulping air, spitting up bits of web. The spiders in her hair scattered. Her eyes burned. The sores that had stopped hurting suddenly exploded in agony.

With what little breath she had, she screamed. And then swallowed as much air as her lungs would take.

She didn't see anyone else around her, barely felt hands on her shoulders, supporting her back. There was a voice, smooth and jazzy, but the words were jumbled and slippery. She couldn't concentrate on them, and didn't care to.

When she finally looked up, Auguste stared back into her eyes. He looked as sad as she'd ever seen a man. And confused.

3.

Darren watched, unable to help, unwilling to let go of Anna. If he put her down, her cold corpse would slip into the earth and she would be dead. Deader than she was. Permanently and forever.

As long as he held her, as long as he kept her close, his heart could beat for the two of them, the blood in his veins could warm her, his breath could keep her alert. As long as he didn't let go, she lived with him, beside him, integrated beyond the reaches of sex or marriage or eternity.

So he watched this other woman hacking up spider webs, and the servant (someone else's servant) went to his knees at her side and kept her steady and didn't let her fall.

Just as Darren wouldn't let Anna fall.

No one spoke. Quiet came as the woman ceased coughing and gasping. She sounded as though she were drowning.

The lady in black stepped past him. The man snapped to his feet, to attention, crisp and clean for his mistress. The woman on her knees nearly fell when she turned her head.

"Your grace," the man said, bowing. "This is...was..."

"Jill," the woman on the ground said.

"Bring me the other," his grace told him, and the man left. The lady, who might've been some sort of queen, knelt beside Jill and touched her cheek. "Deep breaths," she said. "Fill your lungs."

"What about Anna?" Darren asked.

The lady—queen?—turned to him, her eyes sharp and black. "You have come far enough. You loved her? You bled her." She looked at him with distaste. "*Bleed.*"

Darren looked at Anna's soft, once-warm face, and nodded. He set her down on the mausoleum floor, leaning her back against the sarcophagus and keeping a hand on her at all times, and drew the dagger from his belt.

It felt powerful in his hands. Hungry. It wanted blood. He wasn't sure the queen could bleed; she seemed too much akin to the spiders and to the dark, but certainly the woman on the ground, Jill, would feed it.

The weapon pulsated against his palm.

He moved, toward Jill, ready to strike...and realized he'd let go Anna. Let go, and lost her.

4.

Five, ten minutes passed, but nothing changed. The wind remained consistent, neither rising nor suddenly stopping. No lightning, no thunder, no rumbling fissure rising from the earth. No hand reached up from the well. No face became visible in the darkness that hid the water (and nepenthe) at its bottom. The woman who was ravens and night didn't suddenly appear to throw her arms around him or run him through with a sword or kiss his forehead or give him an honest, solace-filled smile.

Another five or ten minutes. Night stretched infinitely in all directions. Darkness prevailed. Time warbled. Kevin's heart kept the pace of a decathlon.

"What now?" he asked.

No reply came.

He stumbled away from Sabine's Wishing, the well where everything started. He retraced Jill's steps. She'd run, laughing, into twilight, to the mausoleums at the top of the hill. And then into the vault, despite the locks in the stone door, despite sanity and despite probability.

To his own amazement, he followed Jill's path through the gravestones. He could nearly see where her feet had left tiny depressions in the grass.

There, ahead: the mausoleums.

5.

Spiders crawled over Kelli's body, weaving a web around her and through her (through the flute sticking out from her chest and back). They bound her tightly as Auguste supervised. She was pretty. Weak-willed, but that wouldn't matter. Brave. That was important.

The Spider-Queen would be pleased.

6.

Kelli opened her eyes. She hadn't expected to do that again. She tried to reach for her chest, but her arms wouldn't move. Tilting her head, she saw the silver flute protruding from her, and her own blood everywhere. She'd been wrapped, like a mummy. The spiders still worked on her.

Realizing she wasn't breathing, she inhaled. It changed nothing.

She saw feet. Followed them up to a man's face. He leaned with both hands on a cane, wore a cape that should've been silly but was somehow amazingly elegant.

She didn't bother with *Who*. Using the lungful of air she'd taken, she said, "What are you going to do with me?"

"I'll be preparing you," he said, unmoving, "for your

apprenticeship."

Surreptitiously, Kelli tried to free her arms. She doubted thrashing would've been any more effective. She wasn't going anywhere. At least the damn lullaby had left her head.

"You are to be the Spider-Queen's handmaiden."

Oh, Kelli thought. That didn't sound too bad. Not needing breath, she thought it might be better than the alternative.

7.

Caught between the target (Jill) and the victim (Anna), Darren hesitated. He was trapped. Death in both directions. There was no escape route, no trapdoor leading out of here, no salvation.

Jill lifted her head and looked at him. Her eyes begged for him to do it, to drive that knife through her chest and end whatever she'd suffered.

He looked back at Anna. She didn't lift her head. She looked at nothing.

He'd failed. Failed Anna, failed himself, failed the presumed queen.

"As far as it takes," Darren said, and buried the knife in his own chest.

It hurt a lot worse than he'd expected. He knew he deserved it.

8.

The queen helped Jill to her feet.

She didn't look at the man with the knife, the stranger bleeding on the mausoleum floor. She'd watched long enough to see him crawl back to the dead girl, and she'd heard him crying. Now that she'd been sick, she felt as though she'd purged her system; she'd gotten rid of everything that was in her, the webs and the venom, the spiders, even the chill. Her moment had passed; she left the stranger alone for his.

"Go," the queen told her.

And she did.

She kept her eyes forward until she reached the street. It cut through the cemetery, winding toward gates on either end. She'd traveled this road before. Auguste hadn't stopped her from going because he'd known she couldn't. This time, it would be different.

Kevin had never come back for her. He must've gotten lost. Which was entirely like him. If he stayed lost, she'd cry for a while, she'd wonder where he'd gone and what fate he had met. But in the end, she'd be happier.

It saddened her to know that.

A stranger had given up his life for the woman he loved without any guarantee that it'd make any difference. Kevin couldn't even find a caretaker with a key.

Or he'd found a *pretty* caretaker.

She slowed when she reached Auguste. He stood over the other woman, Kelli, but Jill didn't look too closely. She didn't like what she saw.

Auguste met her eyes, but made no other acknowledgement. Not even a nod.

Jill walked to the gate which earlier had cast her out. She paused, touched the iron, took a deep breath (a necessary breath, one that kept oxygen in her system, one that kept her feet working and her blood pumping and her head clear), and crossed the threshold.

9.

Slowly, with discomfort but not pain, Anna opened her eyes. First, she felt her back, where Darren had stabbed her. The wound was there, no longer bleeding. Her shirt and skin were wet with blood.

She breathed slowly, deeply, afraid to rupture something if she lost control.

She was alone, within one of the vaults, the door open. A rectangle of moonlight fell on Darren's body. He was looking at her, not smiling, and not breathing, the knife in his chest. The wet blood was his; hers had dried already.

"Oh, God, Darren," she said, shaking her head, wishing she hadn't believed so strongly. As if her beliefs had made everything real. As if her beliefs had led to Darren's discovery of that cursed blade.

She rolled onto her elbow, brushed the hair from in front of his eyes so she could see him better, and whispered, "I don't know if you can hear me, Darren, but I heard you. The entire time, I heard every word you said. I didn't answer because I didn't think I could, but I listened, and I knew you meant it. You know me, I'll believe in anything once." He said nothing. Made no movement. He was dead, and maybe beyond hearing. "I love you, Darren. I should've believed in you sooner."

Anna kissed his forehead, which was cold, and then his lips, which were colder.

He'd come back. She was sure of it. His ghost couldn't keep away, not forever. Using the sarcophagus for support, Anna stood. More slowly than necessary, she walked out of the mausoleum.

Dawn was coming. She could see the faintest hint of blue in the east. Blue and red; the sun hadn't even started to peak over the horizon.

10.

Kevin reached the mausoleum. Here, he'd had his last conversation with his wife. The door was open now. She was gone. There was someone else inside, and a fresh body on the ground.

He didn't want to linger.

When he turned away, the ravens came together as the woman with the green eyes and the colorful slashes around them, the black hair and black clothes that were as much feather as they were night.

"She's safe?" Kevin asked.

"Real men are confident," she said.

After a moment, Kevin stated, without room for argument, "She's safe."

The woman smiled. "She is."

"And me? Do I now belong to the night?"

She shook her head. "To the spiders."

The woman came apart in a flurry of ravens—an *unkindness* of ravens. Three or four settled on the mausoleums in the immediate vicinity. None made a sound.

To the left, a woman appeared, a girl, with a flute in hand and a glimmering gray dress and a big, plastic ring she must've found at a circus. To the right, a man dressed in complete white tie, leaning on a cane, his top hat slightly askew.

Behind Kevin, a lady waited. A queen.

Confidently, he turned and entered the mausoleum labeled King's Vault.

11.

The Spider-Queen smiled as her meal approached.

12.

After stepping out of the cemetery, Jill vowed never to return. She'd later identify her husband's body in a city morgue.

Dawn's light
merely reveals.
—The Book of Lost Fates

Coda: Dawn

1.

In the great city of the dead, dawn breaks.

2.

The Ringmaster strode through the cemetery. The wind was nice to him, not touching his hat, or perhaps unable to touch it. The sequins in his jacket sparkled in dawn's light.

He paused, beside a headstone with only the name *Athene* and the words *She lies*. He knelt, and picked up a camera.

"We tried to warn her," the baton twirler, Nivea, said. She and her brothers emerged slowly from the woods around him.

"We knew you'd come back," the eldest, Gray, said.

The Ringmaster looked at each, meeting their eyes.

"He's lying," the youngest, Ronnie, said. "Gray said you didn't need us anymore, that you couldn't come back."

"We were quite the show, weren't we?" the Ringmaster said.

The children looked at each other. Confused. Uncertain. Nivea asked, "What do you mean, *were*?"

"It's okay," the Ringmaster said. "Death comes in layers. You haven't yet crossed all the way. I understand. Neither have I."

"We're not dead," Ronnie insisted.

The Ringmaster tapped Ronnie's chin with a fist, the kind meant to say *Chin up*, but his words were nothing of the sort. "We lost the whole circus that night."

"You're still here," Ronnie said.

The Ringmaster lay the camera on the grass over Athene's grave. "I've been gathering everybody. You children are the last who remain."

"But I don't want to go," Ronnie said.

"Me neither," Nivea said.

"You don't have to." Then the Ringmaster rose to his feet, bowed, swinging his arms to one side to give them direction, and turned to follow that path away. "We'll wait for you."

AFTERWORD

Necropolis started as a photo. I was just beginning to explore photography, and I had just moved to Sydney, Australia, which gave me lots of opportunities to take pictures. One day, overlooking the Pacific Ocean, I found Waverly Cemetery between Bronte Beach and Coogee Beach.

I shot a lot of stones and paths and vistas. I've always been fascinated by cemeteries, and this one had an ocean view. I came home, went through my photos, and found one that said to me, "Dude, I should totally be a cover."

I'd never shot a cover before. (I've shot several since.) Also, I had what I considered a damn good question: the cover to what? I had no story.

Fast forward a year or so. I was doing a final read on Brian Keene's *Ghoul* before he delivered it to his publisher, and he used a word I knew but had rarely used myself. He only used it once, but I knew immediately I had a title to go with that cover.

Necropolis.

A few days later, on a Friday, I took a holiday from the day job and went to the Rookwood Necropolis (estimated to be the final resting place for a million souls) for an Inspirational Research trip. I took my camera. When I got home from the necropolis, I started writing—and I had the first draft done in a single weekend.

Photos from that trip ended up being published with the novella when Bad Moon Books originally released it (with that original cover shot) in 2009.

Eveningsong

Evening Song

Can you hear the music? It drifts to me on the lightest of breezes, a single note or a measure, sometimes most of a song. I never hear it start or end. Far as I know, it's ceaseless, transcending time, warping reality.

It drifts over the graveyard as the sun sets. It follows in the wake of passing SUVs shuttling noisy kids to soccer matches and baseball practice. It tickles the back of my ears.

Sometimes, I'm sure it's a flute, but often it's something jazzier, a cornet or saxophone.

I asked the trash man about it. He knows things. I said, "Do you know where it comes from, the music I hear?"

He said, "Your head." And then he said, "Your heart." And then he said, "You're crazy."

"But do you know?" I asked.

He shook his head, then leaned closer to confide, "*Do not follow the flute.*"

"Ah, yes," I said. "Wait until it's the fanciful flutter of the piccolo, I understand."

"No," he said. "Not the piccolo, either."

When the trash man left, I knew I would be waiting for the trumpet.

It's always a single instrument, whichever it is, and nightly I can almost decipher its message. The song isn't for everyone. It's meant for an audience of one. One night, perhaps, it's for a twelve year old girl still in pigtails dreaming of New Orleans. She's got something of the dancer in her, and something of the poet, but after hearing, after listening, her soul will belong to the song. Another night, it's the twenty year old college kid struggling for grades, struggling for acceptance, struggling to figure out exactly who and what he is. Maybe this isn't the right path for him. Maybe he's gay. Maybe he's too young to know anything. Maybe, after the song is played for him, he'll find his path, or the end of his path, and the questions will haunt him no longer.

Last week, the tune came for my neighbor. An aging woman, white of hair but sharp of eye—and apparently of ear—I saw her look, almost wistfully, toward the source of the music. She didn't know I was watching. She didn't know the wind brought errant notes to my ears, too. I haven't seen her since. I've been picking up her mail.

I wonder, sometimes, if the piper once played Hamelin. Do rats and children answer his call?

Tonight, I hear the most amazing thing: accompaniment. A girl plays the violin, though not capturing the airy notes as exquisitely. She makes it mourn. She makes me cry. She weaves between the notes I hear and the notes I don't. She seems to be in control of the rhythm, though that's only because I can't always hear the flute. No, the sax. It's definitely a saxophone, a soprano, crafting notes so impossibly high I cannot trust my ears. I'm not alone.

I follow the violin to its source.

She sits in the window of a third story apartment overlooking the street. There are no lights inside, and only the vaguest hint of streetlamp reaches her. Long dark hair, dark complexion. Her eyes are closed. The violin arcs into her apartment, so her bare neck is exposed to the night. It's a beautiful neck, elegant and long and perfect, and it seems to mimic the essence of the song in its gentle curve.

She plays a long while before I realize I no longer hear the master of winds. She pauses, briefly, opens her eyes and takes a breath, sees me staring up in wonderment, and she smiles. She touches the bow to the strings again, caresses notes from them. Tears leave cold streaks down the sides of my face.

Then, naturally but suddenly, she's done. She lowers the instrument from her chin. She looks out the window, smiling again, points at me with the bow. "Would you like to come up?" she asks. "For coffee, perhaps."

"You hear the song," I say.

"Yes."

"I hear it too."

Her smile remains. "Someday," she says, "I hope to hear it from the master of winds himself. But this night, I think, it's only you and me and my fiddle."

"It's beautiful," I tell her.

"In the end," she tells me, "he'll kill us for his song."

I think I'm in love. I say, "I know."

"Shut up," she tells me, "and come on up here. I have the feeling we have much to discuss."

House of Shadow and Ash

House of Shadow and Ash

1.

    Sunday noon. As he walked down King Street, Philip's shadow just stopped, smacking him to a halt like a dog at the end of its leash.

    "What?" Philip said, looking back, down, left and right—and there, leaning against the wall, his shadow grinned.

    "What?" it mocked.

    Philip approached his shadow, which neither moved nor changed in any way. "We're like brothers," Philip whispered. "Bound. United."

    "Enslaved," the shadow corrected, raising a scimitar. Even in shadow, the steel glinted.

    Philip shook his head. "You *need* me."

    "Not anymore."

    Philip jumped back as the shadow swung. The blade missed his flesh, but severed the threads connecting them.

    The immediate rush of weakness buckled Philip's knees. He nearly crumbled. There was no pain. He stumbled, and supported himself on the wall of 319 King Street.

    "That," the shadow said, ripping itself off the wall, "felt good."

    His shadow left. Philip fell to his knees on King Street—and might have cried if he'd had the strength.

2.

    A long while later, two men came and retrieved Philip's unmoving body from the sidewalk. He moaned, but only once.

3.

    When he woke, Philip moaned again. A dull ache reached into every corner and crevice of his body, especially his head. Eyes were watery, mouth dry, limbs deadweight.

    "He's awake," someone said.

    A face loomed over Philip. He was laying on something hard and uncomfortable; his bed seemed bent under his weight.

    The man looking down at him was one of the two who had gotten him. "Can ya speak?"

    Philip worked his mouth, but found no voice.

    "But ya could speak before, eh?"

He nodded—once, because it ignited all kinds of pains in his head and neck.

"It'll come back, *sim*, believe it," the man said. "An' then, you answer questions."

"Don't badger him, Raul," a woman's voice said. She remained out of sight. "Poor soul's lost his shadow."

Philip groaned, recalling his shadow's betrayal. He'd always kept his shadow close—perhaps too close. Despite all his learning and practice, his spell work and incantations had always seemed second-rate—yet something had gone exceptionally wrong.

Consciousness slipped, like the blink of an eye, and the woman stood over him. She was beautiful, angelic, with dark chocolate skin, mocha in her lips, kohl in her eyes. She smiled. Had a hand on his bare chest, another on his wrist. A gold circlet glimmered around her head, its symbols Arabic or ancient, unreadable to Philip.

"Do you know where you are?"

Philip tried his voice, found it weak. "No."

"My name is Cool-Eyes," she said, her voice a purr, melodic, exotically accented. "I do not know yours."

"Philip." Less of a strain this time, but it sounded rough and gravelly, as if stolen from the deathbed of an eighty year old smoker.

"Philip," she said, rolling the name over her tongue. "Delicious. There's much power in the naming of things. Yours brings to mind French kings and knights and crusaders. Are you a king, a knight, or a crusader, my Philip?"

"None of those things," Philip said, but he held back what he might have said next.

"Very good," Cool-Eyes said. "Tell me one thing, so I may help you."

Philip waited.

"Who stole your shadow?"

"Nobody," Philip said, closing his eyes, wearied by the unending aches. "It left me."

Her voice sounded closer, quick and excited. "Of its own volition?"

"Yes."

And Philip drifted again, more deeply this time, dreaming of excessively bright sunlight and harsh shadows enveloping him, smothering him, oozing in through his pores.

4.

When next Philip woke, the aches had lessened—or he'd grown accustomed to them—and he was alone.

He sat up this time. The cart beneath him shifted on squeaky wheels. He wanted to hop off, but didn't trust his feet.

The room seemed carved from stone. It was wide, with many doorways like mouths, a bank of computer monitors and consoles on one wall, shelves overflowing with books on another.

The computer screens were all illegible, or Philip's eyes simply failed to focus.

One doorway had a barred window; another dripped with velvet. From beyond that, he heard panting, moaning, gasps and little cries: Cool-Eyes, with one of the men.

Philip was too exhausted, too hurt, to be aroused by her sounds.

Tentatively, he touched his left foot to the floor. It held. His right next; he clung to the cart for support. It slipped again, but he held on, did not fall.

He was amazingly weak.

And still, he cast no shadow.

So focused on his own movements, he hadn't realized the lovemaking had gone silent until Cool-Eyes had drawn aside the drape and said, "Testing your legs? Good."

She was gloriously nude, cloaked partially in shadow. She wiped liquid (blood?) from her mouth. "In the morning, we'll arrange for a new shadow."

He didn't think that was possible.

"A temporary shadow," Cool-Eyes said, "until we can retrieve your true shadow. A man cannot long live without it."

Her partner stepped through the velvet doorway, also naked, flaccid, his body glimmering with sweat and blood and other juices. Bite marks and scratches lined his chest, legs, and back. He staggered toward a door, opened it without a word, and shut it softly once inside.

Cool-Eyes' grin widened, and she held out a hand. "Come, Philip. Sleep in here with me."

He doubted he had the stamina, but he went anyway. Her room contained nothing but a thousand and one pillows, shimmering satin and silk, a bed of clouds.

She helped him down and, in fact, slept next to him.

When morning came, she was gone.

Philip managed to stand, but preferred the decadence of the pillows. His thick, jelly legs carried him to the velvet, where he grabbed onto the wall before pushing through to the outer room.

The two men worked at the computers. Cool-Eyes sat on a plush chair, reading. She looked up, folded the book shut, and set it on the chair's arm. "Okay, boys."

"I can't..." Philip said.

She rose and came to him. "You never will again," she said, "without your shadow returned, or at the very least a surrogate. It's an awful, terrible thing, to lose your own shadow. I knew a man once who stole and consumed shadows. The vessels never last."

Philip tried to say something, about how he was more than merely a vessel, but he couldn't bear to lift his voice over hers. "You've been hovering over death for three days now, Philip non-King, and only my potions keep you among the living."

The men had gone to their separate rooms, and now emerged with small bags slung across their backs. They were nearly identical, twins in function if not in form.

"Another spell," Cool-Eyes said, "and we may put some might into those muscles, solidity into those bones. Another day, however, and you'll next open your eyes to death's *soukh*."

"We're ready," one of the men said, after the two had checked each other over.

Cool-Eyes wrapped an arm around Philip's waist; an impossible heat radiated off her body. "Walk with me," she said.

One step, two, he noticed his legs worked better while Cool-Eyes touched him. "You're...you're a demon of some sort, aren't you?" Philip asked.

Cool-Eyes shook her head. "No demon. A mortal-born girl, that's all."

Through one of the doors, they emerged on a sandy field. The wall disappeared behind them, leaving them in the middle of a great desert. Nothing but sand in any direction, and the grating wind buffeting them.

"Where?" Philip asked, unsure if he meant where they'd gone or where they were going.

"Hush," Cool-Eyes whispered, touching his lips.

Her finger lingered, distracting Philip. It had more strength than his entire body; his shadow had everything.

He should've been better prepared.

The oasis glimmered before them, as if rising on waves of heat. A few cacti, first, trees behind those, a puddle that soon became a pool, and then a house — a *mansion*. Ionic columns flanked doors and windows. It hadn't been built in any desert, yet its colors blended like a chameleon. Philip blinked, unable to really see the house.

The men set forth. Cool-Eyes leaned close to Philip. "It's a mirage," she said, her voice so soft it tickled his ear. "Teasing you one moment, the next — gone."

He noticed a single bead of sweat on her brow, extracted by the powerful sun, but Philip felt almost nothing of the heat. His shadow had taken that, too.

5.

The house was even larger on the inside, its front room an arena, its floors marble, its crystal chandeliers numerous. A thousand and one statues of men, women, and beasts filled the room. Some were small: a series of cats, mice, squirrels, and birds hanging from transparent wires. Wood, stone, granite, wax, papier-mâché, ivory, marble, iron, gold, even gems glittering in the sun-bright light. Philip, even with such a muted sense of the desert heat, felt the cool, soothing air in here. A lone violin mourned nearby, a song he had never heard.

The front room went straight through to the back of the house, the side walls lined with a series of regal doorways, both familiar and unknown symbology carved on the doorjambs.

"A house of secrets," Cool-Eyes said, apparently sensing Philip's awe. "For you, a house of shadow and ash."

"My shadow's here?" Philip asked.

"Only the surrogate. Come."

She and the men led him toward a set of doors in the left wall. Philip felt fortunate that he had to put so much effort just into walking, and Cool-Eyes' touch was such a distraction, because he felt the eyes of the thousand and one statues follow their progress.

Raul, or the other, opened the door; both men withdrew weapons from their bags and stood aside. Cool-Eyes helped Philip limp under the door's Arabian arch into a smaller room. Here, thick shadows danced, thrown by a raging fire in a brick hearth.

"The flames are white," Philip noted.

"Few fires burn more fiercely," Cool-Eyes said. She brought him closer. Its breeze brushed him.

"I don't feel it," he said.

"You must," Cool-Eyes said. "Cleanse your left hand."

"Burn it?" Philip asked. He knew the basics of some magic casting, of bindings and sacrifice. When Cool-Eyes didn't answer, but instead slipped away from him, he swayed, teetered. When he regained his balance, he thrust his arm into the flame.

He felt no heat, no pain. He expected his flesh to bubble and blister. A tingle tickled his fingers, as if they'd fallen asleep; it spread to his wrist, his elbow, into his shoulder. Still, he held his arm, letting the magical fire do its worst. He couldn't imagine worse than he'd already done to himself.

"Jinn-fire," Cool-Eyes said. The tingling stretched to his organs; his breath caught, his heart stopped, his stomach twisted, his bladder emptied — *that* warmth, he felt spread down his legs.

His vision swayed, and for a moment his thoughts cleared. Who was this Cool-Eyes? Why should she help him? No angel, she, no fairy godmother, no heavenly boon.

He tried to pull his hand from the flames, but his muscles had locked rigid and refused. The tingling seemed to burst from the fingertips of his other hand; it seeped through his nose, his ears, and in the fresh tears flowing from his eyes. His jaw worked, but all his vocal cords vibrated uncontrollably. Every muscle trembled, an electric shock riding him...and behind him, beyond his field of vision, Cool-Eyes sang.

Her dusty words were foreign, not a chant so much as a plea. He tried to look back at her, tried again to yank his arm free, failed to even blink.

Someone — some *thing* — inhaled. The fire shot up, escaping the hearth and dissipating. Philip snatched his unscarred hand to his chest and collapsed.

6.

Cool-Eyes was on top of him in an instant, reaching around one side, the other. Philip hadn't blacked out, but had no strength with which to buck her. Under more normal circumstances, he might not have objected — might even have welcomed it.

All the aches intensified. White edges crowded his vision. She had something in her hands, coal perhaps, or chalk. She reached between his legs, brushing his body as she drew on the floor. Down to his feet. Around his hands, his head. Finishing, she stood and reached into the remnants of the fire.

"Quickly," she said, scooping a handful of ash from the hearth.

Philip rolled out of his chalk outline; he wasn't yet ready to be a corpse. Cool-Eyes smeared the ground, coloring between the lines. "While it's still warm," she said.

He had no feeling in his hands, except iciness in his left, but he reached into the fire and followed her example, filling his silhouette with ash.

She'd used a chunk of coal to outline him. No longer necessary, she'd dropped it carelessly to the side, and kicked it further away when she went back for another handful of soot.

The work, simple as it seemed, tired him, draining what little energy he thought he'd had. But Cool-Eyes' urgency bled into him, and he went further than he thought he could go, exhausting his reserves, finally collapsing in a heap next to his figure.

Cool-Eyes draped herself across him, touching his cheek with an ash-coated hand. "Now just close your eyes," she whispered. "And wait."

Her warmth sustained him during the next...however long it was. Might have been just one minute, but it stretched like hours and days. The violin continued to play. He sensed Raul and the twin, fidgeting in the doorway, weapons drawn, eyes scanning the statuary. He found breath only because Cool-Eyes lent him hers; the thrill of her lips so close to his was enough to keep him alive.

She whispered stories, poems, tales of woe and glory, love and war, trial and treasure, gods and genies. They blended, one into another, intertwining with what he knew of Bibles and Korans and the mystical books he'd stolen. She spoke of Egypt and Babylon, Rome and Gaul, Celtic warriors and Nordic maidens. She smelled of vanilla and cinnamon, and a stirring groaned somewhere deeper than his bones. With his eyes closed, she teased his other senses enough to keep him conscious.

"A thousand and one nights, they made her tell tales," Cool-Eyes was saying, "but all the while her maidens infiltrated the servants' ranks, the court, even the beds of princelings still innocent, and then the king found himself surrounded by her admirers—and his enemies. He was given a thousand and one nights, to tell stories, but should he one day fail to give an engaging tale, she promised the deeper dungeon, as it was never encouraged to sacrifice kings."

"How much longer?" he asked.

The click of weaponry answered him.

7.

Philip strained to look toward the doorway. Raul and the twin had raised their weapons, powerful oversized rifles, too big for anyone else's hands. But these were big men, masses of tense muscle, and they seemed to know what they were doing.

From the ground, looking over his head, Philip's angle was entirely wrong to get a clear view of anything. Cool-Eyes had him pinned, her gaze also focused beyond that door.

"Don't let it close," she whispered, as if the twins might hear.

An enormous figure approached, booming footfalls, towering over the soldiers. Statues fled from its path.

The creature knelt at the door to look in. The soldiers kept both their positions and their aim—directly at the creature's skull. All its bones were visible beneath a skin of white fire.

"You wish to bargain?" it asked, as deep a voice as Philip had ever heard.

"No bargain," Cool-Eyes said. "We've followed the prescription. *We* demand payment."

The creature laughed.

"A body of flesh without shadow," she said, "perishes. We have laid upon this floor a new shadow, of ash, from the fire that tasted the flesh."

"Indeed," the creature said, unimpressed. "For so small a man?"

Philip wanted to object, but Cool-Eyes' weight on his chest drove the breath from him.

"For a mortal man, yes," Cool-Eyes said.

Heat rose beside Philip. He turned, toward his drawn silhouette, as the ashen figure rose from the ground.

"You cannot enter this house," the creature said, "without at least a token."

It moved so quickly, Philip wasn't quite sure what had happened. Both weapons fired. One fiery hand enveloped one twin and took him; the other pushed Raul into the room, and slammed the door shut.

"No!" Cool-Eyes screamed, jumping up past Raul. She threw the door open, onto some other room.

Philip sat up. The blood in his veins warmed him. Aches subsided to ghosts. The ashen shadow followed his every movement.

But looking beyond Cool-Eyes, he saw the statuary had been replaced by a jungle.

8.

Jungle sounds overwhelmed Philip: the calls of birds, monkeys hollering, thunderous rain in the distance. Humidity washed through the room like a tsunami; he was already wiping sweat from his brow. Cool-Eyes immediately swung the door closed, shutting out the green, green vines and leaves and the earthy smell and—had those yellow cat eyes staring at them through the underbrush belonged to a jaguar?

Cool-Eyes cursed in several languages; Philip recognized a few. Tentatively, he pulled himself to his feet. Saw Raul picking himself up off the floor, as well.

Cool-Eyes leaned against the door and glanced around the room, cursing again.

"What of Carlos?" Raul asked.

She shook her head, and locked her eyes on Philip. "You're standing."

"I feel better," Philip said weakly; his feeling better meant nothing compared to losing one of her twin lovers, but it was a relief to stand again under his own power. "A little."

"Only a little, I'm sure," Cool-Eyes said, turned to Raul. "Are you hurt?"

"No, ma'am," Raul said, his voice colder now, detached.

"Your weapon?"

He checked it quickly. "Ready."

"Give Philip a gun," she said, pushing away from the door.

Raul went to his bag.

"What happened?" Philip asked.

"In this house of secrets," Cool-Eyes said, "doors only go one way."

"We're stuck here?" Philip asked. He hadn't noticed earlier; there was a door on every wall.

"No," Cool-Eyes said, "but the ifrit will return. How well are you?"

Philip flexed an arm. "Well enough."

Raul handed him a pistol. "Ever shoot one of these?"

Philip shook his head.

"It's easy," Raul said. "Point, pull the trigger." His voice was slightly strained—whether with loss or fear, Philip couldn't tell.

"Right."

"You will die without your shadow," Cool-Eyes said. "That ashen effigy is bound to us, but will deteriorate. Do you understand?"

"You speak as if I'm stupid," Philip said.

"I don't know that you're not."

Philip bit back his most defensive of answers. "It's bound to *us?* Not just me?"

"You couldn't complete the ritual yourself," Cool-Eyes said. She walked past him, past the hearth, to the door opposite the one they'd used to come in. "Off the statue garden, the doors are more solid, more lasting. But deeper, any door may lead anywhere, and elsewhere the next time. Do not get separated."

She opened the door onto another room.

Skeletons hung suspended from the ceiling, birds with huge wingspans. Others were propped against the walls, some human looking, carrying additional bones in their hands like axes. An elephant, a horse, a snake twined around a bare branch, it reminded Philip of museums he'd seen as a child—and, more recently, alchemical laboratories and workrooms. This was huge, long, stretching further than he could see.

Raul led the way, passing Cool-Eyes in the doorway, scanning both sides and the ceiling with his rifle as he walked.

"The Chamber of Bones," Cool-Eyes said, running her fingers along the edge of the snake—which looked like one tremendously long spine and rib cage and a flat head. Dust rose in the wake of her touch, and the skeleton trembled.

Philip almost shut the door behind them, but Cool-Eyes pulled him away. "Leave it open," she said, "or the next door might bring us back to the Chamber of Ash."

His makeshift shadow followed unsteadily, struggling to keep up, its edges blurred. Philip frowned at it, and the faux shadow shrugged its shoulders as if to say, *What am I supposed to do about it?*

"How long do I have?"

Cool-Eyes smiled at him. "Long enough, Philip non-King."

9.

Like the statues, the skeletons watched their progress.

The hall wasn't infinitely long, just about the size of the wing in the Louvre filled with Italian masterpieces. There, the walls were covered by an endless supply of framed oils, some obscure, some remarkable, some famous, some famous only amongst certain circles; but there was a place, near the middle of that hall, where you couldn't see either end. Philip wished he was there now, with his regular shadow attached, instead of here.

Philip and Cool-Eyes walked ten paces behind Raul, who seemed intent to aim his weapon at every set of bones.

From the darkness of the high ceiling, Philip heard the leathery flap of bat wings, and maybe the click of bat bones. He had expected blue whales in the ceiling, not birds—especially so many hundreds of them, all unmoving on cables or strings that were almost invisible.

Almost. That he could make out those cords offered a small bit of relief.

"It's like the Natural History Museum's Freak Exhibit," Philip said, just to break the silence. His shadow chuckled silently. Cool-Eyes glanced at him and rolled her eyes. "Or its storage unit."

None of the skeletons were labeled. There were no plaques, no guidebooks, no references whatsoever. But those that stood were mounted upon small wooden and marble (and maybe some bone?) bases. Dry tree limbs, mounted in the walls on either side, gave perch to some birds and a place for the monkeys and snakes to hang. One thick branch supported what appeared to be a tiger looking down at them. Stalking.

Just like everything else in this Chamber of Bones.

Philip's faux shadow stumbled; the stagger rippled up into Philip, and he had to pause.

Cool-Eyes looked down at his shadow. "How's it holding up?" she asked, keeping her voice low.

"A little shaky, I think," Philip said.

"Well, it's not very substantial," Cool-Eyes said. "We weren't really supposed to be moving."

"Why are we moving?" Philip asked. "Why not just keep re-opening the door behind us until it leads where we want to go?"

Cool-Eyes shook her head sadly. "There are a thousand and one rooms in this house of secrets," she said. "I built seven with my own hands."

"Really?"

"Long ago," Cool-Eyes said. "Another lifetime, it sometimes seems."

"We're looking for one of your rooms, then?" Philip asked.

"We're in one of my rooms," Cool-Eyes said. "And I know its secrets."

This surprised Philip. "Would you share?"

"No."

"Not even one?"

"Okay," Cool-Eyes said. "The bones are alive."

Philip looked around, then let out a single laugh. "That's no secret."

Cool-Eyes shook her head and continued walking.

Philip looked down at his ashen shadow; it nodded and started walking ahead of him.

"Far enough," Cool-Eyes finally told Raul, who stopped but continued to scan the bone forest.

She turned to Philip and lowered her voice even more, as if they'd just been chastised by the librarian. "Every creature caught within these walls," she said, "except the three of us, sailed upon the Ark."

She knelt, reaching under the wide base of a rhino. The beast looked down at her, the movement dropping little sprinkles of bone dust from its joints. She pressed something, a trigger. Beast and base slid aside, revealing a staircase descending into darkness.

A burst of light exploded behind them. Philip turned, but his makeshift shadow fled into the hole. Just as he recognized the white flames of the jinn behind them, his legs crumbled.

10.

The jinn carried a screaming Carlos, charred to a crisp, blackened, flakes drifting off him. The creature moved swiftly, its stride three times a normal man's, every booming footfall shaking the bones around them.

Raul put himself between Cool-Eyes and the jinn, raising his weapon but not yet firing. Cool-Eyes murmured something, or chanted, or prayed—Philip wasn't sure.

"This," the jinn said, holding Carlos in front of him, "might've been a fine token, mortal-born."

"Kill him!" Carlos cried. "*Oh meu Deus!* Kill me!"

Cool-Eyes ignored him, still chanting, and Philip recognized the cadence of her words if not the language: a summoning.

All at once, the skeletons ripped their feet free of their bases, or with a single flap of wings snapped their wires, or hopped down from their petrified limbs.

Had it happened in the moment before the jinn reached the Chamber of Bones, Philip might've panicked. He'd seen entities summoned before, creatures of shadow or mist, nothing more substantial or horrifying than an imp or dead soul—though imps could be nasty little fucks and the dead were seldom happy to be called upon. He'd managed a thread of smoke once himself; it had choked and blinded him, sent him fleeing into the cemetery—that had been an awful weekend. But to see this girl of maybe twenty, unaided by talismans or fetishes, raise a whole army...it brought tears to his eyes.

Cool-Eyes pointed at the jinn. "This is not your house," she said, not an inkling of fear or tremor in her words, "and this is not your room."

Twenty meters away, the jinn stopped. And scowled. The skeletons had crowded around him, the rhino's horn pointed directly at his groin. "Little girl," he said, "you misunderstand. I do not want blood."

"It doesn't matter to me *what* you want," she said.

Nor to me, Philip thought, crawling toward Cool-Eyes' feet. He didn't think there was anyplace safer in this room than in her shadow, especially since he had none of his own.

The jinn narrowed his eyes. "Bones are brittle and easily broken," he said, snatching one of the larger birds over his head and crushing it to dust.

"Me!" Carlos cried, in the jinn's other hand. "Kill me!"

"I believe," the jinn said, laughing lightly, "you might call this a Mexican Standoff."

"Raul," Cool-Eyes calmly said. "To me."

He retreated so effortlessly, Philip would've sworn Raul had eyes in the back of his head. That weapon never wavered from the jinn.

"Barter with me," the jinn said. "I have had my fill of blood."

Unmoving, Cool-Eyes said, "I have not."

The jinn laughed. "Is that what you would want?" he asked. "Then here, this one, I can give you this." He offered Carlos, who had no struggle left and could barely lift his head.

"You cannot offer what is not yours," Cool-Eyes said. "But maybe we *can* work out some sort of trade."

The jinn dropped Carlos to the ground. He rolled a bit; the animated skeletons moved aside to let him pass. He crawled, his body leaving a trail of burnt remnants, the whites of his eyes red, all other color blackened and crispy. "I knew you were a girl of reason. For what would you wish, then?"

"Your wishes," Cool-Eyes said, "cannot be trusted."

The jinn held out both empty hands. "What, then?"

Cool-Eyes shook her head. "You first."

Good, Philip thought; she knew better than to ask for something without first asking its cost. Even *he* knew that, so he should've expected her to know. Still, she surprised him. He hadn't expected much from a girl so young.

She'd rescued him from the streets when his shadow deserted him; she'd held him up when his legs failed; she'd guided him this far, with intelligence and obvious experience. Philip felt stupid to be surprised.

Stupid, of course, had been his operative word lately.

The jinn sneered. "Okay, girl. I want release."

Carlos, crawling even more quickly than Raul, had reached the top of the stairway. He was halfway up to his knees now, stronger and more capable than Philip without his shadow.

"Too high," Cool-Eyes said.

The jinn's fists tightened. "You cannot leave me here. I won't allow it."

"What you will *allow*," Cool-Eyes said, "doesn't matter anymore. Raul."

Raul pulled the trigger.

The gunfire was louder than thunder, exploding the jinn's face, wracking his body, tearing him apart and even blowing back the white flames of his skin. Simultaneously, the skeletons attacked, bearing down with claws and teeth and horns and clubs of bone.

Cool-Eyes bent to grab Philip by the back of the neck. Some strength surged through him, enough to move—at least, enough to move where Cool-Eyes dictated. They dropped into the staircase, behind burnt Carlos. Raul came last.

The base slid back into place, plunging the stairway into absolute darkness.

11.

The scratch of a match, flare, and then the stick's flame brought to the wick of a candle.

Philip's faux shadow clung to him. It was out of breath, pale and pasty, its existence dependent on Philip's nearness. It wasn't likely to flee again.

Cool-Eyes set the candle on the ground. They all surrounded her at the bottom of the steps.

The room seemed empty, its walls looming just beyond the candle's glow. Raul knelt, gun propped on his knee, over Carlos. The twin's body had been scorched; his breathing was ragged and noisy.

The stairs rose into darkness, which ended at a door in the ceiling.

"Where are we now?" Philip asked.

"The Side Chamber," Cool-Eyes said.

"*Por favor,*" Carlos said, reaching out to Raul.

For the first time since Philip had seen him, Raul seemed uncertain, looking from Carlos to Cool-Eyes and back again, a finger moving uncontrollably along the side of his rifle.

"No," Cool-Eyes said.

Carlos sobbed. Tears of steam rose from his eyes.

"The Side Chamber?" Philip asked.

"The jinn cannot come here," Cool-Eyes said. "And we cannot stay."

"He's in a lot of pain, ma'am," Raul said. His hands floated over his twin, as if afraid to touch the burnt flesh. Either he didn't want to cause even more pain, or he didn't want to get flakes of Carlos on his hands.

"Nothing we can do," Cool-Eyes said. "If one of the jinn require a sacrifice..."

"One of?" Philip asked. "You mean, there's more?"

"I had hoped not to see any," Cool-Eyes said.

Philip hadn't always hoped that, but he hadn't known better. "Those skeletons can't stop him, can they?" Philip asked.

"No more so than Raul's bullets," Cool-Eyes said. "The jinn are of fire, not of flesh."

"Is there a Chamber of Water, then?" Philip asked.

"A Chamber of Ice, yes," Cool-Eyes said, "but I don't know its secrets."

"Is this Side Chamber one of yours, too?"

"No." Cool-Eyes looked up the staircase. "Must you always ask so many questions?"

"How else will I learn?"

"You even answer with questions."

"You have to admit, you haven't told me much of anything."

Cool-Eyes spun at him, her kohl eyes seeming to capture the candlelight, and lowered her voice. "I prolonged your life, I cast you a shadow effigy, *I* am the only reason you didn't melt away when your shadow left you. I have brought you here, to reclaim your true shadow, and you demand answers to questions you don't even know how to ask?"

"You helped me, sure," Philip said. "And don't think I'm not grateful. But why? What do you gain by it?"

She glared at him. Carlos moaned.

"Ma'am?" Raul asked.

"He stays alive," Cool-Eyes snapped, not releasing Philip from her gaze. "Unless you'd rather bargain with your own life."

Raul cursed under his breath.

"You risked yourself, your lovers," Philip continued. "For what? A stranger? A self-taught magician?"

Cool-Eyes chuckled. "You are no magician, Philip non-King. What have you learnt? To lose your shadow?"

The faux shadow laughed silently. Philip ignored it.

"You're a disgrace," Cool-Eyes said. "If I had no candle, you could not have made light. If I have no key, you cannot open the door. If we find your shadow, what then would you do? If I'm not there, how will you retain it? Subdue it? Control it?"

"It can be bound," Philip said.

"You couldn't bind sand to the desert," Cool-Eyes said.

Philip's fists curled of their own accord. The faux shadow lent him strength.

Cool-Eyes didn't stop. "Your failures have cost you greatly. Your feeble attempts at self-preservation have made you weak. Your thirst for knowledge has left you dehydrated. Your desire for power has cost you your life."

Philip punched her.

He didn't know if he'd ever thrown a punch at a woman before. One time in second grade, he remembered, but that had been self-defense; she'd already hit him a number of times, wasn't stopping, wouldn't stop, taunted him with cries of *sissy boy* and *wimp*.

His punch was even less effective this time.

Cool-Eyes ducked beside it, caught his arm, flipped him to the ground, and dropped her knees into his ribs. His breath burst in a surge of pain. He struggled to inhale, gasped painfully, and tried to wriggle loose. Her knees held him tight.

Shaking her head, Cool-Eyes said, "Pathetic."

The faux shadow trembled beneath Philip.

Cool-Eyes bent low—so that her lips almost touched his, her breasts pressed into his chest—and whispered. "Yes, of course, you're right, I help you for my own, personal reasons. If those reasons have kept you alive this long, is it wise to question them?"

Philip held his breath, certain now that nothing would be wiser. Rather than lie, he said nothing.

"I'd appreciate a little thanks," Cool-Eyes said. "Even love, that'd be fine. Trust, maybe? At least some respect. I can unmake that effigy just as easily as I made it, and then where would you be, Philip non-King, non-magician? Alone in the middle of a house of secrets, with nothing to trade, not even strength enough to walk."

In the candlelight, her striking, dark face was darker, more angular, but still beautiful. Philip closed his eyes, turned his head.

After a moment, Cool-Eyes climbed off him. "We cannot stay here," she said, "but I do not know where the next door will take us. With luck, the statue garden, but I doubt that and wouldn't trust it if it did. Raul, can you carry him?"

"*Eu posso andar sozinho,*" the twin grumbled, pushing up off the floor. But his muscles trembled and shed flecks of burnt flesh.

Cool-Eyes, stepping momentarily beyond the reach of the candle's glow, opened the door.

12.

The light from the next room blinded Philip. He held up a hand to shield his eyes. His faux shadow, however, seemed to revel in it, flexing its muscles, boosting Philip's stamina. For just a moment, he felt strong enough to wrestle the jinn—and immediately thought better of it.

Cautiously, a step at a time, he followed Cool-Eyes through the door.

This room was wide, with huge skylights dropping hot rectangles of sunlight in a checkerboard pattern on the floor. Something buzzed.

Philip, last to come through, almost closed the door; a look from Cool-Eyes was enough to stop him. "Where are we now?" he asked.

Carlos, limping behind Raul, stepped too close to the sunlight and moaned.

Then, in a sudden wave, the stench hit Philip.

He'd smelled death before, but never on so large a scale. It assaulted him from all sides, nearly knocked him over. The faux shadow retched. Even Cool-Eyes scrunched her nose in distaste.

The light had been too bright to notice at first; within each of those rectangles was a pile of carcasses. Dead, rotting meat, home to swarms of flies. Dried blood stained the floor. The freshest meat still bled, and it undulated beneath a thick coat of flies.

"Is this another of your rooms?" Philip asked.

Cool-Eyes hadn't answered his first question, and she didn't answer this, either. She was brushing flies from her face. More had settled on Raul's rifle; the gun wouldn't do him much good against bugs.

They were landing on Philip's arms and neck and cheek, buzzing into his ears, crawling along his eyebrows and his lips, reaching into his nose.

He swatted a bunch away, smacking several in flight, but with no effect; more, immediately, replaced them. And more.

Ahead, there was another door. There had to be. But suddenly, the wave of black around them was so thick, Philip could barely see Cool-Eyes ahead of him. Charred Carlos was completely invisible. Raul's silhouette swung his rifle at the flies, as if that might help.

The insects even swarmed over his faux shadow.

Cool-Eyes ducked her head, held an arm up over her eyes, and charged forward.

They ran as a group, but Carlos and Philip lagged behind. Through the flies, Cool-Eyes—and then Raul—disappeared.

Philip tried to call out, but immediately clamped his mouth shut, catching a dozen or more flies. Rather than risk opening his mouth again, he swallowed, then covered his mouth and retched. Hard. Caught only one more.

Some were large as his thumbnail, others small as gnats. Individually, each was a minor irritation on his flesh; en masse, they were excruciating, revolting, overwhelming, and biting painfully.

His faux shadow, coughing, propelled him forward, stealing strength from the intense sunlight.

Carlos stumbled and fell. Philip stooped to help him back to his feet. Carlos looked at him, his eyes wide with fear and red as the desert. His skin crinkled like tin foil and sloughed away in sheets at Philip's touch, but he didn't seem to feel it. His expression had no room for more pain; disgust and panic had taken over.

Up ahead, Philip heard a door open, followed by gunfire. Cool-Eyes cried, "Don't," and the door slammed.

Philip and Carlos reached Raul at the door. Holding his gun up, wiping sweat and flies from his face, Raul panted once, twice, then spun and kicked the door open.

He charged in with gun raised. Carlos staggered through the door. Philip, hesitating, slammed it shut.

A hundred or a thousand flies had come through with them, but they scattered. The three men found themselves in a library. Shelves of books lined the walls and filled aisles that rose six meters to the ceiling. There were no chairs or couches, but several chest-high stone tables and a dozen or more lit candelabra.

Quickly, Philip realized two things. First, the shelves weren't lined with just books. There were scrolls, loose parchments, and papyrus; tablets of stone and marble; engraved egg shells; leather and pelts; skulls with words carved into them. Greek, Egyptian, Babylonian, Mayan, Celtic, even English, dozens of languages he wasn't sure about, some he'd never seen. None of the visible titles were familiar.

The second thing he realized, and this might have been most important, was that they were alone.

Raul slowly lowered his rifle, blinking, looking left and right; this was not the room in which he'd left Cool-Eyes. Since he'd fled while shooting, there was a good chance she was dead.

Part of Philip felt relief. The greater part of him, however, knew they had no guide, no knowledge of this house of secrets, and no magic by which to survive.

From a Chamber of Flies into a Chamber of Words. Philip was sure he could learn everything he'd ever wanted to know right here, now, in this place that echoed Alexandria—except many books were more recent and some were even modern.

"Cool-Eyes?" Raul asked, hesitantly, expecting no answer.

The aisles went off at an angle, so when something moved, they couldn't see anything. But Philip heard it, his shadow quivered, and Raul snapped his rifle back to a ready position.

13.

A woman emerged from one of the aisles.

"Wait," Philip said, reaching toward Raul, but the soldier didn't fire. Neither did he lower his gun.

"Greetings," the woman said. "I am Deshanazza." Red tinted her golden skin—not tan, but gleaming. Gold irises swam in a sea of pale blue. She wore veils, wisps of clothing attached to bracelets and anklets, the blue silk cascading over her, flowing as if made of air and wind, revealing glimpses of thigh and stomach and breast and arm, hiding everything but her face, fingers, and bare feet.

Philip felt himself staring, but couldn't help it.

"Welcome to my library," she said.

"Mary, pray for me," Carlos said, so low he probably hadn't intended to say it aloud.

The nails on Deshanazza's feet and hands were painted the same blue as her eyes. The windless draft parting her veils momentarily revealed a gleaming sapphire in her navel.

"You're a jinn?" Philip said, not meaning for it to sound like a question.

"And you are human," Deshanazza said.

"Lead us out of here," Raul said, threatening her with his rifle.

"That," Deshanazza said, her voice as smooth and breezy as her clothes, "is no way to speak to a *lady*." With a finger, she lowered the tip of Raul's weapon until it pointed at the ground. She smiled, winked at him, and turned her attention on Carlos.

He whimpered.

Then she fixed her eyes on Philip.

It felt as though she sought his soul through his eyes, and Philip felt suddenly possessive, unwilling to surrender to this gorgeous stranger; yet at the same time, he knew he'd give her everything. Even his ashen shadow trembled at the thought.

And as she looked at him, certainly for no longer than she'd looked at either of the others, she seemed to touch every inch of him, caress and smooth his flesh with just her gaze. Her lips did not move, yet she spoke in his head: *I can give you knowledge, I can make you powerful, I can bring you fortune and favors, oh the favors.*

"Out of my head, witch," Carlos said, crossing himself.

She laughed, a joyful sound. "I am no seductress," she told him. "I am the librarian."

"Show us the way out of this house," Raul said again.

"And do you really wish to leave?" Deshanazza asked.

"Straight away," Raul said.

"No, wait," Philip said. "I..."

One at a time, lover, Deshanazza's voice said in Philip's head, even as she spoke aloud to Raul: "Go right through that door, there," she said, pointing, "but leave your weapon and bag."

"Why?"

"Payment," Deshanazza said. "An offering. An exchange. You want to leave, and I grant your wish."

Tentatively, Raul slung the bag off his shoulder and dropped it to the floor. He seemed less willing to give up his rifle.

"Your distrust hurts," Deshanazza said.

Carlos reached into the bag, withdrew another rifle, and pointed it at Deshanazza. "Out of my head," he said, firing.

The gunshots echoed loudly in the library, scaring ravens near the ceiling and sending them flying. The bullets tore into Deshanazza's face, perhaps nine or ten shots before Carlos released the trigger and lowered the weapon.

Raul snatched his bag and ran toward the door behind them. Philip thought it'd open again on a swarm of flies, but instead there seemed to be sand dunes and sunlight to the horizon. Raul ran out, into the desert.

Before Carlos or Philip could react, Deshanazza closed the door. The bullets had left no mark, no trace of blood, no wound.

"God, God, God," Carlos chanted, but there was no magic in his voice or his words.

"You," Deshanazza said, putting a hand on his shoulder, "are not very nice."

"You're in my head," Carlos said, dropping to his knees and throwing the rifle aside.

Be neither rash nor foolish, her voice told Philip, *don't discard me or what I offer.*

She knelt before Carlos, took his head in her hands, and kissed him, hard and long. Then, pushing him away, she stood and faced Philip.

Carlos swayed, teetered, steam once again rising from his eyes.

"What'd you do to him?" Philip asked.

"Kissed him," she said. "I merely kissed him. I do not seek enemies. This is a place of words, not of violence. Not of death. Would you like me to kiss you, as well?"

With all his heart, Philip did, so he shook his head and said, "No." It twisted his stomach to deny her, but he had to; he felt himself slipping. Losing.

The faux shadow clung more tightly to him, its fear draining his strength.

Deshanazza smiled. Her lips looked so soft, so inviting, so terribly luscious and tempting, Philip had to close his eyes—as if she might then cease to exist like some childhood closet monster. "I have nothing to trade," he said.

"I've asked for nothing," she said, and in his head, *I offer all the knowledge in the world.*

"You'll trick me," Philip said.

"Of course."

"You'll give me all the knowledge," Philip said, "all at once, so much and so fast that I would go mad."

"Probably."

Shaking his head, he said, "I can't accept it."

"All the pleasures of the world," Deshanazza said, "and all the pains. Hope and fear. It's all written here." She spread her arms, and even with his eyes closed Philip knew she gestured to include all the shelves in this Chamber of Words. "You would pass up the chance to have all that I have?"

"All of it, yes," Philip said, opening his eyes. "Yes, I pass."

"The others, they didn't have your strength, your potential," Deshanazza said, touching his cheek and neck, her thumb crossing his chin. "All the arcane secrets are here. All the spells. The recipes. The consequences."

A shudder ran from his faux shadow into Philip's bones. He struggled a moment to find his voice. "I pass."

Her smile loosened, losing its wicked edge. "So brave," she said. When she removed her hand, it left a cold spot on Philip's face. She glanced at Carlos, still on his knees; his eyes rolled back and he grimaced, holding back an apparent scream.

Without another word, spoken or thought, Deshanazza disappeared between the aisles.

14.

Carlos continued whimpering, leaving Philip alone—with his ashen shadow—to determine their next move. He knew opening the door behind them would reveal neither desert nor flies, but he couldn't quite convince himself. He felt the weight of Raul's pistol in his hand, useless against jinn magic. And he admired all the books and papers strewn before him.

The Chamber of Words was his to peruse.

Deshanazza had offered all the knowledge in one mind-numbing lump, but nothing prevented him from browsing.

He listened carefully, to make sure she was gone, heard only Carlos, and stepped forward.

The truth of worlds lay before him. Universes and dimensions. Treasures and secrets—and the magic he'd pursued all his life.

He'd started with simple coin tricks. When palming quarters became too easy, he switched to cards, scarves, and eventually sawed a plump girl in half during a junior high talent show. (She'd liked him a bit too much, but no one else volunteered; he'd wanted a lithe and flexible assistant, just like all the greatest magicians.) He started studying the real thing in high school, flirted with minor spells and incantations, actually succeeded in drafting a potion that made Jenny Boone sleep with him.

He'd seen some of the rarest texts, but never had an opportunity to touch them, much less study one.

How long before the door opened and the fiery-skinned jinn found him? *Forever.* It wanted Cool-Eyes, not him.

He scanned the nearest shelves, wishing he understood the order of their filing. He found histories of countries he'd never heard of, tales from Homer and Shahrazad, maps of Atlantis, and too many books he simply could not decipher. Then, there, just above eye level, something sparked his interest.

He glanced at Carlos, now sobbing into his hands.

Good.

Philip slipped the tiny book off the shelf. The author's name was familiar to him, the title written in both Latin and Hebrew—two languages he *could* read—more pamphlet than book, crudely printed by one of the earliest presses. He flipped through the pages and digested every word.

The faux shadow shuddered as Philip mouthed a spell. He wrapped his tongue around every syllable, paying particular attention to the old French words at its center, careful to understand its annunciation. A spellcaster could ill afford mistakes.

But he didn't actually speak the spell. Not yet.

The shadow, paler now than its ashes, shifted nervously. It, and consequently Philip himself, weakened with every passing moment.

"Carlos," Philip said, turning dramatically from the shelf and slipping the tiny book into a pocket.

The burnt man looked up. "You know, it's true, what they say about God."

"What do they say?" Philip asked.

Carlos looked over Philip's head. "At the edge of death, when you know it's imminent, you find Him."

Philip looked over his shoulder, just to verify that Carlos didn't actually see someone (or some*thing*). "We have to go," he said.

"Home?" Carlos asked.

Twisting the doorknob, Philip said, "I doubt it."

15.

Light blue tiles lined the floor. A gentle tinkling of bells filled the air, deep and resonant but soft and pretty.

They left the door open.

Long, slender wind chimes hung from the high ceiling, singing songs Philip might expect at the gates of Paradise. The breeze was light.

The only other sound was the crackling of Carlos' skin as he moved.

"Where are we?" Philip asked aloud, not expecting an answer.

"One step closer to Heaven," Carlos said.

"I don't expect to die." But even as Philip spoke, his faux shadow shuddered, and a wave of dizziness hit him. He had to find his true shadow soon, but had no idea how.

"I do," Carlos said. When Philip said nothing more, lulled by the music, Carlos said, "The pain's gone."

"Your nerve endings were probably burnt."

Carlos smiled grotesquely, white teeth gleaming in the middle of a black smudge of a face. "Comfortably numb," he said. "Just like the song."

Philip walked deeper into the room. It was high ceilinged, wide, and very, very long. He couldn't see the far wall. A white swirl ran through the blue tiles, from the door he'd just gone through and nearly straight down the center of this hall. There were no doors on either side.

"Hello!" Carlos called out, his voice echoing back.

Philip glared at him. "We don't know what's in here."

"There's nothing here," Carlos said. "You. Me. The freaky librarian bitch behind us." He was shaking his head. "Raul's gone home, Cool-Eyes is...gone." This almost stopped him. "There's nothing here."

Unwilling to argue, Philip followed the line in the floor.

It was never perfectly straight, arcing this way and that, shifting, changing, but always leading forward, as if someone had painted clouds into the tiles and those clouds drifted on the wind.

Carlos followed him.

The rhythmic chimes kept their movement slow and quiet. Philip, feeling himself falling under its hypnotic spell, shook his head violently to keep focused. The ashen shadow stuck close, tapping whatever reservoir of strength it had left.

Carlos whistled as they walked.

He'd been right. They *were* alone. The breeze strengthened, pushing them forward, then from their sides. Then in their faces, so they had to push instead of walk, and the chimes quickened their tempo.

"It's like we're inside a giant xylophone," Carlos said.

Philip said nothing. He'd liked the burnt twin better when he'd been quiet.

"Or a harp," Carlos said. "Like the angels play."

"Angels," Philip said, "do not play harps."

"Oh, *Mister I Can't Keep My Own Shadow*, you think you know things?" Carlos asked. "Think I'm just some slob with a gun, is that it? I can point and shoot, so she kept me around? I've never met an angel, not a *divine* angel, anyhow, but I'm damned sure they don't play kazoos and accordions."

Philip sighed. "They *sing*," he said. "Each voice a choir beautiful beyond description. At least, that's how their song has been described." He shrugged, and nodded up toward the silver and wood chimes hanging everywhere. "These dance on the winds. Describable."

Carlos scowled at him, but couldn't hold it and smiled instead. The scowl was easier to look at it, so Philip looked away, forward, following the streak in the tiles toward what had to be another door.

"They're getting faster," Carlos said.

The tempo had risen again. The wind blew harder, too, ruffling Philip's hair. Despite the song's soothing effects, he suddenly—and desperately—wanted to be anywhere but here when it reached its climax.

He started to run.

Carlos apparently agreed; he also ran.

Up ahead, there *was* a door. Even if Philip didn't see it yet. He hadn't seen the way out of the Chamber of Flies until they were on top of it. Here, at least, he'd see it long before he reached it.

He glanced backwards. The Chamber of Words dwindled behind them.

Beneath his feet, the streak in the tiles shifted more actively, until it roiled and the winds gusted and the white of those floor-clouds turned gray and the blue darkened to indigo.

The faster he pushed himself, the more resistance the wind gave.

He glanced at Carlos. Flecks of charred flesh trailed behind him.

The walls on either side receded as they pressed forward, the ceiling rose, and wind buffeted them from all directions.

A gust lifted Philip off his feet. Just for a moment. The faux shadow held him down, but still he staggered. The gales surged at him. He squinted, held up a hand, lost his balance.

Carlos tumbled to the side. The wind ripped sheets of burnt clothes and skin from his back and head; he ducked to avoid the worst of it.

There had been spells to influence the weather, but the ones Philip had seen always brought rain or sunshine. He remembered nothing about wind. He tried to review everything he'd read, all he had seen, even as the wind forced him to his knees.

He crawled forward, finding less resistance when he flattened himself. Unable to look straight into the wind, he followed the path in the tiles. Even with its twists and turns, it led ever closer to the next door, the next chamber.

The wind howled so loudly, Philip barely heard the chimes. They still played, weaving their song like an orchestra, racing toward some incredibly explosive conclusion.

So close to the ground, Philip's faux shadow enveloped him. He tasted its ash, and a scent of Cool-Eyes. He took its strength to push harder, faster, further into the driving wind. What else could he do?

The wind picked him up. He clung to the ground, and the shadow anchored him, but it wasn't enough. He rolled in the air, turned over onto his back, and skid across the floor until he slammed into Carlos. The bigger man grunted, also struggling to press forward.

The shadow clung to them both, weighing them down.

Together, they made their way back toward the gray slash in the now-black tiles.

There were no clouds above. No darkening of a sky. Only the floor changed, and the wind intensified. The cloud slash churned.

No rain. No lightning or thunder. But the chimes screamed, desperate to be heard over the wind.

As a child, Philip had seen hurricanes, and once a tornado. These winds were of that magnitude, darkening the air by blurring it, shoving at them more and more harshly. Philip had been outside during one of those storms, near the beach. The rain pelted him, and sand whipped his face like pellets. He'd managed to find shelter in a post office. Most of the city had been destroyed, the hurricane's name retired, and he'd tried to protect himself within a cocoon of magic.

It hadn't worked, though he had survived.

He tried it again now, doubtful that such a minor and childish spell would have any effect in a place like this, a house of secrets, its Chamber of Winds.

Carlos added his voice, repeating prayers, "Hail Mary, full of grace..."

Philip repeated the spell. And again, each time hoping to add a layer of protection, something to get them through this artificial hurricane, this jinn-designed storm—but without effect. The wind stole the words before he could complete them.

The gale lifted the two of them, together, threatened to carry them off. They both scrambled at the ground for something to hold, finding only the faux shadow's equally frantic hands.

Pulled down, at least for the moment, neither Philip nor Carlos seemed to have much strength to go further. Carlos still prayed, but Philip no longer heard him.

Inch by inch, they dragged themselves forward, following the line of the cloud. Then, suddenly and remarkably, they pulled so hard they were launched forward.

They tumbled, breaking apart, the faux shadow leaping for joy as the wind—and the chimes—fell suddenly dead.

Rubbing the back of his neck, Philip looked at the eye wall behind them. He could see it, the exact point where the wind died: a differentiation of the air's texture, a subtly different shade, like something solid but almost invisible.

"We're through," Carlos said, pushing himself to his feet.

"No." Philip shook his head. The gray slash still led through black tiles. "We're half way." Carlos gave him a quizzical look. "We've reached the eye."

Carlos cursed. And again in English.

Looking back the way they came, Philip saw the doorway to the Chamber of Words, so distant he couldn't be sure it was still open. And ahead, equally distant, he saw a closed door waiting. He couldn't help but smile. They really were in the middle of the Chamber of Winds.

The other eye wall, only a few meters away, stood in the way.

16.

Carlos shook his head. "No way."

Philip saw no other option.

As if knowing this, the winds deepened, the eye walls pulsated. Strangely, little of its roar—or the sound of the chimes caught in the maelstrom—penetrated the serene eye. Above, the same chimes hung motionless and silent.

Philip took a deep breath. "A Side Chamber."

Carlos did not respond.

Philip dropped to his hands and knees and started looking for some sort of trigger, a doorknob, a mechanism that would reveal the hidden entrance into another Side Chamber. The Chamber of Bones, after all, had had one near its center.

The tiles were smooth and tight, but any of them could possibly be lifted.

Except, Philip couldn't get a finger between any. Barely a fingernail.

The gray slash was nearly still, swaying only in response to action outside the eye. Philip concentrated his search here, and Carlos, who might be better at finding secret doors, did the same.

The tiles were huge, one meter squares, so perfectly laid there was no space for grout or even air between them.

"Here," Carlos said.

Philip crawled over. The tile looked no different than any other. The cloud slash went right through it. Carlos pressed down on the edge, raising the other side—but only slightly.

"Are you sure?"

The expression on Carlos' burnt face suggested Philip shouldn't ask such stupid questions.

"But how...?"

There were nothing to use as leverage. Their guns wouldn't catch the tiny bit of marble that was available to grab. With barely any purchase for his fingers, neither Philip nor Carlos couldn't move it.

The faux shadow reached underneath, leaving an ash stain on its neighbor. With its exertion, sweat broke out on Philip's forehead and rolled down his neck. His biceps burned, and the tile shifted.

Above them, the wind chimes trembled, their sound a disorganized cacophony, nothing like the music of the winds.

With an audible grunt, the shadow lifted the tile. Carlos grabbed its edges as soon as they were high enough and heaved it the rest of the way. He stood, pulled the tile away from the hole, and let it drop.

It shattered loudly, scattering black and blue shards.

The chimes jingled. The eye walls surged forward.

Carlos dropped in first, missing the first step and tumbling into the dark. Philip and his shadow followed, more carefully.

Unlike Cool-Eyes, he didn't have a candle to light.

And yet, there was the scratch of a match, a brilliant flare, and then a burning candle.

17.

Carlos threw his arms around Cool-Eyes, disrupting the candle flame but not extinguishing it.

Looking over his shoulder at Philip, not returning the embrace, Cool-Eyes asked, "How's your shadow?"

"Weak," Philip said truthfully.

"Thank God you're alive," Carlos said, pulling away to arm's length. "Where's Raul?"

When Carlos didn't answer, Philip said, "Deshanazza let him out of the house."

She sighed. "Sometimes, he can be so stupid." She looked at Carlos. "You, too."

Carlos backed away.

"I was beginning to believe you were lost," she said. "But I knew you hadn't died." She glanced at Philip's shadow, which soaked up every ounce of candlelight it could. "Your shadow is weak, though. You made it work."

"I didn't make..."

"It's strained, nonetheless," Cool-Eyes said. "I'd like to keep you alive, Philip non-King, and find your shadow. But we cannot do it here." She glanced up and smiled. "You didn't shut the door."

"Don't want to end up back there again," Philip said.

"Eventually, if we open enough doors," Cool-Eyes said, "only the Statuary Garden will remain. That's our goal. From there, we can go anywhere at will. But inside, we're doomed."

Philip watched her as silence fell between them. He had half-hoped she'd died. Something about her unsettled him. Why did she want to reunite him with his shadow so badly? What would she gain?

He glanced at the faux shadow, tied to her just as it was tied to him. *Would you betray me for her?* He didn't voice the question, afraid the thought might reach her.

She, in turn, stared at Philip, and he wondered what went through her mind. How did she see him? Pathetic? Pitiful? Or had Deshanazza's hint of *potential* been sincere? Had Philip merely failed to properly tap into himself? What power brewed just beneath his skin?

Judging from her kohl eyes, she was amused, maybe exasperated, and afraid of nothing.

Cool-Eyes turned to the onyx wall, taking the candle with her, and opened the black door.

18.

It was like walking into Vegas—without the neon.

Tables everywhere. Silken women dealt cards (no Bicycle decks, these). Dice were rolled, bones tossed, coins stacked and pushed and pulled. Tall, lithe men hung from the ceiling by ribbons, twirling and dancing acrobatically. Cheers erupted from one corner. A hundred, a thousand people crowded this massive casino. Haggard crones sat behind crystal balls. Various incenses filled the air with jasmine, citrus, vanilla, and cinnamon. Smokes wafted from tents. An elderly Asian woman poured tea for herself and a very anxious girl. Wheels spun. Heavy sighs and excited gasps sounded from every direction.

Absolutely no one turned to look at the new arrivals.

There were groups of people: Chinese here, Arabian there, Aboriginal and Caribbean and Eskimo, breathing on dice cupped in the hands of their eldest, crawling over each other to glimpse the cards.

"A Chamber of Gambling?" Philip asked. The shadow chuckled soundlessly.

"The Chamber of Fortunes," Cool-Eyes said. "I've been here before."

"But this isn't one of yours?"

"What do they play for?" Carlos asked. "Gold? Jewels?"

"And lives and souls," Cool-Eyes said. "Depends on what you're willing to win." She hadn't advanced far into the room, slowly turning her head as if searching for someone. She seemed neither worried nor hurried.

"We're safe here?" Philip asked.

"As safe as anywhere," Cool-Eyes said. "I don't see her."

"Who?"

"The exotic."

As far as answers went, that wasn't particularly helpful, but Philip said nothing more and instead took in the room.

It was easily larger than any casino he'd seen in Vegas or Atlantic City, like a humongous gymnasium lit by scattered lanterns and cauldrons of fire. Some of the participants appeared human; others, however, most certainly were not. Men of stone, women of fire, some with vibrant pink skin or a third eye in their forehead. Cloaked, hooded, naked. One group of people might have been Wall Street brokers, pressed white shirts and power ties and hard attaché cases. Half a dozen doors on this wall alone.

Carlos lowered his weapon and glanced at Philip. His expression said bewilderment. Despite his claims of being more than *just some slob with a gun*, this was well beyond his experience.

Beyond Philip's, too, but he'd never admit it.

"Soothsayers and alchemists," Cool-Eyes said, "seers and prognosticators, mathematicians, astrologists, readers of palms and leaves and bone dust and yes, even ash." She glanced at Philip's faux shadow and grinned. "Want an idea of your future?"

"Is it safe?" Philip asked.

Cool-Eyes shrugged. "Is any knowledge safe?"

A trio of willowy women in veils danced toward them, nearly singing. "We knew you would come," they said together, their voices in perfect harmony. "We knew you'd end our loneliness."

"We want nothing," Cool-Eyes told them.

Philip, and his shadow, actually moved closer to Cool-Eyes. Beautiful as these women were, they moved liked serpents and smelled of poisonous wildflowers.

"We see your futures," the girls sang, dancing around and between them, touching, caressing, leaving little burns on Philip's skin. "Your pasts. Your lives."

Cool-Eyes shook her head.

"We see the dangers," they sang, "the triumphs and the pains. The ends."

Cool-Eyes pushed away from them. But one woman had a hand on Carlos' scratchy face, and the soldier hesitated. He looked forward, again at Philip instead of Cool-Eyes, and spoke to the sing-song women. "What ends?"

Cool-Eyes stopped abruptly. As if struck. When she turned to look back at Carlos, her eyes were wide with shock and narrowed with anger.

Under her breath, she whispered Carlos' name.

The triplets circled around him now, stroking and swaying and kissing, slipping their hands under Carlo's scorched skin, whispering into his ears.

Philip had said nothing because they were jinn; he could tell by the heat of their touch. To accept their offer meant to pay their unnamed price. Carlos, virtually silent until they entered the Chamber of Winds, must have lost something when Deshanazza touched his mind.

He should've kept his eyes forward and his mouth shut.

Whatever they whispered, Carlos didn't like it. He shifted his gaze to Cool-Eyes. It cried for help. He worked his mouth, but made no sound.

Various cliques and clusters around them paused in their games of fortune to watch.

Philip half expected the women to eat Carlos alive, here, swallow him in three equal pieces before disappearing in a puff of flame.

Cool-Eyes shook her head sadly, and grabbed Philip's arm. "Quickly," she said.

Carlos stepped toward her, reaching with one arm, but the dancing women held him back. "Ours," they said, "ours and ours alone..." They pulled him away, in the opposite direction.

Carlos raised his weapon and, at point blank range, blew one of the women's heads off. It exploded in a rain of fiery blood.

The others laughed.

"Your end is dark," they said, as one yanked the rifle from his hands. "Dismal. Lonely."

One turned to look at Cool-Eyes and Philip. "*All* your ends."

Cool-Eyes stepped toward her defiantly. "We didn't ask..."

The headless woman screeched as she stretched her arms, and a new, equally wondrous head popped out of her neck. She hissed at Carlos, bearing cat teeth.

"But the beginning of your end," one sang to Carlos, "is ours."

"Ours," they sang together, lifting him off the ground. He writhed in their hands, kicking, punching, biting. The sing-song women laughed and carried him away.

Philip moved to follow, but Cool-Eyes held him back.

"You're not going to help?" Philip asked.

"He's no longer important," Cool-Eyes said.

"He was your lover."

"I've lost many lovers."

"He's still alive."

Cool-Eyes glanced back, as close to sad as Philip had ever seen her. "He'll soon wish he wasn't."

The noises of the crowd, having died in those last few moments, came back hushed and quiet as the poisonous jinn women dragged Carlos through one of the doors. A rush of heat emerged from that room—Philip felt it despite the distance—and then the door was closed and the casino's regular cacophony returned.

"They'll string him up in webs and strip his flesh," Cool-Eyes said. "One layer at a time. Overnight, his skin will grow back, and the girls will do it again tomorrow, and the next day, and the next, the skin more tender every day, and thinner, until they expose muscles and tendons and bones. And he'll survive it because he can't feel the heat of their touch."

"You can't stop them?" Philip asked.

"He made the trade," Cool-Eyes said, turning away from the door and moving forward. "*This* is a jinn chamber. When you strike a deal, it's over."

"He didn't agree..." Philip started, but stopped himself.

"He wasn't important," Cool-Eyes said. "*You are.* Only you. Raul, Carlos, they've served their purpose, they were good, but now there's only me, and you, your missing shadow, and that surrogate."

"And what purpose do I serve?" Philip asked.

Cool-Eyes smiled and touched his cheek. "You know, I could have loved you."

That moment, the faux shadow faltered and Philip collapsed.

19.

Since its creation, the ashen shadow had strained in its efforts to go well beyond its actual abilities, drawing every ounce of strength from every available source until finally reaching the end of its reserves.

It was pale beneath Philip, clinging to him like a cub to its mother, shivering, even sweating. Philip wiped his own brow with the back of his hand; it was about the only strength left in his muscles.

A wave of dizziness struck. The ground seemed to tilt underneath him; Philip hugged it like a drunk. A distant throbbing began deep within his skull. White flecks popped into his peripheral vision. The casino's sounds were muted, its scents overwhelmed by that of ash.

"Hold on," he told the shadow.

It whimpered, and held on.

Cool-Eyes dropped to her knees next to him. A hand on Philip's back gave him a surge of temporary strength. Her breath was hot on his ear as she whispered, "I'll bargain, now. I have to."

He looked up at her kohl eyes, lovely things set on a lovely face, framed by all her black hair hanging like a waterfall from her down-tilted head. The diamonds in her circlet sparkled.

The shadow shifted to touch her, climbing like ivy over her feet, her ankles, twining up her shins as she stood. Philip tasted her energy, part fire, part mud. It burned his tongue, but the faux shadow found something it needed.

Cool-Eyes walked away, apparently oblivious, pulling free from the shadow's grip as easily as from cobwebs.

Philip and shadow took deep breaths. On the extended exhale, he pushed off the ground.

The shadow grinned, though it still trembled.

It had stolen something from Cool-Eyes. Since it was bound to her (as well as Philip), she must also be bound to it. Unsteadily, he got a leg under himself and rose.

He staggered, catching someone's back to keep from falling.

"Hey!" The man turned. He was the size of an ogre, broad and muscled, a scimitar hanging from his hip. A rough brown patch shadowed his face. He had to bend his head to look down at Philip.

Philip could barely keep his balance. The ogre raised his fists, the blue illustrations on his arms and bare chest popping and stretching. Slobbering, sneering, he pulled Philip closer.

The rotten milk breath overwhelmed the ashen taste at the back of Philip's throat. "Puny thing," the ogre growled.

The ogre yanked him off his feet, ripping him away from the faux shadow. Vertigo struck so suddenly, he didn't feel if the ogre punched or dropped or threw; he just suddenly found himself on the floor again, sharp pains in his neck and jaw, blood spilling from his nose.

A cape on the ground, the faux shadow swarmed to him.

The ogre's shadow followed.

If there were any other sounds, Philip didn't hear them. Only the pounding of the ogre's thunderous steps made it through, echoing like volcanoes.

Now, Philip thought. Speak the spell. Do it. Do it fast. Those words from the stolen pamphlet.

He worked his mouth, unable to form coherent sounds. Two teeth dropped into the puddle of his blood.

The ogre snatched Philip from the ground, spun him around, brought his face close and breathed that awful, deathly stench. "Oops," the ogre said. "Breaks easy, this one does." The brown of his eyes was all Philip saw.

"Sor...sor..." His swollen tongue got in the way, and nose blood dribbled over his lips. "I...d...sorry..."

"What?" the ogre bellowed.

"Sorry," Philip said again. No other word would come out.

The ogre looked confused. "Oh." He bit the corner of his lower lip. "Oh." He set Philip down on his feet, brushed down the sides of his arms, and took half a step back. "Ah. I see. Yeah, I do tend to overreact, don't I?"

Philip didn't even try to answer.

"Ah, well, then I owe you one," the ogre said, nodding. "Yes, I've done you a grievous wrong. Please, forgive me."

Philip looked left and right, uncertain, unsure, unable to focus, and didn't see Cool-Eyes anywhere. He spit blood. "Sure."

The ogre nodded. "Well met, then." He returned to whatever he'd been doing.

Philip wiped his nose on his sleeve. Still bloody, but not a fountain. He concentrated on two or three breaths, and balance, and realized he felt no weaker than before the ogre had hit him.

The faux shadow, darker now, embraced Philip and soaked the blood off his face.

Philip managed a half turn, looking again for Cool-Eyes. A familiar figure loomed in front of him: a visible skeleton beneath a skin of white fire.

The jinn grinned, tilted his head, and said, "Philip, isn't it?"

20.

Philip stared at the jinn. His head reeled. His knees buckled. He didn't know what kept him on his feet.

The Chamber of Fortunes had, ultimately, been unfortunate for Philip. The faux shadow tried to hide between his ankles. The jinn leaned forward, his toothy smile growing. "Care to bargain now, mortal?"

"No," Philip said. His voice was so weak, it quavered.

The jinn laughed. "You think you have a choice?"

"I cannot help you," Philip said. "I don't know the way out any better than you."

"Oh, I know the way out," the jinn said.

"Then just go," Philip said. "You don't need me."

"If I could *just go*," the jinn said, "I wouldn't need you."

"Excuse me," the ogre said. *He* was supporting Philip with an arm around his shoulders, and only now let go to step between them. Philip almost fell, but absolutely couldn't.

"My friend," the ogre said, "has politely declined."

The jinn glared at the ogre. "He's in my debt."

"Then risk that debt," the ogre said, motioning toward one of the tables. "Play the Wheel."

The jinn looked from the ogre to the Wheel, then back to Philip, and narrowed his eyes. "Agreed."

21.

The Wheel stood vertically behind a table manned by two heavily veiled women. Only their eyes were visible, yellow things that belonged on lizards.

It was similar to a roulette wheel, in that most slots alternated between black and red. Numbers had been replaced by various symbols, most of which were foreign to Philip. There were two consecutive white slots at one end of the Wheel. One woman spun; the other draped an arm on the player's shoulder and whispered in his ear. A pile of coins lay on the black square in front of him.

The Wheel slowed, slowed, clicking from black to red to black to red...to black...to red...

Behind the player, a round, greasy man silently cheered the Wheel, his eyes rapt on the pointer.

The player held his breath and the Wheel settled—on black.

"Yes," the greasy man said, waving his fist in victory.

"Too bad," the whispering woman said as the player stood. The spinner collected the coins. The player faced the greasy man, head downcast, and mumbled something.

The greasy man grabbed him by the back of the head and pulled him close. Bit his throat. Laughed as blood spilled over his mouth.

"Away, away," the whisperer said, shooing the greasy man and his prize.

Philip glanced at the ogre. "I don't understand…"

The ogre, however, either didn't hear or ignored him. He pushed Philip forward, to the player's chair.

"He has a debt," the jinn told the whisperer.

She held out a hand.

The jinn deposited a red crystal into her fist. She examined it, turning it over under her eye, and set it on the table in front of two squares, one red, one black. "Pick your poison," she told the jinn.

"I don't know the rules," Philip admitted.

She whispered so that only he could hear. "There are no rules. Do you want to win or lose?"

"What happens if I lose?" he asked.

"The jinn collects his debt."

"And if I win?"

"We collect it." Under that veil, she grinned; Philip heard it in her voice.

"Black," the jinn said aloud, pushing the crystal into the square.

"Black," both the whisperer and spinner said.

And the Wheel was given a healthy spin.

Philip watched the pointer, around which the colors clicked. It felt nice to be sitting, relaxing comfortably in the presence of these most gorgeous, lizard-like women, the whisperer's voice constant in his ear. "Round and round and round she goes, though I know where she'll stop, don't you know?" When Philip didn't answer right away, she touched the tip of his ear with her tongue. "Delicious. A debt to be paid, but to whom, to whom? The jinn with the fiery soul, or the mistress of the table? Whom do you want? Your destiny awaits, you can choose, but you must do so ever so quickly."

Philip saw nothing but the spinning Wheel, heard nothing but the whisperer. He wasn't prepared to pay any debts. The faux shadow beneath him had faded almost beyond memory. Cool-Eyes had abandoned him. Carlos, lost to the sing-songy women. Raul, gone to the desert. What fate awaited Philip? He saw nothing but shadows and darkness, death and despair.

Good thing, he realized, he was no seer.

The Wheel slowed.

"Make your choice," the whisperer said. "The jinn will want his freedom, the mistress wants your dying love. Which path shall you take? Which fate do you want?"

"It's really my choice?" Philip asked, keeping his voice just as low.

"It's really your choice."

"I want my shadow back," Philip said.

The Wheel clicked to black, red, black, red...black...white...and once more to land on the second white slot.

"White?" the jinn howled. "White!?! No one spins white!"

"White," the spinner said, shrugging.

The whisperer kissed the corner of Philip's mouth with cold lips. "Good choice," she said.

"Tough break," the ogre said to the jinn, putting a consoling arm around his shoulder and leading him away. "Perhaps I should buy you a drink. I've done you a grievous disservice, I fear."

The spinner took the crystal and ground it to powder in her hands. She dropped the grains in front of Philip (the faux shadow absorbed them all).

The whisperer helped him stand. He felt substantially stronger now, as if that crystal had fueled the shadow. "Through the door you entered," she said. "Your third destiny waits." Then, as an afterthought, she added, "Good luck."

22.

Philip, knowing he existed on borrowed time, went straight to the door and opened it.

He had expected some swirling vortex of shadows, where perhaps his shadow had eventually found itself after learning it really did need Philip. He thought there might be a crag upon which he'd stand, in the midst of terrible lightning, where he could raise a fist and call down his shadow. Demonic faces in the mist, jinn watching with their fiery eyes from the mountaintops, a bubbling river of lava below. Wind and flies and skeletal guardians. A bright moon distorted through a gigantic skylight like a funhouse mirror. Cackling creatures clawing at his shadow as it tried to return to him, the faux shadow reaching out in one final, sacrificial act.

He might have imagined trumpets.

Instead, the walls were white, close in, almost claustrophobic. There was another door, yes, and a single wooden chair, a green eyed woman seated upon it, violin under her neck, bow poised to sing. She wore a fancy black evening gown, long and sleek, slit to climb half way up flawless thighs.

She lowered the violin to her lap. With a voice much deeper than Philip expected from such a petit frame, she asked, "Have you a request?"

The ashen shadow, trembling, circled around Philip's leg, but could do nothing to make him retreat. It was afraid.

"I'm looking for my shadow," Philip said.

She tilted her head to look at the faux shadow. "You've come to the right place. This is the Chamber of Shadows."

Puzzled, he said, "You have no shadow."

"Not that you see," she admitted.

"Do you have a name?"

She smiled sweetly. "Jacinta."

"Philip."

"Well, Philip," Jacinta said, bringing her instrument back to its place under her chin. "What gift do you offer?"

Philip thought about that a moment. He doubted he could pry the faux shadow off his skin, and wasn't really willing to part with it. He still carried Raul's pistol, which had been utterly useless in this house of secrets, but didn't think it would be acceptable.

The book.

It was a small price if his life was returned to him. He hesitated, considering all he would lose, then pulled it from his pocket.

Jacinta cocked an eyebrow. "There is powerful magic in that book," she said. "It'll do."

He set the book at her feet, careful to meet her eyes as he knelt, and took a step back.

Jacinta slid the bow across the strings, drawing one long, steady, deep note. It bored into Philip's brain and bones.

And then she was off, a wild and relentless melody, her whole body swaying, eyes closed, red lips slightly parted and moist. He wanted to touch her, to somehow merge with this sound, but couldn't move without risking its ruin.

The walls grayed as she played, shifting like smoke, undulating to the rhythm; this darkening had the effect of a spotlight, and Jacinta shone within it.

She played so furiously, sweat glistened on her forehead and rolled down her neck. Her fingernails, painted as green as her eyes, flashed up and down as she bent the violin to her will. It looked like it might break under the pressure. Smoke rose from the strings. As the volume increased, every individual note burned into Philip's veins.

He almost recognized the song—or the shadow, clinging breathlessly to him now, knew it and howled, its cry matching a suddenly held note.

The tempo changed again. Philip's stomach knotted. His legs trembled. Tears fell from his eyes. Jacinta played as if for all the angels of Heaven and Hell—but for Philip alone.

A shriek echoed from the distance. The walls, beyond gray—beyond pale—had become something translucent, revealing a twilight sky over the desert. Bright reds and oranges surrounded the setting sun. A figure stretched from the horizon, almost human but bigger, both magical and mundane. Philip's true shadow slashed the sky, answering the call of Jacinta's violin.

It circled, first like a hawk and then more closely, and finally landed between the violinist and Philip.

"I've learned a lot since we parted," his shadow said.

"So have I."

The song diverted into minor keys so heart-wrenchingly sad, silver tears dropped from the shadow's eyes. They plopped on the clouded floor, sending ripples through the desert image far below.

"You were right," the shadow eventually said. "I do need you."

"I almost died," Philip said.

Without another word, the shadow stepped forward to embrace him.

All at once, Philip's strength returned. His senses sharpened. He caught the scent of rosin, heard the rolling dice from the Chamber of Fortunes still behind him, tasted honey on his shadow's breath.

With one final, vibrating note, Jacinta finished the song. She laid the violin across her knees and wiped a bead of sweat from her cheek.

"Thank you," Philip said, his voice his own again, everything he'd lost returned.

Jacinta lowered her head, a bow, and closed her eyes. "You're welcome."

Taking a deep breath, Philip turned and walked back toward the Chamber of Fortunes.

"No," Jacinta said. "The other door."

He went through the other door, into the statuary garden.

23.

It was larger than he remembered, crowded with a thousand and one statues. Doors lined both sides of this hall, with more on a higher level, though he saw no stairs.

"We're going home," Philip told both shadows.

He strode through the front doors and into the desert. The sun had dropped, as had the temperature. The faux shadow shivered and drew close.

He had never seen so many stars. The sky was alive with them. Shooting stars streaked by. He picked out a few constellations before realizing he should hurry.

But the doorway was gone.

Cool-Eyes had taken him to this house of secrets from her lab, through a door she had opened onto the sands. He might've been out of it then, but he knew where the door had been.

There were only the remnants of Raul, rifle still in his skeletal hands, bag at his feet. He had made it to the desert, no further, and scavengers had picked him clean.

How much time had passed?

Tattered bits of cloth clung to Raul's remains. Philip didn't dare get too close, in case the house vanished, damning Philip to an early desert end.

Someone approached from behind. He recognized Cool-Eyes' vanilla and cinnamon scent. "I've got my shadow again," he said.

"Good," Cool-Eyes said, taking his hand like a lover. "Now, give it to me."

Before he could react, she reached into his back, through shirt and flesh and bone but without pain, without touching *him*, and grabbed his shadow.

The jinn, unseen, laughed.

Cool-Eyes yanked, sweating with the strain. Philip tried to hold his shadow, but it tore noisily. The shadow resisted, too, but it had no substance.

Cool-Eyes recited words under her breath, causing the faux shadow to swell. It doubled, tripled in size, its ashes sticking to the back of Philip's throat. Its edges blurred into Philip's true shadow, merging, and it pulled toward Cool-Eyes.

"You're mine, too," Philip told the false shadow. He lost his balance, fell to his knees, and his shadow ripped free.

Only strength of will kept Philip from falling on his face.

"Your shadow, then," the jinn said. It stepped forward, the light of its fiery skin brightening the night. "I'll bind it to you on the other side."

"You...wanted my shadow for yourself?" Philip asked, panting.

"Loose shadows," Cool-Eyes said, "make powerful magic. But there were no loose shadows." It hung limply within her fist.

"I can bargain with you now," Philip told the jinn.

The jinn chuckled. "With what? You shan't live to see the morning sun."

Philip lifted Raul's pistol, pointed at Cool-Eyes, and fired. Twice. The jinn snatched the bullets from the air.

"Like I said," Cool-Eyes said, coming close enough to take the gun from his hand. "I could have loved you. Really, I could have. But you were doomed, and I've lost too much in my time."

White spots danced along the edges of Philip's vision. Dropping to his butt, he fumbled with words, stolen words, the spell he'd learned before surrendering the book. It was an unconventional application, but as he'd hoped with the ogre, it might help.

A tingling rose in his chest, and sputtered.

Cool-Eyes shook her head. "You cannot transform living flesh," she told him. She sketched a doorway in the air, creating the opening to her lab.

"Finally," the jinn said.

Philip grabbed for Cool-Eyes as she walked away. This last bit of strength failed, and he tumbled to the ground.

"Please," Philip said. "At least...at least a kiss, before you go." He didn't have a plan; anything to delay her. When she took his shadow through that doorway, he'd die.

She paused to look at him, both of them bathed in the light of the jinn's fiery flesh. Even Philip's shadow cast a shadow, pale as it was; the ash shadow, still beneath Philip, was weaker, and fading.

After a moment, Cool-Eyes shook her head. "I don't grant dying wishes," she said, and turned away.

Philip, as a last effort, cast his spell again. The alchemical magic burned him, rising from his intestines, this time finding its target and making the change. If he couldn't change her flesh into gold, then at least he could get her shadow.

Cool-Eyes faltered. Philip's shadow slipped from her fingers and flowed back to him. Her golden shadow shimmered, and she dropped to her knees.

Since her back was to Philip, he couldn't see her expression. But he was more concerned with the jinn. "I can give you the girl," he said, "*and* her shadow."

The jinn grinned and rubbed his hands together. "And in return?"

"Let me go back to where I started," he said.

"Through this door?" the jinn asked.

"No," Cool-Eyes said, moving her hands. The motion caused the door to swing shut, but the jinn caught it.

"I use this door, as well," the jinn said. "I delivered, mortal-born girl, and so must you." He turned to Philip. "Done, Philip non-King."

The jinn threw the door open so wide, it swallowed them all. On the other side, Cool-Eyes' room with computers and bookshelves and normal, regular doors on its walls seemed remarkably welcome.

"And to you, too," the jinn told Philip, "I have delivered. If I see you again, I shall consume you."

He vanished, taking Cool-Eyes and her golden shadow.

24.

Days later, Philip sat on one of the many pillows from Cool-Eyes' chamber. Some of the doors were locked, but most opened onto small rooms and closets—no exits. The door to the desert was gone, leaving one wall bare.

There were two cots and assorted weaponry where Raul and Carlos had slept. Books in another, but every one dissolved into ash when he opened it. Smoke rose from the computers when he tried to turn them on; a monitor popped, and its screen shattered.

There was a bowl of water. Philip drank often; it refilled itself every time. Another bowl held various fruits, all fresh and ripe.

The jinn had brought him back to where he'd started his journey into the house of secrets. But from this lab, he found no escape.

With his limited spellcasting, Philip managed to open all the locked doors, finding nothing but the shackled bones of the dead.

In frustration, he cast the spell he'd learned and changed the entire computer system to gold.

"Stuck," he said, finally, breaking the silence.

His shadow said, "I learned a lot while I was away."

"Can you get us out of here?"

"I can recite the Chinese alphabet," the shadow said. "Backwards."

165

"Can you get us out of here?" Philip asked again.

"I've been to the palace in which the moon's sister resides."

"Can you get us out of here?"

"I can read the stars."

"Can you get us out of here?"

"I met a former king of France."

Philip looked down at his shadow, unable to ask again. It met his gaze, and then looked away. "No," the shadow said at last. "I cannot get us out of here."

The faux shadow had vanished, maybe with the jinn, maybe because it had reached its end.

On the table, between the bottomless water and fruit bowls, Philip had laid Raul's pistol. It was solid gold now. Gleaming. Still useless.

"I can tell you stories," the shadow said. "To pass the time."

"Until when?" Philip asked.

The shadow shrugged. It didn't know.

AFTERWORD

House of Shadow and Ash was originally released as an e-serial with fantastic artwork by John Pierro--he did a cover and an image for each of six installments. In 2007, Bad Moon Books published the novella with John's artwork and cover.

This is the second story in which we see Cool-Eyes. (The first is *Bablyon Rising.*) I suspect it will not be the last. I have a special place in my heart for her, though I know if we were to meet in real life she would either ignore me entirely--not even ignore, but simply never even notice--or lead me straight to my destruction.

I guess we've all got to go sometime.

You should know: there's an unwritten pornographic epilogue in which the librarian finds Philip. The end results are several paper-thin gold-leaf statues of Deshanazza that disintegrate at the slightest touch and one dried-up, used-up husk, Philip's corpse, entangled in shadowy ribbons hanging from the ceiling of a room full of golden pillows.

Rouen, France 1944

A wisp of a girl, no more substantive than a ghost, no older than ten or twelve, pale and fragile like porcelain, like fine china, she slips from cot to cot, touching a hand here, a shoulder there, sharing a heart-breakingly sad smile to some. She seems not to hear—neither the noises from outside, the whistling of bombs, the explosions, the gunfire or the sirens, nor any word said to her, whispered or cried out. If she has a name, she's not sharing. If she arrived at this makeshift shelter with anyone, no one remembers. She sits beside you, perhaps for only a minute or throughout the whole long night. Does she sleep? No one's seen her sleep. No one believes she causes death, not in a place like this, not when everyone is already hovering at the far edge of life; perhaps she gives, to some but not to others, some small comfort, some warmth, maybe something so abstract as innocence or joy, before their final breath.

THE
DRY
DUSTED
SANDS

Someone had folded the map into thirds, stuffed it into an envelope, scribbled Joe's name on it with a number two pencil, and left it under his car's windshield wiper while he slept. So when morning came, he woke, showered, did all those morning things you do before going to work, and trudged out into the bitter pre-dawn chill and started the car before he noticed it. He had to get out of the car—and pluck it off the windshield.

The envelope was wet with dew, but the temperature hadn't dropped so far as to form frost. That was good. He was running late to work already, some problem with getting up two hours before sunrise just to make the trek across town; five minutes with an ice scraper would've made it worse.

He glanced at the envelope, his name barely legible in big, looping letters, and slipped it into the front pocket of his briefcase.

His wasn't an exciting job, nor a glamorous one, but he liked it well enough. And they liked him. But whenever he tried to explain exactly what he did to an attractive member of the opposite sex, her eyes would roll into the back of her head and her attention would shift to any other place available. He learned long ago to keep it simple. "I work with computers," he would say. Keep it mysterious. Keep it dull and boring and, essentially, outside of conversation.

At lunch, Joe climbed into his car and remembered the envelope. But it was in the office and he was hungry, and he forgot about it again until quitting time. After shutting down his computer, after picking up his briefcase, he noticed the edge of the envelope just sticking out, teasing him. It was barely sealed. He opened it easily, withdrew the map for the first time, and looked at it for an entire sixty seconds before he realized what it was. Yes, sure, he knew immediately it was a map. But it was a map of where he lived, his condo complex and the neighborhoods immediately adjacent. His unit was marked in red. So was another. The map had a box for a legend, but it only had a series of numbers. It didn't take long to translate them to a date and time. The date was today. The time was soon.

If he drove straight home, if he didn't stop for dinner somewhere, or at a bar, or at the supermarket to pick up some box of frozen tasteless sustenance, he could make it back to the condos before the appointed time. It sounded like a good idea. Joe refolded the map, stuffed it back into its envelope, returned the envelope to his briefcase, and carried the case out to his car.

His wasn't a red sports car. It was gray. He called it the Gray Lady when no one else was around. It drove smoothly and effortlessly, and he guided it home in good time. He pulled into his parking spot, carried the briefcase into the living room, and withdrew the map again.

He glanced at the clock. It was art deco, a lot of straight lines on the sides, exposed gears, all gray and black; and it told him he had ten minutes until the time indicated on the legend of the map.

He poured himself a glass of water, ate a piece of chocolate, then looked to the clock again. Seven minutes.

He looked at the arrangement of condominiums on the map. His was east of the entrance. The other red condo was on the other side, the newer section, where the condos had continued being built until the real estate market decided it wasn't a good idea. Half of those never sold. Joe wasn't sure, but the other unit marked on the map might very well be vacant.

He took his keys, locked his home just as he always did when he left, and walked along the sidewalk. He passed his car, the trash compactor, the front office, and the mailboxes. He passed empty and occupied units; he knew some of those people, if not by name then at least by face. He passed no one on the sidewalk. You didn't see a lot of people walking this little circular route after dark—not because it was dangerous, or roughly kept, but because there was nothing to see but other condos that looked just like yours.

None of the units on the map were numbered, but they were situated on the map to match the angles and shapes of real life. When the sidewalk turned left, the units on the map showed the turn. The last unit in the next block of four was the other marked in red. The windows were dark. No car waited outside. Either no one was home, or no one lived there. But the door, slightly ajar, invited him in.

He knocked anyhow. Looking in, he saw it was empty. There was no furniture, but the painting had been finished and the carpets had been laid. Stairs led to the second floor. Upstairs, in the loft overlooking the living room, a light flickered. A candle. Joe pushed the door open but still hadn't crossed the threshold. "Hello?" he said. "Anybody here?"

Predictably, no one answered.

It was dark, but no curtains blocked the windows. A combination of streetlights and moon penetrated deeply enough into the condo to see there was nothing to see. Joe, who never could resist a mystery, climbed the stairs. He wished he'd thought to bring a flashlight, but when he got to the top of the stairs the loft was lit well enough by the candle. It stood on a café-styled table, the kind you might find in Paris or London. Also on the table: a bottle of red wine from Argentina, two empty glasses, one folded slip of paper, and two envelopes. Both envelopes were sealed. Both had names on them. One was his, in the same messy handwriting. The other said Janice.

He pocketed his envelope, unopened, and picked up the slip of paper. It said, "With my compliments." It was unsigned. It was the same handwriting. Someone was playing a game with him. Someone named Janice? He didn't think so.

Downstairs, someone knocked at the door. She called, "Hello?"

"Up here," Joe said, looking over the edge of the loft. He didn't recognize the woman, but there wasn't enough light for a man to recognize his own mother.

She hesitated. "Why?" she asked.

"Haven't got a clue," Joe told her.

There were no chairs around the table. He glanced into the bedroom; it appeared to be empty, but it was even darker there than in the loft. The bathroom was virtually a wall of thick shadows.

The woman, Janice, had reached the top of the stairs. She looked at Joe, then at the table, and said, "What are you up to?"

"Nothing," he said. "I didn't do this. Did you?"

"No." A slight pause. "Why should I believe you?"

"Don't know," Joe said. "I found a map."

"On my back porch," she said.

"On my car," he told her. "Are you Janice?"

"How would you know that?"

"There's an envelope for you on the table," Joe said.

Janice picked it up and opened it without taking her eyes from Joe. She stepped closer to the candle, putting the table between them, and read the note. It was another folded piece of paper. When she finished with it, she folded the paper back up and put it in her pocket. She dropped the envelope on the table.

"Shall we?" she asked, indicating the wine.

"Might not be a good idea," Joe said.

"Might not," she admitted. The bottle had already been uncorked. She filled both glasses generously and waited for Joe to claim his before lifting hers to her lips. She smiled as she drank, and her eyes stayed on Joe the entire time. "Not bad, for a cheap table wine," she said, then sipped some more. "What now?"

"I don't know."

"Have you read your note?"

"No."

"I'll wait," Janice said. She leaned against the railing, putting her back to the living room downstairs, and drank more wine.

Joe opened his note, tearing the end of it as he did so, and read it quietly. Janice watched. The note said, "Midnight. The Witching Hour. The Transition from Day to Night. The Crossroads. North." He turned the note over, just to be sure the other side was blank. It was.

"Yours says the same thing?" Joe asked. "Midnight?"

She shook her head. She dug out her note and flipped it open. "Says nothing of the sort." Her voice altered as she read the words. "Railroad Station. Passenger platform. Stop. Main line. No connections. One way tickets." She closed the note.

"Tickets?" Joe asked. "Plural?"

"Tickets. Plural." She finished her wine and refilled the glass. Joe had barely touched his. He felt obliged to keep up. "So we have a time and a place."

"What's the place?"

"The old Amtrak station," Janice said. "They don't stop there anymore, haven't for years, but trains still go through this place."

"It was easy enough to get here," Joe said. "I only had to walk."

"I have my car out front," Janice said.

"You think we should go?"

"Why not?" She grinned. "I'm always up for an adventure."

"You didn't write these notes?" Joe asked.

"And neither did you."

She seemed certain. So was he. "Okay," Joe said. "Should we leave now?"

Janice shook her head. "Might as well finish the wine. It's only ten minutes away, and we've got more than two hours."

Joe didn't keep up. She drank three glasses to his two, but they finished the bottle. The candle burned lower and dripped wax on the table. They didn't say much. He couldn't think of anything to say. But she looked at him, up and down and sideways, and he did the same. She wasn't beautiful, not in a conventional way, but she had beauty, and she held herself with confidence. She looked smart, chic and professional, a business suit designed to show off her legs. The light of a single candle did neither of them any justice.

"Ready?" Janice asked.

Joe nodded. They left the glasses on the table. He blew out the candle. They descended in darkness. Outside, the edges were further away, the streetlights closer and unobstructed, but it wasn't much brighter. She drove a convertible. The top was down. Portishead streamed out of the speakers. She made no effort to turn it down or change it in any way. He recognized the song but couldn't name it.

Beth Gibbons' haunted vocals accompanied them through the dark, winding streets to the other side of town, off the map, where the old Amtrak station waited. The platform was well lit, but the ticket booth had been closed years back. Trains passed through every day, but none stopped here. One set of tracks ran alongside the platform; a second set ran parallel. A series of wooden columns supported a roof over the platform. On the third, someone had attached an envelope with a nail. It was unmarked. Janice ripped it down, opened it, showed Joe the two train tickets inside.

"Guess our benefactor wants us to go for a trip," Janice said.

Joe glanced at the clock on the tower. They were ten minutes from midnight. The air was brisk, but not quite cold. The platform was completely empty.

"Why?" Joe asked.

Janice leaned against the pole. "Not *who*?"

"That's another good question, sure," Joe said, "but it's not my first."

"That's one way in which we differ," Janice said. "I'm much more interested in who." She looked up and down the tracks; in both directions, they faded into the shadows. "Will be impressive, though, if a train actually pulls in and stops, don't you think?"

They saw the train, or at least its one gleaming headlight, before they heard it. Its brakes screeched, its horn called out to the night, and the iron locomotive lumbered to a stop in the station. It was an old-fashioned passenger train, with steps at either end of the cars leading to a door. The car, a faded yellow in the yellowish light of the station, was the only door that opened. A conductor, in uniform and spectacles, leaned out and looked down the platform. Though there was no one else, he called out, loud as he could, "All aboard!"

Janice leaned closer to Joe. "I think I'm beginning to be impressed. Too bad you didn't arrange all this." Then she climbed aboard. The conductor tipped his hat to her as she entered. Joe, fully aware this wasn't a dream, and despite that the note had clearly said the tickets were one way, followed.

A dozen rows of seats lined the car. Besides the conductor, and Janice standing at the start of the aisle, there were six other passengers, men and women looking as bewildered as Joe felt, and just as curious, as though perhaps these people boarding now, Joe and Janice, might have answers.

"Enjoy the ride," the conductor said. He pulled the door shut behind him, locking eight passengers into the yellow rail car.

"You all got notes, too?" Joe asked.

In response, they murmured or nodded their heads or simply looked out the window, but no one actually said anything.

"Do we know where we're going?" Janice asked the passengers. The train lurched, beginning its forward momentum. Joe could feel the iron wheels straining to pull beneath them. The train struggled, briefly, before picking up any speed. The station receded slowly.

Janice walked forward a few rows, not so far as any of the other passengers, and turned. She motioned to one set of seats. Joe followed her suggestion, sat at the window. She took the seat next to him, leaving the aisle empty. She whispered, "They don't seem to be a talkative bunch."

Joe nodded. "I wonder what they've seen."

Janice shook her head. "I don't."

"No?"

"I know what they've seen," Janice said. "They've seen their lives reach stopping points. They've watched their forward progress screech to a halt. They've watched their dreams, their aspirations, their very souls dissipate like smoke on the wind."

"That's rather cynical," Joe said, though he didn't refute it.

"It happens to a lot of people," Janice said. "It happened to me. It happened to you."

Joe thought about it for a moment. He thought about the Gray Lady he drove, and the condo on which he paid a mortgage, and the job that had him getting out of bed and out of the house sunrise. He thought about the things he'd wanted to do, the mountains in need of climbing, the trails in need of hiking. He didn't feel like he'd taken a wrong turn, but he couldn't argue with Janice. It made too much sense. He'd grown numb.

"How did it happen?" Joe asked.

"How does it ever happen?" Janice asked. "It was time, for you and me and these people, to take charge again, to command our own destinies."

"I'm not sure answering this—invitation—is really taking charge."

"It's not. We've all failed."

"*That*," Joe said, "is worse than just cynical."

Janice shrugged.

"So where does this train go?" Joe asked.

"Isn't it obvious?" Janice answered. "It goes nowhere."

They rode a while in silence. The conductor never came to collect their tickets. Joe looked at his, turned it over, read the fine print, but found nothing to indicate either destination or cost. It said *One Way*, and it had a train number, the platform and station at which he boarded.

He got up, looked at the other passengers. One woman averted her eyes. A man turned to looked down at his feet. Another man, however, met Joe's gaze, narrowed his eyes, and rose to his feet. "Okay," the man said. "Let's get this done."

"Get what done?"

The man emerged from his row with his fists raised like a boxer. He didn't look like a boxer. He looked like a man who might have watched boxers, as a child, but had forgotten the general look of them, had eaten too much rather than exercised. His clothes fit well, but didn't hide that. He carried no muscle, and probably no technique. Neither did Joe.

"I'm not going to fight you," Joe said.

"Someone will."

Joe shook his head once. "Not tonight."

"Then when?" the man asked. No—pleaded. The look in his eyes was nothing less than desperation.

"How long have you been on this train?"

"I boarded in May."

"May?" Joe looked at Janice. "It's not May, is it?"

"It's almost May," she said. She, too, was standing now, along with half the other passengers.

"Long enough," one of the others, a woman, said. "The train stops, it starts, it sometimes picks up passengers, sometimes lets us off."

"Does it *prevent* you from disembarking?" Joe asked.

No one admitted that it did. None of these six had even tried.

"It's just a train," one of the other women said, an older woman, whose rough edges should've been soft. "Have you never ridden the rails before?"

"No," Joe admitted.

"Then just sit down," she said, "and enjoy the ride."

The train rocked rhythmically; outside, trees whipped by too close to the train to get a real feeling for where they were. "There's nothing to enjoy."

"There's the entertainment," the youngest passenger said. He wasn't much more than a boy, maybe fresh out of college, sitting in the farthest possible corner seat and wearing a printed tee and crisp blue jeans. "The entertainment can't be beat."

"What entertainment?" Joe asked.

The boy didn't answer.

"He," the old woman said, "was already here when I got here. I think he's always been here."

"I think maybe," the non-boxer added, "it's his train." He turned on the boy. "Are you responsible for this?"

The boy actually looked a little scared. "I've never been responsible for anything my whole life."

Joe believed him. "Why don't you just get off the train?" He didn't know who he was asking, and wasn't sure he cared who answered.

When no one else spoke up, the old woman said, "If you don't know where the train has stopped, you'd be foolish to get off there. What if there are bandits?"

"Bandits?"

"Men in masks," the woman said. "Desperados. Gunmen. Outlaws. Could be anyone."

"There were no bandits on our platform," Joe said.

"How do you know?"

"It's pointless," Janice told Joe. "They don't know anything. They can't tell us anything."

"Next time the train stops," Joe said, "I'm getting off."

The old woman looked astonished and offended and somewhat pleased. She sat. The train tilted slightly as it took a curve.

The non-boxer was shaking his head. He said, "You can't do that."

"Why not?"

"The train won't stop."

"The train *just* stopped," Joe told him.

"Because none of us were ready to get off."

Janice touched Joe's shoulder. She whispered, "You and me, we're in this together, don't you think?"

"I'm not sure about that."

"Well, *I* think it, and I don't really care if you agree," she said. "Sit down and shut up for a bit. Don't antagonize the locals."

Joe wanted to say something else, but there weren't any words. But he didn't sit, not immediately. He discovered another question inside him. He let it out. "Where's the conductor?"

"Went out that way," Janice said, nodding to the door through which they'd entered.

"If we're in this together," Joe said, stepping around her to get to the aisle, "then let's go."

"It's cold out there," the old woman said.

Joe ignored her and strode toward the door. The train shook and rumbled. The whistle sounded. Janice, without a word, followed him.

The next car was empty except for the conductor. He smiled. He beckoned them with a wave of his fingers and said, "Close the door behind you, it's cold out there."

It wasn't cold out there. Janice came in behind him. She closed the door. None of the other passengers had followed.

"Where is this train going?"

"It's a train," the conductor said. "It goes where the tracks take it."

"That's not an answer," Joe said.

"That's because you're asking the wrong question."

"What should I be asking?" Joe asked.

"Ask why we're here," Janice whispered to him.

"Okay," Joe said, nodding. "Why us? Why were we invited?"

"Everyone's invited," the conductor said. "On a day, some day, I can't say which, each of us gets a summons, and you either respond or ignore it. You'd be surprised how many ignore it. It takes a certain level of curiosity, a certain level of courage, to go into a house and drink poisoned wine and then board a train at the wrong station."

"Did you say *poisoned?*" Joe asked.

"Wasn't that obvious?" Janice asked.

"So this is, what, a hallucination?"

"That would make me not real," Janice said, "or you part of my hallucination, and I'm not sure that's right."

"The lady is correct," the conductor said. "This is neither a hallucination nor a dream."

"Then what is it?"

"A train."

"You're not funny," Joe said.

"The poison takes a few hours to work through your veins," the conductor said, "but you're fortunate. Time isn't the same here as it is elsewhere. Your hours might be years here. Who am I to say?"

"You're the conductor."

"And therefore neither chemist nor pharmacist," the conductor said. "I agree, it's not an agreeable situation, but you didn't have to come."

"What happens now?" Joe asked.

The conductor shrugged. "I suppose, when we reach your destination, you climb off this train."

"And?"

The conductor shrugged again, as though it were a statement of innocence, an admission of ignorance. "And you get off the train," he said. "Beyond that, it's not for me to say."

"Whose train is this?" Janice asked.

"Ah," the conductor said, rising, "that's a question worthy of an answer. That's a question not everybody thinks to ask. Whose train is this, anyhow?" He grinned. "I'd hardly say it's your train, though it is, and I'd hardly claim it's mine, because it's not. No, this train, and all the others on this line, belongs to the Station Masters."

"What's a Station Master?" Joe asked.

"Not what," the conductor said, "but *who*. Why, I believe there's a Station Master's house at the next stop. You might ask them directly." His grin broadened. "You might not."

"That's not an answer," Joe said.

"In another country," the conductor told him, "in another time, the Station Master was a man of high regard. He lived in a good house. He oversaw the stations, the trains coming in and out. He was a busy man, often a rich man, and his daughters commanded only the best husbands." He paused. "But we are far from that country, and far from that time. You can, with minimal effort, meet one of the Station Masters, but I doubt they'll give you the answers you seek."

The rhythm of the train changed abruptly. Joe noticed it through the bones of his feet. The conductor rose. "This must be your destination."

The train rolled to a stop. The conductor stepped forward and opened the door between cars. He looked outside, up and down the platform, and called, "All aboard!" Then he turned to Joe and Janice. "The train will depart in thirty seconds."

No one boarded. There was no one outside. The sky had lightened. More precisely, it had paled. The platform was a slab of concrete, not unlike where they'd boarded. Another track ran on the other side. There was no overhead, no roof of any type, and the few benches provided no protection from rain. Fortunately, no rain fell. The wind was cool but weak. The Station House, presumably, was the big brick structure just past the far end of the tracks.

Joe looked at Janice. Janice looked at Joe. She said, "Let's see what there is to be seen."

When the train lurched forward, it left Joe and Janice alone on the unlit platform. Besides the house, there appeared to be only a single dirt road leading away from the station. There was no one and nothing else to be seen but patches of brush amid the plains.

Only one light on the house's second floor windows had been on; as they walked the platform, a lower level light came on, then a porch light.

"I think we're expected," Janice said.

Their footsteps left swirling dervishes in the dust, and a trail behind them. At the end of the platform, a winding dirt trail led to the house. Fallen leaves crunched underfoot. The trees around them, Joe realized, were bare branched and white barked, nothing like other Florida trees. They hadn't been on the train that long. Combined with the bizarre nighttime atmospherics, it felt like a different world.

Joe wouldn't concede that, not yet; but once the idea formed in his head, he found it hard to shake.

Janice noticed it. "We're not in Kansas anymore, Toto."

"I think I know what they meant by one way," Joe said.

As they reached the porch, before climbing the two steps, the front door swung open. A tall, lithe man dressed in black stood there. His arms and legs seemed excessively long, or his torso was just abnormally undersized. The arms of his black suit were long, covering nearly half his hand. The shirt he wore under the jacket was also black. His face looked like the face of a man who had worked under the sun all his long life, scarred and cracked, dry, permanently tanned. He wore wire glasses with small round lenses. He smiled, but it didn't look right on him. "Welcome," he said, gesturing for them to enter. "I rarely have the opportunity to entertain guests."

"We're not here for entertainment," Joe said. But they followed him into the sitting room with a half dozen chairs, chaise lounges, and a variety of tables, one of which supported glasses, several bottles of wine, and a platter of meats and cheeses.

"Please, sit," the Stationmaster said. He poured wine into glasses. Joe and Janice exchanged a glance and, together, sat on one of the lounges. Joe didn't feel like getting comfortable; Janice didn't look like she meant to stretch out anytime soon. The Stationmaster sat opposite them, leaned forward, showing that the lenses magnified his eyes, and asked, "You came in on the train?"

"Yes," Janice said.

"I'm pleased," the Stationmaster said, leaning back. "So few ever disembark. It's as though you realize there's absolutely no need to do so. You grow accustomed to having your needs met by strangers and watching the worlds pass on the other side of those windows. I should admit, windows on trains always seemed, to me, to give a false sense of reality. I think that's why I prefer subways."

Joe said, "Subways have windows."

"Yes," the Stationmaster admitted, "but they travel through tunnels of darkness, and there's nothing to see but darkness, perhaps other subways, and the only indications of life are the posters selling perfume and jeans and concerts. Inevitably, those show other people, and you soon find yourself wanting to see other people, and touch other people, and speak with other people. It's so much more civilized."

"But you don't work on a subway," Janice said.

The Stationmaster shook his head, sipped his wine, and said, "Alas, no."

"We were summoned," Joe said suddenly. "Why?"

"All people are summoned, at some time in their lives. Some answer the summons. Some ignore it."

"This sounds familiar," Joe said.

"Who wrote the notes?" Janice asked. "Who left us the maps?"

The Stationmaster's gaze went from Janice to Joe, locking eyes with them, showing his sincerity and trustworthiness and compassion. Joe didn't believe a bit of it. The Stationmaster said, simply, "I did not."

"No, of course not," Joe said. "But you know who did."

"Knowledge is a tricky thing," the Stationmaster said. "Do you know really the names of places? Do you understand the uselessness of maps? Never trust a map. They lie. They lead to places that don't exist, or pin things to places where they aren't. Are you familiar with trap streets?"

Joe looked to Janice. She shook her head. "No," Joe said.

"Cartographers of a certain age would create false locales on a map to confound those who would recreate their creations," the Stationmaster said, "and also to hide places the cartographer did not want you to see. I was a cartographer, once, though I admit it feels like a lifetime ago."

"You're not answering our questions," Joe said.

"And you're quite rude, young man, to accept an invitation into my home and demand anything more of me," the Stationmaster said. "However, I am, in fact, answering your question. Certain trap streets, besides bewildering treasure hunters and tricking unwary travelers, might be used to lead the less fortunate to disreputable houses, perhaps of ill repute, the homes of bandits and highwaymen, and thus into a trap that, indeed, proved fatal." He finished his wine. Joe realized Janice had finished hers, too, though he hadn't had any himself.

The Stationmaster refilled his glass, and Janice's, and said, "You might take some food, if you're not thirsty." Then, without waiting for Joe to react, he said, "If an unknown person left for you a map, then it was, undoubtedly, meant to entrap you. Did it lead you somewhere seemingly benign and uninteresting but perhaps a little enigmatic?"

"It did," Janice said.

The Stationmaster tsked and shook his head. "Then I'm afraid there's no hope for you. You've fallen into a trap. And, I should warn you, you're now *off the map*. Off the map entirely. There's no atlas of these lands, nothing to set down the tracks in a single place, no means by which you can find your way home. In a way, you're like me, except of course that you're not, not at all. For in a short while, I'll invite you two strangers to leave my premises, but I shall continue to be the Stationmaster, and I shall continue entertaining the rare guest. You, on the other hand, may find work in a field, or go back to the station and hope for another train. I should, however, warn you: the next train is not scheduled."

"What do you mean, not scheduled?" Joe asked.

"This is an unusual station," the Stationmaster said. "Only when there's a passenger who needs to come here, to this place, would the train stop at this station."

"What place is this?" Janice asked.

The Stationmaster shook his head. "I've talked all I can for an evening, and must retire. There's no rest for the weary, or the wicked, or, unfortunately, the Stationmaster. There's much to do, and my day begins quite early. There's a bedroom on this floor, across the hall, if you'd care to stay for the night. I won't put you out without notice. I'll see to it you have breakfast, if you wish, and then see you on your way." He rose, bowed slightly, and said, "Good evening, strangers. May your dreams be pleasant."

After he was gone, leaving them alone in a lonely room, Janice said, "Why do I get the feeling our dreams won't be pleasant?"

"Maybe it's the house," Joe said.

"Maybe it's the Stationmaster."

"He didn't actually tell us anything."

"I think I've learned something," Janice said. "No one will tell us anything."

"You seem so nonchalant about this whole thing," Joe said, glancing out the sitting room window. "Do you think they drugged us?"

"No."

"With the wine," Joe suggested.

Janice sipped hers. "No. But it's sweeter than I would prefer."

"How can you be sure?"

"Because you've barely touched yours, and you've seen all the same things I've seen, and been to all the same places."

"Was it a mistake, getting off the train?" Joe asked.

"I don't believe in mistakes." She finished her glass of wine and refilled it.

"We have to find a way back home," Joe finally said.

"There is no way."

"I know," Joe said. "But I don't believe in that, either." He fished out his one way train ticket. "Maybe we just need a return ticket."

"You think the Stationmaster will give us one?" Janice asked.

Joe didn't think so. He didn't have to answer that. He put his ticket back into his pocket. "There's no destination on the ticket," he said.

"Maybe we're going nowhere."

"We're already *at* nowhere," Joe said. "Maybe we determine our own destination."

Janice smiled. She kept smiling, and kept looking at him, until Joe felt obliged to ask, "What?"

"You're a philosopher."

"I'm a lot of things," Joe said, standing. "I won't argue one more."

Janice also rose. She touched Joe's arm, leaned close, and whispered, "Should we go straight to bed, or should we explore?"

Beyond the sitting room, the hall was spacious and neatly decorated with old, unknown oil paintings, landscapes of places Joe didn't know and portraits of people Joe had never seen. There were a variety of doors and a big, utilitarian kitchen. There was, as the Stationmaster had said, one bedroom with a gigantic bed and still plenty of room for chairs, dressers, and a shelf full of books. A crystal chandelier hung in the foyer. The library contained walls full of books, and also an assortment of musical instruments; trumpets and violins hung on the walls, an upright bass stood in one corner, and a grand piano dominated the center of the room.

It was a large brick house, so all the rooms were large, filled with an antique, affluent style. Joe wondered if the stuff came with the house, and if the house came with the job; and he wondered if such a job were something he'd want.

They were in the library, Janice still drinking wine, Joe standing over the piano keys and wishing he could play, when a woman asked, "Can you play?"

She stood in the doorway. She had the same elongated features of the Stationmaster, but they made her seem like a model. Her almond shaped eyes were a startling blue. Her hair was black, her silk robe black, her fingernails and lips red. She said, "My husband told me you might be restless after your journey, and suggested I might check on your progress, and I find you in the music room."

Joe almost commented on the books, but didn't.

"So I ask again," the Stationmaster's wife said, "do you play?"

"No," Joe said.

"Pity."

"I can," Janice said.

"Then please, by all means," the Stationmaster's wife said, "play for us a sad song."

"Why sad?" Janice asked.

The Stationmaster's wife picked one of the violins off the wall. "There is beauty in sorrow," she said. "The trick, of course, is to not wallow within it, but to celebrate it. So play us a song, and I'll do what I can to keep up."

Janice played. She started slow, a little unevenly, finding her way through the unfamiliar ivories, pulling together notes and musical phrases until she found a minor progression she liked, and then she got into it. She played her heart out. The melancholy was palpable, and forced Joe to sit. He was in love, he realized suddenly; he'd never known it, never felt it, but now he understood. He wanted, more than anything else in the world, to ease the suffering of the songstress, to care for her and save her.

The Stationmaster's wife joined with the violin, adding depth, bringing pain to the sorrow. She eased through the most agonizing array of notes anyone had ever heard, perfectly weaving around the piano's melody, perfectly matching the pale, barren landscape outside.

There was a difference between listening to a recording of perfectly played and produced music, and being caught between two desperate, anguish-driven instruments. Joe's heart stopped. He finished his wine and refilled it and finished it again. He cried, silently, and was still wiping the tears when the song reached its natural conclusion.

Janice stared at the Stationmaster's wife with her mouth hanging open and her eyes wide. The Stationmaster's wife smiled radiantly. Joe closed his eyes.

"How...?" Janice asked.

"It was in you," the Stationmaster's wife said.

"I said I could play," Janice said. "But that was extraordinary. It was almost like my hands moved on their own."

"They did."

"I've never played anything like that," Janice said.

"Of course not," the Stationmaster's wife said. "Neither have I." She returned the violin to its hook in the wall.

For a while, no one did anything else, and no one dared break the silence. Joe would've sworn the echoes of the song continued to bounce through the house, passing the library/music room several times before finally dissipating.

"You have a talent," the Stationmaster's wife finally said, causing Janice to blush. "It's true," she added, "and it's rare. I appreciate that, and thank you for your gift."

"You, too," Joe said to the Stationmaster's wife. "I don't know much about music, but I do know the way the two of you played together — I don't think either by itself would've been near so..." Failing to find a word, he settled on, "Nice." Then, having something better, he added, "Beautiful."

"I'm sure," the stationmaster's wife said to Joe, giving him a full smile, "you have talents, as well." Joe couldn't tell if she was teasing or making fun.

"So," Janice said, leaving the piano and turning her full attention to the stationmaster's wife. "Do you know why we're here?"

"Of course. We're so far removed from any town, there's no inn nearby, no other place to rest your head."

"The maps," Janice said.

The stationmaster's wife shook her head. "I know about maps." But she looked confused.

"What do you know?" Joe asked.

"They're tricky things," the stationmaster's wife said. "They can lie, they can cheat, and they can lead you to harm. The stationmaster, before he was stationmaster, was a mapmaker."

"We know," Janice said.

"He was particularly talented," the stationmaster's wife said. "His were the hands of an artist, and the heart of an artist, as well. He could play the piano, though not as well as you. And his voice...he sang like a nightingale, he did, once upon a time."

"You make it sound sad," Joe said.

"Of course it's sad," the stationmaster's wife said sharply. "He does none of these things now. He works at the rail yards, the switching station, the train graveyard, but he makes no time for art anymore, or music." She looked, now, adversarial. "Or maps."

"I didn't mean..."

"I know what you meant," the stationmaster's wife said, "and what you didn't. But there *are* other mapmakers, other mischief makers, other liars and thieves who would bend their inks to such purposes. Here," she stuck out a hand, "let me see this map."

Joe, being closest, offered his.

The stationmaster's wife pursed her lips and narrowed her eyes as she examined it. She turned it round and round, and turned it over to see the back, and finally gave it back. "This is no map. There's no art here."

"No one ever claimed it was art," Janice said.

"Maps," the stationmaster's wife said, "just like lies, just like poetry, should be *art*. This, that you have, is an affront to the senses. You mean to tell me you took it to mean something? You followed it from one place to another? You *listened?*"

Folding the map and returning it to his pocket, Joe said, "What should we have done?"

"You should have walked away," the stationmaster's wife said. "You should have struck a match and set fire to this fallacy. There are neither lies in that map, nor truth. There's nothing. It's hollow and empty and meaningless and..." She paused a moment, took a breath, shook her head. "You should have ignored it."

"It was an invitation," Joe said.

"One addressed to each of us," Janice added.

"It was hard to ignore."

"Not hard," the stationmaster's wife said. "Impossible. I see that, of course I do. I'm no fool. So, the map led you to a place, and something in that place somehow led you here, to the train, to this station?"

Joe and Janice exchanged looks. It all sounded so simple, and also ridiculous.

"You're brave," the stationmaster's wife said. "Courage is as rare a virtue as your talent with the piano." She closed her robe about herself, held her hands across her chest as though she were cold. "I'll help, in the small ways that I can. Ask your questions."

"Someone left these maps," Janice said. "Someone enticed with mystery, with intrigue, then gave us wine to dull our senses. Next thing we knew, we were on a train to nowhere, from nowhere, from a station back home where the train doesn't even stop anymore." The stationmaster's wife nodded as Janice spoke. "The conductor told us the stationmaster would have answers."

"And so here you are," the stationmaster's wife said. "That's simple enough. There's one problem that I see."

"What's that?" Janice asked.

"You don't have questions."

"No," Joe said. "We do."

The stationmaster's wife shook her head. "You only think you have questions. You want to know who drew that lackluster map, who tricked you here, and you think you want to go back home. But you don't really know what that means, do you? *Home?* What waits for you, a job? A house? Friends you think are friends who will drift in and out of your lives until you find yourselves old and abandoned?"

"That's awful," Janice said.

"But true," the stationmaster's wife said. She turned to Joe. "Look at me. Guess, if you will, my age."

"I can't do that."

"Why not?"

"I've made it a rule," Joe said. "Never guess a woman's age. Or weight."

The stationmaster's wife smiled. "It's a wise rule," she said, "but I promise not to be offended. If you wish, guess high."

Joe frowned. He hesitated. Janice almost said something, but the stationmaster's wife held up a palm to stop her. "This is for him."

Finally, Joe said, "Thirty."

"You're not being honest," the stationmaster's wife said.

"Maybe thirty-five."

"Or perhaps forty?" she asked. "Fifty? Would you believe seventy-nine?"

"No," Joe said.

"Tough," the stationmaster's wife said. She turned to Janice. "Would you like to know the secret?"

"Yes," Janice said.

"Honesty. Trust. Love. Art. Devotion." She let the words linger on the air. "My husband," she added, "is one hundred and two." She smiled. "Of course, there's one additional secret, if you'd care to know. *We're not human.*"

Silence followed. Joe didn't intrude upon it because he had nothing to say. His thoughts were jumbled; and since he believed the stationmaster's wife, his thoughts were also confused.

"My husband is the stationmaster, true," she added after a moment, "but it's not just his title, it's our race. We're from the race of stationmasters. Also cartographers and dramatists and musicians and harlequins."

"Where are we?" Janice asked.

The stationmaster's wife smiled. "You're at a railway station, a switching station, and the end of the line for some. You're at a crossroads, and possibly a new beginning. There are things you haven't seen yet, things that will amaze you. Come."

She left the room with impossible speed and grace. Joe and Janice stumbled to follow. They went through the massive kitchen and onto the back porch. A barren landscape of skeletal trees greeted them, and train tracks stretching in myriad directions. In the distance, they saw what must be a bonfire; they heard music, albeit muffled and distant.

"Children," the stationmaster's wife said, referring to the music. "Every night, they gather and sing, and bring color back to our world every dawn. But forget them for now, you'll never see them. Like the will-o-the-wisp, they'll always be off in the distance, just a bit closer than the horizon, further this way or that. No, for now just look up."

The night sky was a blanket of stars, thousands of stars, some bright and some brighter, some swirled, some streaked; some were red or orange or blue; some shifted, though only slightly, and some faded when Joe looked directly at them. Shooting stars lit up the sky with some regularity. And some stars looked, instead, to be like galaxies and nebulae and other astronomical oddities that could not, normally, be seen by mere eyes. Joe recognized no constellations. The longer he looked up, the more he could see, as his vision adjusted to the near-darkness that was anything but complete. Some stars were ringed. Others were not round, but amorphous, shapeless, obscured by their own clouds. Distant, intergalactic fireworks exploded silently and randomly.

Instinctively, Joe took Janice's hand, or she took his. They stared at things they shouldn't see.

"The stationmasters have been here a long while," the stationmaster's wife said. "Before your trains, they were watchmen and sentinels and marauders; before that, scouts and explorers, hunters and assassins. They were bricklayers and glassblowers and tradesmen, and always, they were cartographers, the makers of maps, ever trying to understand the worlds and put some order to them, never understanding that maps could be folded, shifted, erased, and forgotten. They became clockmakers and playwrights and seamstresses, and eventually, one by one, by the hundreds and by the thousands, whilst slipping between worlds, they lost their way."

Startled, Joe looked at the stationmaster's wife. "What?"

"As a race, the stationmasters are gone," she told him.

"Gone where?"

"To the places between places," the stationmaster's wife said. "Through the slips and holes and wrinkles." For a long time, no one said a word. The stationmaster's wife wiped a lonely tear from her cheek and offered a quiet, reserved smile. "Personally, I like to believe they've stumbled into other worlds, other landscapes and cities, and make their way again as pipers, poets, and pastry chefs."

"Your husband is a stationmaster," Janice said.

"Yes," she admitted, "and not the last. But that's not enough." She shrugged exaggeratedly and said, "Enough of that. We've had our sad song for the night." She looked directly at Joe; he almost had to look away. "It's your turn."

"My turn?"

"She has shown us her music," the stationmaster's wife said, "and I have shown you the night sky. Show us something."

"I have nothing to show," Joe said.

"You lie," the stationmaster's wife said, without malice or anger. "You don't even know it."

"I don't play an instrument," Joe said. "I don't sing. I don't dance."

"You *don't* dance?" the stationmaster's wife interrupted.

"I don't do anything," Joe said. "I watch computers. I make spreadsheets. I start jobs and reports and other programs, but I'm not an artist."

"Everyone is an artist, at heart." She laid her palm over his chest, over his heart. "Find your art."

Joe shook his head.

"What do you do, then?" Janice asked. "It doesn't have to be an art."

"What do you mean?"

"Show us something," Janice said. The stationmaster's wife still held Joe by the chest, but her head was turned toward Janice. "Show us *something* we haven't seen before."

Joe looked left and right, up and down, but avoided the night sky. He felt suddenly cold, and awkward; he tried to pull back, away from the pulsating heat of the stationmaster's wife's hand, but she refused to release him. She leaned close and whispered. "You would not have received a ticket."

Joe felt deflated and defeated. "I can't *do* anything."

Again, the stationmaster's wife said, "Liar."

Joe shook his head.

The stationmaster's wife kissed him.

It took him by surprise. He stumbled backwards, but there was no place to go; one of the porch columns caught him. Her kiss was soft, warm, and tender. She held the side of his head in one palm as she kissed him and gently pulled him closer. It was a long kiss, thoroughly indescribable in its beauty and depth. It aroused a jumble of emotions within him, both joy and sadness, a certain degree of lust, and an overwhelming sense of solace.

She pulled gently away, her excruciatingly blue eyes holding him to her, but it was her red lips he found himself staring at. "See," she said. "You can do *something*."

"That's not exactly fair," Janice said.

The stationmaster's wife pulled away and looked down. "You're right. I apologize. You mustn't tell my husband. I've been a poor host, and you've been a naughty guest." She turned sharply and opened the door.

"Wait," Joe said.

She waited, but he had no more words.

"Nations rise and fall with a single breath," the stationmaster's wife said, not turning, "or a single kiss. What have you come for?"

When Joe still couldn't talk, Janice said, "The map."

"The map," the stationmaster's wife said. "You think that excuses us?" She took one step into the house and continued waiting.

Janice punched Joe in the arm. It broke his trance. He found a few words, stumbled around them, and said, "I can show you something." He then looked at Janice. "Both of you."

"What?" Janice asked.

"I can..." Joe paused. "I need a piece of paper."

"And something to write with?" the stationmaster's wife asked.

"No," Joe said. "Just the paper."

She left them out on the porch, under the stars. Brief bits of music, mostly drumming, drifted across the field. These were echoes, mostly, ghosts of pipes or strings, a single note of voice, but for the briefest of snippets it was as if they were right there at the bonfire, surrounded by teenagers drinking and dancing and smoking and laughing.

The stationmaster's wife returned with several leafs of paper in a variety of colors and sizes. Joe took a relatively regular sheet of white, then changed his mind and opted for red. It wasn't much bigger than a regular sheet. He folded it, and again, and several more times, turning it as he did so, bending bits backwards or forwards as necessary, until he finished. Janice and the stationmaster's wife watched; the stationmaster's wife's eyes went wide in surprise or delight several times.

When he finished folding the red sheet of paper, he held up a paper butterfly.

"Beautiful," the stationmaster's wife said.

A breeze lifted the paper off his hand. Caught in the slight wind, it was as though the butterfly were alive. It flittered up, then down, then went straight to the ground just beyond the porch. The stationmaster's wife was there in an instant. She picked up the paper, held it pinched between two fingers, and turned it over and over as she examined it. "This is exquisite," she said. "I've seen masters of paper folding from Chinese empires not do so fine a job."

"It's not that good," Joe said.

"No," the stationmaster's wife told him. "It's better. Watch." She cupped her hands around the paper butterfly, hiding it from view. She closed her eyes, puffed a breath of air between her thumbs onto the origami, then flung her hands up, releasing the butterfly into the air. It flew again, caught on the air currents, but it wasn't simply riding the wind. Its wings fluttered too swiftly, and its path was both too erratic and purposeful. The butterfly landed high on the wood column, flexed its wings, then took off again, around the eave and up to the roof.

"That was real," Janice said, following its path and, hanging over the edge of the porch railing, peering up at where the butterfly had disappeared. "You made that butterfly real."

"I merely gave it a breath of life," the stationmaster's wife said. "It won't live for but a moment. It's paper."

"You're a magician," Joe said.

"No. I am the stationmaster's wife."

"That means more than it sounds like it means, doesn't it?" Janice asked.

The stationmaster's wife shook her head. "It's not a title," she said, "or a duty. It's just what I am." She turned to Joe again. "I'm sorry about the butterfly. I think it's gone away. And I'm sorry about the kiss."

Joe almost said, *It's nothing*, but that would've been a lie.

"Where'd you learn to do origami?" Janice asked.

Joe shook his head. "I wanted to impress a girl once."

"It's always about a girl, isn't it?" Janice asked.

"It should *always* be about a girl," the stationmaster's wife said to Janice. "Especially if that girl is you."

The music stopped.

Until that moment, the music had been a subtle undercurrent, constant but distant and virtually unintelligible; the silence, meanwhile, was overpowering and oppressive and a little bit frightening. Simultaneously, all three of them turned to look out across the fields, seeking signs of the faraway bonfire, but there was no orange glow, no line of smoke, no sound of dancing or music or laughter. Indeed, the sky seemed to have darkened, dimming the stars and swirls and planets and galaxies they had seen so clearly. A cloud of dust advanced toward the stationmaster's house. It was far away, almost to the horizon, but coming closer quite swiftly. Joe's stomach dropped. Janice moved closer to him, and to the door. The stationmaster's wife closed her eyes and sighed.

"What is it?" Janice asked.

"I'm afraid it's my fault," the stationmaster's wife said.

"What?" Joe asked.

"Your butterfly."

The butterfly, still alive, as much paper as flesh, fluttered back into view, skimming off the side of the roof. It seemed, for a moment, not to know which direction it wanted to go. Instinctively, Joe held out his hand, palm up and open. The red butterfly landed there, flapped its wings one last time, and became paper again. He folded the butterfly in such a way that he could hide it in his pocket.

The cloud of dust approached, revealing itself to be three people on horseback, the horses huge and fast as lightning, black as shadow, breathing smoke. The riders wore muted colors, dark red, green, or brown. They came to a halt only a few meters from the porch.

The rider in red was a woman, though she would never be called a *woman in red*. She had a scar on the side of her face; it stretched from the corner of her eye diagonally back to her lower ear. It was barely noticeable, but she wore her hair in such a way that it was accentuated and proudly displayed. Holsters hung on her hips.

The rider in green was a hefty, unshaven man with a shotgun and a permanent sneer. He carried the shotgun like a dance partner.

The rider in brown, in the center, had come forward to head a V formation. His hair was light and sandy, his face young. A patch covered one eye. If he carried a weapon, it wasn't immediately noticeable. He raised a hand in greeting, cast his eyes across the three of them, and settled on the stationmaster's wife. "I hate to be here," he said to her.

"You needn't be," the stationmaster's wife said.

"Ah, but I must," the brown rider said. "Please, fetch your husband, as this most certainly concerns him, as well."

The stationmaster's wife held his gaze for a moment, but she ceded quickly and disappeared into the house.

"The two of you," the brown rider said, "are strangers. Guests?"

"Guests," Janice said.

"We were invited," Joe added.

"Of course you were," the brown rider said. "I suppose you came in on the train, the train that's not supposed to stop here."

"You should take that up with the engineer," Joe suggested.

The brown rider smiled. "I may very well do that, stranger. But first, we're to have ourselves a word."

"We're having a word now," Janice said.

"You may think that, yes," the brown rider said. He didn't look away from Joe. "You've come a long way. I can tell by your clothes, and your accents. You're not merely strangers. You're lost."

"I don't think we're lost," Joe said, turning to Janice. "Do you?"

"I don't think we're lost at all," Janice agreed.

"Sorry," Joe said to the brown rider. "Not lost."

The green rider's horse shuffled back a step. The rider steadied himself. His grip on the shotgun had changed. He held it now as a lover. The red rider remained motionless. She smiled with half her mouth. It was a hungry, vicious, wicked grin; Joe didn't like it.

The brown rider said, "That's too bad. I'm sorry to hear that. If you were lost, perhaps, we might overlook the fact that you are simply not supposed to be here."

"Here?" Joe asked.

"And," the brown rider said, "you shouldn't be doing the things you've been doing."

The stationmaster and his wife came out onto the porch. The stationmaster wore a robe and an exaggerated frown. "What do *you* want?" he asked. He said *you* like it was a curse, and aimed it at the brown rider as though intending to be rude and dismissive and derogatory.

"I'm afraid you know what I want," the brown rider said. "It's what I do, what I must do. There's been a bit of magic, I'm afraid, and we're here to extinguish it."

"You're crazy," the stationmaster said. "There hasn't been magic this side of the dusty clouds since the days of James. There are laws."

"There are laws," the brown rider admitted. "Someone has broken them. Perhaps one of your guests?"

The stationmaster looked briefly at Janice and Joe. "I'd forgotten they were even here," the stationmaster said. "But they're incapable of magic. They're from the farthest side, the darkest corner, the place from which the trains derive."

The brown rider spared another glance at Joe. "They do look rather senseless," he said.

"No need to be rude," Janice said.

"There are laws," the brown rider said, "and it is my sad duty to enforce them. Now, I ask each of you here, the four of you, to do the right thing and tell me where and how and who. Answer these questions, and I'll send..."

The stationmaster interrupted. "You have no authority here."

The green rider's horse shuffled again. The red rider's smile grew more malevolent. Surreptitiously, perhaps not meant to be seen, she unsnapped the holsters on both her hips.

"There is no authority," the brown rider said, "but mine."

The stationmaster started to respond, but the green rider lifted his shotgun and aimed it straight at the stationmaster before he could utter a word. The red rider's guns were aimed at Janice and the stationmaster's wife. Joe felt oddly neglected.

The brown rider said, "I'll ask kindly, if I can, because you know I'd rather not have bloodshed here at the stationmaster's house. Now, again, calmly if we may: who has been practicing magical arts?"

"I played the piano," Janice said.

"I made a paper bird," Joe said, but he kept it safely hidden.

The stationmaster looked at each of them in turn, then at the riders. "I was asleep. Perhaps I dreamt some arcana in my sleep?"

The green rider's horse huffed. It was as good as laughing.

"And you, lady?" the brown rider asked. "What have you been doing?"

The stationmaster's wife shook her head. "Nothing," she said. "Watching the stars," she said. "Conversing with our guests," she said. "And maybe drinking a little wine."

The brown rider narrowed his eyes. "You've done much," he said. "You're outnumbered, and you're outnumbered and outgunned."

Joe did a quick count. It was a reaction, yes, but the rider was wrong, unless he was counting the horses.

"Confess," the brown rider said, "and I'll be lenient."

"You know nothing of leniency," the stationmaster's wife said.

"No, perhaps I don't," the brown rider said. "Shoot them."

Immediately, there were three thunderous gunshots, a single roiling sound that echoed across the field and down the railroad tracks and off the swirling stars in the sky. Janice and the stationmaster's wife flew backwards. The stationmaster crossed his hands before him and somehow stopped the shotgun pellets from hitting him.

Before Joe could respond or react, before he could think about what happened, before either Janice or the stationmaster's wife hit the ground, the red rider had both her weapons, Colt Peacemakers, aimed at his eyes, and the distance separating him from her seemed suddenly to shrink. She cocked both guns but held off from shooting when the brown rider held up his hand.

"You know the law," the brown rider said to the stationmaster. "You suffer the law just as we all suffer it. I'll take your guest, your stranger, and leave you to tend to your dead and dying. You do me a grave disservice, stationmaster, to think you might thwart me."

The red rider bound Joe's hands with rope. The green rider took Joe on the back of his horse. They rode swiftly away. Joe didn't see Janice or the stationmaster's wife, or even the stationmaster, and soon they were too far from the house to see anything.

They galloped alongside the rail. They rode hard and far, through the night, through the fields and scattered trees, at some point crossing the tracks and veering away from them. Bound as he was, and senseless as he'd been described, it took all Joe's effort to stay on the back of the horse. The going was rough. He wasn't sure he wouldn't be better off slipping off the horse intentionally. But before he convinced himself to do this, they reached the riders' camp.

Camp was a series of tents alongside a pond. Joe had seen no other water, neither streams nor rivers nor lakes nor rain. This was, in fact, only a big puddle surrounded by thick bushes and a few white-barked trees. He looked back, toward the railroad tracks they had left behind, but could see neither the tracks nor the stationmaster's house. The last thing he saw, in fact, was blood and bullets. His ears still rung. His wrists hurt from the rope cutting into them.

The green rider pulled Joe unceremoniously off the back of his horse and shoved him toward a fire pit. The brown rider had just lit the kindling. The red rider stood slightly aside, examining her Colts one at a time, polishing them with a burgundy handkerchief.

Logs circled the fire. The brown rider settled on one and held his hands over the infantile flames. Joe managed to get himself into a sitting position. His hands weren't just hampered; they hurt. "Are you going to keep me tied up?"

The brown rider regarded him. The red rider continued to clean her guns; the green rider ignored them all and stroked one of the shadow horse's manes. The hair was long and ethereal, and blacker than the night.

"Yes," the brown rider said.

"Why?" Joe asked. "I haven't done anything."

"Haven't you?" the brown rider asked. "You're our evidence."

"Evidence of what?"

"Of magic," the brown rider said.

"I'm not," Joe insisted. "I'm just a man."

The brown rider arched his eyebrows. "That's quite an assertion," he said. "Would you care to back it up?"

The red rider holstered her guns; Joe noticed that they were already cocked. Single action pistols—she kept them cocked so she'd have an immediate shot. He didn't think that was safe. She wandered toward the fire, her eyes on Joe. She grinned.

"Forget it," the brown rider said. "You're a stranger, and it's mighty inhospitable of me to be issuing challenges. Do you have a name, *man?*" He said it with amusement.

Finding no reason not to tell them, he said, "Joe."

"We're of the riders," the brown rider said. "We enforce the laws here. Some are stronger than others. You broke one of those."

"I broke no law."

"Magic," the brown rider said, "has been forbidden since the cataclysm."

"I don't know what you're talking about," Joe said. "There's no magic."

"What have you got in your pocket?" the brown rider asked.

"Nothing."

"You cannot lie to us," the brown rider said. Still grooming his horse, the green rider grunted in agreement.

The red rider wiped her mouth with the back of her hand. Her voice was a deep contralto and impossibly resonant. "Maybe he's stupid."

"No," the brown rider said. "I do not think our friend Joe is stupid. Are you, Joe?"

Joe didn't answer that. He didn't really think he needed to.

"Now, if you would," the brown rider said, "please empty your pockets."

Joe hesitated. Then he held up his hands. "I can't."

The brown rider glanced at the red rider. She responded instantly, withdrawing a small knife from some hidden fold of her clothes. She stepped around the fire, cut the rope, and returned to her seat in a single motion. The rope fell apart grudgingly. The red rider used the same knife to start cutting an apple.

"Now," the brown rider said, throwing all sorts of intimidation into his voice. "Your pockets."

Joe emptied his pockets. He carried his wallet, a pen, a tiny notepad, some coins, a handkerchief, and a folded-up piece of red paper that had been a butterfly. Reluctantly, he passed the whole lot to the brown rider, who examined every item individually. He opened the wallet slowly, as if expecting it to explode in his face. He thumbed through the bills inside and showed the license to the red rider. She shrugged.

The brown rider gave everything except the butterfly back to Joe.

"This," the brown rider said, holding the paper up, over the fire in an implied threat, "is rather interesting, wouldn't you say?"

"It's a piece of paper," Joe said.

"You have a whole pad of paper," the brown rider said. "But not a page as interesting as this. Can you feel it?" He handed it to the red rider.

She sneered. "Magic'd."

"Magic'd," the brown rider said, taking back the butterfly. "You created this."

"It's a paper butterfly," Joe said. "Origami."

The green rider came over, held out a hand to the brown rider, requesting the red paper butterfly. There wasn't a trace of life to be found in it. It neither fluttered nor sighed. Its wings were paper. Its head was paper. It was, quite thoroughly, paper from one end to the other. The green rider made the wings move and smiled.

"It's a toy, now," the brown rider said. "But it hasn't always been."

The green rider looked at Joe, then tore the butterfly in half. He grinned some more, then stuffed the two halves into different pockets.

"It breathed," the brown rider said. "So tell me, who did the magic?"

"There was no magic," Joe told him. The green rider, chuckling, went back to the shadow horses.

"Our laws are strict," the brown rider said. "We watch for the slightest bit of magic. Since the last time...well, we have to be on our guard constantly. So many think that a little something here or there won't amount to much, but it does. It's cumulative. So punishment must be swift and judicious."

"You shot Janice," Joe said, turning his eyes to the red rider but meaning to speak to the three of them. "And the stationmaster's wife. That's not justice."

"What would you call it, then?" the brown rider asked.

"Murder."

The brown rider frowned. "Strong word, that. I advise you to withdraw it."

Joe met the rider's eyes and held his ground. He said, "No."

The brown rider sighed deeply. "I don't reckon I like you much."

"I don't care," Joe said.

"You do realize you're our prisoner, don't you?"

"I did nothing," Joe said.

"I'm afraid I cannot accept that," the brown rider said. "But I'll tell you what. Justice has been served. Blood has been spilt. And I believe that, while you created the butterfly, while you gave it form and function, you did not give it life. Did you?"

"Of course I didn't," Joe said.

"That was the stationmaster's wife," the brown rider said.

Joe said nothing.

"We've long been aware that she harbored something," the brown rider said. "There's no law against the acquisition of knowledge or skill. A day may come in which we rely upon magic again. But the practicing of those arts..." He shook his head. "I'm afraid we cannot tolerate the slightest act of magic, no matter how small and meaningless. We resist magic. We resist another cataclysm. We will not break open our world again. We are the law."

Joe said, "Your laws suck."

By now, the fire was going strong. The brown rider stuck out his hands again, turning them in the heat. He no longer looked at Joe; and the green rider seemed to see nothing but the horses. But the red rider—she looked straight at Joe from under her brows, one half of her lip arced in a dangerous smile. She'd been cutting the apple and eating the pieces, but she looked perpetually hungry. Tossing the core into the fire, she spoke to the brown rider. "You should've let me shoot him."

"There's no magic in gunpowder," the brown rider said.

The red rider seemed pleased by that. Joe was quite certain he was not pleased.

Abruptly, the brown rider rose and brushed the dust off his hands.

"Sleep. We break camp and ride at dawn."

"I can't ride," Joe told him.

"Nor do you have a horse," the brown rider said. "Nor do I much care. Sleep here, next to the fire and under the stars, if you're able. You can, if you wish, escape. I will not have you bound. However, it is more than a day's travel, by foot, in any direction, and we've got the best tracker in the realm."

The red rider grinned. "It would be a pleasure to hunt you like an animal," she said. She went into one tent, the brown rider into another. The green rider stopped at the fire, looked Joe up, down, and up again, and without a word entered the third tent.

They left Joe, but there was nothing for him to do. They could track him, cut him down, shoot him, leave him to die in this wasteland. He might never find the train tracks, and certainly not the stationmaster's house. Or the dead he'd been made to leave behind.

He felt guilt. He felt despair. There was no sleep for him.

Over time, the fire burned itself down, the flames dancing less and less, until only embers remained. The stars and galaxies and nebulae made their way slowly across the sky. Thin wisps of clouds drifted aimlessly by. When Joe could close his eyes, he saw only Janice—on the train, playing the piano, getting shot—and the stationmaster's wife—those impossible blue eyes, that mischievous smile, getting shot—and even the stationmaster—not getting shot.

That image went round and round in his head. Arms crossed. Jaw set. Eyes flaring. The stationmaster had deflected the scattershot of the green rider's shotgun.

When lying down and staring at the sky failed to bring sleep or solace, Joe sat again on the log, back to the dying embers, staring toward the stationmaster's house. He had no sense of direction, so he might be facing exactly the wrong way, but the actuality of it wasn't as important as the symbolism. He tried to peer through the darkness, over the sands. He tried to follow the train tracks back to the stationmaster's house, but the tracks were straight and the world curved; he couldn't make his imagination conform to reality.

The shadow horses slept standing. Their hair and bodies melted in and out the darkness, shimmering, here one moment and somewhere else the next. They were impossible to see clearly, and best seen peripherally. He had ridden horses in the past, but could not claim any real knowledge or skill. These were easily three of the largest he'd ever seen, and the darkest, and the most shifting. He doubted they were completely real. He doubted that they would take him away from his captors; if they brought him anywhere, it would be no place Joe wanted to see.

The night stretched infinitely through time and space.

Joe thought about justice, and the lack thereof; the purpose of the riders; the cataclysm. He could easily picture a person, unskilled, unleashing something they could not control. Had that happened here?

Sometime during the night, he heard the music again, the children dancing around a bonfire he couldn't see.

He wondered if he was foolish, not trying to run away.

A shooting star burned its way halfway across the sky. It flared up out of nowhere, brightened half the night, and arced suddenly downward. Somewhere distant, it crashed into the ground; Joe heard the muffled impact and felt, however mildly, its vibrations under his butt.

Joe knew it was an omen. He couldn't read omens.

The riders emerged from their tents. The green rider came first. He lumbered toward Joe, looked in the direction Joe looked, then went to comfort the horses. The crash had awakened them, as well.

The red rider came second, Peacemakers in hand. Under other circumstances, Joe knew he might be enchanted by the look of her, the dark, sensuous, scarred beauty; as it was, he saw her as a murderer, and, quite rightly, feared she meant to end his life next. She took a position outside her tent and muttered curses under her breath as she stared in the direction of the shooting star.

The brown rider came last, fully dressed and ready to ride. He looked at the other riders, then at Joe. "What did you see?" he asked.

"Nothing."

"This is important," the brown rider said. "Don't lie to me."

"I saw stars," Joe told him.

The brown rider arched an eyebrow. "You have no reason to trust us, I know. You're a stranger. But we do carry the authority of law."

"You're right," Joe told him. "I don't trust you."

"The earth shook beneath us," the brown rider said.

"Only barely," Joe said. "Have you never been to California?" In fact, Joe had only been to California once, for a week, during which time the earth never quaked.

"There was a light in the sky," the red rider said. "I saw it through my tent."

"Couldn't sleep?" the brown rider asked.

"Nightmaring," she admitted.

The brown rider nodded. "Saddle up, riders."

"What is it?" Joe asked.

"Could be nothing," the brown rider said. "Could be the end of everything."

"That's not an answer," Joe said.

"If they detected magic in the night, and they've come back," the brown rider said, "you may have just witnessed the return of the cataclysm."

It didn't require a lot of work to ready the shadow horses; they were anxious, pawing the ground, snorting smoke through their nostrils, and they knew where to go. The riders mounted their beasts. The brown rider held out a hand to Joe and said, "You better come with us."

"No," Joe said.

"Or we put a bullet in you and leave you, unburied, to rot."

Joe climbed onto the back of the brown rider's horse. Immediately, they were racing into deeper darknesses, in exactly the direction that the shooting star had landed. This time, Joe was able to look forward; there was nothing to see but more of the same until they reached the impact crater.

The crater was massive, easily the diameter of a football field. The shadow horses ascended the loose earth easily enough, but it took effort for Joe not to fall off. When they reached the top, the horses and riders paused. The red rider cursed. The green rider grunted. The brown rider said nothing, but Joe rode closely enough to him to feel the strength sap from his back and shoulders.

The hole went deep. They could not see the bottom. The sides were steep, nearly vertical. Steam rose from those walls. The presence of the shadow horses caused little bits of dirt and rock to tumble into the hole.

"It can't be bottomless," the red rider said.

"It might've punched a hole to the very center of earth," the brown rider said.

The green rider dropped something over the edge. At first, Joe wasn't sure what it was; it fluttered, like paper, and Joe realized it was the two halves of the red butterfly he had fashioned and to which the stationmaster's wife had breathed life. They turned, end over end, falling far more slowly than they ought to fall, until the shadows swallowed them.

"Throw the stranger in," the red rider said, "Maybe they'll accept him as sacrifice."

"I'm afraid it's gone beyond mere sacrifice," the brown rider said to her. "Ride north, get with the other riders, make them aware of everything that's happened." He turned to the green rider. "I need you to stand guard. If anything rises out of here, anything at all, you come get me. You hear that?"

The green rider grunted. He heard.

"Where are you going?" the red rider asked.

The brown rider had already turned his horse and was about to descend the outside of the crater. "I'm afraid we'll need an army to face this."

The red rider did not look pleased. Joe didn't have a lot of time to revel in it. They were off.

The shadow horse rode swift, more swiftly than Joe ever before saw. A dust storm followed them. They would've ridden without pause, but a tremor shook the earth and disrupted the shadow horse's pace.

On the horizon, directly to Joe's left, the sun peeked over the edge. Reds and oranges stretched across the sky and painted the few clouds. But the clouds were gathering, all drawn in the direction of the crater. When Joe glanced back, he had to cling to the back of the rider lest his balance shift. He could still see the crater, just as he saw copses of trees and other rises in the distance, wooden structures set far apart from each other, the smoke of a bonfire, a glimmer of railway tracks.

The sun rose gradually. The sky brightened, the colors paled to a dusty blue, the clouds stretched and tore. The brown rider leaned forward the entire time, urging the shadow horse farther and faster. They rode without pause. The shadow horse twice let out a sound that could best be described as a roar or a war cry. The air warmed up quickly, but the wind they created never ceased.

Another shockwave reached them. The tremor threw the shadow horse off balance. The brown rider, in an effort to regain his own footing, reigned the shadow horse to a halt. He looked back, toward the crater they could no longer see. They'd ridden flat out for three or four hours.

"That wasn't a quake," the brown rider said. "Something's emerging from that hole."

"What is it?" Joe asked. He thought it was merely a chunk of moon rock or comet dust, but he suspected the riders had reason for the degree

THE DRY DUSTED SANDS

of their reaction.

The brown rider spurred the shadow horse to ride again. Apparently, there wasn't time enough to answer.

Gradually, the terrain changed. The dusty dirt gave way to rock. They left any trace of greenery behind them, though most of it had been scattered solitary bushes and trees. The ground rose and fell on all sides, until rises became hills and dips became something like valleys. Ahead, trails of smoke rose into the sky. Eventually, a village came into view, a collection of gray huts matched perfectly to the color of the rocky ground.

Another shock wave reached them. The shadow horse complained noisily, slowing and stopping and rearing up on its hind legs. Joe fell. The brown rider managed to stay on. He glanced at Joe, took a moment—perhaps to consider abandoning his prisoner—then reluctantly held out his hand. When Joe didn't immediately get up, the brown rider said, "We're wasting time."

Joe hurt. He ached from riding. His legs were weak. It was a risk, rising to his feet. But he had no choice. He rose. His wrists hurt from the fall, and one of his ankles, and his ass, but nothing was broken. The brown rider showed no compassion or tenderness when he pulled Joe back onto the horse.

By then, village riders had come out to greet them. There were seven, not riders in the same sense as the brown rider. They were all tanned to leather. Their eyes were too close and too bright, their coats dusty and gray. The leader, a dusky woman with long, golden hair, said, "You're one of the riders from the north."

"I am," the brown rider said.

She wasted no time. She didn't even look at Joe. "You're not welcome here."

"I don't come for welcome," the brown rider said. "I come for an army."

"We will put you down," the woman said, "and send your horse back with a corpse."

The brown rider held out both hands to the sides, showing that he held only reins and no weapon. He said, "There was magic."

"Magic," the woman said, "is not our problem." Clearly, a few of the other riders seemed more concerned than she; they looked left and right, and back the way Joe and the brown rider had come, but they said nothing. "In the north, perhaps, you've used and misused magic," the woman said. "Not here."

"There was magic," the brown rider said, "and something came out of the sky."

"Something?"

"Something enormous," the brown rider said. "This man witnessed its fall."

"This man," the woman said, "is your prisoner, and will say what you will have him say if it serves to save his hide. I don't trust him anymore than I trust you. And make no mistake, *rider.*" She said it like a curse. "I don't trust you."

"It will bring the cataclysm to your lands as well as ours," the brown rider said.

The woman narrowed her eyes. She looked toward the horizon, then back to the brown rider. "What, exactly, is *it*? A creature? A machine? A piece of magic?"

"I didn't wait for it to rise," the brown rider said.

The woman did not seem amused. "So it might have been nothing more than a rock from the sky?"

"It was more than a rock," the brown rider said.

"A *big* rock," the woman said, laughing derisively. "I understand."

"I came seeking aid," the brown rider said, "I came seeking an army. I came under the auspices of long ago treaties."

"I know the treaties," the woman said. "I dare say, I know them better than you."

The brown rider seemed genuinely confused. "You won't help us?"

"Two decades ago," the woman said, "you riders came to our lands under a white flag. You were young then, I'm sure, so maybe you won't remember, but I certainly do. I was here. There were nine riders, blue and brown and gray. They came with weapons of war. They came seeking assistance against a traitor."

"There was never a traitor," the brown rider said.

"Don't interrupt," the woman told him. "They came seeking this assistance, saying one of their own kind, a stationmaster, had unlocked a mystery, had opened a doorway, had performed an act of magic."

The brown rider shook his head but said nothing.

"They said the stationmaster brought forth a deluge of frogs," the woman continued. "A plague of locusts. A drought that stretched fourteen months. They warred against their stationmasters, and one among them came to believe there had never been any magic."

"What happened twenty years ago," the brown rider said, "has no bearing on today. We riders are scattered. The stationmasters are all but gone."

"The cataclysm you so greatly fear," the woman said, "was of your own creation."

"It came, then, from the sky, just as it does now," the brown rider said.

"Rocks fall from the sky," the woman said. "As do frogs, and insects, and sometimes water. These things are natural, or not, but they are not portents of disaster." The brown rider seemed about to speak again, but she raised a finger to stop him. "And if they are, indeed, omens, how do you think you can possibly battle fate?"

"The mistakes of the past," the brown rider said, "do not have to be repeated. We can survive, together, or perish apart."

The woman considered her next words before speaking. "I have an army," she admitted. "They are well trained and can be ready at a moment's notice. You see the seven of us here, but do not see another seventeen around you, and another seventy ready to join should I give the signal. Should you bring your cataclysm to our borders, we will meet it with the all the skill and talent and weaponry at our disposal. And if your cataclysm is, indeed, a real threat to your people, then maybe your stationmasters will save you and maybe not. If it comes to our borders, we will turn it back."

"You, too, will die," the brown rider said.

"The real cataclysm of the past," the woman said, "was the installation of you riders. Now, because I'm feeling generous, I will allow you to live, but only if you turn now, ride away, and never return. *However.*" She raised a finger again. "Your prisoner, if he so chooses, may stay." She turned to Joe for the first time. "Whatever hold this rider has over you, we sever it. We will give you sanctuary."

"You don't know what you do," the brown rider said.

"I'll never get home again," Joe said.

"You'll never go home, either way," the woman told him.

"Then I'll stay."

With an elbow to the ribs, the brown rider shoved Joe off the back of the shadow horse. "Stay, then," the brown rider said to him. "The damage is already done."

Joe, on the ground, watched the brown rider turn his shadow horse and ride north again. A moment later, the earth shook again. The seven horses whinnied, and the riders ducked low to stay on their mounts. The woman offered Joe a hand and said, "Ride with me."

He took her hand and mounted the horse. "What happens to me now?" he asked.

"What do you want to have happen?"

"I...I'm not sure anymore," Joe admitted.

"When you have that answer," the woman said, "tell me." Then, to her contingent, "Go back, tell the Commander of the Huntsmen everything you just saw and heard. Tell him to be ready. War may be coming."

"And you, Lady Ariantha?" one of the riders asked.

"I'm scouting," she said.

She turned the horse and spurred them forward, chasing the dust trail of the brown rider. Joe hung on. He asked, "You believe him?"

"Yes," Lady Ariantha said. "The facts, not the suppositions. We saw the star fall. We felt the ground shake."

They rode neither as fast nor as hard as the brown rider. He was easy to follow. They also didn't ride as smoothly; Joe had to hold on to Lady Ariantha more tightly to keep from being thrown. He ached, and he was exhausted, and he was unable to do anything but react. He didn't know the land, the people, the places, the world. He didn't know the stationmasters or the cataclysm, and he didn't know what had crashed to earth overnight. He couldn't discern right from wrong without context. He did know the riders had shot Janice and the stationmaster's wife in cold blood. That, he understood. He had an enemy. He had a ticket for the train, should it ever stop here, should he ever find himself at the station again. He doubted the stationmaster would welcome him; he might blame Joe for the magic and the bullets. All he'd done was fold some paper. He no longer understood cause and effect.

Joe tried to stop thinking. It did no good, coming around to the same thoughts again and again. There was nothing to see, nothing that he hadn't already seen, nothing but scenery that repeated itself and suffered under the stark sunlight. The sun burned, the wind they created was rough on his face, so he closed his eyes and tried imagining another world: his condo, his job, his life. It failed to inspire him. It failed to ground him. Quite simply, it failed.

"Stay with me," Lady Ariantha said, tapping his ribs lightly with her elbow. The ride had lulled him nearly into a meditative state. When he opened his eyes, the light was still stark and the colors of the world muted, but he felt more alert. Had he learned something?

Lady Ariantha glanced at him over her shoulder. "Tell me," she said, "how you ended up on the back of a rider's shadow horse."

Joe gritted his teeth. His stomach clenched with the anger.

"Tell me how you came to be here," she said.

"The train."

"No train stops here," Lady Ariantha said.

"It stopped," Joe said. "We got off, met the stationmaster and his wife."

"We?"

"The riders killed her," Joe said, "and the stationmaster's wife."

"Why?" Lady Ariantha asked.

So he told her. He started at the beginning, with the map on his windshield, the wine, the train, and the conductor. He said the stationmaster had been abrupt and unhelpful, but the stationmaster's wife had been wondrous and enchanting. He didn't mention she'd kissed him, but he told Lady Ariantha about the piano, the night sky so different from his own, the paper butterfly.

Lady Ariantha was silent until Joe told her about the butterfly and how the stationmaster's wife had brought it to life.

"Not life," Lady Ariantha said. "Mere animation. But that was enough to attract the damn riders, wasn't it?"

"It was," Joe told her. She didn't interrupt again until he reached the crater.

"What did you see inside?" she asked.

"Nothing," Joe said.

"Nothing at all?"

"It was dark," Joe said. "Still night. And it was deeper than I could see. Darkness all the way down."

"But it was a big hole?"

"Tremendously so."

Lady Ariantha reined her horse to a halt. "We'll rest here a moment," she said, though *here* was no different than any other place on their path. Around them was dirt, sand, dust, scrubland. They dismounted. From a pack on the horse's side, Lady Ariantha found food and a canteen. "You need this more than I," she said, giving Joe the water first.

It wasn't water, though. It burned a harsh trail down his throat. He coughed.

"Whiskey," she told him. "You don't have any where you're from?"

"Oh, we do," Joe said. "I was expecting water."

Lady Ariantha shook her head. "I wasn't meaning to journey. I didn't need much by way of provisions. But you never take to the trails without something."

She gave him half her sandwich. It might've been pastrami or turkey or ham; Joe couldn't tell. The bread tasted sweet. He washed it down with another swallow of whiskey, then passed the canteen back.

"You're on a journey," Lady Ariantha told him. "I think yours might be a one way journey."

"The ticket says it's one way," Joe said, "but it's blank."

"You're not on the train anymore," Lady Ariantha said. "You need to accept you're probably never going to be able to go back. If the falling star is, in fact, a behemoth of any sort, it may destroy our world, and you with it."

"That's not much of a journey," Joe said.

She smiled. "Everyone's journey must come to an end. Are you ready?"

He only hesitated briefly. "Yes."

Before they climbed back onto the horse, however, the earth shook again, far more violently this time. The horse whinnied. Joe stumbled and fell. Lady Ariantha managed to remain standing, but only barely. Sands shifted. The clouds in the sky seemed to tremble.

The brown rider's trail of dust, however distant, still guided them. Joe knew where he was going: back to the crater.

"Maybe we should leave," Joe suggested.

Lady Ariantha helped Joe stand. "No."

"If it's the end of everything here, couldn't the train take us somewhere else?"

"The train won't stop."

"We can follow the tracks."

"We can't," Lady Ariantha said again.

"What's wrong with it?" Joe asked.

"We don't run," Lady Ariantha said. "I'm not going to abandon my people, and neither are you."

"I don't have any people here."

Lady Ariantha said, "It's your journey, of course, but you realize you are your own people. You'd leave a part of yourself here, dead, if you can't face the unknown. You don't know this is the rider's cataclysm. It may simply be an earthquake. It happens."

Joe said nothing, but he didn't look away from her eyes. She was right, of course. He was acting the coward. Under some circumstances, retreat was certainly acceptable; but what was he retreating from?

"And if it is this great cataclysm," Lady Ariantha added, "we survived the last one."

They rode on. They rode mostly in silence. Joe steeled himself for what was coming. He sought his inner strengths. He knew he had them. Cubicular work never required such a rough, physical manifestation, but that didn't make him incapable. The ride, in fact, strengthened him, even as the sky grew starker and more barren. Sunlight reflected off the sands, obscuring his vision. The sound of their own wind made it difficult to hear anything else. He felt nothing but Lady Ariantha and the horse and the riding and the wind, which was more than enough. He tasted copper in his dry mouth, smelled blunt dirt and acrid dust. His sense of equilibrium was constantly challenged.

Just beyond the horizon, Joe could almost sense the stationmaster's house, his dead wife, and Janice lying beside her. It fueled his anger. He worked it through his veins, channeling it into strength, using it to build a wall against his emotions. If there was to be a fight, or a cataclysm, he needed action and instinct, not emotion.

Up ahead, the dust trail converged with other dust trails and dissipated. They were close, now, to the crater; Joe could almost see it, if he squinted. Lady Ariantha slowed her horse but pressed forward.

"We're still a good distance away," Lady Ariantha said. "They'll see us approaching, if they haven't seen us already."

"What do you intend to do?" Joe asked.

"I intend to look into the abyss," Lady Ariantha said. "I intend to learn what fell from the sky."

"It's deep," Joe told her.

"It's daylight, still," she said.

A shock wave passed them, shaking the earth; another came immediately after. On the horizon, though the crater itself was only barely discernible, and the individual riders completely invisible, something rose from the hole. It roared as it did so. The sound echoed across the land and shook the ground again.

Even the horse hesitated.

"Just a little further," Lady Ariantha whispered to her horse. It whinnied in defiance, but she didn't stop.

As they came closer, Joe could better see what it was that had climbed from the hole. It looked like a statue assembled with bits of iron, granite, and marble. It stood like a wall, like a building, with molten magma for eyes and an unreadable expression on its stony face.

Closer, Joe could see the riders, at least eleven on their shadow horses, some with repeating colors—there were at least two other reds and another brown.

Closer still, he felt the heat of the creature, and heard the gunfire, and listened to the barking commands of the brown rider. "Take it down! Shoot out its knees!" Joe didn't know if it had knees. "Cripple the thing or kill it, I do not care which!" As far as Joe could tell, their weapons had no effect on the thing. It turned its head slowly, very slowly, examining the attacking riders who fired, fired, reloaded, and fired again.

"That's senseless," Joe murmured.

"The riders," Lady Ariantha said, "are senseless." Still, she rode closer. He heard the scraping of stone and metal and glass as the creature shifted its gaze. When it finally struck, it sounded like thunder. With an open hand, it swatted one of the riders like a fly, squashing him instantly.

"The eyes!" the brown rider cried. He circled the other riders, circled the creature that had emerged from the fallen star.

The creature smacked him, his whole body and horse, with the back of its granite hand, tossing horse and rider through the air in a spray of blood and smoke. The horse never hit the ground, evaporating completely; the brown rider broke into pieces in the air and tumbled away messily.

Lady Ariantha reined her horse to a stop, but it was too late. The creature's face turned in their direction.

The riders scattered. The green rider tossed his shotgun aside so he could lean lower into his shadow horse and spur it to even greater speeds. He came straight toward Lady Ariantha and Joe. The red rider, meanwhile, with her two Peacemakers holstered, rode toward the train tracks.

Lady Ariantha held her horse steady. It did not want to obey, but it did. Joe wanted to flee with it, but he wouldn't. He had no weapons, and looked nothing like the riders. He trembled, but so did Lady Ariantha, and so did the horse. The creature's every stride was the length of a football field and sent shockwaves through the ground.

The green rider reached them and stopped. The shadow horse, too, seemed compelled to run, but the green rider had control. He didn't look at Lady Ariantha, but at Joe. He was frowning. He was sad. He wasn't scared at all. He turned his horse, put himself between Joe and the creature.

The thing reached them, stopped, and stooped. It bent its head low. Joe felt heat radiating out of its magma eyes, smelled smoldering iron as it exhaled. Its head was roughly cut, perhaps the size of a locomotive, its fists twice as thick as Joe was tall.

It was looking past the green rider, ignoring him completely, and paying no attention whatsoever to Lady Ariantha. Joe felt the heat of its gaze on several levels, and he met that gaze. What else might he do? He held his chin up and took a deep breath and said, "What do you want with me?"

Lady Ariantha and the green rider both turned to look at Joe. Yes, all eyes were on him. The creature extended its stone hand, palm up. At the center of its palm, easily seen because of its contrast with the black and gray rock, were two pieces of folded red paper, two halves of a butterfly that had lived and breathed and flown for but a moment.

The green rider, seeing this, cried. He made no noise, but tears were plainly visible on his face and he shook with the sorrowful horror of what he saw. He had, after all, ripped the paper in half.

Joe shook his head. "I can't make it whole again."

The creature shoved his hand forward some more, brushing aside the green rider's shadow horse. Joe climbed off the horse, climbed onto the hand, scraping his knees and palms as he did so, tearing his pants, almost slipping twice. He crawled to the center of that palm and retrieved the two pieces of red paper. He held them next to each other, but apart, and said, "See, they won't go together again."

The creature spoke, but its whisper was incredibly loud and windy. "It lived."

"Once, yes," Joe said. "Briefly."

The creature blinked. Joe had no idea what black substance made up the eyelids. It said, every word slow and carefully enunciated, "We all live briefly." Then it closed its fist around Joe.

Joe cowered, expecting to be squashed, but the creature enclosed him in its palm. When it moved, the rocky ground that was the creature's hand beneath Joe's feet shifted violently. He fell, then hugged the ground as it continued moving. It did him little good; the motions were short, sudden, and irresistible. He was thrown around, shaken and stirred, bruised and bloodied and, by the time it stopped, dizzy.

When the creature finally opened its fist, Joe, still clutching the ripped paper butterfly, tumbled off the hand and onto the dirt outside the porch of the stationmaster's house.

The stationmaster stood on his porch, unarmed but defiant, staring at the creature. The stationmaster said, "I know what you are."

The creature did not respond.

"I'm the last," the stationmaster said. "There are no more. My wife is dead."

The creature did not respond.

"Shot," the stationmaster added. "Murdered."

"No," the creature said. "Not the last. Him."

The stationmaster turned his attention to Joe. "*Him?*"

"And his," the creature said.

"Dead," Joe said.

After a moment, the creature said, "No."

The green rider and Lady Ariantha were nowhere to be seen. The other riders had gone in other directions, except for the red rider; Joe didn't see her, either.

"We're done," the stationmaster said. "I was about to close my house."

The creature, again, said, "No."

The stationmaster sighed. He said, "I can do no more."

The creature smiled, or seemed to smile, though it was horrific and unnatural and, somehow, sad. It said, "No. You cannot."

The stationmaster bowed, then turned to Joe. "Good luck," he said.

"You're leaving?" Joe asked.

"There's nothing for me here anymore," the stationmaster said.

"I don't believe you," Joe said.

The stationmaster looked sharply at him. "My wife is dead," he said. "My station is abandoned. You and yours were the only guests in a dozen years or more. My time here is done. I have served well." He raised his arms to either side, closed his eyes, and dissolved into sand as black as his clothes. The wind took the bits of him and scattered them across the barren landscape. He hadn't needed a train to leave.

The creature said to Joe, "You."

"Me, what?" Joe asked.

"Butterfly."

Joe looked down at the two pieces of red paper in his hands. They were beyond help, beyond hope. Joe took a deep breath, held it, and started unfolding the pieces. They were nearly equal in size, but devastatingly rough along the edges. Joe put one piece in his pocket and worked on the other. Because the paper was smaller, torn, crumpled, and abused, it was more difficult to work with. It didn't help to have hot magma eyes watching him.

Joe abandoned the first attempt, but finally finished with something that resembled a butterfly. It was smaller and asymmetrical, but it had red wings and a happy little butterfly face.

It was easier to duplicate the effort on the second half.

Joe held them out to the stone giant. "There," Joe said. "Two butterflies now."

The creature held out its hand, palm up. Joe did not climb onto it this time. He threw the butterflies toward the center of the palm. Neither made it all the way, but they were close enough. The creature cupped its other hand over it, mimicking the fashion by which the stationmaster's wife had done the same, and lifted his closed hands into the air. When he released the paper butterflies, they fell lazily for a moment and then, with a tentative flap of wings, started fluttering. Instead of falling, they flew. They circled each other where the creature's hands had been. They made no sound. Looking up at them, Joe smiled. The creature, looking down, smiled.

"Butterflies," the creature said.

They came down toward Joe, darting left and right and up and down, then circled him until he put up an open hand. One landed on his pointer finger, the other on his middle finger. They were paper, partly, but they were butterflies. They seemed to look at Joe, as if to thank him, or at least acknowledge him, and then fluttered away, up and over the porch's awning again, back over the stationmaster's house.

"Again," the creature said.

Joe shook his head. "I need paper."

"No," the creature said. "Women."

Joe laughed, briefly, but stopped himself. "I can't make a woman out of paper."

"No," the creature agreed. It was its favorite word. "Inside."

The porch door leading to the kitchen was open. The stationmaster had stood there a moment earlier. Joe looked at it, back at the creature to make sure he understood, and crossed the threshold.

The house was darker now, more solemn, as if the wood itself was sad, the paint melancholy, the floors depressed. There was nothing in the kitchen. He expected to find, and found, the stationmaster's wife and Janice laid out, side by side, in the first floor bedroom. The stationmaster had carried them there and arranged them neatly, arms crossed over their chests. They looked almost alive, almost as if they were acting. They hadn't paled or gone blue or anything to indicate they were dead. They simply didn't breathe.

At the side of the bed, looking at them, Joe felt the same oppressive despondency the house seemed to feel. He touched the hand of the stationmaster's wife. She had shown him wonderful things during their brief encounter. He would never forget her. Her hand was chilled, but not icy, and getting warmer. Joe snatched his hand back.

He watched her, sure she would open her eyes, but nothing happened. Cautiously, he reached out and touched her hand again. So cold. Had he imagined the warmth? No. He felt it again, spreading as if from his hand, intensifying, pulsing. He could almost see the essence of life spreading across her, pulling bits of it from her deepest places, the bits of life that hadn't quite yet fled. The stationmaster's wife twitched a finger.

Joe jumped back. Her eyes had been closed, but they were open now, wide, surprised, staring straight at where he'd been standing. But the life eased away from her again. Her mouth, open now in an O, deflated.

"You're alive?" he whispered. She said nothing. She didn't look at him. He touched her hand again. The cold had returned, but again it fled. When her finger twitched, he held his ground. She looked around frantically. She moved her mouth, blinked her eyes. The heat spread.

She gasped, coughed, sputtered, and said, "More." Her voice barely worked.

Joe held her hand now in both hands. He didn't know what else to do.

Her breath came in heaves. Her body quivered. She finally locked her gaze on something, on Joe, on his lips, and put all her little bit of strength into her voice. "Kiss me."

He did.

It was passionate, like their earlier kiss. It revived her. It strengthened her. Joe felt some sort of energy passing between them, circulating, taking from him and giving to her. When she pulled away, when it was over, the magic was complete. The stationmaster's wife lived. She was sitting up now, breathing heavily, supporting herself with her hands on the bed and looking at nothing but Joe. She said, breathlessly, "I was dead."

It wasn't a question, but Joe said, "Yes."

"Your magic," the stationmaster's wife said.

Joe shook his head. "I have no magic. That was you."

"No," she told him. "It was never me." The speech seemed to exhaust her, but she wasn't weak anymore. She looked at Janice, lying dead beside her, then back at Joe. "Revive her."

Joe looked at Janice's corpse. So beautiful, so peaceful, so beyond the pale. He said, "I can't."

"Of course you can't," the stationmaster's wife said. "Do it anyway."

Reluctantly, Joe walked around the bed. It felt like walking the long last mile to the gallows. He wasn't afraid of success, or any of its implications. He feared failure. He stopped at Janice's side and realized the stationmaster's wife had made the journey with him. She touched his shoulder. She said, "I didn't raise the butterfly. And I didn't raise myself."

Joe reached out, took Janice's hand in his, and squeezed. She was cold and stiff, and, up close, an indistinct shade of blue, as though a spider had woven its unnaturally translucent web around her. He felt the warmth spreading through her hands. He looked at her eyes. He didn't know the color. He might have seen, might have noticed, sometime last night between the train and the stationmaster's house and the red rider's Peacemakers, but he couldn't recall. The stationmaster's wife had blue eyes, unnatural and startling and unreal; he remembered the shock of them clearly. They seemed somehow less unimportant.

Janice's eyes flickered. She gasped. She snatched her hand from Joe's. She dropped back into death. He grabbed her hand again. He leaned closer. He said, "Don't leave me." It didn't matter that he had no right to say it. He held her hand in both hands, just as he'd done with the stationmaster's wife. He held her hand tightly, and this time would not let her go. She opened her eyes again. Her lip quivered. A moment passed, and though Joe felt the heat coursing between them, she said, she whispered, she breathed, "*Cold.*"

"Not much longer," Joe told her.

The stationmaster's wife pressed her mouth to Joe's ear. She didn't have much voice yet. She whispered, "Kiss her."

Janice clutched Joe's hands now with both of her own, but her lips were still blue, still clinging to lifelessness. He looked at her, looked at her brilliant amber eyes, eyes that were not the same now that she'd passed from life and back. She looked nervous, anxious, frightful, and hopeful; she looked devastated and devastating. She looked back at him, and maybe there was pleading or maybe Joe only imagined pleading, but he took that as permission. He leaned down and kissed her.

She returned the kiss. She let go of his hands and held his face and, for long, long moments or years, something passed between their lips, an energy that shifted back and forth, grew stronger, receded, strengthened again. She kissed him like he'd never been kissed before, like a woman in love, and Joe lost all track of all things outside of them.

When the kiss ended, it started again, briefly, before the stationmaster's wife said, "We'll be needing water and food and rest, Janice and I."

Joe nodded. Janice laid her head back and said, "I was dead."

"Yes," the stationmaster's wife said.

"I was dead," Janice said again.

"Briefly," the stationmaster's wife said.

Janice looked at Joe. Her eyes had shifted from light brown to amber and now settled somewhere between. "I was dead." Joe, unsteady on his feet, had strength enough to nod. "You brought me back," she said, looking again at the stationmaster's wife.

Shaking her head, she said, "Not me."

Janice closed her eyes. "I feel weak. And cold."

"That will pass," the stationmaster's wife said.

"How?" Janice asked.

"You brought magic back," the stationmaster's wife said. Though she answered Janice, she was speaking to Joe. "The two of you, here, brought something you didn't have there, wherever there might have been. Now go, do something good with it before it's too late."

"I've already done something good," Joe reminded her.

"There's someone outside," she said.

Joe had forgotten about the creature. How could he forget such a thing as that? He walked through the house, onto the porch, and looked up at the face of the creature sitting in the yard. Its molten eyes had darkened and seemed less fluid; when it didn't move, it could pass for a statue. It made Joe nervous.

But it wasn't the unmoving creature the stationmaster's wife had meant. The red rider, perched on her shadow horse, approached ahead of a cloud of dust. She slowed as she neared the stationmaster's house. She sneered when saw Joe standing there. She was alone, and had no one to speak for her, but she still carried those two Colts on her hips. "I thought you'd be dead," she said. "I thought you were gone. I knew we should have killed you then, last night, here on this porch." She glanced at the unmoving stone and granite and marble statue. "It's not too late." She drew both guns, which had hung in their holsters already cocked, and let loose with both.

Joe stood his ground. He held up a hand to deflect the bullets, just as the stationmaster had done last night. He didn't understand how, but the lead never hit him.

"It is too late," Joe told her.

"It was you all along," the red rider said.

Joe nodded. "It was me."

"You've brought cataclysm," the red rider said.

Joe shook his head. "I don't think so." He stepped down from the porch, so he had to look up if he wanted to meet the red rider's gaze, but he didn't bother with her. That wasn't his intent. Instinct drove him. Knowledge of which he was not aware gave Joe strength and courage. He knelt on the ground. He touched the dirt with both hands, palms down. Warmth moved through him first, then heat, as if the sands seared his skin, and the hot spread through his whole body. It was too much, but he endured it. He suffered the heat in his bones. He suffered the heat in his flesh. In his suffering, he looked up at the red rider and smiled for her. She'd returned her Peacemakers to her hips, her mouth hung open, and her eyes were not only wide, they were moist.

Joe looked down at the ground where he knelt, the sand now soil, the dust now sprouting grass, a little patch widening in uneven lurches. A meter here, two there, tendrils of ripe earth overrunning the dry, dusted sands. The green stretched far and farther. Above, clouds gathered, dark clouds, rain clouds and storm clouds, the kind of clouds that had not been seen over this land for a long time. The scattered barren trees erupted into greenery when the new soil reached them. From the distance, he heard the sounds of a blaring train's whistle.

The storm arrived first, letting loose a torrent of warm rain. The drops sizzled when they reached Joe. He felt heat like the creature's magma eyes, which were completely dark now, solid and unmoving. The green rider and Lady Ariantha arrived after, soaked to the bone, both of them smiling and laughing. The stationmaster's wife and Janice emerged from the house, stood on the porch, looked up at the sky and down at Joe and over at the arriving train.

The train, of course, had not stopped at this station for a long time, with one exception the night before. The train stopped now, the conductor called out the name of the stop, and even behind the stationmaster's house Joe heard him clearly. People disembarked, a great number of travelers and tourists and pilgrims; they bustled around the platform, they made their way to the place where carriages and taxis would soon arrive to take them to their final destinations, though of course some would linger and some would question and some would wonder and some would dream.

Eventually, Joe bowed his head. He couldn't see anymore, or hear, through the heat passing in and out of his hands. Bolts of lightning might have struck him. Janice might've put her hand on his shoulder and, later, held him, but he was barely aware. He was working. He was busy. He was enraptured, enslaved, and emboldened. He felt alive, alive like he'd never felt before, all the way until the moment his heart stopped and his senses fled him and the sky darkened to blackness and he collapsed.

His heart had missed only one beat, but it was enough to separate him from the earth. The power that had surged through him continued moving through the land. It didn't need him anymore. Janice and the stationmaster's wife led him into the house, into the bedroom, and gave him water and wine and bread and meat. Janice sat with him, stroked his hand, pressed a cold cloth to his forehead. The stationmaster's wife, too, sat a while with him, and said things like, "You are brave, but also foolish," and, "You did a great thing but at a great cost."

But it wasn't a great cost. Though Joe's consciousness faded in and out through the night, he woke, ravenous and parched, at dawn, and found the two of them had not left his side. The stationmaster's wife stood, leaning on each other, at the doorway, while Janice sat at his side and held his hand. The extraordinary heat had gone. His body heat was his own only.

"Good morning," Janice said.

"There's a crowd outside," the stationmaster's wife said. "They're here because of you."

"I don't want them," Joe said.

"Doesn't matter," the stationmaster's wife said. "Some are here because they fear you overmuch. Some are here because they don't fear you enough. Some will beg for your help or your vanishing. Some will pray and some will try to kill you."

"The red rider," Joe said.

"She," the stationmaster's wife told him, "has pledged her Peacemakers to you. The green rider, too, though he doesn't speak. The remaining riders will not be pleased."

"The creature from the sky?" Joe asked.

The stationmaster's wife shrugged. "A mystery to me."

"And you?" Joe asked.

She smiled. She said, "This is no longer my house. This world has no more need of the old stationmasters."

Joe sat up. He was still weak, but he knew he'd be fine. He looked at Janice. "So we're staying, then?"

She smiled. "We are."

The stationmaster's wife stepped closer to the bed. She said, "You'll need each other, just as we needed each other. I hope your magics continue to prove complementary."

Janice smiled at her. Joe squeezed Janice's hand. The stationmaster's wife left. Outside, a train was pulling into the station; she had already packed a bag and maybe knew where she was going and maybe not.

AFTERWORD

I have an inexplicable and purely irrational fascination with maps. When I started writing this story I only knew what you, as a reader, learned with each paragraph. Until Joe opened the map, I didn't know where it might lead. Until he found the envelope addressed to Janice, I didn't know her name. I had no idea they'd be boarding a train, or where it would take them.

The Dry Dusted Sands, I feel, can be part of something larger, and maybe someday I'll explore it. At the moment, it seems to be about the Stationmasters and the changing of the guard and the reawakening of magic and the blossoming of loyalty, trust, and love. But it's also, at its heart, about the art of cartography.

We never did learn the identity of the mapmaker, did we?

THE THOUSANDTH DREAM

"After a thousand dreams,
one is either a god
or one is doomed."
- Book of Lost Fates

"A thousand dreams, and I had to dream you."

He smiled at Kerri's words, cocking his head to one side. His teeth gleamed in the unworldly light.

The scene was familiar: a long hall, barren and desolate, dominated by granite and gray. Bare cement walls, cracks like captured lightning in the ceiling. A series of industrialized windows. At the center of four rows of folding tables, Kerri faced *him*: a flickering memory from one sweaty, long ago night (and morning). Cool. Cold. Calculative. He'd claimed he was dangerous. He was just a pretty boy with an attitude.

Dirk Conner. She'd left him there, in that bed—*breathing*, for God's sake. Of all people, what reason did *he* have to haunt her?

"Nothing to say?" Kerri asked.

He tilted his head to the other side, a puzzled look plastered on his face.

She understood the setting: her old Catholic school cafeteria. To the right, there should have been an assembly line of mediocre food skillfully kept at room temperature, and Mrs. Angerly standing at the door like a British sentinel, eyes never wavering, a thin wooden stick in hand.

"Well?" she asked, stepping closer.

Dirk retreated. "It's your dream," he reminded her.

"So, you do talk," she said, looking around. Only the tables, the doors—no sign of any of the other girls. No boys, no teachers, no nuns.

Just Dirk.

"You dreaming, too?" she asked, tapping the top of the nearest table. Its hollow echo bounced around the hall like a bullet, returning and returning again. The pressed wood felt real under her knuckles.

Dirk shook his head.

"So sure?" she asked.

"Your dream," he said again. "I'm not even alive."

This surprised her. She held up both hands, revealing empty palms. "It wasn't me."

"No," he said. "It wasn't."

"So what do you want?"

He shook his head again, but said nothing. Kerri sighed and tightened both fists. It was only a dream. She'd taught herself, long ago (before the pretty boy) to be aware of her dreams. To use them. Direct them. To know when she was caught in a tide.

And to ride with it, when she had no control.

Because if this had been controllable, she would have dreamt Dirk naked and enjoyed it. At the very least, she would have relived their one-night, beginning with the smoky corner of that neon and mirror club. Breakfast had been damned good, too, now that she thought of it.

Was there something else to remember? Was that why she was stuck here, going nowhere in this useless dream?

"So," she said casually, "wanna screw?"

"No."

She rolled her eyes. "What, you're dead, you don't want it anymore?" Dirk gave no answer, simply standing and staring, as if waiting for *her* to do something.

Like what?

"Wake up," she told herself, partly an answer and partly a command. Nothing happened. The dreamscape didn't waver. The walls didn't fade. Her eyes never opened. Dirk shifted his weight between his feet.

"Wake up," she said again. Her voice echoed in the empty hall. She shouldn't have heard it. Her eyes should have opened on her dark, quiet bedroom. Kerri refocused her attention on Dirk. "You did this."

He took a defensive step back. "So what if I did?"

Kerri shook her head. She hadn't done anything to him—well, nothing beyond what he wanted. She had left so many others in pools of sticky blood. Town to town, via Amtrack or Greyhound, or her thumb and a supple set of curves. No one ever questioned her.

Dirk never did, then or now. "I didn't kill you," she reminded him.

He blinked, then shied away. "Not directly, no."

"What do you mean, not directly?"

"Nance did it," he said, staring down at his feet. "A 9mm. Point blank in the face when I woke up." He shrugged. "It didn't hurt, at least."

Kerri struggled with the reins on her anger. *He* kept her in this dream, a prisoner in her own memory. Did he plan to kill her? Revenge? She felt the twin butterfly knives in her back pockets, the ever-present babies she'd picked up one night after school—after leaving *this* school, near the end of spring, when one assignment on top of the others seemed a bit too much.

She'd overreacted. But she enjoyed it so much, the memories brought tears of joy to the edges of her eyes.

Dirk misread the wetness. "I never had a chance to beg," he said. "Plead, cry, I had none of that. I never should have told her about you."

"Is that it, then?" Kerri asked. "Your wife—Nance, I take it?—offed you because you mentioned our grimy hotel room in St. Louis."

"It changed me," Dirk said. "It changed everything."

Kerri laughed, short and hard. "It didn't change me." But then, why hadn't she killed him? Maybe a half dozen of her lovers still lived; one was scarred and drinking his dinner through long straws, but that hadn't been entirely her fault.

"Tell me what it was like."

"What *what* was like?" Kerri asked.

"Killing all those people. How did it feel?"

She grinned. Maybe this was her own dream, after all. A conscience, after so many years? "It makes me feel like a god."

For a long time, he said nothing. She fantasized about splitting him open, sticking her blades between his ribs, maybe stealing one final kiss as he breathed his last. But in a dream—in a dream *he* controlled— what would that cost her?

"How did you do it?" he asked.

She reached back and drew the knives from her pockets like a gunslinger. They twirled prettily around her hands, flashing and glinting, ending their dance with two sharp blades waist-high and pointed at Dirk's groin.

He nodded, and again looked away. Perhaps she smiled too wickedly for him. She felt the power in her hands, the strength and bite of steel. It brought her close, dangerously close, to ecstasy. Dream be damned, she wanted him. Again.

Before she took the first step, he looked up with glistening eyes. "You ever meet my wife?" Kerri shook her head. "She's nice, really. And awfully beautiful." She was about to say something, *screw your Nance*, perhaps, but he held her gaze. "It's about time you meet her. *Wake up.*"

With a flash, the cafeteria disappeared. Kerri swam in the darkness of her bedroom, arms pinned to her sides by her sheets.

No. Not the sheets. Someone knelt over her, straddling her, a knee on either side. The woman leaned closer, not smiling at all but as beautiful as Dirk suggested, though the light through the window only revealed the basics of her features—and the 9mm, its barrel directly between Kerri's eyes.

Nance shot.

BENEATH MIDNIGHT

JOHN URBANCIK

BENEATH MIDNIGHT

A Dream

Falling, lost in darkness...hot breath...putrid...unable to move yet so fast, wind roars past...through a web of secrets...outside of time, no, *under* time...the clock ticking, ticking, threatening...and from the darkness, teeth, sharp and wet, snapping...

1.

Fourteen year old William Warde rose from the Metro, climbing the cement steps to see the lights like so many hundreds of his friends and neighbors, and enemies, had done throughout the week. Maybe thousands of people, from all corners of Midnight, had seen this spectacle, the strings of flashing white lights, the colored arcs and streamers, the huge red letters proclaiming, quite proudly, that this was the only carnival that ever mattered. The gate was wide, a grinning clown's face, its mouth open for all to enter, its teeth straight and even and white, its eyes set far apart and lit up by red globes.

From within, music emerged, calliopes and harpsichords playing discordant songs, and also laughter and chatter, screams of delight, and the barkers and pitchmen with their shouts of "Win a prize!" and "First try free!"

Then, the scents washed over William: cinnamon, cotton candy, apples and chocolate, caramel, horses, hay, salt and sweat and tears, all kinds of smells overlapping and drowning in each other. It was a smorgasbord, a kaleidoscope assaulting all the senses.

Dozens of people stepped around him, everyone headed first toward the tickets tent or through the clown's mouth, but William found himself frozen to the spot. He clutched a fistful of cash, and no one waited for him at home. This was the night he'd been waiting for all his life, with neither parent nor older sister, no hint of a chaperone, just one William and the infinite carnival. There were a lot of games to be played, rides to be ridden, and freaks to be seen. When it came time to write the story of his own life, William knew this night would feature prominently. This was a time for beginnings, perhaps endings, and certainly mysteries; and this was a place of magic and wonder, a place where dreams were realized, where the rest of the world didn't exist, the carnival's last night in Midnight.

William ran beneath the hungry clown, whose mouth devoured the city's residents as eagerly as they fed themselves to it. And inside, where the sounds were crisper and louder, where the odors were strong enough to drag you by the nose, William, too, would have surrendered himself to the general undertow, except for two things. First, he was a fourteen year old boy, and therefore neither able nor willing to give himself entirely to anything. Second, Penelope had promised to wait by the Spider Dragon, that fastest and scariest and most dangerous of all the carnival rides. Penelope waited—and she waited for him, William, the kid no one waited for, whom no one ever noticed. He was neither picked first nor picked on; he was just William, passing like a ghost through school, and Penelope waited for *him*.

He moved through the crowd like a shark in water, an unstoppable force, his eyes focused on the farthest mountain wall of the fairgrounds, against which the carnival had erected its mighty Spider Dragon. It seemed to grow as William came closer, and though not quite as tall as the Ferris Wheel, it was unmistakable in its menacing glory.

Every other week of the year, the fairgrounds was an empty field, barren, a stop on the Metro at which no one boarded or disembarked, a dimple in the ground cut into the edge of the mountain wall. It was the lowest land in Midnight, far enough from everything else to be surrounded only by abandoned warehouses and neglected streets. There was city, surrounding the fairgrounds, but no part of the city any sane person visited, certainly not a place in which to find William. People came here to die—so they always said in school—or to be absorbed by the carnival.

But for one week at summer's end, life erupted in the fairgrounds— or a pantomime of life. The carnival went up in a day, came down in a day; for the week between rising and falling, it lent its frenetic energy to Midnight.

That energy pulsed in the lights, in William's blood; it powered his feet as he darted around carts selling spun sugar and offering games of chance and skill. Every step brought him closer to the Spider Dragon, the monstrosity that even his father had risked as a child, and to pretty red-haired Penelope. He didn't pause to see the things around him, though William knew better. His heart pounded. His palms sweat. He wasn't about to keep Penelope waiting, no way, not him.

Around a dirt corner, passing an ice cream stand and nearly running

into the legs of a stilt-walker, William finally stopped when his view of
the Spider Dragon shifted from *that thing snaking over all other things*
to *the ride at the end of this lane.*

William caught his breath.

So many people still separated him from the Spider Dragon, he
couldn't be sure if she was there. But she had to be. She promised.
Promises were meant to be kept, even if they were small, even if you
didn't mean them. You couldn't make one otherwise. There were laws,
rules at least, so William knew she was there.

Compared to that knowledge, the Spider Dragon didn't scare him at
all.

And there she was, like a flower visible through the swaying weeds,
alone in the middle of this great field, surrounded by nothing that
mattered. "Penelope!" William called, but she was still too far away. He
couldn't run anymore, couldn't betray how desperate he was to ride
together with her on the Spider Dragon, to share red ice shavings and
hot dogs.

Through the sea of people, many of whom were taller and wider
than Penelope, William only caught glimpses of her. Peering into the
crowds. Glancing at her watch. Looking to the heights of the nearby
Ferris Wheel. Talking to a tall stranger in a black suit. Smiling.
Nodding.

Gone.

Gone. William ran again, racing toward where he'd seen her, near
the entrance to the Spider Dragon, on the other side of the winding line
of people waiting to be thrilled near to death, where now stood only a
white wooden fence post and a clod of earth.

How could she be gone?

But no, there she was, listening to that stranger, just a few feet closer
to the Spider Dragon line. Pushing through one last throng of people,
William reached Penelope.

She looked at him, no trace of the stranger anywhere, and smiled.
"Ready?" she asked, looking up toward the Spider Dragon's peaks.

William tried to look nonchalant, as though he hadn't just been
driven mad with the fear she'd abandoned him, and said, "Absolutely."

2.

The best place for a secret rendezvous was out in the most open, public place imaginable, especially when there was no one from whom to keep the secret. It sounded more exciting when you thought of it that way. At least, Mileah had convinced herself of this.

No such meeting had been planned, secret or otherwise. Mileah wandered the carnival, snapping pictures every few feet, catching unsuspecting people with caramel dripping down their chins or overshooting rings and rubber frogs.

She didn't ride the rides, but captured screaming faces distorted by centrifugal force and the constant flickering of a thousand tiny lights. *Click-whirr*, Mileah's camera caught another. *Click-whirr*, and another.

The pictures were partly for fun. She assembled albums of collages, painting 35mm stories. They were partly her job, too. *The Midnight Sun* paid freelancers good money when they wanted a shot, and how could they not want an entire pictorial from the carnival's final night? One week a year, that was all they got, and Mileah had made the best of it.

Click-whirr, she caught the fire-eater running across stage. Mileah moved closer as the lithe woman displayed flaming swords in front of her like a deck of cards, the tips held in one gloved hand—delicately gloved, not a gauntlet of leather or mail, but red lace that matched her thread-like costume, the flames apparently dancing in her palm. The mechanisms or magics of her act were unimportant; it was the expression on her face, the abject delight as she gripped blades that neither cut nor burned her flesh. *Click-whirr*, another shot, as the fire-eater drew one sword with her other hand and swallowed it, steel and flame.

On another stage, an illustrated man had the colored inks on his chest dancing with his pectoral muscles, up and down as he flexed, a lewd display Mileah absolutely needed to have on film. *Click-whirr*.

The night had almost been lost, until she'd had the most brilliant of ideas. Her parents had saddled her with William, disappearing for their weekend away (they were never clear about where they went, but took such weekends every few months). "But I can't drag him around the carnival with me," she'd protested. Mom and dad shrugged and said goodnight.

And then it struck her, as suddenly as any good notion: she didn't have to drag him along. Sure, he wanted to go, and she *had* to if she wanted to sell something to the paper, but there was no reason he had to stay with her.

"Here," she'd said, shoving money into William's hand. "Go enjoy the carnival. Be home before me."

They'd parted at the top of the Metro steps. It was almost as if he'd forgotten she was there, and that was certainly best. He had a secret rendezvous to attend; she had her own, with the faces.

Click-whirr, she captured an older woman dragging a frightened child behind her. The woman scowled, and turned away, but once caught the images belonged to Mileah—and maybe *The Midnight Sun,* if she was lucky.

Nine pages, maybe twelve. That's what she wanted. A huge display, maybe a teaser on the front page.

"You'll have to stop," someone said, so abruptly Mileah didn't realize he was speaking to her until he said it again. His voice was low and soft, without any hint of malice.

"What do you mean?"

"The camera," he said, nodding toward it. "You can't go around stealing pieces of people's lives."

Mileah smiled. "I'm not stealing anything."

He moved closer, so that the breadth of his shoulders became a wall and his chin jutted down at her. He lowered his voice to a whisper. "Souls," he said, "for memories. You may refer to it as a trade, and thereby ease your mind, but I call it theft."

She refused to back down. "Your soul," she said, "is safe from me."

"I would not be so certain," he said, but the argument was gone from his voice. He couldn't maintain it.

"What are you after?" she asked. "Who are you?"

He sneered, snorted, and narrowed his eyes. "It's bad enough, the carnival entices and seduces our brothers with all its lustful and gluttonous ways. Win this, eat that, see this most beautiful woman in all the world." He said these words like curses, clipped, unclean as they came off his tongue. "And you, here not to immortalize but to further inflame the vices of Midnight. All those suffering souls, the lost and the wandering, trapped in the grip of this heathen carnival, not just tonight, but by your *camera*"—another curse—"forever."

Mileah had stepped back as he spoke; he didn't seem to notice, and she slipped into the crowd and away. Five minutes later, she snapped again—*click-whirr*—three carnival workers headed through one of the blockades, toward the trailers and tents behind the scenes.

With furtive glances in all directions, Mileah snuck behind the temporary wooden barrier. There, the three carnies argued, bitterly, words lost beneath their fury, arms flailing, eyes and nostrils blazing, shouts that went unheard in a background filled with screams and boisterous come-ons.

Click-whirr. The argument ended abruptly, and three faces turned as one toward the interloper, Mileah. She blushed, waved, and stepped back into the carnival.

3.

The line wasn't too long. In fact, William didn't mind waiting at all. Penelope stood with him the entire time, looking pretty and smelling wonderful, so it didn't matter that they were densely packed with dozens of sweaty, dirty, grungy carnival goers.

"There's a story about the Spider Dragon," Penelope said. "My father was telling me about it."

"A story?"

"It was named for something that really existed."

William smiled. "No way."

Penelope insisted, and maybe there was some truth to it. William was still young, and knew it; there was a lot of world out there to find, and maybe spider dragons crawled in dark corners beneath the mountains.

Their turn on the ride came, interrupting their conversation, but William didn't mind. The carnie running the ride sat him and Penelope close, so their shoulders and knees rubbed together, and locked them in with a metal bar over their laps. The guy's teeth were crooked and dingy, visible as he chomped his gum. He never said a word, but after glancing at Penelope he gave William a wink, one that said, *You're doing things right.*

And he was. William was sure of it. He wasn't as nervous as when they were talking; he could concentrate on something other than Penelope's eyes or hands or lips, something as abstract as the beast for which the Spider Dragon had been named. Already, the cars clacked as they were slowly drawn forward.

"It lives under the sewers," Penelope said, "and feeds on blood. Human blood."

"Do you want me to go down into the sewers and find it?" William asked. "Maybe slay it, or just get a photo. I can take one of my sister's cameras..."

But Penelope was shaking her head. "No, no, not at all. That would be...foolish, for one, and then, you being the hero and all, I'd *have* to kiss you."

Williams' cheeks flushed. "Oh," he said, slightly thrilled at the suggestion but mostly disappointed by the tone.

"I'd rather kiss you just because," she said, "with no reason whatsoever."

And she did.

On the cheek, light and fast, but still those were her lips, glorious and warm and soft, touching his skin. Her lips. No one else's face but his. He couldn't help but smile. "Thanks," he said, and suddenly wished he hadn't.

"It's just a story," she said, as the rising cars reached the peak. "To scare kids..." With a rush and a roar, they plummeted, guided by wooden tracks, wheels buzzing and clicking beneath them. The roller coaster banked hard to the left, pressing Penelope against William's side, and then rose sharply for another swift decline. Wind in their hair, their faces, their ears, made it impossible to hear anything else.

William's grin was indestructible.

4.

Mileah expected a pursuit, angry carnie faces waving their arms in her direction, running, loping, chasing her down the hilly lanes and between attractions. But even that was a romanticized vision of what might have happened, had she stumbled upon—and photographed— something she shouldn't have. Shouts and warnings, commands to stop, perhaps a pistol fired into the air.

Instead: nothing.

She walked from the side of the carnival, away from an argument she only partially witnessed, and back into the throng of revelers.

The carnival was always a celebration. What the people of Midnight had *to* celebrate, Mileah didn't know. There might be marriages, anniversaries, births and even deaths, promotions and new jobs, first dates, *third* dates, illnesses overcome, friends reunited. Mileah could list dozens of reasons. Hundreds. Maybe they were just enjoying life.

She smiled at that thought.

Click-whirr, she captured another mini-party in front of her, an entire family, child a step in front of parents whose arms wrapped around each other's waists, still obviously and wonderfully in love. *Click-whirr.* They smiled at her as they passed, and the kid even paused in licking the side of a flat, round lollipop to give her a better pose.

"Thanks," she said.

They beamed and walked on.

In fact, the only person to talk to her (not with her, as she would have preferred) had been that preacher. *You can't go around stealing pieces of people's lives.* She shook away the memory, and the stirrings of depression. Damn, she couldn't allow that to sink in. Wasn't room for it. No time. She had a life, a real one, and whenever she realized she'd begun to slip into the maelstrom of self-pity and hatred, she had to stop it or she'd be lost—to the world and to herself—for days, weeks, even months.

She fished money out of her jeans and went, instead, to the nearest food cart. Oddly enough, a funnel cake (showered with powdered sugar) might help her.

5.

Riding the Spider Dragon took about thirty minutes out of William's life. For the first twenty-seven minutes, give or take, he waited on line—with Penelope, so it was an effortless span of time. Climbing into the car took thirty seconds at most; emerging afterwards the same. That meant the trip lasted a mere hundred and twenty seconds, during which he and Penelope were yanked this way and that, and often thrown into each other. They hurtled down long, steep slopes, circled in loops, and rose so high he could make out the outline of City Hall against the mountain across town.

It was too short.

People screamed, waving their arms over the heads, reaching out as if to grab a layer of tracks above them (reminding William of all the stories in which hands were severed at the wrist by thin, nearly invisible cables—and those who tried to stand got it at the neck). The Spider Dragon was an exhilarating rush of wind and adrenaline, but nothing compared to the nearness of Penelope.

The ride was way too short. William wanted to go again.

"No," Penelope said, taking his hand. "Let's walk around a bit, see what else there is."

He looked down at her hand, soft and warm, fingers curled across his, and his brain short-circuited. She could have said, *Let's go deep into the sewers and feed ourselves to the Spider Dragon, that beastly thing for which they named this monstrosity, and maybe die together like Juliet and Romeo*, and despite that the star-crossed lovers had not quite died *together*, William would have followed Penelope into the deepest, darkest caverns, under subways and sewers and crypts, into caves filled with darkness and abysses, sharp-toothed and winged creatures, and one hungry Spider Dragon—just to keep his hand in hers. Walking, therefore, was a no-brainer.

"Sure," he finally managed. He hoped his hand didn't sweat, betraying nervousness and excitement, and wished his heart didn't sound so loud in his throat.

They passed too close to the games.

There were a hundred from which to choose, rubber frogs to toss and clown-faced balloons to fill with water, darts to throw, baskets to shoot. The barkers called out their prizes, and people wove around William and Penelope to test their luck and skill.

"Win a prize for your girlfriend," one pitchman said to William, tossing a softball back and forth between his hands. "I guarantee you'll win a prize, no matter what, promises and scout's honor and everything."

"Do it," Penelope said. "Win me that stuffed tiger."

"Why the tiger?" William asked, scanning the pink elephants and purple flamingos hanging in the back of the pitchman's cart.

"Because it's blue," she said, "and it's the only one."

But William hesitated. He wasn't any good at throwing balls— baseball, soccer, volleyball, none of them, and certainly not a softball. He couldn't get his grip all the way around it, so it always felt just about ready to slip out of his hand.

"The blue tiger," Penelope said softly.

William fished money from his pocket, stepped forward, and paid for three big, hard softballs. He stared at the plastic milk bottles, prayed, closed his eyes, and threw.

And missed entirely.

"Nice arm," the pitchman said, glancing toward the back corner where the errant ball had disappeared. "Aim's a little skewed."

"A little," William conceded.

The pitchman leaned closer, so Penelope couldn't hear, and whispered, "Why don't you try it with your eyes open this time?" He winked. "Visualize."

William nodded. Two of the milk bottles were red, one yellow, and he wasn't quite sure how that third balanced on top of the others. He squinted at it, trying to narrow his focus so he wouldn't see anything else, wound his arm back, and threw.

The ball bounced off the corner of the ledge, in front of the bottles, popped into the air, and flew over William.

Another boy caught it, one-handed, before it crashed into Penelope.

"Good catch," the pitchman said, applauding. "That alone deserves a prize."

The kid grinned. "Cool." Then he pointed. "That tiger."

"No," William said.

The kid shrugged. He was older than William, maybe a year or two, taller and more athletic, with bluer eyes (anything was bluer than brown). He had stolen his grin from Tom Sawyer.

Behind him, Penelope's face contorted into something between sour, angry, and amused.

"You've got one more chance," the pitchman said to William. "Take out the bottles, you get first choice."

The kid leaned with one arm against the side of the cart, nonchalant as he waited for William's last attempt.

The pitchman nodded, giving him permission to go again. He had been close, very close, with that last one; a few inches higher, it would have hit at least one of those bottles. No one else would be having this much trouble, he was sure of it. His father, even his sister, could knock down those bottles without trying. William shouldn't have any trouble, either.

He tried to ignore the kid's smirk, which gleamed in William's peripheral vision. When he realized he couldn't do that, he transferred that image to the spot directly between the bottom two bottles. Knocking those down would be the same as wiping that grin away. With that in mind, William smiled, took a deep breath, and threw.

The ball brushed the neck of the top bottle. It wobbled, teetered, and threatened to fall—on top of the others, William hoped, trying to knock it down by willpower. The balance tipped backwards. The bottle dropped, behind the others, not touching them.

"We have a winner," the pitchman announced—but it wasn't William. He tossed the blue tiger to the other boy, the interloper, the stranger whose eyes sparkled and grin widened.

Penelope made some sort of disapproving noise, half grunt and half moan.

"And you," the pitchman said, fishing a fist-sized yellow bear from a tub filled with them, "like I promised, a winner every time." He lobbed the bear over. William fumbled with it, almost missing the pathetic consolation prize.

"Tell you what," the kid said, giving the pitchman some money. "You want this thing?" He dangled the tiger by one of its hind legs. "If I can't knock down all three on one shot, it's yours."

Penelope grabbed William's hand. "You don't have to wait for him to show off."

"Oh, it's not showing off," the kid said. "Just doing my part. The tiger's for you, ain't it? Would you rather *he* gave it to you, or me?"

She glared.

"That's what I thought." He picked up one of his three balls as the pitchman reset the bottles. "One throw, that's all. But if I make it, you"—he looked at Penelope—"buy me ice cream."

"No way," William said.

"And sit with me while I eat it, and *he* goes somewhere else. And I'll take a good long time eating my ice cream. Three scoops. With toppings. Right over there." He nodded toward a nearby cart. "Either way, " he said, flipping the tiger in the air and catching it by its tail, "this thing's yours." He set it on the counter in front of the pitchman.

"No way," William said again. But Penelope was nodding.

"One shot," she said, "from here."

Here was five feet back from the edge of the cart, where William had stood. Penelope didn't look at him as she spoke, and she no longer held his hand. Everything had gone horribly wrong—and was about to get decidedly worse, since the kid obviously expected the bottles to jump out of his way.

Shaking his head, the kid stepped five feet further back. "How about from here?"

William cursed under his breath.

"One shot," the pitchman said, beaming as he backed into the corner. "Go on, Rex."

William hung his head. Not only did the kid have a name, he was known at the carnival—if not the whole attraction, at least at this tent, here, where he probably spent all his spare hours imagining new and different ways of knocking down bottles and stealing other kid's girlfriends.

(Okay, girlfriend was a bit premature, but the pitchman had said it and Penelope hadn't flinched.)

Impossibly, Rex's lips stretched even further to the sides, as if he could always grin just a little more widely. He glanced left and right, nodded to the pitchman, and winked at William.

If he didn't think Rex could flatten him without breaking a sweat, William would've hit him.

The windup came, as if in slow motion, and William almost threw himself into the path of the ball. Instead, he glanced at Penelope. She watched Rex, hands curled into fists.

Rex threw the ball hard. Fast. It smacked the lip of the table under the bottles, the very place William had hit on his second attempt. It bounced back, just as fast—and again, straight at Penelope. William lurched forward and snatched it from the air, one-handed, surprising himself more than anyone else.

The pitchman, looking at Rex, shook his head. "Off your game tonight, Rex." He threw the tiger to William. "Congrats, kid. You earned it."

Penelope hugged him, which would've made the whole incident worth it, except Rex, grinning over her shoulder, mouthed, "You owe me," and winked again.

6.

Mileah put aside her camera long enough to try some of the rides. The House of Horrors, of course, was always fun, with day-glo skeletons and purple neon ghosts popping out from behind Styrofoam tombstones. And the Whirly-Bird made her dizzy, again, just like every year since she was six. Atop the Ferris Wheel, she took a few pictures of Midnight. This highest point of the carnival faced inwards, so most of the city's skyline was visible.

She also stopped and got something more substantial to eat, and was walking aimlessly sipping lemonade when the bells sounded midnight.

Even in the fairgrounds, the church bells could be heard.

She paused that moment.

Midnight—the time—was a divider of days, an impartial and blind jury that determined one day to be over and another to begin. Thus, many decisions were made at this arbitrary cut in the fabric of reality. People who went to sleep and awoke with a solution to some problem, or a decision on some weighty issue that had plagued them, did not arrive at this new place because of a sound night's sleep or a particularly beneficial dream. Rather, the days were cut, cleaved as if on a guillotine, a moment of simultaneous death and birth, and many, many things were, at that very moment, decided.

All around, people paused, but not everyone; some continued blindly, or deafly, unconcerned with the passing of another day.

"Saturday," Mileah said, under her breath, as she finished her drink.

"The carnival," someone said, "is consuming its full."

She turned. The tall, black-clad preacher stood behind her, smiling broadly, shielding his eyes from the moonlight as he stared off in the direction of the church. It was too far away to be seen, and the bells had already echoed into silence.

"Like your camera," the man said.

"We've already had this conversation," she reminded him.

"There's something I didn't tell you," he said. "Something I should share."

She rolled her eyes, not wanting to even look at him. If this had been some awful Romance novel, of course, she'd find herself unable to tear away from his chiseled good looks or the lilt of his voice, and she'd eventually fall in love with him, despite any misgivings, and he'd eventually protect her from some invisible evil of which only he was aware.

First, however, he was a preacher; the collar around his throat meant he was unavailable. Second, his voice didn't lilt or sing or caress or seduce. It wasn't exactly unpleasant, low pitched as it was, but it was rough in a way Mileah didn't appreciate, and it lacked resonance. Third, his looks were neither chiseled nor good. Fourth, she didn't believe in Romance novels (romance, yes, of course, but that was completely different). The idea only filtered through her head because she'd been taking pictures of so many couples and families.

"My name is Joshua," he said. "They call me the Wandering Reverend."

"So?"

"I've been watching you."

"You're a freak."

"Snapping bits and pieces of lives all around you," he continued. "You particularly like the children, and delight in their innocent joys. That's a good trait, I think, but you're failing."

"Failing?"

"You can't take what isn't yours," he said. "You can't steal the things you want. You must earn them. God helps those..."

"I've heard it," Mileah said.

The Wandering Reverend smiled and bowed his head. "That's it," he said. "There's sin all around, and you're tempted, I can see, but you won't give in. You won't surrender. These evils will depart shortly, as they leave us every year, and they will return. Will you be strong enough to resist, next year, if you haven't found what you seek? First lives, then the souls of others...will you sacrifice your own soul in your pursuits?"

"You don't know me," Mileah said.

"No," he told her. "I know people."

"You're a freak."

"As you've already said."

She turned sharply and walked away. The Wandering Reverend said nothing more, and made no noise if he chased her (but he'd been *watching* her all night, what in Hell was that about?), but his words remained. Echoed. Pulsed inside her brain and tortured her mind. What *did* she seek? Was her photography a crutch, a method of living vicariously through the lens?

No, damn it, no, the photography wasn't in lieu of her wants and desires, it was a vital and inescapable part of it, her primary source of joy. She wasn't about to let some eerie, voyeuristic creep ruin her night—her *life*—with a few disjointed and invalid assignations of "the human condition" on her.

Will you sacrifice your own soul?

What did he think she was trying to steal, people's families? Their children?

Without even being aware of it, Mileah walked straight toward the exit, beneath the clown's teeth, and down the Metro steps. In the dimness of the subways, she tried to shift her thoughts to home, to her darkroom, where she would begin developing the pictures she took.

It almost worked.

7.

Penelope had been in the middle of a string of nasty names, all meant for Rex, when the bells sounded twelve. Together, without another word, they paused.

William thought he was the luckiest guy in all of Midnight—in all the world. Only the stuffed blue tiger was luckier. First, Rex had missed. Second, most importantly, Penelope couldn't be happier. She clutched her prize to her chest, held William's hand, and they wandered aimlessly.

They'd stopped only for some ice cream.

"Oh," Penelope said, looking inward toward the city. "I can't believe it's that late already. I better go home."

All night, William had feared this moment. "I can walk you to the Metro, at least," he said.

Penelope looked at him slantwise. "I should hope so."

They weren't far from the entrance. She still held William's hand as they passed beneath the clown's teeth.

The stairs to the Metro were darker than at most stations, and narrower. "Tonight was fun," Penelope said as they descended. "Well, mostly fun."

"I was afraid for a minute there," William said, but it was thoroughly untrue; he'd been nervous most the night, and now he feared he'd said exactly the wrong thing. *Again.* How many times had that happened? Maybe he should wait another five or ten years, until he had something of a brain controlling his voice box, before asking another girl out. Except...except that just maybe, if he asked Penelope, properly and immediately, before the *mostly fun* memories faded, she'd go out with him again.

The carnival was over. By dawn, the carnies would have torn it all down. By Sunday, the Fairgrounds would be empty again, a barren wasteland in the farthest corner of Midnight. William didn't have a clue what else to ask Penelope to—a film? Concert? No, dinner, that was it, but where could he afford that was decent?

They reached the landing and turned to face each other. Penelope's subway was just arriving; William's would arrive on the other tracks. He wished the end didn't have to come so abruptly—or at all.

"That's it," Penelope said, squeezing his hand.

"We...we should do this again," William said.

Penelope raised her eyebrows. "Next year?"

"Sooner, I hope."

"Then we'll have to do something other than *this*," Penelope said, nodding up the stairs. Her train screeched as it stopped. She leaned forward and kissed him, lightly, on the lips.

Then she was gone.

It was like the whole world ceased to exist that moment, and William's mind dissolved. The brief, light contact tripped his heart and blurred his vision. There she was, already on board, waving even as she turned toward a stranger on the train, and the doors slid shut.

It was a tall man, in black, whom she'd been speaking with at the Spider Dragon.

"Pretty," a voice said behind him.

William turned. From the shadows alongside the stone staircase, Rex emerged. "Very pretty," he said. "I can see why you like her."

William's hands bunched into fists—instinct—though he wasn't any more a fighter than a ball thrower. He tightened his jaw, narrowed his eyes, but said nothing.

"You weren't afraid I was gonna steal her away, were you?" Rex asked.

"What do you want?"

"Want? Me?" He shook his head. "Don't think I want anything, really. Just trying to be friendly, is all. I mean, I made sure you got her that animal she wanted, made it look good and tough and scary, didn't I? Maybe I just want you to thank me."

William said nothing.

Rex stopped about a yard away. The platform was rather empty, and none of the available eyes seemed to pay any attention to them. "Listen, I'm sorry if it came out wrong," Rex said, "or if you didn't realize what I was doing. I just thought you and I could be friends."

"Friends?"

"You know, pals," Rex said. "Buddies. Chums. We can get into trouble together. Create mischief." He looked around, though there was nothing to see inside the tunnel except granite walls, bare fluorescent bulbs hanging over the two sets of tracks, and twenty gigantic copies of the same red poster. "I'm still new here. Don't go to school. I thought, maybe, since I helped you win the girl, maybe you'd show me around a little. The sights. I haven't seen much of Midnight yet, except down here, and down here ain't all that pretty."

William wasn't used to disliking people; he couldn't hold onto it. And he also wasn't used to someone offering to be his friend. He didn't have many, not in school; he was something of an outsider, but not far enough outside to be accepted by the *true* outsiders, who were a clique all their own.

The tension fled his muscles, but he still didn't know what to do.

After a moment, when it seemed Rex would say nothing more, William asked, "What do you want to see?"

8.

There were no lights on inside the house as Mileah approached. It was crowded between other houses, about as far from the mountains as anyplace in Midnight. It was narrow, three flights high, with two basement levels—which meant somewhere along the line her parents (or their parents, most likely) had had a bit of money.

Mileah climbed the three steps to her front door, keyed herself in, and turned on the hall light.

Rather than upstairs, to her bedroom, or even to check on her brother, she instead went immediately to the upper basement. There, she'd converted one of the three rooms into a darkroom; another stored equipment and shelves with books of her photography.

She'd taken four rolls of film tonight, and wanted to start developing them immediately.

She loved the smell of the darkroom, the chemicals, the promise; and the dim red bulb made her feel like she lived in a fantasy world, away from the fluorescent and neon brightness of the city.

Mileah had to keep even the red light off for the first step of processing. She prepared all of the rolls, spending maybe an hour in total darkness. Since this was her world, she never worried, and only sometimes thought about how comfortable she was in the dark. Here, she existed outside herself, beyond the boundaries of her own body, as if she didn't have a physical existence at all. She knew her lab so well, she never bumped anything, and sometimes seemed to see black outlines and silhouettes. She'd built it herself, and spent as many hours here as she did in bed.

Here, too, she forgot the things that bothered her, the missing pieces, the loneliness. She wasn't alone in the dark; rather, she was complete—or something like complete, so that even the Wandering Reverend's little diatribe faded into nothingness. She knew she used this room, this whole process, as an escape—but not the way he'd described it, not in some sickly, abnormally obsessive manner. It was Mileah's form of meditation.

After cutting the negatives into strips of six, she arranged them on the enlarger to print contact sheets, exposing one roll at a time and taking it through the various chemical pools until setting it adrift in the fixer solution.

The sounds of her own home failed to penetrate the darkroom, making it something like an isolation chamber. She smiled as the images took shape on the paper, happy with most of what she saw. She expected to have three, maybe four good shots per roll, easily enough for that pictorial essay in *The Midnight Sun*.

She brought the contact sheets into the other room, where she could examine her results on a light table with a loop—a magnifying lens similar to what a jeweler would use to examine a diamond. With a grease pencil, she circled the shots she wanted to enlarge, the ones she thought would be best for the paper and her personal collection. There were six on that first roll, which thrilled her, and another five on the second.

On the third, however, she paused. "That's not right," she said, squinting. The image was distinct and crisp and, in fact, compositionally interesting: the Wandering Reverend in the foreground, obviously ranting (in the way he ranted, soft-spoken but intense), closer to the right side of the frame. Moving toward the center, but seeming to come from behind the man, was a shadowy shape, something like a snake rising up to spit its venom. In the background, on the left, the carnival was visible, distinct with its roller coaster set against the mountainside.

She blinked, rubbed her eyes, took a deep breath, and looked again. The picture didn't change. "But I didn't take that," Mileah mumbled.

She went back to the darkroom, found that negative, and set it on the enlarger. She turned on the light without sliding paper into the machine, and studied the image. That was definitely the Wandering Reverend, though she knew she hadn't shot him. And she'd certainly not seen any twisting smoke-like creature at the carnival. It wasn't quite a snake, maybe some sort of arachnid. Its tail twisted like a serpent's, and disappeared behind the Wandering Reverend. By its appearance, it *should* have continued past him, maybe even out of the frame; it looked, to Mileah, as if the creature emerged from his back.

9.

"I really ought to be getting home," William said. "My sister's waiting for me."

"I don't have a sister," Rex said. "Not anymore."

They hadn't left the steps, though William's train had come and gone. There'd be another in about twenty minutes.

"What's that mean?" he asked.

"She died," Rex said, shrugging. "I barely remember it anymore. Long time ago."

"Sorry."

"No need."

"I...I never thought how it'd be like without Mileah," William admitted. "Except, of course, that I'd have a bigger room, and more gifts."

"You have the greatest gift," Rex said.

William laughed.

"No, it's true," he said. "And I have it, too, and your sister, everyone on this platform." There were maybe a dozen people waiting for their trains, most headed home from the carnival. A few seemed to watch the others from (and in) the shadows, as if this was their home and they weren't accustomed to having it invaded every night for a week, nervousness visible in their eyes and the way they shrank behind stone columns or peered around the sides of magazines they didn't read. "You'll figure it out," Rex said. "So, you gonna show me some sights?"

"Nothing's open."

"Nonsense. The trains are running."

"The trains always run."

"And doors," Rex said, his grin returning, "can always be opened. Doesn't matter when they were locked, or by whom."

"I don't know what you mean," William said, but it was a lie. He knew exactly what Rex meant: breaking into whatever he wanted to enter, picking locks, smashing windows, kicking in doors—whatever it took, things William had never considered doing. They could get caught, in trouble, maybe even arrested. Or they could have free reign...

"Forget it," Rex said.

A group of people descended the stairs, a pair of families with parents and grandparents, children and infants, all noisy, spreading like water to fill every available spot. To get out of their way, William and Rex stepped to the side of the staircase.

"Better idea," Rex said, lowering his voice. "We don't have to get in the train with *them*. Have you ever been inside St. Lazarus' at night?"

St. Lazarus' Cathedral was not too far from the fairgrounds. It was a few hundred years old—no one knew for certain when it had been built—and home to hundreds of gargoyles. There were iron bells in its towers. William had seen them once, and touched them, these massive bells that reminded everyone of old stories. To reach them, he'd had to climb a spiraling stone staircase barely wide enough to fit one person. The steps were steep; graffiti scarred the walls (though William knew, in that absolute way he knew things because he'd have run it that way, there were other stairways not open to the public, where no one had scratched in their names or sketched comic characters). There was a huge organ in the back of the church, played through two rows of pipes flanking the altar. Rose windows on either side cast a murky tint. And there had been candles everywhere, white pillars half as tall as William, thin tapers, and tea lamps no more than half an inch high, flames dancing at the tops of many.

His parents had taken him there twice. They lived too far away to attend services, but that didn't stop his father from pointing out the faces interspersed on the friezes inside, between prayers carved in ancient languages.

Rex waved a hand in front of William's eyes. "Hello?" he said. "Can you hear me?"

"We can't get into St. Lazarus'," William said. "They'll find us."

"Nobody lives *inside* the church," Rex said. "All the priests are in the rectory, across the street. There's no caretaker at night, and God has never struck me down."

"You've been inside by yourself?"

Rex laughed once. "And we don't even need to go through the doors," he said. "We can get in through the crypts."

10.

No matter how long Mileah examined the picture she didn't take, there was no denying that it had come off her roll of film (between a woman dragging a child—unhappy despite the caramel apple in his hand—from an ice cream cart, and another of a grinning stilt-walker leaning down to offer an orchid—which Mileah had refused).

She looked through the negatives again, and then the contact sheet, and finally at the picture she'd eventually developed. The smoky beast was translucent, revealing edges of carts and rides behind it, and people walked either right, left, or away—but none toward—the camera. Only the Wandering Reverend seemed aware of the camera; he spoke directly at it, not her, as if the camera itself had stolen from him.

But she hadn't taken the picture.

"How did you get here?" she asked.

She expected no answer. A part of Mileah didn't want to know—that small iota of hopeless, foolish romantic who believed that maybe even this Wandering Reverend, Joshua, was the white horse-riding knight, come to rescue her from dragons and evil princes—and therefore wanted nothing more than to find this man and tell him everything, all of it—even if there was nothing to tell.

Another part of her wanted to snip that negative out of its strip and burn it, with the contact sheet and finished photo, in a great big bonfire into which she could cast all her demons and fears.

Except she had no demons. She knew no fear.

It was obviously a portent of something, either threat or hope, and it was up to her to act.

Mileah thought to try to phone him, but there were probably a hundred men named Joshua living in the city, a thousand, and certainly the phone company wouldn't have a listing under Wandering Reverend. Would it?

She tried information. No luck.

She took the photo upstairs and stopped in the kitchen for a snack. On the way, she glanced at the ivory-faced clock (an antique, passed down to her parents from their parents and their parents before then). Both hands pointed just past the three.

"That early?" she said aloud.

The clock gave no response.

She made a sandwich, poured a glass of milk, and picked up the picture again as she ate. A little too much mustard, she thought, but the milk cut through it nicely. By the end of the meal, she'd reached a decision.

She had to go back.

11.

If someone asked what he was doing, William would have said, "Making a mistake." He knew this with all his heart. There was no reason to go anywhere with Rex. To follow him into the darkness under the subway system, that was entirely unreasonable.

He did it anyhow.

Behind the staircase, the platform narrowed so only one person could walk on it. There were no garbage cans or signs written in the tiled walls, and none of those advertisements William found so interesting. Perfume, jeans, cars—he wanted the world based on those images, but that world did not include the thickening dark of the underground.

The platform ended at an iron ladder. There, between tracks, they waited until William's train had passed (he could be headed home, but had instead chosen adventure, action, all the things fourteen year old boys were supposed to choose). After it had gone, and they were safe, they crossed the railings (careful to avoid the third), walked alongside the track a few yards, and reached a recessed door. It was wooden, unlocked but tightly jammed; Rex forced it open with his shoulder, revealing a narrow set of stairs.

"They're quite elaborate, these tunnels," he said. "There are aqueducts down there, where they still bring water into the city." He pulled a small flashlight from his back pocket and pointed it down.

The steps were uneven, the rusty railing covered with dust. The passage had been cut into the stone but never finished, so rough edges jutted out at odd angles in the corners of the ceiling.

"Careful," Rex said, leading the way. "Wouldn't want to sprain an ankle or something."

"What's it like, inside?" William asked.

"Find out when we get there," Rex said. "We're here now, going deeper than the subway, maybe into places that no man—well, few men—have seen in generations." He paused in mid-step and turned to William. "That's it, that's our deal then. I'll show you the secrets of Midnight Underground. You show me the city at street level."

William hesitated, but only for a moment. There were hidden corners to find, mysteries to solve, stories and rumors to be proved or disproved. He didn't even know all of them. There was always something under Midnight, beasts or treasures, magical toys and weapons, the burial chambers of gangsters and their vaults, the paths used by criminals and runaways, and the remains of whatever stood, before, where Midnight now stood. "Deal," he said.

Rex offered his hand. "Shake on it."

They did, and William felt a hundred, a thousand times better than he had. Who needed the kids at school? Well, there was Penelope—pretty, red-headed, wonderful Penelope—but the rest of them didn't matter. They didn't know what he was about to find out. They'd never seen what he was about to discover.

Rex was right. Why worry about what St. Lazarus' would be like when they got there? They still had this mystical, mysterious underground system to explore first.

The steps deposited them at the end of a long corridor. Doors lined both sides; William tried one (though if he let Rex get too far ahead, he'd have no light), but it was locked.

"It's at the far end of this hall," Rex said. "These were apartments once. Might still be." There were numbers on the wall next to the knobs; most had been painted and had faded until they were barely visible. Others were etched in, or raised, and had been worn almost flat. They were four digits, all beginning with sixes.

"Who lived here?" William asked.

"Don't know," Rex said. "They might at the Historical Society." Which, of course, was something of a joke, as no one ever went inside that building. "But now," he added, "I guess whoever found or inherited the keys. I live in one of these."

"No way."

"Not on this hall, no," Rex said, "but not too far from here. Maybe, after St. Lazarus', we'll head that way."

Above them, a train rumbled past. Dust fell from the ceiling, doorknobs rattled...and from behind one of the doors, there was a loud thump.

Rex looked back, still grinning, but quickened his pace.

Twice, they crossed other hallways leading further into the dark than William could see (looking back, the shadows consumed their path). Rex never shined the light into any of these.

Now, the doors were further apart, and the first of the four digits seemed to be three. The hall had been sloping gently downward since they left the stairs, but suddenly it was steeper.

"This is one of the old districts," Rex said, keeping his voice low. "The miners used to live here, and the factory families, all the slave-wagers, because they couldn't afford anything better. They rented from the factory owners, so there was never any chance of them getting anything better."

"What happened?" William asked.

"Don't they teach you history?"

"I don't remember anything about miners or factory workers," William said.

"Maybe they were never here," Rex said. "But then, they never would have needed these apartments."

Up ahead, the hall branched off in two directions. Rex motioned down the left hall with his flashlight as another train passed overhead, sounding duller and more distant this time. "The library's that way," he said. Then he pointed to the right. "St. Lazarus, straight ahead."

There were no doorways on the sides of this hall, but it ended, rather quickly, at a narrow, stone door. "It's secret," Rex whispered. "Looks just like the wall on the other side." He tugged on the handle, straining, pulling it open slowly. Stone scraped stone as it moved. He shined his light in, revealing a two foot drop to the ground, and let William jump in first.

Rex landed beside him, leaving the door open. There were panels, on which epitaphs had been etched, and statues in alcoves; ahead, steps led down into a sanctuary lined with stained glass — in front of stone walls.

"The crypts," Rex said, sweeping the light across the walls and floor, "of St. Lazarus'."

12.

The subway rocked to a halt at Fairgrounds Station. It had been empty most of the way, and the few who boarded while Mileah rode exited before her.

The station lights had been dimmed, as if the powers that be knew no one roamed around this part of town so early in the morning. This time was meant for bakeries, newspaper deliveries, coffee shops, and end-of-graveyard shifters. But no one worked here, except the carnies, and they had their own trucks and trailers. No need for mochas or breads. Just one man sleeping under a patchwork coat on the far bench.

She wished she'd brought her camera.

She climbed the stone steps and found herself facing the grinning clown-face entrance. A wire fence had been drawn beneath the teeth, blocking the way in, and already the carnival was coming down. The carts were closed up, and some had disappeared. Most of the streamers of light had been shut off. The Ferris Wheel and roller coaster stood off in the distance, skeletal monuments to stillness. The cars didn't even rock.

She pounded on the wooden plank shut over the ticket taker's booth. "Hello!" she called.

Silence.

Which was strange, because she expected to at least hear the carnies tearing their rolling festival to its bits and pieces, packing up to head out into the world before returning next year. No one ever left Midnight, not for long.

She paced a while, and then followed the fence as far in one direction as she could. But it seemed to continue forever, curving around so it enclosed most of the fairgrounds, and ended at the mountain wall. She peered between carts and down alleys, unable to find any sign of life on the other side of the fence.

Eventually, she gave up.

She headed back toward the entryway. She thought she saw someone working in the carousel, behind the lead horse, but it was only her reflection in the mirror.

Anyhow, she wasn't seeking one of the carnies. She wanted the Wandering Reverend. She had the photograph folded in her pocket, and questions rolling around her head. She kept trying to convince herself she was crazy, she'd imagined the picture and needed only a good, solid dream to give her mind a chance to clear. Six hours, eight, in bed with herself and no thoughts of the accusing stranger or his shadowy companion. She'd wake and find the picture was actually of a girl with pigtails and a bright yellow lollipop, or the near-naked contortionist swallowing torches and swords.

Mileah half expected to see the snake-like shadow slipping over the funhouse like a breath, around the side of the House of Horrors where it belonged, or maybe slithering between the games of no-chance—as if capturing it on film meant it really existed.

Maybe it was only real on film, captured, stolen like the lives the Wandering Reverend so vehemently meant to defend. Chuckling at that thought, she reached the clown's mouth.

As far as she could see in any direction, she was completely alone, but Mileah didn't believe it. She shivered, overcome with the certainty of eyes in the dark, malignant and lascivious. And if those eyes emerged? Fight or flight? Would a hero follow them out of the dark and capture her heart?

Could she go in? The flimsy fence beneath the clown's teeth would bend aside rather easily, and she could wander inside the carnival. But what purpose would that serve? They'd closed. There was no one left inside, not even the Wandering Reverend. She'd be better off going home and forgetting it, burning the picture, sleeping it off.

She unfolded the photo again to look at it, to be sure that contortionist hadn't snaked her body around someone who happened to share the Wandering Reverend's shape.

The smoky creature stared up at her.

Frustrated, she shoved it back into her pocket and kicked a stray rock on the ground. It clattered against the fence and echoed loudly.

She stomped down the stone steps into the subway station. Her platform was empty still, except for the man in the multicolored coat. No longer asleep, his eyes followed Mileah's every movement. Trying to ignore him, she read the schedule board and then glanced at the clock.

The next train wasn't due for another ten minutes. In Midnight, that was a lot of time.

13.

The crypts were as wide and long as the cathedral itself. The main hall went around the perimeter, but there were a dozen or more corridors and doorways moving inwards, leading to burial chambers and prayer rooms, several sanctuaries, and at least two immovable iron doors.

William wondered how many secrets passages there were, and if anyone alive still knew about them all. Granite markers in the walls signified the bodies of past priests and holy men, at least two bishops, and a woman named *Elizabeth* (which was, in fact, the strangest of all the epitaphs, as nothing else had been written on that slab, and there seemed to be no other women).

"Who was she?" he asked Rex.

Rex read the name for a minute or two, much longer than needed to discern the nine letters, and finally said, "Damned if I know. A girl, I suppose."

"Some girl."

"Not as pretty as your girlfriend, I bet," Rex said.

Anger flared up inside William, but he held it back. He hadn't forgotten Rex's offer to have Penelope buy him ice cream, regardless of his explanation. It was William's first date ever, a good one all around except for those few tense moments at the softball throw.

"She probably fucked someone," Rex said.

William's fists tightened. "What?"

Rex nodded at the inscription. "Elizabeth. She probably slept with all the priests."

"Priests don't do that," William said.

"Sure they do," Rex said. "They're men, aren't they?"

William touched the cold stone. "Yeah, but then why bury her here?

Why acknowledge it?"

"Maybe she was something else," Rex said. "Like a vampire. Maybe she had to be interred on holy ground."

"The cemetery."

"Nothing's holier than a cathedral," Rex said.

"Maybe there's not even a body in there," William suggested. "Someone carved the name of a girl in the wall, and she was all impressed, and later people thought, *Oh, there's a body there already, we can't use this space.*" He didn't believe it; the block letters were too even, too precise.

"Maybe if you say her name three times in a mirror in the dark," Rex said, lowering his voice, "she'll rise up and give you a kiss."

"And pass along maggots from her mouth? No way."

They found a sanctum, three steps down from one of the inner rooms, in which there were two oversized chairs, a table carrying a leather-bound tome, and a candelabra with three burning candles; the other two had died out, leaving empty arms and a few drippings of wax.

"Someone's been here," William said.

Rex nodded, trailing the flashlight along the walls. It was a narrow and short room, barely big enough for the chairs, and an adult would have to bend down to not scratch his head on the ceiling. Rex was only an inch away himself.

If someone had been there recently enough to light those candles, they might return. William edged toward the door, glancing up and down the darkness of the hall. Without the flashlight, he couldn't see beyond the reach of his hands. At least, if someone came back, they'd have some source of light that would give them away.

Rex, however, stepped fully into the room and opened the book. "It's a Bible."

"You said no one would be here." William tried to raise his voice and whisper simultaneously, and it almost worked.

"I think it's Latin," Rex said. "This isn't Genesis."

Glancing one last time in all directions, William gave in to his curiosity and stepped closer. "What is it, then?"

"Can you read Latin?"

William shook his head.

"Why *do* they make you go to school?"

"You read Latin?"

"No," Rex said, "but I have an excuse. I don't go to school."

One of the candles reached its end. It flared, its flame stretching heavenward, and went out. A wisp of smoke curled from the candelabra.

Rex stared at it a moment, and then looked at William. "Let's go upstairs, shall we?"

"Into the church?" William asked. He didn't know whether to be scared or excited.

14.

The guy in the coat did nothing but watch her.

He sat on the end of the bench, motionless as a statue, eyes trailing Mileah's every move. His coat couldn't quite be called a rainbow, because of the browns and creams and one patch of neon pink, but it was definitely unique. He didn't rock back and forth, adjust his legs, twiddle his thumbs, or even yawn.

It took forever for each minute to pass. Every second took its time. Mileah kept glancing at the big white clock. It was lit from within, with straight black hands and Arabic numerals, nothing exciting or interesting or aesthetic about it, so she tried to envision the Moonstar Clock at home. Its smooth, ivory face and ornate etchings. Roman numerals. A moon moved across the top, every day. It counted every moment with an audible click; the second hand popped into each new position. Like the minute and hour, it was shaped like a musician; tall, straight, pointing its clarinet upwards; the minute, long and slender, played a violin, and the hour had a saxophone.

Yes, thinking of the clock gave her a precious diversion, and the colorful stranger only stared and stared and stared.

Her clock's base ended abruptly, an ornate design that seemed to have been broken off something larger. Its history was lost, like many histories in Midnight. Her family had been influential once, far wealthier than now, and it might have been a gift or a prize. The uneven bottom had never been fixed, so the midnight hour, which should have pointed straight down (up indicated dawn and twilight), instead aimed half a space to its left.

Maybe when her parents died and left the clock to Mileah, she'd have the bottom leveled off.

The man in the coat remained so still, she began to wonder if maybe he wasn't real—a wax figure, perhaps, or a carnival worker. She didn't dare approach it (and *it*, of course, was easier to accept than *him*); she stood near the steps, so if he moved she could ascend quickly.

And go where?

She didn't worry that far ahead. The man stayed still, the minutes passed, and her subway approached, bringing cars emptier than this platform. The sound of metal screeching on metal echoed, the air shifted. She imagined the conductor's electronicized voice announcing, "Next stop, Fairgrounds Station."

The clock said her ten minutes had passed. She'd survived, despite the unmoving stranger. The train rumbled as it neared, the grating sound suddenly so comforting and peaceful.

It rolled to a halt. Doors slid open. Mileah didn't look at her silent companion as she boarded. If luck was on her side, her presence made him too nervous to sleep, and now he'd lay back and relax. She took a seat several yards from the door, though the car was empty, and sat with her back to the platform. She felt his eyes still on her and didn't want to give him the pleasure of her looking back.

The doors slid shut...almost. At the last moment, they bounced open again. Mileah looked toward the front of the train, wanting to keep her eyes averted from the platform. The man in the multicolored coat stood in the doorway, one foot on the platform and one in the train, looking at Mileah, hands in his pockets.

Her breath caught in her throat.

"You oughtn't go," he said, his voice as dry and cracked as the station's concrete walls.

"Carnival's over," she told him, knowing there was no real logic, but also doubting reason would be useful here.

After a pause, in which the doors tried to close again, he said, "I know 'bout your brother."

"Home," Mileah said. "Asleep."

The stranger shook his head and did not smile. "William," he said, "ain't comin' home tonight."

15.

The stairs up from the crypts were just as claustrophobic as those to the towers, without the annoying scribblings of braggarts and idiots seeking immortality with magic markers. With Rex leading, the dark solidified behind William.

In some places, the steps were gravelly or crumbly, eroded by time, and one step was entirely missing; already steep, that was like mountain climbing.

The steps led to a vestibule, which opened onto an apse at the front corner. It was too dark to see the dome above them.

"They sacrificed virgins here," Rex said.

"No way."

"Not the church," Rex said, "but it happened."

The apse was at the end of the hall separating the outer doors from the inner doors; the ceiling was several stories high and the many windows were thin as arrow slits, allowing just enough light to give the shadows texture. There were massive closets out here, and chapels, and somewhere a door opening onto a narrow hall to the church offices.

If Rex turned off the light, William was sure he could stand in the middle of the hall and see neither ceiling nor walls.

However, Rex did not pause. He went straight for one of the pairs of massive wooden doors. They were usually open during the day, closed now, but Rex did not hesitate. He yanked the door by its iron grip; the door resisted and protested, and its hinges creaked, but he pulled it open wide enough for them to enter.

Comparatively, the hall they'd just left had been miniscule.

Rows and rows of heavy wooden pews, darkly oiled, faced a glowing altar. One light blazed, hanging on a chandelier and pointing straight down at the golden chalice, book, and doilies behind a wrought iron fence.

"I want that cup," Rex said.

William shook his head. "They lock the altar," he said. "Even during the day."

"Oh, I don't think I'll get it," Rex said. "There are other things I'll get long before I drink from that cup. But I still want it."

"It's a sin," William said.

"Says who?"

Distracted, William couldn't answer. He had never seen the rose windows at night before. They flanked the nave; during the day, they were beautiful, higher than the arched windows displaying Biblical scenes, with lots of blues and reds and the profiles of saints and angels. But in the dark, with moon and stars and streetlights outside, they became luminescent, like halos, like their own little suns. And immediately, William thought everyone had to see these, everyone in the world; such beauty should not be locked away to be witnessed only by bats and mice.

Rex dropped a hand on William's shoulder. "Wonderful, ain't it?"

"I've never..." William had no words to express what he felt, and no capacity to feel it. He was numb.

"Under that one," Rex said, pointing to the window on their right, "they buried St. Lazarus' first bishop. The tomb's out in the open. I've tried to pry it open, but the damn lid won't budge."

"It's solid," William said, not looking down from the window. "They cast the marble to cover his tomb and go into the ground. There's no lid. You'd have to lift the whole thing."

Rex shook his head. "Must weigh a ton."

"See," William said, "I did learn something in school."

Rex laughed.

They walked around the chancel, unable to get to the altar through the iron gate; it rose straight to the ceiling. Inside, bathed by that one light, gold glimmered, gems sparkled in the side of the altar and the chalice, and even the words in the Bible (open, apparently, to one of its last books) glowed.

"They don't know about your door, do they?" William asked.

Rex shrugged. "They don't care," he said. "Visitors stay away on their own."

"Why's that?"

"We're near the fairgrounds," Rex said, "the lair of the Spider Dragon."

Penelope had mentioned that, though William had never heard of it. He wanted to see her again, hold her hand...another kiss...

"Some think it lives in these crypts," Rex said, "but it's not true."

"How do you know?"

"No webs."

Directly behind the altar, on either side, organ pipes rose into the darkness. The ceiling was too high to see, no matter how much light came through the windows, and at night the flues also disappeared. William touched the brass, then tapped on it with a knuckle, creating a tiny, tin echo. Other pipes were made of wood, and maybe copper; William tapped a few, listening to the differences.

"Can you play the organ?" William asked.

Rex shook his head. "It's one of those instruments that requires both of your hands and both your feet, and it's not like I can practice here without making noise."

"It'd be cool," William said.

Rex nodded in agreement, and started down the side aisle toward the rear doors. William followed, a little disappointed, wishing he had his own flashlight. "There's treasure under Midnight," Rex said.

"Oh," William said, rolling his eyes—he'd seen enough of the world underneath Midnight to know it was no place for treasure—"I suppose the Spider Dragon guards it."

"Every family has its treasures," Rex said. "Yours, I'm sure. Even mine."

William thought about it a moment; what treasures did he have? Heirlooms? Grandmother's wedding ring or an original da Vinci? No, it was the Moonstar Clock, in the main hall, which his sister liked so much.

Rex paused, turned, and asked, "Want to see ours?"

16.

Mileah stood. The subway doors tried, again, to close, bounced off the man's patchwork coat, and a proximity alarm began to buzz.

If he hadn't known William's name, she might have— *would* have— ignored him. "What'd you do to him?"

The stranger shook his head once and stepped out of the subway.

The doors started to close.

Mileah rushed toward them, but failed to get her arms between them before they kissed shut. The man looked through the plastic windows, again unmoving, his eyes small and sharp and black. She pounded on the window as the train lurched forward. "Where is he, you bastard!?"

The train pulled out of Fairgrounds Station. Mileah glared at the stranger for as long as she could, unable to see much but concrete, empty benches, and red advertisements on the walls. The tunnel was mostly dark; they passed an occasional light on the wall. When the tunnel receded, they were in a vast, wide cave of cement and steel; a distant light revealed a subway moving in the opposite direction. Then they were enclosed by a tunnel again, and slowing for the next stop. The conductor's voice came over the loudspeaker: "Paladin Court. Paladin Court."

Mileah got out. The ride had been all of a minute, maybe two, not too far to walk, even in the dark. Since she'd seen a passing train on the other track, she didn't want to risk waiting for another. It couldn't be more than a five minute walk; the train never moved that fast.

She'd have to be careful, especially in the darker parts of the tunnel.

But a walkway hugged the wall, at least part way out, and she'd stay on that. The patchwork coated stranger hadn't moved much while she was there; now that he wanted her back, she didn't expect him to leave.

She wasn't really prepared for exploring the Metro system. The darkness was absolute in places, broken only by passing trains; she had no flashlight, no torch, no matches, not even her camera.

But Mileah did not hesitate.

She jogged around the side of the staircase, pausing to climb a waist-high security bar. On the other side, it was remarkably darker. Since she was past the platform, there wasn't two feet between wall and ledge, and a four foot drop to the tracks.

She passed a couple of recessed doors, a post with a red and green light (the red glowed dimly), and reached a ladder at the end of the walkway. She climbed down, glad she hadn't worn a dress and heels to the carnival—which, of course, would have been as foolish as traipsing through these tunnels in the hours before dawn, when who-knew-what lurked around every corner and beyond every pool of light.

She felt the subways' vibrations through the ground, though she heard no trains here. She passed one of the high wall lights, a bare bulb behind a steel mesh cage.

The floor wasn't as littered as she'd expected. No rats ran across her feet, at least not yet, and she didn't trip over discarded refuse or bodies. If not for her feet slapping the ground, quietly as sneakers were wont to do, there would have no sounds at all.

Maybe her heartbeat—but she didn't hear that so much as feel it trying to break out of her chest.

If he'd done anything to William...Mileah wasn't sure what she'd do, but it'd be mean. Nasty. She'd kick ass. Take names. She'd tear another hole in that coat, one that would never be patched. No more colors for that vagabond. No more nighttime wanderings. The thoughts made her tense.

She emerged from the tunnel and entered that wide, open area, where parallel tracks lay as far as she could see, though that wasn't far. The light she'd seen from the train still shone, way off in the distant gloom.

The ceiling here was higher, a labyrinthine network of thick pipes and cables, ventilation shafts, and support beams. Mileah didn't examine them, but slowed because of how little she could see. If she lost these tracks and accidentally followed the wrong set, she might find City

Hall before she realized she'd gotten lost.

A dripping sound echoed from nearby, soft and light, consistent and annoying.

Mileah walked around a signpost. The words were too high to read, designed to be seen from the trains.

She heard fluttering, like the wings of owls or butterflies, something quiet that should not normally be heard.

Bats.

She was sure of it.

Positive.

The noise came closer, as well as something that sounded like rushing wind. Sweat trickled into her eye, burning. She wiped it away quickly, blinking, pausing...and someone coughed.

17.

The variations in the tunnels surprised William. He expected everything underground to be identical, one long series of those old apartments and hallways leading to other crypts.

Instead, they passed basements, where doors were labeled with names he recognized from the streets (*The Poppery*, where they made popcorn, and *Old Possum's Kitty Supplies*, which Rex insisted was a whorehouse).

They passed an aqueduct, a huge hall stretching as far and wide as a coliseum, and filled with narrow walkways and manmade rivers atop stone columns. It smelled awful, like someone had died and been shoved in the closet, forgotten, with a half ton of feces. Rusting chain link fences guarded one side of the bridge they crossed; if William leaned on it, he'd fall into the vat of sewage below

"This is how it leaves the city," Rex said, after they left the hall.

"How does water come in?" William asked.

"Looks the same," Rex said. "Doesn't smell as bad."

William had no idea how long they'd been walking. He should've been home, he knew, sleeping, with his sister in her basement lab and their parents expected home by twilight. As long as he got home before them, he figured he was okay. There was no school, no one expected him anywhere—though he should call Penelope. It was a law or something; if he called too early, she'd have complete control over him for the rest of their lives, but if he called too late she'd never speak to him again. He didn't understand, had never dealt with it before, but it was common knowledge.

He didn't feel in danger, like he might if he was by himself. Rex seemed to know where he was going, and which corridors to avoid (like the one under the asylum; Rex said he had a key to it, but never carried it and intended to never use it again).

And there were treasures.

Sure, most belonged to *someone.* "Can we get into the museum?" William asked.

Having descended a long flight of stairs, they'd reached a series of intersecting tunnels with solid, heavy looking doors.

"Which museum?"

"Any," William said. "They only put maybe a tenth of their collections on exhibit."

"There's a reason for that, I'm sure," Rex said.

They were descending again, in a sloped corridor. Each area seemed to be its own community, despite that William never saw anyone. He heard things, usually behind doors or from the dark, but nothing close or threatening. Some tunnels, like this one, linked underground neighborhoods just as main thoroughfares connected sections of the city.

The walls here were ridged and segmented, almost as if they passed through the skeleton of a giant worm. The pieces had been placed like buttresses, climbing the walls and connecting in the arched ceiling. The air was damp, cold, and still. If he didn't know better, William might have believed there were human bones in the walls.

But he knew better. He was sure of it. Even cemeteries only buried their dead six feet.

They turned a corner, where recesses were carved on both sides of the bony walls, one above another, each high and long enough for a person to lay inside. The first few were empty, but the next was occupied by a skeleton.

Tattered clothes hung on the bones. His hands were crossed over his chest, and it looked like his fingers had once curled around something. Now, they seemed brittle, like dust.

The next set had a skeleton in each. One had been overturned. The other had been ravaged, removed once and shoved back in, a pile of bones, the skull looking out from the middle, a hole at its top that shouldn't be there.

"We're in the catacombs," William realized. "I didn't know they really existed."

"We're almost home," Rex said.

"I heard they know nothing about who's buried here," William said, "that these bones are older than the city."

"There were cities, here at Midnight, before Midnight," Rex told him.

"Yeah, but I didn't believe it."

"You don't believe a lot of things."

"Of course I do," William said.

"You believe in magic?"

"Who doesn't?"

"How about Destiny?"

"Destiny," William said, "is ours to make."

"You *do* read," Rex said. "But that doesn't mean you understand."

"Hey."

Rex laughed. "I think destiny is unavoidable," he said, "like a test, and what matters is what we do when we reach it. Tonight, our meeting like we did, don't you think that was destiny?"

"How so?"

"That we have so much in common," Rex said, "and also so little, and yet how fast we've become best of friends."

It was apparently William's time for making friends; Penelope and Rex—maybe more kids at school when he got back. He'd played with others when he was young, real young, but even at five he knew he was different. His mom said it was because of his destiny, but William never gave it much thought.

"Destiny," Rex said, "that the founders should settle Midnight right here, over these catacombs, where some civilization a thousand years ago settled. That's more than coincidence, don't you think?"

"Because of the water," William said. "Makes sense to me."

Rex shook his head. "No it doesn't, not really. Look around. We're in a city surrounded by mountains. Isolated. There's a world out there, somewhere, but have you ever seen it? Heard about it?"

"Of course I have," William lied.

"You're making that up."

"Everyone knows there's other places," William said. "People come here all the time."

"Yeah?" Rex asked. "Who leaves?"

William didn't know of anyone who had left.

"Midnight should be inhospitable," Rex said. "My family lived in the mountains, before we came back here, and there was sunlight up there. Dazzling and bright and so overpowering, you can't even imagine it. And snow, everywhere, when you get high enough, all year round, and you can touch trees that, here, you only have pictures of."

After a moment, William asked, "Then why'd you come back?"

Rex shrugged. "No one leaves Midnight. Not for long."

In most of the graves, the skeletons laid undisturbed, though some had been vandalized and a few were missing. Ahead, skulls lined the arched doorway, hundreds of them. It was a lot like entering the carnival under the clown's teeth, except the skulls were real, somehow more sentient, possibly aware of who passed through them.

Safely beyond that doorway, and apparently out of the catacombs, William said, "Who would want to leave Midnight, anyhow?"

"Some people are driven out."

"How?" William asked. "Why?"

"Maybe they were criminals," Rex said. "Or maybe someone convinced the city they were criminals."

"Like they were framed?"

"Exactly. Happened, still happens, all the time."

Then Rex stopped, in front of a door William might have missed, camouflaged perfectly by age and neglect. He took a key from one of his pockets and said, "Scenic tour's over. This is where I live."

He unlocked the door, leaned on it to push it open, and flipped a switch.

There wasn't much light, nor much to brighten. Rex turned off the flashlight and left it on a little table next to the door. There were two chairs, old and wooden, a table, a fire pit surrounded by rocks, and several black pots and pans around it. There was one bookshelf, filled and double-stacked, atop which was an ornately designed box.

"My home," Rex said, forcing the door shut behind him, "and our family treasure." He nodded toward the shelf.

William approached it, interested in the books but more intrigued by the box. It seemed to have been broken at the top, its intricate ironwork snapped but not twisted, as if waiting for its other half to be returned. Celestial etchings covered it, stars and comets and various phases of the moon, and the centerpiece represented a sunburst — something he'd only ever seen in pictures. The rays seemed to stretch an inch or two in all directions—no, twelve directions, like on a clock. The upward pointing beam was broken.

"It looks familiar," William said after a moment. "I've seen something like it."

"The ironwork," Rex said. "There was a famous clockmaker, Tiernan, a hundred years ago, commissioned by the Mayor to make something extravagant for the city, something powerfully magical. He did a wonderful job, don't you think?"

William shook his head. "This isn't a clock."

"Not the whole thing, no," Rex told him. "It was broken and stolen. There were three pieces, scattered among the more *influential* families of the day. They were so afraid of one person having that much power, they put out the clockmaker's eyes so he couldn't build another, destroyed all records and plans, and at great cost broke the clock and its magic."

"At great cost?" William asked.

"There was a massive storm," Rex said. "Lightning set off a fire. One-quarter of Midnight burned in 1902. They teach that much in your history classes, don't they?"

William nodded. "Not the clock, no, but the storm and the fire, yes. Hundreds dead, thousands homeless. It took decades to recover."

"Longer," Rex said.

"So this is one of those pieces?" William asked. He didn't have to ask; his parents had inherited a clock, passed down through generations, and he knew it was part of this marvelous sculpture.

"No," Rex said. "Two pieces, fused together. There's only one piece left before we can return to our rightful place in Midnight."

"One?"

Rex nodded. "We had to steal back these pieces," Rex said. "My father's father's father, or something like that, he was the clockmaker. Blinded, and forced to live the rest of his days as a beggar, and when his sons thought to have revenge, they were cast out of Midnight. And that, William, is when we learned there's no place else to go. We can't leave."

"That was a long time ago," William said.

"Very long," Rex agreed. "None of it matters anymore, does it?"

"No," William said.

"Of course not. Come on, my room's over here."

There were three doorways off this main room, but no doors. All the rooms were dark. William followed Rex into the leftmost room, where

Rex cracked open a glow stick. It gave off a blue halo, warmer and more comforting than the flashlight, but William felt decidedly uneasy now. Did Rex know who had the third piece of the clock? Was that why Rex found him at the carnival and then again on the subway platform? No coincidence, as Rex would say, but not destiny either; had their meeting been orchestrated?

Rex's small room contained a stack of books, some thick and old, and a bedroll. Nothing else, not even a lamp.

"This is it," Rex said. "I've been sleeping here since we came back."

"How long ago was that?" William asked.

"Long enough." Rex glanced at his wristwatch. "Better get you back to the surface. Your parents will be home soon, won't they, and what will they think if you're not sound asleep in bed? And that Penelope girl, you'll be wanting to call her. I would." That grin reappeared, the nasty wicked one William found so unsettling.

Rex grabbed the flashlight on their way out and locked the door behind them. William noted the number on the side of the "apartment," barely visible even in the light of the glow stick. *1970.* It might be important to remember that.

They walked in silence, taking many twists and turns, climbing one long set of stairs before William's curiosity pushed to the surface. "What kind of magic?"

"Powerful magic," Rex said. "Strength and riches and secrets. The clockmaker put a lot more into it than just what they asked, more than they ever knew. It can kill, and heal, and it can bring the dead back to life."

"No way."

"I thought you believed in magic," Rex said.

"Death is death," William said. "The end, fini, fat lady's done with her singing."

They followed the curve of the corridor and ended at a small room with a well in the center. A rustling sound came from within.

Rex leaned over the edge. There was a ladder in the side of the wall, reaching down as far as the glow stick illuminated.

"We have to go down there?" William asked.

"It's not *too* deep," Rex said, "but it's the quickest way."

The shaft went straight down, an abyss without end, the threads of spider webs so thick and multi-layered they hid the darkness.

Rex dropped the glow stick. It broke through some web, tumbled and bounced, and then remained still, caught, doubling the visible depth and highlighting things trapped in those webs.

It took a moment for William to recognize them. "More bones." The ladder went down five rungs, but no further.

Rex didn't even look at William. "Yep."

Then he pushed William in.

18.

Mileah paused.

Only for a moment. She didn't want to give anyone—whoever was with her, in the dark—any reason to think she knew she wasn't alone.

Was she being followed, or had she stumbled upon someone?

It was possible, but only barely, that the cough came from someone who didn't know she was there. Possible—but unlikely. If you lived in the dark, you developed senses for it. Her own night vision was rather acute, developed in the darkroom.

She glanced around, moving only her eyes, unable to make out more than tracks and columns.

She pressed forward, sure she'd gone more than halfway through the open area. Light up ahead indicated the tunnel. She could make it.

Cough.

Ahead of her. This time, she stopped. Two people—or one, moving like she was? If she waited, maybe the next cough would be further up the tracks.

Clink. Metal hitting metal, a pipe casually tapped on one of the rails, off to her right.

Two, at least, maybe three. More? Was this some sort of street gang, or vagabonds just passing through? She tried to focus on the not-so-negative options, like old men meandering alone in the dark, not seeing her and not caring if they did.

She tried, but it felt wrong.

Whispers. Furtive, quiet, too soft for Mileah to hear.

Then, on her left, they laughed.

She could almost see their silhouettes, black on a darker black, a deep canvas through which they danced around her in a perversion of ancient ceremonies. Maybe gypsies, but Mileah didn't think they lived in the city.

One said a word, sharp and clear though still under his breath, and Mileah's heart skipped a beat. "Warde." There was no mistaking it, and no one could have guessed at a whim. Almost a million people lived in Midnight; only a handful shared her name.

She sprinted forward, sticking close to the tracks, swerving to avoid the man ahead of her.

There were three, at least, she was sure of that now. One followed on her right, pacing her, mocking. The others chased, laughing.

A thousand feet or miles, the tunnel was too far away. She saw its light clearly. It offered no sanctuary.

The guy on her right started making monkey sounds, jumping as he ran, swinging his arms, more visible with every step.

Someone tapped her shoulder. She hunched to the left, trying to duck. He fell behind, laughing. Another slammed into her from the right. She stumbled away from him, lost her balance, and tripped over the next set of tracks. She crashed into the floor, scraping palms and knees, kicking up dirt and finding concrete underneath.

One of her pursuers leapt over Mileah and straddled her.

He spun her onto her back and grabbed fistfuls of shirt under her collarbones. He jerked her head up, to an angle from which she had no leverage. She pounded on his arms, without effect.

He bent so close, his sour breath rushed over her in heavy waves. "Warde," he said, spitting out her name like bad wine.

"Let's take her home," one said.

"You don't belong under the city," the guy above her said. "Stupid girl."

"Yeah, stupid," the other said.

"But I think..." He paused, purely as a demonstration of power. "This might just be your lucky night. See, it's not you we want."

"Of course it is," the other said, much closer than before.

"You have something that doesn't belong to you. It's mine. Ours. We want it back."

"Yeah, yeah!"

"And," he added, dropping her head so it cracked against the hard floor, "we're willing to trade for it. For your brother."

19.

William fell through the webs, dragging the sticky stuff and resident spiders to the bottom. The strands were so thick in places, they actually slowed his fall, so no bones shattered when William hit the bottom.

The glow stick clattered next to him, illuminating four metal walls and a matching floor. The sides went straight up, tapering at the top to form the well.

The beam of a flashlight shined down at him. "Oops," Rex called down. "Don't worry, I'll come back. It's just an abandoned gas tank."

"Worry?" William said. "You pushed me!"

"Yes," Rex said. "Yes I did." And nothing else. The flashlight vanished.

William checked the walls and ground, but everything was smooth, without doors or latches, and the ladder rungs only lined the very top of the well. It was like a giant cauldron, and still smelled faintly of fuel.

Spiders were everywhere and all over him. He wiped away as many as he could, and lifted layers of web out of his hair and clothes. His shoulder ached where he'd landed on it. Tears gathered in his eyes, but he did not cry. Somewhere in the back of his mind, he preferred that it was Rex who betrayed him; the only other person who could was Penelope.

Sitting in the dark, he tried to picture her face.

Eventually, the glow stick started to dim.

20.

"We've been away for a while," one of the men said.

"Our knives are old," another said.

"Rusty." A third.

"Not real sharp." That was a woman's voice.

"And we'll use them," the one holding Mileah by the scruff of her shirt said, "unless you return it."

"Trade," the woman said.

"We don't *want* your brother. Though you...you look delicious..." Someone slapped him; Mileah heard the swat and the man's grunt afterwards.

"We don't want you, either," the man holding her said.

"I don't know what you do want," Mileah said.

He laughed. "What could we possibly mean, little Warde girl? The Moonstar Clock."

"*Our* clock," the woman said.

Two or three of them laughed.

"We don't need trouble," the man holding her said. "We don't even need revenge, not really. We just want what's ours."

"Why is it yours?" Mileah asked.

He slapped her, hard, smacking the back of her head on the cement ground. Then, with the one hand still holding a wad of her shirt, he yanked Mileah to her feet. He steadied her, not gently, and shoved her toward the tunnel. "You have until dawn."

"That's not a lot of time."

"Our blades are dull," he told her.

"Painful," the woman added.

"And we'll start carving the Warde boy at dawn."

"So go," the woman said.

"Yes, go, go, go!" one said, jumping up and down beside her. He pushed her, hard, toward the tunnel.

Mileah ran for the light.

They laughed around her, running alongside until she reached the first sphere of dim light at the very beginning of the tunnel. She didn't know who they were, why they wanted her parents' clock so badly, or what they really planned to do to William.

Did she have time to get the police? Maybe. But she doubted that would help. No hostage negotiations; that had been mentioned several times on the news. And this was different. This wasn't some random drive-by-and-grab, or a ransom of millions, but rather small and simple. A clock, a *broken* clock, something that didn't yet belong to Mileah but would eventually. It wasn't valuable, just an heirloom, something passed down through generations. It was at least a hundred years old.

Which meant, of course, they were crazy; there was no way the Moonstar Clock had belonged to them.

But if that's what they wanted for the safe return of her brother?

She didn't really know they had her brother. It could be a bluff. Or the lie might be the assertion that they'd trade. What if after taking the clock they simply killed Mileah? William might already be dead, or someplace else entirely.

The long tunnel eventually brought her to the platform. There was no indication of a train from either direction. She climbed to the main level and finally reached Fairgrounds Station.

The man in the patchwork jacket still sat at his bench, watching her approach. His lips were so thin and cracked, his grin was a scar across his face.

Reaching him, she stopped. "Who are they?"

He said nothing for so long, Mileah didn't think he'd ever answer, and she didn't have time to force the issue. But as she began to walk away, he said, "Rourke."

Mileah stopped. She recognized the name, not from history or school, but from legends. "The exiles?"

The man shrugged, almost imperceptibly, and said nothing more.

21.

The year was 1902. The summer had been long and hot, and unusually bright. That much was reported in the newspapers. A fire in August had burned a chunk of the city, killing some four hundred people—mostly poor families living in tenements, which were never rebuilt but replaced with more "modern" apartments. Thousands were hospitalized, many for smoke inhalation and some for burns, but most for bones broken during the crush of people trying to escape.

The fire swept through Midnight like a nightmare, a wall of flames consuming everything in its path. Fortunately, that path included none of the museums; it left the Historical Society standing, and City Hall, the opera house, the churches...anything of historical or architectural importance survived.

There, the newspaper stopped, and the legends began.

You couldn't kill hundreds of innocent people and not blame someone. After the smoke cleared, but before the ash was removed, blame fell on a man named Charles Rourke. His family had been more influential in the past, and wealthier, but had fallen on hard times after the death of a worker in one of their factories. In response, someone (they never determined who) set fire to the factory, in 1898 (again, a story Mileah could verify in the library).

Nothing was saved. Not even Charles Rourke's wife and infant son.

Revenge was, of course, the motive. A mob drove Rourke and his surviving family—an elderly blind father, two sons, and a daughter— beyond the city limits. No arrest. No trial. No murder. But they were told never to return, under penalty of death, neither them nor their descendants.

The penalty was included in the penal codes.

The story of their exile appeared in no history books and no official records. Instead, it was passed down, every year, in the schoolyard.

Two of the Rourkes returned some years later. They killed one of the city councilmen while ransacking his house. One, Thomas Rourke, was caught and hanged. A thousand people attended his public execution. They didn't care so much about him as his father, the arsonist, who had destroyed so many lives, and maybe he wouldn't have been put to death otherwise.

Thomas Rourke, too, appeared in the papers; his pictures were on the cover of the *Midnight Sun* the next day, one before the hanging and one after. The headline read *Justice.*

Other stories were credited to the Rourkes. When children disappeared at night, even those who probably ran away, whispers suggested they'd been taken by Rourkes who still lived in the mountains with gypsies and animals. Unsolved murders were, sometimes elaborately, linked to the Rourkes. They became like the boogeyman and the Tooth Fairy, a story, a *legend,* told to keep young kids in line: "Eat all your veggies, or the Rourkes may come out tonight," or "If you're not good, we'll send you to live with the Rourkes."

The stories persisted, warping and shifting, so that any and all of it might have been true, but probably only the part about Thomas Rourke. And even the newspaper reports might have been exaggerated.

Mileah hadn't believed in the Rourkes any more than she believed in love at first sight. Until tonight.

22.

Eventually, the next train arrived. The man nodded, moving his head almost a full inch, as Mileah boarded. This time, they watched each other. The doors slid shut. The subway lurched and moved. As it pulled out of the station, the man lifted himself off the bench.

Then Mileah was in darkness.

She hoped the train would catch one or two of the Rourkes, smash them, split them apart, whatever speeding Metro cars did to a human body.

She thought she saw them out there, in the darkness, watching the train with anticipation and hunger.

Those were the longest thirty minutes Mileah had ever spent in a train.

She relived the events in the tunnels, seeing her assailants better, watching from different vantage points, right, left, above. What could she have done differently?

Staying on the train, that's what.

Then she'd never see William again. Though she sometimes wished for just such a thing, she couldn't possibly be a party to it. It was unthinkable. Daytime fantasies never involved him dying so much as his simply not living, as if never born, and momentary death wishes between siblings were normal.

If she didn't go to the cops, her parents would be pissed. How was she going to explain the clock?

But if she said the name *Rourke* to anyone, they'd laugh, or take her to the asylum in a white jacket and remove her shoelaces, just in case. She didn't have to name them; how trustworthy was the average vagabond hanging around a Metro station so late at night, anyhow?

When the train finally pulled into her station, she paused only long enough to glance at the boring white clock, and suddenly she didn't want to give up hers. The Moonstar Clock was unique, a piece of art, functional and beautiful and engaging.

Damn it, it was almost six already. She didn't have time. Dawn was coming. The trains were filling up. How was she going to hop off the platform, in full sight of all the morning commuters, with that heavy clock?

She'd manage. She had to. Otherwise, they'd kill William, and then her parents would kill her.

If they didn't kill her first.

Why didn't they just steal the clock from the house? Why make her get it? Why take William at all? They were alone for the weekend.

Maybe they didn't want to get caught. No fingerprints. No chance of stumbling upon an enraged, shotgun-wielding father. No repeat of the public hanging ninety-some years ago. Better to let Mileah take the risks and reap their rewards in comfort—assuming they considered the subway tunnels comfortable.

She hopped up the stoop, inserted the key, and shoved her way inside.

No one was home.

Just to be certain, she ran upstairs and checked William's room. He should've returned hours ago, and found his way to bed. But the door was open, the sheets undisturbed.

Dawn was an eerie time in Midnight. High above, the mountaintops glowed; that light penetrated the city with a red tint and never got any brighter than a desk lamp. Twilight was similar, a time when colors were saturated and angles sharpened. Neither flash lasted much longer than ten or fifteen minutes.

Dawn approached without prejudice.

Mileah stuffed the clock into a duffel bag. It was heavy, but not so she couldn't carry it. She thought again about phoning the police. *They want to trade my clock for my brother.* But she felt this was something *she* had to do, something personal. The Rourkes had claimed the clock was rightfully theirs. She didn't believe it, but would worry about retrieving the clock after getting her brother back. He was more important, wasn't he?

She heard the clock's mechanisms through the bag.

Outside, down the steps, to the Metro station and into the subway, Mileah tried not to look as guilty as she felt. *Thief,* she kept telling herself. *But how can I steal from myself?*

As the subway started to roll, she sat with the bag between her feet. Somehow, the clock seemed bigger, more important, than it ever had in her house, like it had kept secrets she'd never have a chance to discover.

Someone sat across from her, and spoke with a rough, low voice. "Whatever sin you're thinking of committing," he said, "I cannot allow it."

She looked up into the face of the Wandering Reverend.

23.

William sat for a long time. He'd wiped most of the spider webs away but couldn't shed the stickiness. He swatted at over a dozen spiders on his arms and legs, but more than half were imagined.

He called up to Rex several times.

No response.

He tried reaching the bottom rung of the ladder, but fell short at least two feet when he jumped. Even Rex wouldn't be able to reach it.

There were no doors. He tapped on the sides; everything sounded hollow and tinny. He stomped on the floor, hurting his feet more than the metal tank.

The glow stick continued to dim.

He flung another spider off his hand (and wished one bite would transform him into a superhero), but his worst fear was elsewhere. He heard the scampering of heavy legs, an arachnid perhaps as large as him. When the little spiders told the Spider Dragon what William had done—trespassing, destroying their intricate works, squashing their brothers and cousins—it would be angry. And vicious.

Penelope had told him about the Spider Dragon; he had never heard of it before tonight. Then Rex had mentioned it, two people who had nothing to do with each other, entirely different sources of information—enough to write a news article.

Therefore, it was true. Real. The Spider Dragon lived in these tunnels, crawling uncontrolled and undeterred, seeking meals just William's size.

He jumped again and again, slapping his sweaty palm on the side of the tank's mouth but unable to reach that rung.

One more jump, and he gave up. That wasn't the answer.

Then what was?

There was only one way out of this gas tank, and his light was fading fast. *Think*, he told himself. *Think, think, think*. As if such commands worked.

And as if by magic, they did. He looked up, at the rungs of that ladder, slivers of iron protruding perhaps three inches from the wall. If they had rusted...

William shook the thought away, and pulled down his jeans.

24.

Mileah stared for a moment at the Wandering Reverend's dark brown eyes (she wasn't about to call him Joshua, not even in her mind). He leaned back in his seat, hands on his knees, the epitome of serenity, in direct opposition to words she couldn't believe she'd just heard.

Calmly, he shook his head, and turned his eyes down at the bag between Mileah's feet. "That's too important."

"You don't know what you're talking about."

"Don't I?" He glanced to the right and left; apparently satisfied no one was close enough to hear, he leaned closer and lowered his voice. "You carry a part of the Moonstar Clock that has been protected by your family for over one hundred years, and you intend to give it to the very people from whom you're supposed to keep it."

Mileah ignored the parts she didn't understand. "They have my brother."

The Wandering Reverend closed his eyes. Nodding, he leaned back again. "There are greater sins than loyalty," he said. "But do you think this will help get him back?"

"They said they wanted a trade." It sounded as ridiculous as Mileah had expected; she was relieved she hadn't called the police. She sounded off-balance, and certainly she needed sleep, but she didn't have six hours to spend in bed. "Dawn," she told the Reverend. "I have until dawn."

He shook his head. "Dawn is upon us, a new day, however brief."

"I ran as fast as I could," Mileah said. "It's heavy."

"The burden?" the Wandering Reverend asked. "Or the clock?"

"What's so special about it?" Mileah asked, angry. "It's just a clock."

"Hush," he said. "No need to attract attention. It's a difficult enough situation as it is. You should have gone to the police."

"And tell them what?" She didn't wait for an answer. "They didn't give me enough time to get home and back, and then..." She fished the photograph out of her pocket, unfolded it, and thrust it at him. "What in hell is this?"

The color in his face turned ten degrees lighter as he took the picture and examined it. "My life you stole."

"I stole nothing."

"Your intention is not the issue," he said. He refolded it and handed it back. "The thing in that picture is dead."

"The *thing*?" Mileah asked.

"The Spider Dragon."

Mileah nodded. "I bet that's supposed to make sense."

"I can tell you all about it another time. Presently, I am here to prevent you from making a mistake that will cost far more than the life of your brother."

"Tell me, then," Mileah said. "What will it cost?"

"There's magic in that clock," he said.

She believed him. She waited a moment, expecting him to continue. When he didn't, she said, "It's never done anything that I've seen."

"You've never seen it whole."

"So?"

"You don't ever want to see it whole," the Wandering Reverend said. "*The earth will tremble, blood will fall from above, fears thought dead will rise from the depths.*"

"That's not from the Bible."

"I work from other books."

The train had stopped several times as they spoke, but no one came close enough to hear their conversation. As they rolled away from this station, the conductor's voice over the intercom said, "Next stop, Paladin Court."

"You have one stop to convince me," Mileah said, "or I go trade for my brother."

"You must, of course, do what you feel is right," the Wandering Reverend said. "Sacrifice generations of caution, or turn around and go home. Either way, your brother is lost to you. Choose the former, and you will also be lost."

He looked down, either sad or contemplative, perhaps calculating the effort and risk in snatching the bag with her clock and making a run for it at the next station.

The train slowed to a halt. "Paladin Court."

Mileah rose and picked up the bag. "If there's a chance," she said, "I'll get him back."

25.

On the first try, William missed completely.

He held one leg of his jeans tight in one hand. Ignoring the spiders (and who knew what else) crawling all around him, he flung the other leg, trying to loop it through the ladder.

The second try, he hit the rung, and the pants fell back in his face.

Third, fourth, fifth tries all failed. The sixth slid through the three inch opening. William jumped, but couldn't reach the bottom of that leg before the jeans slid out and he had to try again.

He could keep trying as long as there was light, but the glow stick probably had only a few minutes left and barely emitted enough light to aim.

Three more tries failed.

He tried a different approach, throwing the top of the jeans up, hoping the extra weight might pull more easily through the rung, but there wasn't enough length to go through that opening.

Finally, he threw the jeans into the air. If they caught, but were too high, he'd be stuck in his underwear.

They fell. A second attempt, however, did not.

For a moment, William feared he couldn't reach his jeans. Rex would come back, shine a light into the utter darkness of the gas tank, and find an embarrassed William trying to hide in the shadows and avoid the spiders.

He jumped, managed to grab both dangling ends of his pants, and hung from the ladder.

He would've leapt for joy, but was already in the air—and now faced the hard part.

He pulled himself up as best he could, an inch at a time, wishing he'd been better at the rope climbs in gym class. He had to make sure he held both legs of the pants or he'd drop. He used every muscle, every ounce of will, and earned a thick sweat. His fear now was that the denim would rip, he'd fall, and be left without any second chance.

Dangling, he grabbed the lower rung first with his left hand, then his right. It was tougher, climbing the ladder, since he couldn't ascend an inch or two at a time but had to reach high enough to catch the next rung.

He wasn't strong enough for this.

He thought of Penelope, how she'd feel if he allowed himself to die in this pit, never calling her at all. Too-early would slip into the perfect time, then to too-late, and finally into whatever-happened-to-him. *His bones rotted in the belly of the spider dragon*, he thought, hanging by strength he didn't really have.

After reaching the second rung, he pulled his jeans free and wrapped them around his neck. Whether he reached the top or fell, he didn't want to spend the rest of his life in underwear.

The third rung was hardest, because his thighs banged against the wall and the bottom rung, but he was still too low to get his feet up.

He had counted five. He looked up, saw nothing above the next rung, and reached for it. His hands were slippery with sweat, but he wasn't willing to fall. He'd already done that once. It hadn't hurt too much, but he'd gotten lucky. What if he twisted an ankle? Then he couldn't try again. He'd have to wait either for Rex or the spider dragon.

He reached the fourth rung and managed to swing his foot onto the bottom. The rest of the climb was easy, comparatively, but still slow. Above the fifth rung, there was nothing else to grab except the lip of the well, and he had to pull himself over the edge. He dropped, panting, to the floor next to the gas tank.

He'd left the dying glow stick at the bottom of that pit; none of its light reached him. Only now, in the dark, did William wonder if Rex was waiting for him.

He looked around, but saw nothing.

His jeans were ripped, at the bottom of the legs, nothing to worry about. He pulled them back on, and wondered what to do next. He didn't want to speak, didn't want to reveal himself to Rex or anyone else—assuming they weren't already aware of him. He hoped his eyes would adjust to the absolute darkness, but doubted it. Looking down into the tank, he watched the glow stick finally wink out.

Taking tiny steps, William found the wall and walked alongside it until he reached the doorway. He remembered the corridor had been curved, intersecting another passageway not too far away. He wouldn't know which way to go, and would probably find himself deeper and deeper under the city, lost, wandering in the dark until he went mad—unless the spider dragon found him first.

Out of the tank, William had nowhere to go.

26.

Mileah walked calmly down the platform as the train pulled out of the Metro station. She glanced at the clock but didn't notice the time; rather, she checked the reflection in its glass to see if the Wandering Reverend had followed her off the train.

He had.

There weren't too many people out yet. It was early for a Saturday; the crowds were on their way, but they'd pay little attention to her, either lost in their own little worlds or not yet awake. Unless there were police or security officers, she ought to be able to walk off the platform, through the tunnel, and to the Rourkes.

She dreaded the meeting.

The Wandering Reverend was right, of course; they were as likely to kill her as not, and if they had her brother she'd never see him again.

Mileah walked around the stairs unnoticed, and looked over her shoulder only after going halfway to the end.

No one. Not even the Wandering Reverend. Damn him. She was confused now, and worried.

The bag grew heavier as she traveled, or her shoulders wearied. She didn't want to believe the clock performed magic; she'd never seen it do anything except tell the time—and even that had been slightly askew on its uneven base.

She climbed down the ladder and set out for the depths of darkness. They were there, ahead of her; she couldn't quite see or hear them, but she felt their presence, their eyes, their stench. They smelled of mountains, of exile and desperation, even through their pungent, unwashed stink.

Walking slowly, she gave her eyes some time to adapt.

They were there, silhouettes and shades, three sitting or kneeling, one standing, maybe another hidden, all much closer to the tunnel than earlier. She'd already committed herself, crossed the point of no return, by bringing the clock willingly into their trap.

At the end of the tunnel, before entering the vast chamber connecting so many railroad tracks, Mileah stopped. "Where's my brother?"

One of them laughed. The woman said, "You'll see him soon."

They moved, randomly perhaps, like predators around their wounded prey. Mileah held her ground. Here, within the last bulb's sphere of light, she'd be able to see their faces and, if later necessary or possible, identify them. She set the bag down at her feet. "Get him first."

"Girl," one said, "I don't think you quite understand where you are."

Another laughed. The man who had grabbed her earlier said, "You have our clock."

"*My* clock, yes."

"It was never yours," he told her. "In the old days, thieves had their hands severed, liars their tongues."

Mileah picked up the bag and stepped back. "William," she said.

"Soon enough," he said.

One of the laughing men, the hyenas, suddenly grabbed her arm. She hadn't realized he'd gotten that close. He yanked her forward, away from the light, and snatched the bag.

"Quickly," the woman said, pressing forward.

His hands on Mileah's arm were too tight, cutting circulation; he dragged her further into the dark while another opened the bag and removed the clock.

Even in the dark, its ivory face seemed to glow.

The woman sighed. "Still beautiful."

They put it back in the bag. "C'mon." The grip tightened even more, fingers pressing into Mileah's bones. He dragged her with them, through the darkness of the subways, toward the next tunnel, through a door, and down.

27.

William barely started moving before he heard footsteps.

He backed up as quietly as possibly. A flashlight came into view, scanning the floor as someone approached.

Rex.

William was sure of it. He hadn't gotten to the end of the first curve yet, hadn't made any decision to turn left or right, and now Rex was returning to...to what? Taunt him?

Rex came into the room, looking to neither side as he approached the well. He peered down and shined the flashlight into the tank. "What, did the spider dragon get you already?"

William, pressed against the wall next to the entryway, remained still.

"My dad wants you to see it," Rex said, setting the flashlight down on the edge of the well and uncoiling a rope he had around his shoulder. "If you'd rather stay down there, that's fine. I won't do this again."

He dangled an end of the rope. "Hey, William, you awake down there?" He leaned lower, trying to get a better view. There wasn't much down there to see.

It wouldn't take long for Rex to realize William wasn't in there. He had to act fast. He could flee down the dark corridor, certainly making enough noise to attract attention, and possibly get ten yards before slamming blindly into a wall or being tackled by the bigger boy. Or hide in the shadows and hope Rex didn't cast his beam of light around the room searching for him. Or...

William rushed forward, jumping at the last moment, smashing Rex's back with all his strength and weight and will.

He bounced back, away. Rex toppled over the edge. The flashlight fell off the ledge, not too far from where William fell, and did not even blink.

Rex yelped as he fell, and again when he hit the ground.

William retrieved the flashlight.

"Damn, damn, damn!" Rex yelled, echoing.

William pointed the light into the tank. Rex was sprawled on the ground, his leg twisted oddly beneath him, bone protruding through bloody jeans.

"You fucker!" Rex yelled. "You broke my leg!"

William turned and went down the hall, thankful for the gift of light, but still with no sense of direction.

28.

Mileah had been invited to quite a few parties in her life. Most were basic affairs, someone tapping a keg while the parents were away, birthdays, weddings, but she'd always been free to decline when she had other plans.

Her plans, this moment, had included a darkroom, the thick aroma of developers and finishers, and lots of photographic paper. She would have declined this invitation, and not felt the least bit depressed over it.

The Rourkes dragged her through several twists and turns under the subways. The trains rumbled above them, shaking dust from the ceiling; it clung to her hair and eyes and lips. They had, between them, one flashlight, up at the front, so she saw nothing of their trip except the frenetic movements of that beam, several feet ahead of her.

Of the four, two laughed incessantly.

She could have listened to Joshua—the Wandering Reverend—and left her brother to his fate. Obviously, she'd been in no position to change it, and her own was now the same: death, probably after plenty of humiliation and disgrace.

They banged her against the walls as they moved, a little more quickly than normal walking. The leader, who had grabbed her earlier, whispered excitedly, words Mileah couldn't quite catch.

In a Romance novel, the role of knight would belong to Joshua, with that weird title (who called themselves *Wandering Reverend*, anyhow?) and those steady, intense eyes; he would sweep out of nowhere just before it was too late, defeat the villains with fancy swordplay, and rescue the distressed damsel.

In real life, there were no such heroes. Mileah would have to rescue herself.

But she wasn't sure she'd be able to get back to the subway platform by herself.

The leader used a key to open a door, and they brought Mileah into a crummy, dingy, deathly room, in which they had two decrepit chairs and a bookshelf. A fire burned in a pit at the center.

In the firelight, she saw the features of her kidnappers better: weather-roughened skin, wrinkles, unkempt hair, eyes wild as the wind. Her attention was diverted to the intricate sculpture on top of the bookshelf, the only hint of aestheticism visible. There were stars and comets, even a sunburst, and it was obviously missing a piece. Not just any piece: the Moonstar Clock.

"Okay, you've got it," Mileah said. "Now let me go."

Laughter.

The leader opened her bag and withdrew the clock face. If there had been any doubt before, there was none now. The arcs and angles coincided precisely, fashioned by a single hand, and maybe now midnight hour would point properly downward.

"Where's that boy?" the woman asked.

"William?" Mileah asked.

"Shut her up."

One of the hyenas yanked her backwards, off her feet. Clutching her tightly her, he leaned close to her ear and whispered, "You're a pretty one. I'm gonna like you."

"He'll be along," the leader said. He turned to Mileah. "I thought you should see this. You've been keeping our treasure so long, you ought to witness the why of it all."

"I don't know what you're talking about."

"Our clock." He shuddered, as if in ecstasy. "Finally. My grandfather never saw any of it. Not even the first piece. We didn't get that until the 60s. They were well hidden, but secrets have a way of...being discovered."

"I have no secrets for you," Mileah told him.

"No," he agreed. "You don't."

29.

William tried to backtrack as best he could, but tracing his steps all the way back to Fairground's Station was impossible. With luck, he might find St. Lazarus' again, but he didn't even think he'd manage to return to Rex's home.

Not that he wanted to.

He couldn't tell if these were the same corridors he'd used earlier.

He shined the flashlight on the wall next to one of the doors, searching for the apartment number. The etched symbols were barely legible.

"1932," he mumbled, managing to make it out.

Rex had lived in 1970. He remembered that.

If these were like the first set of apartments he'd seen, there ought to be a stairway leading straight up to the Metro.

He was afraid to explore too far on his own. He'd never get out.

He stopped. One of the doors, just a few apartments down, was open. They'd all been closed before. Quickly, he turned off the flashlight, though that did him no good. Did he have the courage to pass that open door? While it was possible the resident might happily lead William back to the surface, the opposite was far more likely. The gas tank had been bad, but at least he'd been alone down there, without rats or madmen, and the spiders hadn't really taken much interest in him. (This wasn't true; at the thought, he had to scratch more away, and bumps on his arms indicated where they'd bitten him.)

William couldn't see inside the open door, so no one inside could see him, either. Eyes just couldn't adjust to the complete absence of light, no matter how long a person lived in Midnight, the City of Night. Absolute darkness was, well, absolute. Impenetrable. Only the flashlight could give him away. Unless he crashed into a wall, tripped over something, or accidentally walked *into* the open apartment.

It's not an invitation, he told himself, trying to shake the idea that everything was prearranged. If he'd been the hero of a movie, and he walked through that open door, without fail it would slam shut, giving the villain the upper hand for at least another third of the film.

William didn't know how much longer this movie of his life would continue.

Tentatively, he stepped forward, using the wall on his left as a guide. The next set of steps he found, he would climb, as high as they went, and then he'd look for another flight, and another, until he reached something familiar, a Metro station or the streets of Midnight.

He knew the hall stretched well beyond the open door before splitting off in any direction. He hoped the stairs weren't hidden behind doors or locks. Without any real confidence, he moved forward, and knew he passed the open door by the fragrance. It was citrus, orange, a delicacy in Midnight, a fruit you couldn't find. There was a light inside, a flickering so thin it didn't escape into the hall. A woman sat behind a candle, the source of the scent, which burned on a tiny round mirror. Her hands lay on her knees, palms up. Her eyes were closed, her head tilted slightly back.

Abruptly, she opened her eyes. William froze, caught by her stare.

"A little young to be out and about so early, don't you think?" She nearly sung as she spoke, so softly and delicately, like the wind through lace.

"I'm lost," William said, and instantly regretted it. Just because she was pretty, maybe even as much so as Penelope, didn't mean she was *good*.

She smiled. "I know."

"Will you help me?"

"No," she said, shaking her head, "I will not."

The candle went out.

William fumbled with the flashlight a moment. By the time he switched it on—not more than three seconds—the door had closed. The orange scent vanished.

He looked up and down the corridor, in case he hadn't stopped at the right door; every one was sealed, as if not opened in centuries.

He couldn't have made Rex take him home. The other boy was bigger, stronger, as much a fighter as William was not. He'd had no other options. None. He had to think of this as a maze, albeit one filled with strange women, maybe hidden treasures, and doorways into all the forbidden parts of Midnight.

In another part of the city, underground apartments were common and well-known, appearing on maps and home to real people who worked in shops or factories. His teacher lived in one of those, not too far from City Hall, and would be no further away if she lived on another continent. Another day, William might come back down here and explore—after he was sure Rex wouldn't come looking for him. Right now, all he wanted to do was get home.

He paused in front of Rex's apartment, 1970. Not too far away, a stairwell waited to lead him up another level. Only two, three, four more to go after that.

30.

The Rourkes were anxious—especially the woman, who paced the room, spit into the fire, and snarled at every opportunity. "Where is that damned boy?"

The annoying pair of laughers continued doing what they did best, sounding at best uneducated and at worst like mean third graders who never grew up. Despite forcing Mileah to the ground, they never let go; one knelt behind her, pressed rudely into her back, and the other, standing, clutched her wrist. She couldn't think of a worse situation.

Should've listened to Joshua.

She'd stopped referring to him as the Wandering Reverend. A name made him more human, more real.

She clung to the idea of reality with all her will; this room, these people, were part of some deranged fantasy concocted by some drug-addled perverted madman.

The woman kicked the dirt by the fire, scattering a flame or two, and said, "Damn it, Jeffrey, do it. Do it and get it done. I'm *tired.*" She said *tired* like she'd carried the weight of the city on her shoulders, like Atlas supporting the world, as if every problem ever experienced had to be solved by her and she'd done it, damn it, revealing all the solutions until her skin was bare and chaffed, her bones brittle, her muscles burned to their last tattered fibers. A curse, worse than any Mileah had heard or used.

Jeffrey, the leader, lifted the Moonstar Clock and sighed. "Okay."

The guy behind her jumped up, yanking Mileah to her feet. The other released her wrist and also hopped, excited, repeating his hyena bit.

Jeffrey turned to Mileah. "You hid the face of our clock for a hundred years," he said. "You broke it, stole it, exiled our fathers."

"*I*," Mileah said, "did nothing."

"*You*," Jeffrey said, "are a *Warde*, the worst of the offenders. You may have forgotten, but we have not. You stole the eyes of our patriarch, in case he should create another, and then his dignity. By all that is right and fair, this machine"—he lifted the clock's face—"and all its magic belong entirely and completely to us."

"I gave it to you freely," Mileah said. "Give me back my brother and let us go."

He shook his head. "The Moonstar Clock has many talents. Tiernan Rourke was a good man, a strong man, and he gave this greatest achievement of his life everything he had to offer. He put a lot more into it than he was asked, more than they ever knew. It heals and kills, and it can bring life to the dead." He hoisted the face of the clock over the base. "First, it'll bring Tiernan back, so he can know he has been avenged. Then it shall heal his eyes, plucked from his skull by a man named *Warde*." He snarled. "And then, it shall kill."

He lowered the face of the clock. The pieces clicked together, fused, and emitted a white glow. Mileah tried to shield hey eyes from the heat, but had to watch. The ivory face brightened; the musicians that were the hands danced and played their song, clarinet, violin, and saxophone, louder and louder as they spun to point straight down, indicating midnight. The fire flared, startling even the man clutching Mileah.

The smoke, which had had been wafting through some hole in the ceiling until then, writhed around the fire pit, spinning and twisting, darkening the brightening room.

"Come, great-grandfather," Jeffrey said. "We wish you would return."

The smoke roiled. Mileah's heart pounded. The clock chimed the midnight hour (though outside, dawn had stretched red across the mountaintops). She expected a heavy knock at the door as the dead man returned, nothing more than bones now, not even rotted flesh, eye sockets empty.

Instead, all sound was sucked away as if into a vacuum. The light of the clock, and the fire, flared and imploded, drawn into the rolling, thickening cloud, where it disappeared.

When the darkness broke, the smoke had solidified into something resembling a snake, thick as a man, curled, half floating, too hidden in shadow to be clearly seen. The beam of a flashlight fell on it, from the hands of Jeffrey Rourke. There were gasps, a scream from one of the men, and Mileah lost her breath.

The creature struck. The light vanished. Jeffrey cried out; his blood sprayed across the room, drenching Mileah. She jumped back, no longer restrained by anyone.

Web struck her like a fist—throwing her to the wall; thick, sticky, it covered her face, chest and abdomen, and one of her arms, and bound her there. The creature crashed through the door.

She'd seen it once before. She still carried the photo.

31.

As William reached the stairs, two things happened simultaneously.

First, he saw a familiar man standing in the shadows. He wore all black, had his hands pressed together as if in prayer, and a knife hanging from his belt. His lips moved, silently speaking, chanting, singing as far as William knew. This was the tall, black-clad stranger he'd seen with Penelope; William had forgotten all about him.

Second, a bright heat rose behind him, throwing his hard shadow at the man in the stairs. William turned. Light poured from Rex's apartment, evaporating the door (a trick of the shadows, William thought). Then, just as suddenly, the light was gone. The door shuddered, and then the whole corridor. There was a distant sound of straining metal, followed by two thunderous booms.

The door burst apart, shattering. A snakelike thing slithered into the hall. It turned its head toward William, blood dripping from its snapping teeth, and then shot down the hall, away from him.

William stared until the shadowy thing melted into the darkness.

The black-clad man put a hand on William's shoulder. "You'll be safe," he said. "I hope your sister is."

He strode toward 1970, stepping over the splintered remnants of the door, and into the apartment.

William, not knowing what else to do, followed.

32.

Mileah fought against the webs, struggling to take every breath. She tore strands away from her face with her free hand, but they were tough and soon thickly entwined around her fingers. In the firelight, she saw little other than a lump on the ground in front of the clock—half Jeffrey Rourke's body in a spreading pool of blood.

Joshua—no, too late to save her, he was the Wandering Reverend again—and who really needed a Romance novel knight?—strode into her line of vision. He went straight to the Moonstar Clock and started working on it with a knife.

"Mileah!"

It was William's voice. He ran to her, and helped with the webs. Mileah gasped, finally able to take a full breath again. "What are you doing?" she asked the Wandering Reverend.

He glanced at her and went back to work. "*The earth will tremble, blood will fall from above, fears thought dead will rise from the depths,*" he said.

The earth *had* trembled. Jeffrey Rourke's blood had splattered everywhere and now dripped from the ceiling. Whatever that shadow was, surely it was someone's embodiment of fear from the depths.

The Wandering Reverend broke through one piece of the ironwork, and the clock broke apart. He separated the sections and bagged the face. Then he came to the wall with his knife to cut the rest of the webbing. "You should learn more about yourself, your history," he told her, freeing her other arm.

"Who are you?" William asked.

The Wandering Reverend looked down at him. "I am me," he said, "though to different people, that means different things." He cut carefully around Mileah's head. "To you, William Warde, I am Penelope's father."

"You told her about...*that* was the spider dragon, wasn't it?"

He nodded, and cut the last thread holding Mileah to the wall.

Around the room, the two hyenas and their woman were also pinned to the walls, struggling—no, one hung limply. A look of shock had been permanently etched onto Jeffrey Rourke's face. His legs were nowhere to be seen.

"Let's get you out of here," the Wandering Reverend said, thrusting the bag into her hands. "I'll take care of the rest of this later. *You*," he narrowed his eyes, "take care of this."

Numbly, Mileah nodded.

"And you," he said, turning to William, "better go home, call my daughter, and be nice to her."

"What about...that thing?" Mileah asked.

"Your father can tell you about the spider dragon," he said. "It wasn't that big last time."

"Last time?"

"The carnival brought it here, part of the freak show," he said. "It escaped. Killed a few people. We followed it underground and it got a few of us. Finally, we cornered it, and killed it."

"Then why tell Penelope it was still down here?" William asked.

The Wandering Reverend looked at him. "She was pregnant. When we struck the killing blow, a hundred babies burst from her belly, none any bigger than your fingernail, and...and we had to kill every one of them, by hand." He closed his eyes. "But what if, maybe, just one of them got away?"

"Obviously, one did," William said.

Mileah shook her head. "Not quite." Her brother shot her a quizzical look, but she could explain later. "Can you take us out of here?"

"Back to Fairgrounds Station, yes," the Wandering Reverend said. "I killed the spider dragon once before. Now, I'll kill it again."

33.

Rex Rourke, future King of Midnight, who stood to inherit first the mountains, then the underground, then the entire city, would one day be sole possessor of the Moonstar Clock. He knew its powers in ways his brothers, dim as they were, could never fathom. His father, Jeffrey, knew this, as did his mother, and they'd raised him to build a kingdom. Midnight had never had a king before.

Nothing as simple as a broken bone was about to stop him, either. That whiny brat, so easily tricked to believe someone like Rex could actually want him as a friend, had stolen his flashlight but not the rope. After the throbbing in his leg died down some, Rex climbed out of the tank. It hurt, a lot, there was no denying it, but a future king should be able to withstand a little pain.

34.

A man standing alone in the Fairgrounds opened a cage door. He couldn't stop smiling, not at all, and his heart pounded so heavily, he thought tears would burst from his eyes. He was older now than some of the carnival rides, all of which had been folded away, packed, stowed, and shipped. The city awoke to an empty field cut into the side of the mountain, empty except for one solitary truck and its driver.

He was nervous, of course, how could he not be. He'd lost his favorite pet so many years ago, under this very city, back when he was still young. But he forgot everything when the spider dragon surged from the open sewer hole. She paused, seeing him, and he wondered if death had made her forget her master.

AFTERWORD

Ah, Midnight.

This was the first. Well—the first was a title, which became the novel *Once Upon a Time in Midnight*, but even then, before that was begun, this novella was my first walkabout in the City of Night.

Originally published as part of *New Dark Voices* from Delirium (2004) with Mike Oliveri and Gene O'Neill, I wrote "Beneath Midnight" as an initial exploration of the city. I've learned much since then, but I already knew the basics: a city tucked between two mountains in such a way the sun never shines there.

Must be a dark place. Eternal night. Lots of vampires, eh? Well, no, I don't think there are vampires in Midnight. There are, as you know, Spider Dragons, and a Wandering Reverend, who first appears here but wanders through *Once Upon a Time in Midnight* and a number of other stories. He's a power in Midnight, and not the only one.

I think, in part, Midnight is an answer to my own desire to live in a bigger, richer city than the one I in which I lived at the time. I wanted depth and history. Like any city, I suspect there are a million stories to be told, in all sorts of genres, some of which I have never tried and some I never will.

I have discovered, since "Beneath Midnight", a few things I didn't suspect at the time, including an overarching storyline that involves more than just the history and legends of the city itself. There's a crisis brewing in the undercurrents, and maybe there's something else, something more, beyond this single accidental inescapable beyond-the-mirror world.

Me
and the
Magic
Beans

You might not believe in magic beans. Doesn't matter. Jack believed in them, and he grew a beanstalk. So when I got my hands on a whole dozen of the dry little beans, I figured I'd at least get me a golden goose.

I planted them carefully in the backyard, separating them by a good two yards each, and made something of a grid. I apologized to the oak. Since I didn't know how crowded the beanstalk would make things, I figured I ought to give a warning. I waved to the squirrels, too, who played up and down the side of that oak as though they owned it.

I watered the garden. I sat on the back porch and watched. The birds, when I saw them, ignored the magic beans.

I chatted on the phone with my mother for a while, and then a friend from college, and a girl I liked. I drank red wine, but skipped dinner. I played Solitaire with an old deck of Aviators. I kept drinking, and I kept playing, and eventually the sun went down and the battery in my phone died and I fell asleep.

I dreamed of climbing through the clouds, which tasted remarkably like vanilla ice cream. I kept hearing, "Fee fi fo fum!" but never saw the giant. Or his wife. Or the golden eggs. It was only a dream, after all, and couldn't be expected to fill in the blanks for me.

I woke with sunlight in my eyes. For a moment, I couldn't see past the rising sun; it, and the red wine, hurt my head. My eyes adjusted, though, and in the morning mist, I saw...I saw...well, it wasn't beanstalks. Were they? They were narrow but tall. They were about as high as my waist, which is a fair amount of growth for a single night, but nothing to touch the skies. There were twelve, arranged just as I'd arranged them. Rubbing my eyes, and holding up a hand to block the sun, I approached to survey my garden.

Twelve sticks, in red, green, blue, and yellow. With a clockwork sound, they began unwinding their outer petals. Out popped twelve little people. They were no more than a foot tall, reed thin, dressed in the colors their leaves had sprouted. They raised their legs high when they walked, and as a group they moved to encircle me. They sounded like wind-up toys. The one in the middle, straight ahead of me, bowed and said in a high-pitched, nasally voice, "Master." The others bowed, too.

"You're not what I was expecting," I told the little man.

"Our apologies, Master," he said. "We rarely are."

"So what's it to be, then?" I asked. "Golden geese? Giants? How does this work?" I figured I'd missed a part of the story.

"Oh, that," the little man said. "It was a hen, not a goose, and it's long since dead. And the castle in the sky has decayed into cloud stuff, so there's no use in even making the attempt. It's a dangerous climb, too, Master, not one I would recommend."

I have to admit, I was confused. "What, then, would you recommend?"

"We are your servants," the little man said. "Command us."

"But I have no commands," I said. "I only wanted a little gold. Something to chase away the economical blues."

"We can find you gold," the little man said. And off they went, all of them, in varying directions. I rubbed my eyes again. I figured I'd awakened into another dream, so I gathered my phone and my wine glass, went inside, and found my bed.

This time, I slept dreamlessly. I was awakened by the metallic clicks and scratches of twelve little people crossing the wood floor. They surrounded my bed. I yawned, big, and this time came fully awake.

Their leader hopped onto the foot of my bed, held out his hand, and dropped a piece of gold between my ankles. It was gold, yes: a school ring.

One by one, the other eleven little people—about half were women—deposited their treasures. A vial of gold leaf. A three inch coil of wire. A gold tooth. Another ring, this one much smaller, a woman's engagement ring, complete with diamond.

"Wait," I said, picking up the ring. The diamond looked real. So did the tiny drop of blood. "Did you steal all this?" I looked around at each. With one exception, they hung their heads.

The exception puffed up his stick-like chest and said, "I stole nothing, Master. This was an honestly found object, of which no one can complain." He dropped a penny onto the pile.

"That's not gold," one of the others said.

"It looks like gold."

"It doesn't even look like gold," another said, one of the women. "You're a fool. It's copper."

"Not copper," said another, leaning close and sniffing, then licking the side of it. "Zinc. Definitely."

"It's a penny," I said.

"We acquired the gold you requested," the leader said.

"And this ring?" I showed them the diamond. "Was it still on her finger?" When no one answered, I said, "Was it?"

"Yes, Master," one of the little people said.

"Bring it back," I said, throwing it down onto my sheet. "Return it all. I didn't raise you to steal for me."

"But Master," the leader said, "did you not intend to climb into the sky and steal from the giant?"

At first, I didn't answer, and none of the little people moved.

"We did nothing less than what you required," he added. "And via your own intended means. Master, I cannot help but believe we've done nothing wrong."

"No," I said. "No, of course not, nothing wrong. It was me. I didn't phrase it right. I expected magic gold. Not stolen. Not even found. Created."

"Ah," said one of the little women.

"Ah?" I asked.

"Ah, indeed," she said. "We've a fool for a Master. You cannot create gold out of thin air."

"You need base metals," added their little leader.

I grinned. "That, we can do."

Babylon
Rising

1.

March 2003

Sunset painted the horizon like a fire.

Gabriel had walked a long way, wet sand sucking at his toes. He'd left his shoes in his car. And for the moment, he'd lost sight of the few other beachgoers he'd seen.

Someone had left an enormous sandcastle. The turrets and spires were already eroding, but the surrounding wall stood strong.

As a boy, Gabriel had built sandcastles every chance he got. The ocean provided his moats with water; his imagination supplied them with alligators.

Looking out across the Atlantic, where a few ships lingered at the darkening horizon, Gabriel inhaled deeply. *This* was what life was about: escaping the mundane. The office, his apartment, even his car— all this became part of some other life, abstractions he needn't worry about.

He didn't escape often enough.

When he turned back toward the sandcastle, an old man stood in front of it. He wore brown sandals and a long, thick robe, and leaned on a walking stick.

For a moment, Gabriel's serenity broke. He'd been surprised, even ambushed, and his solitude was ruined. He started to say something, but hesitated. The old man hadn't done anything wrong; maybe he came out here every night, making Gabriel the intruder.

"Lovely night, isn't it?" the man said. His face was dark and wrinkled; his voice matched perfectly.

"Yes," Gabriel said, nodding. He wanted to get away, to reclaim his aloneness.

Gabriel turned to walk on.

The old man laughed.

It was not a joyful laugh, as if he'd seen something funny. It was not maniacal, either, like a madman on the edge of victory. Rather, it was a little of both, inappropriately timed, and it stopped Gabriel.

He looked back. The old man, who had not moved and still gazed straight onto the ocean, said, "Turn around."

Gabriel didn't have to. The silence struck him immediately, the absence of distant birds crying and waves crashing. The salt was gone from the air, which was now terribly dry and stifling. The Atlantic was gone.

Gabriel turned. Sand stretched to the horizon, where the wind lifted it in sheets. Instead of blues, he saw shades of brown, and waves of heat rising from the ground. A road bisected the desert; he stood in the middle of it.

The old man laughed again. The sandcastle was gone. Instead, there was a vast city. Facing it, Gabriel felt like he'd been struck down by a speeding truck. The curved wall cast a long shadow well beyond Gabriel. Two towers flanked the huge, closed gate. He stared in awe.

"Arabia, perhaps," the old man said. "Babylon."

2.

The old man closed his eyes, facing now toward the gate, and gripped his staff with both hands.

Slowly, rumbling, the gates opened inwards.

Towers, spires, huge minarets like overturned hearts came into view—and many vibrant reds and oranges and gold. Artistry everywhere: in the lines of the architecture, the curve of the road, the textures of fabric and brick and sand, the fragrance of jasmine and lavender. Snakes climbing ropes suspended in air, camels with one or two humps and reins like horses, llamas, monkeys with collars, children laughing and running. In this grand, overcrowded marketplace, acrobats performed, jumping and flipping, contorting unnaturally; cartographers sold maps; astrologers offered fortunes.

It was too much. Gabriel shut his eyes—but still heard the crowds and smelled the scents—and was touched, lightly, by a woman.

He opened his eyes. Her hand rested on his shoulder, and her kohl eyes locked with his. Heat shot from her fingers; for a moment, he forgot to breathe. Behind the gates was this surreal marketplace filled with noisy merchants, distant singing, and exotica Gabriel could barely register; yet the most wondrous sight of all was this woman. Her flawless skin was the color of dark chocolate, her hair long and black, her crimson clothes wispy like veils. She wore gold bracelets and dangling earrings, and her fingernails were painted like cream. A diamond-encrusted gold band circled her forehead.

She took his hand. She led him inside the gates as they started to close. They passed men with swords hanging from their sashes, guards with hard, unwavering eyes.

He felt weak, unable to resist the woman's gentle tug. He had no idea what had happened, and couldn't follow this chain of events. It was too much to absorb. Glancing over his shoulder, Gabriel looked for the old man.

All he saw was the distant sandstorm rushing closer, a huge brown and yellow wall undulating as it swallowed the horizon.

"Silks, sir," a merchant said, thrusting a fistful of fabric at Gabriel.

"Scents," another offered, coming too close, "cinnamon and vanilla, spices from the east."

The pitches came from every direction as they entered the crowd.

"Sweetmeats, mead."

"Dancing girls...or boys, if that is your pleasure."

The woman paused, leaned close and whispered, "The *soukh* is always busy, this time of day. Especially with the coming storm. People think they'll never buy again."

Then she pulled him again, weaving through the press of people, camels, chickens, horses—and a rhino, its horn bejeweled, one big eye on the side of its head.

They escaped the throng, entering a massive adobe building through an elaborately carved wooden archway. There, on the black and white marble tiles, Gabriel stopped and said, "Wait."

She glanced down at his hand in hers. Her eyes narrowed like a cat's. "We cannot wait."

"I don't understand," Gabriel said. "I was on the beach."

She looked left and right. "There is no beach."

"There was."

"Come." She tugged, pulling Gabriel off balance. When he resisted, she jerked him forward.

"Okay," Gabriel said, again walking, "at least tell me who you are."

"Cool-Eyes," she said. "Now, hurry."

She led him through a maze of dim corridors, passing tapestries and statues, huge mosaics made of tiny tiles, and doors and dark passageways. Finally, exiting beneath another arch, they came to an atrium. Here, trees grew as high as the sky. Ripe fruit hung from vines. A fountain cascaded softly. Cool-Eyes let go of Gabriel and waved one hand to encompass it all. "Most people never see this garden."

It was very green, especially for the desert, and too large for Gabriel to see to the other end. "Why not?"

"Forbidden fruit," Cool-Eyes said, picking an apple from the tree. She bit into it with a crunch, squirting juice.

"You're not Eve," Gabriel said, disbelieving.

"And you're not Adam."

"Where am I?"

"Babylon," Cool-Eyes said. "One of the great gardens."

"One of...?"

"You should see the hanging gardens." She smiled, and took another bite.

"I don't understand any of this."

"It'll be easier," Cool-Eyes said, "if you forget all the things you knew."

"How did I get here?"

She shook her head. "No more questions," she said, "and I'll tell you a story."

3.

Years ago, so many years that I lose track, there was a boy who wanted to be a great hunter like his father. This child, Ali, tried to draw back the strings on his father's hunting bow, but it was twice his height, and very tightly strung. He pulled and pulled but nothing happened.

Every year, on his birthday, his father let him try to draw an arrow, promising Ali could join the hunt when he succeeded. Every year, Ali gave it his all, but every bit of strength he had wasn't enough to budge the string.

On his ninth birthday, he cut his fingers on the string.

On his tenth, he again drew only blood.

On his eleventh birthday, despite all his training and prayers, Ali was unable to draw the bow. But he did not cut himself, and his father congratulated Ali on his progress.

Ali grew tall very quickly, and strong for a boy, yet on his twelfth birthday he still failed to set an arrow.

So the night before his thirteenth birthday, Ali went to the soukh in search of something, anything, to help him. He ignored the men touting strength elixirs and went instead to a woman whose skin was as fair as the moon. She'd come from the north, and even her hair was pale, her eyes the color of sky. To men, she was an exotic. Women called her a witch. Ali believed she'd been sent by Allah to answer his prayers.

He told the exotic his story, that tomorrow was his thirteenth

*birthday and he should be a man by then. She agreed, and introduced
him to the ways of manhood.*

*Afterwards, she took two dinars as payment, and told him where to
find the student of a jinn, a girl who could help him.*

*It was well past midnight, the moon was setting, and he needed to
be home before dawn, but Ali followed the exotic's directions to a home
at the farthest corner of the city, and there was the girl.*

*He'd never seen one like her. She promised nothing, demanded all
his money, and showed him her bow. "This," she said, "is the weapon of
a true master."*

Ali said, "But there is no string."

*The girl pulled back on the bow, released, and sent a shaft into the
wall. Then she gave the bow to Ali. "Shoot," she said, "but think not
about what you do."*

*Ali drew back, as if there were a string, and released an arrow. They
laughed together for a while, and played, until the girl said, "You should
go before my husband wakes."*

*Ali reached his home with the sun's first rays, where his parents
threw a huge birthday party. There were magicians and jugglers, Eastern
acrobats, all the spectacle a boy would want. His father took out the
bow, gave it to Ali, and told him to try again.*

*Ali pulled back the string and shot an arrow. This arrow split a tree
and plunged into his father's chest, stealing his breath and the beat of
his heart.*

4.

"That's not a very happy ending," Gabriel said after a while.

"No," Cool-Eyes said, "but it's an honest ending."

"It doesn't help me any," Gabriel said. "It doesn't tell me how or
why I'm here."

"I didn't say I'd tell a story about *you.*" She smiled, and confided, "I
just meant to warn you about jinn-taught girls."

5.

Night fell quickly in the desert. The wind intensified, despite
protection from walls and buildings. The sky darkened to a velvety
indigo, a blanket with neither moon nor stars. Layers of sleek clouds slid
underneath each other rapidly.

In the garden, greens sharpened, shadows grew, and Cool-Eyes seemed content with silently strolling along a winding path.

Gabriel followed because he didn't know what else to do.

What, exactly, had happened?

"I'm in Hell," he said under his breath.

But it wasn't Hell—at least, not how he'd envisioned it. The demons weren't supposed to be beautiful, and the oppressive heat shouldn't ease as the sun set.

"Did you bring me here?" he asked.

She gave no answers. Every few minutes, he tried again. She ignored most of his questions, and merely shrugged when he started repeating himself. Finally, he tried a different approach. "I'm Gabriel."

She looked back at him, cocked an eyebrow, and said, "My husband, if he was alive, would have your head."

"Did you kill him?"

She looked at him steadily and did not smile.

Gabriel stopped walking. "You have to help me," he said. "I don't understand any of this."

"There's nothing to understand," Cool-Eyes said. "Would you like another story?"

He shook his head, and they resumed walking.

"Are we going anywhere in particular?"

"The moonflowers may bloom tonight," she said. She glanced at the sky. "Unless..."

"The storm?" Gabriel asked.

"Have you ever experienced a sandstorm?"

He shook his head.

"Well, this isn't *just* a sandstorm. That's part of it, yes, but look there." She nodded upwards. "Does that look like a desert sky?"

"I'm not sure."

"I've lived here all my life," she said, "longer than you might imagine, and I've seen such a sky only twice. The first time was the night of my wedding."

"And the second?"

She only smiled.

"At least tell me *something*," Gabriel said. "Anything. Please."

"Okay," Cool-Eyes said, meeting his gaze. "I'll tell you one thing, and only this, and then you ask no more questions. Deal?"

Reluctantly, Gabriel agreed.

"Okay," Cool-Eyes said. "Your coming here this night is not a coincidence."

"The night of the storm?"

"The storm, too, is no accident."

"Then someone's responsible for this," Gabriel said. "For my being here."

Cool-Eyes shook her head, touched his lips with a shushing finger, and lowered her voice. "Questions are done."

"But..."

She shook her head. "No."

A flash of lightning briefly tinted the world in blue. Thunder crashed close enough to echo in Gabriel's bones.

"Anyway, would you really want to go back?" Cool-Eyes asked.

The rain began.

6.

Drops fell thick and fast and heavy, splashing on the ground.

Cool-Eyes ran, arms outstretched, mouth open to catch raindrops. Gabriel chased after her. She turned onto an intersecting path, headed toward an arched doorway. Before reaching it, Cool-Eyes spun, her eyes wildly excited, her grin as wide as possible. "Isn't this wonderful!?" she cried.

In that doorway, eyes glistened—and also metal. Men with scimitars emerged, their robes and turbans all purple, their beards heavy and black.

With a yell, they raised their swords and charged.

Cool-Eyes laughed.

Gabriel stepped back. The men parted around her, their weapons and enmity aimed at him.

"Run, if you can!" she called, laughing.

Gabriel turned and ran. Lightning touched down inside the garden. Thunder drowned all other sounds. In the intermittent flashes of electricity, Gabriel turned down other paths.

He felt the swish of a sword near his neck—or maybe just the wind. He glanced back; the soldiers pursued him as if their lives depended on it.

A lightning bolt, barely missing Gabriel, exploded a shrub. Heat and twigs struck him, followed by thick smoke. He turned sharply right, just behind the burning bush, and saw the soldiers retreating from the fire.

Another jagged bolt came down, splintering a tree. Half the trunk fell in Gabriel's path. Again, he turned, suddenly afraid the lightning was aiming for him.

Rounding a corner, he collided with one of the soldiers.

They bounced apart, both surprised. The soldier growled, and slashed the air with his sword.

"Halt!" the soldier commanded, lunging.

Gabriel slipped. He grabbed a tree limb for support. It snapped, and he fell.

Lightning struck the tree. Bark flew in every direction, and flame, just as the soldier came forward with his sword. Blue electricity jumped from the tree to the weapon, illuminating bones beneath the soldier's skin. His beard caught fire, his eyes charred, and he collapsed in a mess of burnt flesh.

Gabriel scampered backwards, sure that had been meant for him. He jumped to his feet and almost grabbed the fallen weapon. But he didn't know how to wield it.

Through a wide doorway, Gabriel escaped the garden. Thunder echoed behind him, and rain pelted the roof without mercy.

The corridor twisted frequently, and Gabriel took several side passages. Sconces held open flames that revealed other hallways and stairs.

He heard soldiers behind him.

Gabriel opened one of the doors and entered absolute darkness. Panting, he closed himself in.

He tried to remain perfectly still, as if his slightest movement might attract attention. A quick scratch broke the silence, and a hissing flame sprang to life. Unhurried, a woman bent low, guiding the match to a candle wick, then to a second and a third. Apple and cinnamon scents filled the room.

Rain continued to assault the rooftop like gunshots. In the hall, men ran and shouted. But Gabriel's heart pounded so relentlessly in his ears, he was surprised he heard anything at all.

The woman's eyes reflected the candles. Her skin was a perfect shade between coffee and cream, neither dark nor light. Her hair was short and fine, as if each strand were the master stroke of a painter. Her curves were supple—hips, breasts, lips, shoulders, neck—her face soft and round. She gazed right at Gabriel—sad yet hopeful, strong and unexpectedly vulnerable—for a long time.

"You think this isn't happening," she said, her voice soft and perfect, melodic, tinted by an unfamiliar accent. "This is all a dream, isn't that right?"

Gabriel nodded; he could do nothing else. In this room, time had ceased to exist. He could stare for hours—days—*years*—and every moment notice something else: the shape of her eyebrows, the hint of skin where her robe closed, the triple silhouette of her shadows on the wall.

7.

"Do you know what day this is?"

"Saturday."

She shook her head. "Today is not your today," she said. "Nor is it mine. But today does belong here." A crash of thunder rocked the candle flames; her shadows danced.

Gabriel tried to focus on her words, not her lips, but he didn't understand what they meant.

She stepped forward and extended her hand. "I am India."

"Gabriel." Her warm, soft touch thrilled him, and her hand lingered in his a moment longer than necessary, which he liked, and squeezed gently before sliding out of his fingers.

"When you woke this morning," she said, "you were someplace else."

"Someplace else entirely," Gabriel said.

"I know. Long ago, I woke elsewhere, as well."

After a pause, Gabriel asked, "Do you know how I got here?"

India nodded, slowly. "Magic."

"That's not really an answer," Gabriel said.

"It's the only one I've got."

"Is it?"

"We were stolen," India said. "Neither you nor I belong here."

"But the old man does," Gabriel said.

"He was here when they started building the tower to Heaven," India said, "though some know their god will demolish that tower and scatter the people. Tonight, Shahrazad is telling about Sindbad's seventh voyage. No one remembers when she wasn't telling her stories."

"Time works differently here?" Gabriel asked.

"I wouldn't say time works."

"And I'm here...why?"

"We should go," India said, "before someone opens that door."

Voices in the hall grew louder; Gabriel hadn't noticed them until that moment; he was too intoxicated. India lifted a candle, turned, and walked through a doorway. The arched top tapered off, like a minaret, and was inlaid with tiles of violet and gold.

They descended a wide, rock staircase, within a tiny sphere of candlelight. The stairs were cool and rough under his bare feet.

When he glanced back, Gabriel was sure the door was gone and the darkness hid only walls.

8.

They paused at a landing. The stairs were broad, the ceiling high, but to Gabriel they felt restrictive. He was afraid if they stopped, the wall—closing behind them, he was sure—would crush him. And India.

"Why are you helping me?" he asked.

"I've been here a long time," India said.

"How long?"

"A day," she said. "A year, maybe a lifetime. I don't know."

They resumed walking, climbing now. "How do I know I can trust you?"

She turned, then, and stepped down toward Gabriel. So close, Gabriel felt the tiny candle's heat between them. She lowered her voice, smoothing it, and said, "If you trust me, I will break your heart, so don't."

9.

The stairs rose to an archway that brought them into a room as dark and shadowy as the one they'd left. India set her candle on a tall, narrow table. Wide, deep settees lined the walls. Tables supported unlit oil lamps and flowers. India's candle barely penetrated the dark, leaving the corners murky.

"I didn't think you were coming," she said. "I visited a fortuneteller, an exotic. She told me where to be, and when, and I've waited every night since."

"When was that?"

India shrugged. "Time has a way of...shifting."

Someone knocked on the door.

"They're going to take me," she said. "Don't worry about me. You have to get away. Do whatever you must." Softly, she kissed his lips, and nothing else mattered. But then India pushed him toward the corner.

"Hide in the shadows until you can get out."

The kiss had left him dazed. "And go where?"

India moved to block the candlelight. The door burst open, and a broad, scimitar-wielding soldier entered. He pointed his sword at India. "We should've known."

India straightened, almost as if she'd grown taller. Two soldiers followed the first, stepping to his sides.

Gabriel froze, unable to move. He wanted to help her, to save her, but could do nothing. If he had retrieved the fallen weapon earlier, he could have used it...and in stabbing one enemy in the back, he'd find himself facing two trained swordsmen. He felt his stomach knot, not from fear but from helplessness.

"The Wazir will not be pleased," the soldier told India.

She glanced, briefly, at Gabriel, and said, "I've done nothing. *Again.*"

The soldier turned his head to follow India's gaze. Gabriel hoped the shadows hid him well, but the soldier's eyes widened. "What, exactly, are you?"

"Shadows are tricky," India said, grabbing the soldier's arm. "Don't trust them."

He shrugged her off. The others, too, had turned. Rather than answer, or wait to be recognized (they wore the same purple uniforms as the garden soldiers), Gabriel ran out the door.

He pulled it shut behind him and chose a direction randomly.

All the halls were the same; he might be passing the same corridors and doorways he'd seen earlier. Statues turned their heads to follow Gabriel's flight. "Over here!" one called. "He's running, running, running over here!"

The passage spilled into an alley. Baskets lined the sandy path. There was no sign of rain, not even a puddle, though the sky hadn't cleared. Either direction would be a long, straight run, but the walls had many cubbyholes and crevices. Gabriel took one.

The statue continued singing inside, and footsteps echoed.

Only one soldier came into the alley. His eyes were black dots under thick brows. His clothes stretched to cover bulging muscles. He looked both ways, sweeping every crack.

Gabriel crouched lower into his hiding place, hoping, praying, crossing his fingers and remembering the rabbit's foot he'd had when he was ten. If time was as funky as India suggested, his childhood good luck charm might help him now.

"Sir!" someone called.

Gabriel risked turning his head. Another soldier raced down the alley, sword hanging from his sash.

"What?"

"Sir, there are wise men at the gates," the new soldier said. He was young, a boy, and the weapon on his side seemed to tilt him to the left. "From the east, sir."

The soldier hesitated. "Allow only three to enter," he said. "What do they seek?"

"Myrrh. And frankincense. They say they have plenty of gold."

"Gold?"

They were a few yards away, just out of reach with their swords, but Gabriel was backed against a wall with no place to run. It was only a matter of time before they saw him. If he had a genie, he'd wish himself invisible.

"I'll see to it myself, then." The soldier pointed at the archway. "Let no one in or out. Do you understand?"

"Absolutely, sir!" The young soldier snapped a salute, an arm to the chest. The other returned the gesture and strode down the alleyway.

The boy watched his superior leave, then looked the other way, and finally settled with his eyes on the arch.

He wasn't going to move.

But he couldn't know who, specifically, he sought, could he?

Gabriel eased out of his corner and, very slowly, approached the guard from behind.

The soldier turned abruptly. "Halt!" His drew his sword. "You cannot pass."

"No?" Gabriel asked, looking from the soldier to the archway and back again. He shrugged. "No, I suppose not. Good night, then." Holding his breath, Gabriel turned and walked away, down the alley, struggling to control his trembling and not look back.

10.

Gabriel wandered. He wanted, desperately, to see India again. That brief kiss lingered in his memory. He could still smell her, like roses, clean and fresh, and he wished he could touch her hand again. And her lips.

He thought of nothing else.

Eventually, he reached a *soukh*. The crowd swelled as he pressed forward. He felt less exposed here. Shaggy men offered spices and foods and games. A woman in veils swayed suggestively at one door, beckoning. Musicians played stringed guitar-like instruments, dazzling flutes, and violins. Alchemists promised to shift metals. Scribes sold tales in rolled scrolls, while poets recited verse and performers acted out the words.

A thick, chiseled man bumped into him. Gabriel stepped back, and some of the man's armful of silks slid to the floor.

"Sorry," Gabriel said.

The man glared, trying to pick up the fallen cloth without dropping more. Gabriel bent to help, and draped some on top of the pile. They slid off, dragging others with them.

"Just bring them," the man snapped.

Gabriel shrugged, gathered what had fallen, and followed the man to his tent.

The merchant dropped his stack on an even larger heap. Gabriel added his. As they shifted, the man caught them and stuffed them in properly. "Thanks." He fished two coins from his pocket and pressed them into Gabriel's palm.

"That's not necessary."

"Take them." The merchant's voice said, *Don't you dare even think about refusing.*

"Thanks." Gabriel hesitated.

"You look like a man preoccupied. I know what that's like." The merchant stuck out his hand. "I'm Cogia Hassan."

"Gabriel." Cogia's grip was strong and unyielding.

"So, I'm a silk merchant," Cogia said, gesturing toward his product. "Would you care to buy one?"

"I don't think…"

"Your clothing screams outsider," Cogia said, choosing something red from the pile. "You'll blend better in this."

"How much?" Gabriel asked.

"For you." He paused. "Ah, one dinar will suffice."

Gabriel looked at the coins in his hands. "These are all I have."

Cogia took one, helped Gabriel pull the shirt over his clothes (it fell loosely to about his knees), and whispered, "I'm not always a silk merchant."

"No?"

"I'm a rich man," Cogia said. "A king."

"You're the king of Babylon?" Gabriel asked.

"Oh, no," Cogia said. "The king of *thieves*."

"Ah." Gabriel checked his back pocket, but his wallet was in his car—with his shoes. He glanced down at his dirty feet.

"You wonder how a king such as I came to peddle silks in the *soukh*?"

"I was wondering that," Gabriel admitted.

"I was the leader of many men," said Cogia, "the most skillful thieves the world has ever seen. We had a great many treasures, gold and jewelry, gems, diamonds, magnificent weaponry, silk tapestries and beautiful musical instruments, all of it stored in a place I thought safe. Then one day, a dishonorable man came and helped himself to our gold."

"He stole from the king of thieves?" Gabriel asked.

Cogia smiled broadly and patted Gabriel on the shoulder. "There are," he said, "honorable methods of theft. This crook returned again and again, bringing his friends, and when the day came that he returned and found some of my men, he murdered them."

Cogia tightened both fists and furrowed his brows. "We waited for his return and ambushed his friends. They told us who he was, and I found the extravagant home of this formerly poor man easily. Yet somehow, he knew we were there, and he slaughtered my men."

He looked Gabriel in the eye, hatred burning in his gaze. "He buys much and often, this man made rich off my wealth. I shall be his best source for silk, and I shall be invited into his home, where I will avenge my men."

Gabriel had no response. He was afraid to simply walk away.

"You seem like an honorable man," Cogia said. "I did not want to lie to you."

"Thanks, I think."

"And I see," Cogia said, "you are on a mission of your own. Maybe I can help."

"I have no money," Gabriel said.

"I have a cave filled with gold," Cogia said. "I need no money."

The intensity of Cogia's stare kept Gabriel from hesitation. "Do you know a woman named India?"

Cogia considered a moment, and then shook his head. "But there are many people in this city, and my mind is on only one. One of the seers, perhaps, might help you. The gypsy, perhaps, or the exotic."

"The exotic?" Gabriel asked. "Where can I find her?"

Cogia smiled devilishly. "Ah, Gabriel, you are a man who knows what he wants. She's a feisty one, the exotic. Good luck to you."

11.

The exotic's tent was off from the main crowd, a few steps into an alley. The din of the marketplace didn't reach her. She sat patiently, cross-legged, on the ground, palms upturned over her knees, eyes closed. Her hair was as blonde as could be, and she was more generously curved than any other woman in Babylon. Her skin was pale, lighter than his, unmarked and unadorned. She wore no jewelry, only wisps of pink.

He suspected her eyes would be blue.

"I knew you were coming," she said. She patted the ground next to her, just beyond the reach of her skirt. "Sit, please."

Tentatively, Gabriel knelt.

"You seek answers," the exotic said, "but the answers you've found have only given you more questions."

"Isn't that common?" Gabriel asked.

She opened one eye, peeked slantwise at him, and smiled. "Very much so." The lid shut again. "The answer is, there are no answers."

"That's not much help," Gabriel said.

"Did I say I would help you? Did I say I'd answer your questions?"

He didn't answer.

"There are forces at play," the exotic said. "You've been here long enough now."

"Long enough for what?"

"To bridge back," the exotic said. "Or forwards."

"I don't understand."

"Haven't you said that enough today?"

Too many times, Gabriel thought.

"You are a link. A bridge. Just as we all are links to the places from whence we came."

"So I can go back?" Gabriel asked.

"And lose the girl?"

"Which girl?"

"Which do you want?"

"I didn't realize I had a choice," Gabriel said.

"You don't. But it's an interesting question, don't you think?" She looked fully at him with extremely blue eyes. "There are men who want you. Women. Ifrits."

"Ifrits?"

"Jinn," the exotic said. "Genies. Like gods, compared to men, but nothing compared to God."

"Allah?"

She shrugged. "If you insist."

"Why do they want me?"

"Each for their own reason."

"The old man?"

"The bridge maker," the exotic said, nodding. "The Wazir. Next time you see him, he'll be flesh and bone."

"He wasn't before?"

The exotic inhaled deeply. "Your time is a long distance from this place. The things I see in your world, they amaze and frighten me. I cannot describe them. People move too fast. Unnaturally. Language is fractured. Wars are still waged. I would have expected that to end, at least." She looked suddenly confused. "You work in a box?"

"A cubicle," Gabriel said.

"She loves you," the exotic said. "I knew she would. You're different, like she is, and you can send her home." She cocked her head to one side. "You do not have magic, do you?"

"What?"

"In the place you are from, they've forgotten many of the old ways. Not everyone, no. But you, you have never seen magic. Only illusion."

"There's a difference?"

She paused. "You confuse me."

Gabriel laughed. "I confuse you?"

"You don't want to go home because of anything you miss," she said. "There's nothing there for you. No love, no joy."

"I love the beach," Gabriel said.

She ignored him. "No purpose. No *life*. You want to return because you're afraid."

"They tried to kill me."

"No, they didn't," she said, and then nodded. "Okay, someone did, but the soldiers have explicit orders. You are to be taken, not killed. But that's not the fear that drives you."

"No?" Gabriel wanted to hear nothing except the magic words to get home, but he couldn't stop listening if he tried. It was like her voice sucked him in, drawing him closer and closer like a moth to electric death. He was blinded. And she spoke truthfully.

"No," the exotic said. "You are afraid to live."

12.

The exotic closed her eyes again.

Gabriel waited. Should he close his eyes, too? Put his hands on his knees? (He was kneeling, not sitting, afraid the soldiers might find him.)

Running was not a solution. Every corner, every day, might lead him to something else he'd have to flee. He was already tired.

Gabriel's thoughts strayed again to India. Even though he'd only seen her in the candlelight, he could vividly recall the curve of her lips as she spoke, her floral scent, the depth of those eyes—like looking into Heaven itself.

How could he have developed such a romanticized image of a woman he'd only just met, and would likely never see again?

That realization sank his heart. The exotic grabbed his hand. "You'll see her again," she said. "She'll be at your side until the end. You worry too much, especially for one who had nothing to lose."

"Had?"

"Perhaps," the exotic said, squeezing his hand, "you've found something to lose, after all."

"Must you always speak in riddles?" Gabriel asked.

"No," she said, opening her eyes again. "No, and I shall speak as plainly as possible. You are being sought. You will be found. The question is, by whom? The answer is yours."

"Circles again," Gabriel said.

"Right." She nodded. "You are about to be captured. Go willingly. It'll be less painful."

"What?"

"You're fortunate," the exotic said. "She sees the potential inside you, the artist you might be, not the failure you've allowed yourself to become."

It was like she'd slapped him. Gabriel still loved art, he did, but he hadn't touched a brush since college.

She pulled her hand away and shook her head. "Nothing else," she said. "Now pay me."

"Pay you?"

"Five dinars, at least," the exotic said, "as I've told you much. Sight is not without consequence."

"But..."

"But," she said over him, "you haven't got five dinars. You came here empty handed, without sandals even, and you cannot pay me. I know. I forgive you." She patted his hand. "But you can give me one dinar, at least, before you lose it with everything else."

He had one dinar, which Cogia Hassan had given him. Gabriel fished it from his pocket and gave it to the exotic. She brought it to her breast and slid the coin under her clothes. "Good luck, friend," she said. "It will feel like you're losing everything, but it doesn't have to end that way."

"What?"

She closed her eyes again. "They're coming."

Soldiers entered the alley.

"They may take you," the exotic whispered, "but do not trust the ifrit."

"You," one of the soldiers said, pointing at Gabriel with a spear. "On your feet."

Cautiously, Gabriel rose. Soldiers grabbed his arms from behind. One, he recognized—the boy he'd left in the alley.

"Thought you were funny, did you?" the boy asked, and then spit in Gabriel's face.

They dragged him away.

13.

They moved through the city quickly, giving Gabriel no chance to notice anything in particular. Merchants and buyers at the marketplace parted like the Red Sea to let them pass, but the noise of selling never ebbed, and the spectacle persisted.

They forced him through the streets at a jog. Above, clouds obscured the night and thickened. Briefly, two of the soldiers talked about the coming storm.

"I thought it passed already," Gabriel said.

The soldier took time out of their run to punch Gabriel, hard, in the face. His nose bled. His eye hurt, but did not swell—much.

They entered one of the many buildings through a wide set of doors, which they closed and locked behind them. One soldier carried a torch, its flame dancing wildly and throwing shadows. The others, except the pair dragging Gabriel, drew their swords.

"Is he angry?" one of the soldiers asked.

"I have never seen him so mad."

"We have taken far too long."

"It's the girl's fault," one of the guards said. "If he punishes anyone, it should be Cool-Eyes."

Silence persisted after that, until someone else broke it: "Halt."

The soldiers stopped, facing two giants, shirtless and bulging with muscles, standing at either side of a doorway. Fires roared in the sconces behind them.

"Our Sultan's Wazir wants this man," the torchbearer said.

"And our Sultan?" one giant asked.

"This man is not significant enough to bother the Sultan and his new wife."

The giants looked at each other, and Gabriel realized any response they gave would be bad for him.

The vocal giant came forward and lifted Gabriel's face by the chin. The fingers, like vices, ignited pain in his jaw and nose.

"The Wazir," the other giant said, "has been very busy these days."

"This is a common criminal," the guard said. "A thief."

"The Wazir would have no interest in a common criminal," the giant said.

"No," a voice said, appearing in the shadows where before no man had stood. Everyone went silent. It was the old man, still cloaked in brown, using his walking stick to step closer. "But this common thief, as you say, is uncommon."

"Of course," the giant said.

"Your father was an ifrit," the Wazir said.

Both giants nodded. Gabriel thought he saw fear.

"An ifrit who serves our Sultan," the Wazir added.

Again, they nodded.

"Whom do you serve?"

"Sultan Shahryar," the giants said together.

"Then perhaps," the old man said, "when the Sultan's minister requests the presence of even a common criminal, you would be wise enough to not delay his arrival."

The giants said nothing.

The old man stepped closer and looked at Gabriel. "He's been hurt."

"Only slightly."

The old man scowled. "Bring him to my lab."

As one, the soldiers said, "Yes, sir!" and snapped their fists to their chests.

As they took Gabriel further down the hall, the old man turned toward the giants and asked, "How shall I deal with you?"

After rounding two corners, Gabriel heard one of the giants bellow in agony.

14.

The lab was a long way down.

The steps were jagged, uneven and sharp. They cut Gabriel's feet, but he barely felt it anymore. Blood had dried under his nose; he'd never had a chance to wipe it off.

The two soldiers dragged and carried him, not allowing a moment's respite. The torch cut through the darkness. The walls were too tight here, the ceiling too low, as if designed to encourage claustrophobia.

There were a few doors at brief landings. Most had tiny, barred windows, behind which Gabriel saw nothing but darkness. But he heard chains rattling, pained moans, whimpering, and desperate, whispered pleas.

One door was rock, without windows. It was bolted, chained, with warnings in an alphabet Gabriel couldn't read. The soldiers swerved toward the opposite side as they passed, and hurried—nearly tripping over themselves. They lifted Gabriel off his feet so he couldn't slow them down.

Within his mind, he heard the prisoner's plea: *Come back, release me, and I shall grant you riches beyond your imagination, a harem filled with a thousand and one eager women, a circus of your own, flying carpets and magic potions. I'll teach you to shoot a cordless bow. Only break the seal, let me loose, and all you want is yours.*

Gabriel was in no position to break any seal or free any prisoner.

At the bottom of the steps, they reached a wide, red door. The soldiers hesitated, only briefly, until the torchbearer stepped forward and opened the door to the lab.

The old man was already there. He was not alone.

15.

Cool-Eyes stood beside the old man (the Wazir, bridge maker—
Gabriel didn't know what to call him). She smiled broadly, prettily, and
with utter sincerity—and it made Gabriel shiver.

The old man came closer, without the aid of a staff. He was neither
frail nor slow—just old, shriveled, and small. His hands were sun-dried
to a deep, reddish brown. He spoke, revealing gaps between his yellow
teeth. "Finally, my link."

The soldiers propped Gabriel up, though he was plenty strong
enough to stand on his own. He met the Wazir's gaze, but remained
silent. He wanted to look around, see what hid in the shadowy corners,
but there wasn't much else to see but a few stone tables and tablets, and
one large, overflowing bookshelf.

"Not very talkative, are we?" the old man asked. "Fortunately, we
have no need of your tongue here."

Cool-Eyes turned to a table behind her, grabbed something, and
came forward. She held the knife—like a scalpel—in front of her. It
glinted, but not as brightly as her kohl eyes. "May I take it?"

The old man chuckled. The soldiers, except those holding Gabriel,
stepped back. "Would you keep it as a trophy?" he asked her.

She leaned close enough to Gabriel to kiss him, and stared at his
lips. He kept his mouth tightly closed. Finally, she shook her head. "No.
There are other parts I might keep." She glanced down.

"I've been waiting a long time to meet you," the old man told
Gabriel. "A thousand years, and one, you might say." He laughed at
himself.

Cool-Eyes returned the scalpel to its tray. There were dozens of
silver implements there, knives and skewers, scissors, scoops and hooks.
Now that he'd seen it, Gabriel couldn't look away.

"Oh, you'll be a fortunate one," the old man said, touching the tray.
"Most of these, I'll be needing later, for summoning Kandara. You'll not
witness that."

Cool-Eyes stepped around the soldiers, and slid a finger along the
back of Gabriel's neck. "Can I taste him?"

"If you must," the old man said. "I don't need him until dawn."

She laid her head on Gabriel's shoulder, and whispered, "Good."

16.

Cool-Eyes pushed Gabriel toward one of the doors, some of which were only hanging beads or cloth. None were rectangular; rather, they'd been cut to mimic the minarets outside. They lined all the walls but one.

Cool-Eyes shoved Gabriel through a doorway of red silk.

Inside, brightly colored pillows with tassels and ribbons, were piled in a corner.

The soldiers had left the lab the way they'd come in. Their manner, their nervousness at approaching the Wazir, hadn't eased Gabriel any.

In fact, he was petrified.

He didn't show it. Couldn't. He'd never been in a situation like this, but in all the movies, the worst thing to do was show fear. Villains thrived on that. Sucked it up like vampires.

The pillows, however, were very much more welcome than medieval medical tools.

"I gave you every chance," Cool-Eyes whispered. Behind him, her lips touched his ear as she spoke. "I gave you clues and hints and suggestions. Are you just stupid?"

"What clues?" Gabriel asked.

"This could have been avoided," she said. "My love need not die. Because of you, he may."

"Why doesn't anyone say anything I can understand?" Gabriel asked.

Cool-Eyes chuckled. "You can't read, can you?"

"Of course I can."

She spun him to face her. "My circlet," she said, pointing to the gold band around her head. "What does it say?" The diamonds formed letters, apparently, but not any Gabriel knew.

He shook his head.

"You can't read," she said. "Not here. I understand now. Where you live, or when, there are many languages, not just one. They build a tower now, and Allah will come and cause that fracturing, but not yet."

"There's only one language?" Gabriel asked.

"One speech, yes. That's why you can understand me. If we were in your world, we could not communicate. Not verbally."

"So what does the circlet say?" he asked.

Cool-Eyes smiled. "That I've been jinn-taught. I'm the girl with the cordless bow."

17.

"Doesn't matter now," Cool-Eyes said, leading Gabriel to the pillows. "My lover will die, and you and I with him. They will stop him."

"Who, they?" Gabriel asked.

"The ones who brought the rain," Cool-Eyes said. "The creatures who gave me my hunger."

"Who?" Gabriel asked again.

"My teachers," she said. "The jinn. The ifrits."

18.

Thunder rumbled above, shaking the lab and all the adjacent rooms. Gabriel felt it even as Cool-Eyes pushed him down on the pillows. Her hands were soft, yet unyielding. She held him down and ripped the silk Cogia Hassan had sold him.

She tore his shirt and kissed his chest, twice, above the heart, and then bit him.

He cried and struggled, but her grip was steel. She tore a chunk of skin. Blood dribbled down her chin. She looked up at Gabriel, licked her lips, and winked. "Too bad we need you alive," she said.

Then she bit again, lower. She chewed his flesh, swallowed it, and took a mouthful from his belly.

19.

It might have lasted hours. Days. Years. In this place, where time meant nothing, it was impossible to tell.

But it didn't last very long at all—four bites, maybe five—before the noise.

The crash echoed like the distant thunder (which had a lot of earth to get through), followed by a muffled—and abruptly ended—scream from one of the soldiers.

Cool-Eyes looked to the silky doorway and cursed. Then she was gone, grabbing a cordless bow from the corner of the room.

After a moment, Gabriel sat up. Whatever was happening outside, it didn't concern him. He could slip behind the pre-occupied guards.

It sounded like a fight, things being thrown, people whelping incoherently. Whatever was out there, the soldiers were no match for it.

The ifrits, of course. The exotic had also mentioned them; they were coming for Gabriel. What the Hell made him so important to everything?

He peaked through the curtain. The fighting was outside the lab, through the open door. One of the soldiers came flying through the door, a bloody arc streaming behind him.

His severed head followed.

Gabriel slipped out of Cool-Eyes' chamber and sneaked alongside the wall. He stayed low below the little windows as he passed door after door.

Just outside the lab, soldiers surrounded a man-like thing formed out of blue smoke. He had six arms; two carried scimitars. The men stabbed and sliced, but their weapons slid through the ifrit as if he wasn't there.

He shot electricity from his fingers, blasting a hole in the chest of one of the soldiers.

Gabriel saw neither the old man nor Cool-Eyes.

The hall fell silent. The smoky ifrit floated into the lab, its arms swinging like tentacles, swords glittering in the torchlight, luminescent eyes emitting steam.

"No," Cool-Eyes said from somewhere in the dark. An arrow struck the ifrit in the chest. Unlike the swords, it pierced something solid. The ifrit looked down at the shaft protruding from his chest.

A second struck his eye.

With a howl, the ifrit lunged forward, all his arms flailing, eyes glowing so brightly they illuminated Cool-Eyes where she stood, in a doorway, bow in hand.

She loosed another arrow.

The ifrit did not stop.

Gabriel reached the doorway, and the hall behind it, where five broken soldiers laid in pools of gore. The smell of burnt flesh made him nauseas, but he couldn't stop. Couldn't hesitate. He wouldn't get another chance.

Gabriel raced up the stairs.

20.

The silence behind him was thick, almost overwhelming. Gabriel refused to look back, afraid of what he might see. He only had another hundred million steps. He could manage this, as long as he didn't turn around.

(Gabriel knew he mixed his myths; he was not Orpheus.)

He stumbled several times. Blood from Cool-Eyes' bites left an easy-to-follow trail.

Without realizing it, Gabriel reached the ifrit's rock door. *You've come back! You're a wonderful and fortunate man, you are! Yes, open the door, the chains are old and weak. Even a mortal can break that lock. I've been here a very long time, but I can grant wishes. Anything within my power, I will give to you. Whatever your heart desires most.*

Gabriel paused, and glanced over his shoulder. Either the ifrit or Cool-Eyes had died by now, he was sure of it. He didn't care to meet the winner.

The chains were rusted through in places, hanging by threads no thicker than spider webs. The lock crumbled to dust at his touch. The door swung inward. A stone man emerged, his booming feet cracking the steps.

"You," the ifrit said, "are either very foolish or very fortunate."

"Fortunate, I hope," Gabriel said.

"Then your wish," the ifrit said. "What is it you want most?"

"To go home," Gabriel said, and instantly regretted it. He wanted to see India again, wanted to touch her, to breathe her and love her. Nothing else mattered, especially not a home of excessive monthly bills and mundane slave-like work.

"Ah, but that is not within my power," the ifrit said. "You want a *when*, not a place. Something else?"

"India," Gabriel said, relieved. "I want to be with India."

"That," the ifrit said, "I can do." He snapped his stone fingers. Dust fell from his hand, whirling, and expanded into a funnel of smoke. The ground shifted under Gabriel. He fell backwards, smacking his head against the rock wall.

The air cleared. India stood in front of him, smiling sadly.

He reached for her, whispering her name.

"You made a wish," India said.

"Yes."

"You wished to be with me."

"Yes."

"I'm so glad," she said. "I've thought of nothing but you since we parted. But..." She paused, looking at the single door to this tiny room. A small window looked into the lab. "Well, here we are."

21.

"No."

Through the window, most of the lab was visible—including the door where he'd escaped, the tray filled with the Wazir's special cutlery, even the silk curtain of Cool-Eyes' room.

The smoky ifrit was a mass of oozing black oil on the ground. Cool-Eyes' bow leaned against the wall, but she was not there.

Gabriel tried the door. The knob wouldn't turn.

"Sealed," India said. "Magically."

"Damn."

"Wishes," India said, "seldom give you what you want."

"I suppose I'm lucky he didn't lock me in his cell," Gabriel said.

"You're lucky to still *breathe*." India touched his bare back, softly, and turned him around to better see his wounds.

"What do we do now?" Gabriel asked.

"Wait," India said. "The Wazir will cast a spell to find you. He'll come back, and then use you to bring him to your time."

"What?"

"That's what he wants," India said. "I was the first experiment."

Gabriel turned his head to look outside again. "He said he needed me at dawn."

"Just a few more minutes," India said.

"I met your exotic."

"She's not mine," India said.

"She knew they were going to capture me," he said. "She said to let them. To not resist."

"You've been captured," India said. "Now, I believe, would be a good time to resist."

"How?"

The door opened. Cool-Eyes—favoring one leg, scrapes and cuts everywhere—grinned. Her chest was charred, but she seemed unconcerned. The diamonds sparkled in her circlet. She looked over her shoulder and said, "I've got him."

22.

The old man stood before the solid wall, sprinkling dust into a burning bowl. "The future takes many paths," he said as Gabriel and India were brought forward. "I've seen paths I do not like. Babylon will fall, and again, and some things cannot be changed. But my city, my realm, will continue into your time. *Through* your time."

Cool-Eyes shoved Gabriel forward. He fell to his knees in front of the Wazir.

"There are bindings," he told Gabriel, "which require pain and blood, while others need only incense." He scowled as he spoke, intent upon the contents of his bowl. His eyes raged in the firelight. "Today, I need a doorway."

He added another ingredient. The fire flashed, and the outline of a door formed in the rock behind him. It shimmered. Gabriel felt sick again.

The old man touched the center of that doorway; the rock wall faded, replaced by the beach where Gabriel had stood at dusk, the ocean and seagulls, even the sandcastle which had survived the night. The sun peeked over the eastern horizon, sparkling on the Atlantic like diamond dust. "I sent only shadows of me, until now," the old man said. "Ghosts. You know, you are little more than that here, either of you." He looked directly at Gabriel. "I should thank you. Without you as an anchor, a mindless, drone-like slave to your own time, I could not open this door."

Cool-Eyes giggled.

"There will be a war," the Wazir said, "and I will ensure Babylon's victory." He shrugged. "With jinns bound to me, of course."

Then he split apart.

Two old men stood there now, one leaning on a staff, the other grinning broadly. "I go," the old man said, "to shape your future in my image."

"No," India said.

She'd managed to sneak away from the door, unnoticed. She lifted the cordless bow and aimed at the Wazir—the one without the staff. She pulled back an invisible string and released an arrow.

It went deep into the old man's chest. He staggered backwards, knocking over the bowl and spilling flames.

Cool-Eyes screamed something incoherent, a foreign curse, and leapt at India.

Gabriel ran to the old man's side; he'd landed on his back, blood spilling from his mouth and eyes. He smiled and closed his eyes.

The image inside the doorway wavered. Unnatural fire spread across the rock floor like water, reaching for India.

Cool-Eyes was on the floor, shot with her own weapon. "Go!" India cried, pointing the bow at the fading doorway.

Gabriel shook his head. "I won't leave you."

India threw the bow aside, jumped over the flames, and dropped to her knees next to Gabriel. She grabbed his face with both hand and kissed him.

He closed his eyes. The unnatural smoke circled around him, warm and thick. The fire's heat intensified. And nothing mattered, nothing except India.

She drew away. Her eyes glistened. "Now," she said, shaking her head, "is simply not our time."

Cool-Eyes knocked India aside.

23.

Cool-Eyes had a knife in her hand, a long, curved blade. She slashed at Gabriel and tackled him.

They tumbled backwards as the flames flared higher and hotter.

She raised the knife to stab him. Gabriel found the strength to catch her arm. The blade wavered over his face. She bared her teeth, hissed, and rolled forward.

They crashed into the wall, next to the barely visible beach within an illusory (and disintegrating) doorway. The knife clattered away.

"You can't stop me," she said through clenched teeth. "I'm going in."

Cool-Eyes was stronger than Gabriel—stronger than any of the soldiers and even the giants.

Gabriel tried to push her off as she shifted to the side. They rolled again, together, through the doorway and onto the beach. They demolished the sandcastle.

The sun and ocean were behind them as they splashed in the surf. The brisk water gave Gabriel a burst of energy. He kicked Cool-Eyes away and scrambled to go back.

On the beach, the door floated, showing the lab with its high flames and thick smoke. India was there, behind a wall of those flames. She called to him and waved.

"No!" Gabriel cried. He lurched forward.

The portal closed before he reached it. Babylon, its people and ifrits, its merchants and giants, were beyond Gabriel's reach—and India with them.

"No," he said again, dropping to his knees.

The sun blinked.

Gabriel turned. Cool-Eyes was gone. Over the Atlantic, a giant bird flew toward the sunrise. It was enormous, its body bulky and its wingspan impossibly wide. It had blocked the sun.

Further in the distance, there was a second such bird, both of them Rukhs, and Gabriel knew what had happened. One of the old men had died; but he'd split, and the second version—the shadow with the staff— had come through the door.

He watched until they were specks, and then they were gone.

Just like India.

On the beach, Gabriel cried.

24.

Two hours later, Gabriel locked himself in his apartment. He found a CD with Rimsky-Korsakov's *Scheherazade* and turned out the lights. He showered, bandaged the worst of the bites, and stumbled into bed.

He slept long and well.

In his dreams, he saw India. They hadn't had much time together; their love was untested. They'd lost the potential.

He watched her approach the doorway, heedless of the growing flames. In the beach image, Gabriel saw himself and Cool-Eyes, and the Rukh already in the distance.

He tried to speak, but found no voice.

The image wavered. Gabriel knew how this ended. Smoke curled, thickening, obscuring the magical door, and even India. He was behind her, unable to move, as if watching a movie.

He hated it.

As India neared the wall, the beach disappeared. Briefly, it was replaced by a long, tree-lined pool leading to a palace—with minarets like those in Babylon, all white, and Gabriel thought it may be the Taj Mahal.

As the smoke thickened around her, India stepped through the door, which the Wazir had used Gabriel to open, and into to her own land and time.

Maybe, he hoped, this had actually happened. Otherwise, she'd died in the lab.

25.

Gabriel woke with the alarm at six, Monday morning. He was sore, his eyes red with tears, and his dreams not completely fulfilling.

The radio talked about the war in Iraq.

26.

March 2004

A tall, skinny woman with a clipboard stared through black framed glasses at the painting. One finger pressed against the side of her chin, as if keeping her head straight on her shoulders. After a long while, she said, "You're improving."

"Thanks," Gabriel said, standing behind her.

"Don't you have anything without this Babylon theme?"

AFTERWORD

This memory may not be entirely accurate.

I got a call one day. Or an e-mail. It doesn't matter. Paul Miller from Earthling Books said, "Hey, why don't you do a flipbook with another author?" When I asked who, he said, "Brian Keene."

Brian and I had been friends for years already, but Paul didn't know this. He contacted each of us separately. We both agreed. This was about the time of Bush and Iraq, and Brian wanted to focus on that. I suggested the stories should have something that ties them together.

Thus was born *The Rise and Fall of Babylon*. I got the *Rising* part. Brian took care of the *Falling*. He finished his story first (shut up, it's not a race), so I incorporated one of his characters into this, to further tie them together. (The wizar, though he plays a slightly different role in Brian's.)

I thought I'd make my Babylon a land out of time, a shifty sort of place, and I scattered several events around it to give it that other-timely feel. It's also the place where I found Cool-Eyes, who was still something of a servant in this piece, though of course she grew to become so much more. (She stands completely on her own in *The House of Shadow and Ash*, and she will rise again, I'm sure.) It's partly an exploration of my own feelings at the time, not pursuing my art as I should, locked in a day job, that sort of thing. It's also something of a love story. A forbidden love story. Or a story of forbidden love. Which, of course, in a very real way, it's not.

THE MAGIC MARBLE

"Give me a dollar."

Jake looked up from his marbles. Except for the girl standing over him on the stoop, the street was empty. He'd never seen her before. She was older than him, but not much, and the way she leaned over him it was as if she was curious but unwilling to get too close. The way she spoke, she obviously expected him to obey.

"No."

"A dollar," the girl said, straightening and taking a step back. "It's not like that's a lot of money."

"No." Jake rolled up his marbles, gathering them in one hand and dumping them into a plastic pouch.

"I'll give you a marble."

"I have plenty," Jake said. "You want me to give you a dollar, you have to give me something I want."

She grinned. "You'll want this marble. It's a cat's eye."

"Is it an actual cat's eye?"

"That's gross," she said. "No."

"Then I don't want it," Jake said. He stood and dangled the pouch in front of her. "Got all I need in here."

"It's magic."

"Marbles aren't magic," Jake said. "You're being stupid."

"I'm a girl," she said. "I'm never stupid."

"You're a girl," he agreed. "You've got cooties."

"I do not," she said. She fished the marble out of her pocket and held it out on her palm. "I've got this."

It was bright, sparkly, blue glass with red veins inside, and it was definitely prettier than any of Jake's marbles. And bigger, too, twice the size of any of his shooters. He reached for it, but she closed her hand around it and shook her head. "I need a dollar."

"What do you want a dollar for?" Jake asked.

"Doesn't matter," she said. "Once you give it to me, it's mine, and I can do what I want with it. And I'll give you this marble, and you can do what you want with it."

"It ain't magic."

"It's very magic," she said. "A fairy gave it to me."

"There are no fairies."

"A fairy elf."

"There's no such thing as elves, either, 'specially not fairy elves," Jake said. He thought he was being reasonable. But he wanted the marble, and he wished he actually had a dollar to give her.

"Of course there are. You don't know everything."

"I know there's no elves or fairies."

"Who takes your teeth, then?" the girl asked.

That wasn't a fair question. Everyone knew about the Tooth Fairy. "Not the same."

"I'm just saying," the girl said, "that you don't know everything, and you're wrong, and this is a magic marble and I'll give it to you if you give me a dollar." She was showing the marble again. Sunlight glinted off it.

"If it's magic, what does it do?"

"It wins."

Jake looked up and down the street. They stood on this stoop, but all the others were empty. No kids. No adults either. He hadn't seen much of anyone since the evening sunrise. Days ago. "I'm not playing with anyone."

"You can play with me," the girl said.

"You're a girl."

"So?"

He didn't have an answer. "Why don't you play with the marble?"

"I'm a girl," she said. "I have dolls."

"That's silly."

She shrugged. "Just give me a dollar. Please?"

"I can't," Jake admitted. "I don't have a dollar."

She frowned. She dropped the marble into her pocket. She looked up the street, then down, then up the side of the apartment building as if someone might look down from one of the windows.

He thought she'd go away now. Or say something else. She looked at him again, and she frowned, but that was all.

"If I had a dollar," Jake said, "I'd buy your marble."

"It's not for sale."

"You said..."

"I said I'd give you the marble if you gave me a dollar. I did *not* say I'd sell it to you for a dollar. That's different."

"Oh." He thought about it, and said, "Then can you give me the marble anyway?"

"But then I won't have the marble and I still won't have a dollar."

"What about dolls?" Jake asked.

"I don't know. You're a boy. What do you know about dolls?"

"I know where to find some."

"Is there a doll shop?"

He shook his head. "Better. A five and dime."

"I don't want a cheap doll."

"I don't want a cheap marble."

"I just want a dollar."

"Why?"

"Because. Why do I have to have more than *because*?"

"That doesn't make sense," Jake said. "Do you want to buy something? Are you saving dollars for rainy days?"

"That's pennies," she said.

Jake reached into his pocket, pulled out three of those, and held them out. "Pennies, I've got."

She took them, one at a time, taking a time to look at each (maybe to check the date, or the face, Jake didn't know). "Thanks," she said. "I suppose you want the marble."

"You said it was magic."

"It wins," she said.

"How would you know?" he asked. "You're a girl."

"I told it I wanted to find a doll," she said. "It led me to you."

"A doll, or a dollar?"

"I really wanted a dollar," the girl said, "so I could buy my doll. But I don't know who to buy it from."

"I can sell you a doll," Jake said.

"From the five and dime?"

"Right."

"That'd be nice." The girl sat on the stoop, smoothed her skirt, and smiled. "Is it a nice doll?"

"I'm a boy," he reminded her. "I don't know if it's a nice doll."

"Will you pick it yourself?"

"Of course."

"Then it will be nice," she said. "Thanks."

"You don't want to come?"

"The five and dime," she said, "is your secret. The fairy elves and their magical marbles are mine."

the making of a shadow

the making
of a
shadow

1.

The shop had a wood door. It was once painted a bright, vibrant red, but most of the color had peeled off and the rest was curled and cracked and ready to jump. The window revealed shelves full of books, but the window hadn't been cleaned for a long while so the glass hid more than it revealed. The etched letters on the glass were so old, they predated whatever was inside now. It said *Apothecary*, when it was clearly something else. It could all be so misleading.

Susan pulled the door open. It resisted, briefly, but she didn't think that might be an omen. She didn't believe in portents or mystical warnings or any of the other things she expected to find within the shop. A bell announced her arrival.

It was small and cramped, stuffed between larger antique stores, across from a fledgling art gallery and a local ice creamery. The bookshelves were a little too close to each other, and each seemed to lean in one direction or another. Books were stacked two or three deep, and stuffed in one on top of the other, and again on the top of the shelves. Piles of them littered the floor. The high ceiling mimicked the antique shops, open and bare, showing air conditioning ducts and solid wood beams that held up the second floor.

An NCR cash register held down the counter, behind which an old man sat. He'd been reading, but put aside the leather-bound tome when Susan arrived. His wrinkled, stubbly face demanded a photographic portrait. His gray eyes were sharp and steady. He looked a lot like you would expect a magician to look, or an apothecary, though he wasn't either.

He watched Susan, but did not greet her, did not ask if there was anything he could help her find; nor did he offer her a finger of scotch, or a cigar, or a Petit Four. He barely moved; when he did, even if it was only his neck, the bones creaked and dust became momentarily unsettled.

The walls were unadorned except for a black Kit Cat Clock, its tail ticking off every second. Other than the floor creaking under Susan's footsteps, there was no other sound.

Susan took a moment to straighten her skirt, which was already straight, gave the shopkeeper a brief nod, then moved through the bookshelves. There was order, of some sort, though it might be a challenge to explain it. Some of the books were new, or nearly new, as recent as the latest nonfiction bestsellers, but most were well-worn, well-used, and well-loved.

She scanned the spines of a dozen books on stage magic; fairy tales of German, Celtic, and Slavic origin; Hollywood's silent era; and historical texts whose subject matter seemed obscure, mysterious, or surreal. After a few minutes, she looked at the shopkeeper, who still watched her, and said, "I'm looking for a book."

He grunted. "Look harder."

"My father had a book," she said. "I've been to a hundred shops, at least, up and down the east coast, and the best anyone else can do is point me to you."

He didn't move. He said, "That so?"

"It's important to me," she said. "My father only wrote the one book."

"Wrote it, did he?" the shopkeeper asked. "I have no time for authors. They're delusional, the lot of them, and if they're not drunk, they probably should be."

"That's an odd sentiment for a bookseller," Susan said.

He grunted again. "I don't have you father's book."

"I haven't told you the title."

"I know the titles, and the workings, of every tome in this shop, in the back, and upstairs as well. Not a single word of them was written by a man who might be your father."

That sounded like an insult. Susan tried to ignore it.

"What I might have," the shopkeeper said, "is a suggestion for breakfast. There's a café around the corner. Make good eggs, and corned beef hash, and squeeze their own orange juice."

Susan glanced at the Kit Cat clock. "It's almost dinner time."

"Right," the shopkeeper said, not taking his eyes off her. "I'm closed. Come back tomorrow, after you've eaten."

Susan stood there, hip jutted to one side, hand on it, posing, meeting the old man's stare. There was nothing particularly malignant in his gaze; he neither challenged nor defied her. He only told the truth, however he perceived it.

Finally, Susan said, "*The Making of a Shadow.*" He didn't react. "That's the title of my father's book. It was a limited edition, only a hundred copies, maybe less, and most of them have been destroyed or lost."

"Intentionally?" he asked.

"Very possibly."

"What did you say your father's name was?"

"I didn't."

"Then tell me now."

"Howard Creighton."

The shopkeeper gave a curt nod of his head, so brief a movement it might've been only a trick of the shadows. But Susan knew about such trickery and illusion, and she would have no part of it.

She said, "Tomorrow, then," and left.

2.

Susan didn't go far. There wasn't far to go. She was three hours from the airport, less than thirty minutes from the Georgia border, surrounded by antique shops that were closing up for the night, a general store just like old time general stores that wasn't even open today, and a tea shop that served tea, biscuits, and little else. She went to the ice creamery, associated with no national or international chains, and got a razzle dazzle cone with sprinkles for dinner. She sat at the window, through which she could watch the bookshop with the Apothecary sign.

The shopkeeper never emerged. A light went on in the window above the shop, but the blinds were closed so nothing was revealed. Susan kept a notepad in her purse. She had a list of similar bookshops in similar towns throughout Virginia, the Carolinas, upstate New York, downtown Baltimore, and a variety of other places she never imagined she'd see.

Seven times, in four different states, a person suggested she try the Apothecary's bookshop, but all they could say was that it was somewhere down south—until she got down south, into Georgia and Florida, where everyone shrugged and suggested maybe Havana, or maybe Cairo, or maybe St. Petersburg.

They all lied, of course. That was okay. Susan lied, too.

She ate her cone slowly, letting the ice cream melt down the sides and onto her hands. She wasn't interested in nourishment. She had a mystery to solve. She knew the solution hid inside that bookshop.

When she finished her ice cream, she washed up, crossed the twilit street, and tried the red peeling door. Grudgingly, it opened. The bell tingled again. It sounded tinny and incomplete, and it failed to compete against the metronomic seconds Kit Cat counted off.

The overhead light was out, but there was still a lamp near the old cash register. It threw a different set of shadows across the room, and made the books appear more menacing. She examined titles, looking for something slim enough to be the volume she sought, as she made her way to the back door.

She knocked. She didn't care much for protocol, but she was rarely intentionally rude. When no one answered, she tried the knob and found it unlocked. This door swung more easily, though it creaked, and led to a very small hall with two more doors and a stairway.

One door led to a water heater, an air handler, and a collection of brooms, mops, and cleaning supplies under the stairs. The other door led to a room just like the one up front, filled with bookshelves overstuffed with books, no cash register and no clock, and one overstuffed comfy chair. The book on its arm was about witchcraft, but the pages were handwritten, like a manuscript, in elaborate and unintelligible cursive, the words an older form of English. One floor lamp provided all the light; another, nearer the window, was dark. The window was small, blacked out, and shuttered; it presumably faced the alley that wasn't an alley so much as a crawl space between old brick buildings.

The books here were not arranged in any particular order. A history of Boston stood between Shakespeare and a book collecting West Virginian folk songs as heard along the newly forming railways. The title hinted that the rails were created by magic, rather than muscle and sweat and sledge hammers and drills.

She found several handwritten journals; where she could read the authors' names, they were unfamiliar. A handful of Little Golden books were stacked together. Chinese calligraphic arts. Tasmanian caves. Cats. She found nothing that looked like *The Making of a Shadow* by Howard Creighton.

At some point, she realized she was being watched. Slowly, she turned to the doorway, from which the shopkeeper's steady gazed once again was fixed upon her. "It's not morning," he told her.

"There's no place to stay," she said. "I want to find my father's book tonight."

He shook his head, but again the movement was brief. She'd never really seen him move; either he was there, or he wasn't. It unnerved her.

350

"Won't find it here."

"Then where?"

"You break into my shop after hours," he said, "break into my storeroom, interrupt my *work*," with so much emphasis on *work* that he clearly saw it as important, whatever it was, "and expect to demand answers of me that I'm not inclined to give."

"But you have the answers, then," Susan said, stepping forward. "What would incline you to give them?"

He grunted. It seemed to be something of a catch-all for him. It involved little movement, except perhaps in the shoulders and the throat, but it was perfectly dismissive. Only problem was, Susan was unwilling to be dismissed.

"I have money," she said.

"Don't need money."

"What do you need?" She asked it point blank, without any hint of play or seduction; she said it the way she meant it.

"Tell me," he said. "It's your father's book. Why don't you already have a copy?"

"I never knew my father."

"Oh," he said. "One of those."

"Not one of *those*," she told him.

He gave her another of those curt nods, then said, "You can stay here tonight, on the sofa. It's not comfortable, but I'll give you a blanket. Come morning, you go out, get your eggs and hash, leave me to my morning things, and we'll talk more after that."

3.

Susan followed the old man up the stairs. He moved with some speed and a great deal of grace, which surprised her. She wasn't a woman used to surprises. The stairs went up half a flight, turned around, and continued to the second floor. It reached no higher than most of the buildings in this town.

The door was open, but had both a lock in the knob and a deadbolt, and then a chain on the other side. They entered through the kitchen, where a number of cylinders and mason jars and beakers dominated the table, as well as unlabeled spice jars, a few old books, a notepad, and a beautiful Waterman fountain pen. The pad was open, the notes written in a neat but tiny handwriting. She didn't look too closely. This wasn't the grand tour.

"There's stuff in the fridge," the shopkeeper said. "Don't touch any of it. You need water, there are glasses above the sink." The shelves were open, without doors, so three glasses were visible, a coffee cup, a few plates, a variety of boxed and canned food items, more spices and herbs, a handful of books, and a few framed photographs.

There were, in fact, no doors in the apartment, except the one separating the bathroom. Far as Susan could see, there was only the one bathroom. The sofa was in the living room. It was old, beaten down, worn near to death, and its cushions looked as comforting as the shopkeeper promised. Beyond that, facing the ice creamery, was the old man's bedroom, but she couldn't see that far from the kitchen, where they stopped.

He appraised her appraising the place. He judged her judgments. She purposefully made no assumptions. One of the beakers stood atop a burner; the flame was low, and the bubbles did not appear to be all that excited. She asked, "What are you working on?"

"Things," he said.

"You don't have to tell me."

"Great and wonderful things," the shopkeeper said. He pointed to the couch. She noticed there was no sign of a television, but there was a black rotary phone from some time before she'd been born. It probably worked.

Susan shook her head. "I couldn't possibly sleep yet. It's too early."

"Read something," he told her.

The living room, besides the couch and a coffee table, contained only books, half as many as either room downstairs, but a more finely discerned collection. She recognized few titles and few authors. She searched for any sign of her father's name or title. "He wrote the book the year I was born," she said, as if in answer to a question.

She touched one or two books, pulling them partway out of the shelves before shoving them back. Nothing sparked her interest. She didn't come here looking for just any book. She hadn't spent the better part of the past two years seeking bedtime reading.

The shopkeeper had taken his post between kitchen and living room; from there, he watched her and, finally, after the silence became uncomfortable, said, "You think you're the shadow he created."

She met his gaze. "The thought had crossed my mind."

"You're a fool."

"Of course I am," she said. "Aren't we all?"

He ignored the question. "You think the book will explain why he abandoned you."

"I never felt abandoned."

He narrowed his eyes. For him, this was a grand gesture. "You lie."

She turned back to the books. "Don't we all?"

He said, flatly, "No."

"You have a copy, don't you?" Susan asked.

"Tomorrow," he said.

"I really can't wait."

"Then I really can't help you. Get out."

She looked at him again, struck another pose, found her poses failed to intimidate, exasperate, infuriate, or otherwise affect the shopkeeper. "The morning, then," she said. "What about your work?"

He grunted, or growled, some barely human noise that could only come out of a throat roughened by a century of whiskey and tobacco. There was no sign of either in the apartment. It smelled vaguely clean, and vaguely like old books, underneath the various scents wafting off the kitchen table. She returned to the beakers and vials and notepad, her intentions obvious. She read the top paragraph. The words were not English, nor any other language she recognized. They weren't Latin.

Quite suddenly, without a sound, he was looking over her shoulder at his own pad. He said, "Can you read it?"

"No."

"Look again," he said.

She did so. Some of the words were, in fact, numbers. She understood these, though they were neither Arabic nor Roman. Mathematical symbols appeared at regular intervals. One of the open books—there were several—showed the same formulae but without the calculations. These weren't strictly words, or text, and these weren't sentences. "It's scientific," she said.

"Be precise."

"Chemistry? Physics?" She shook her head. "I don't know that stuff." But some of the symbols represented stars, moons, and geographical shapes. "Alchemy?"

"Was your father an alchemist?" he asked.

"No," she said quickly. "He was a handyman. A wanderer. A jack of trades. My mother would say he was useless."

"*The Making of a Shadow*," the shopkeeper said. "You know what alchemy is?"

353

"Changing lead into gold."

He shook his head. "It's not about gold."

"What is it, then?"

"The transformation of one thing into something else."

"Something better?"

"You would hope."

"This here," Susan said, gesturing at the contents of the table. "This is alchemy?"

"This is nothing," the shopkeeper said.

"You're trying to create something."

"*Transform* something."

"What?" Susan felt a small bit of excitement; she didn't have room for much. Whatever they were talking about, it would eventually lead her to her father's book.

"Sleep," he said. "We'll talk in the morning."

"You know that's not going to happen," Susan said. "I can look through all this tonight. I'll figure out what you're doing here. Why make me go through all that work? Just tell me."

"That's not the way you learn."

"You're not teaching me anything," Susan said. When he didn't respond immediately, she added, "You're not teaching me alchemy."

"I can give you something to help you sleep," the shopkeeper said.

"I don't need anything."

"It will help your dreams work out your problems."

"I haven't got problems," Susan said. It was a lie, of course; everyone had problems of some sort, and everyone lied about them.

"Tea, then," the shopkeeper said.

"I don't know if I'd trust your tea."

He smiled. It was an ugly smile. No wonder he didn't do it often. "Sleep without it, then. I don't care."

"What are you trying to make?" Susan asked, meeting and holding his gaze.

It was a staring contest she couldn't win, but he eventually conceded. He said, "Gold."

"You lie."

He nodded.

Susan looked down at the page again, the transcript and the original, noting the changes, the variations, both the flourishes the shopkeeper removed and the ones he added. She noticed something. She bent closer, pointed at the pad in which the shopkeeper had been writing, and said, "There's a mistake."

"What?"

"This is wrong, here," she said.

"It's not a direct copy," he told her, looking down at where her finger pointed. "It's an interpretation, as alchemy is ever-changing, and..." He frowned. He picked up the pad, flipped to another page, read something, flipped back, and frowned more deeply. "You're right."

Of course she was right. She wasn't a woman used to making mistakes. She didn't mention that.

"You're right," he said again. "It's wrong." He thrust the pad at her. Rather than be forced back a step, she took it. "Fix it," he said.

"I can't fix it."

"You found it," he said. "You can fix it."

"I can't."

"There's a pen, there," he said, pointing to the Waterman.

"I'm not an alchemist," she said.

"You know something of mathematical theory," he said, "and of philosophy, and probably chemistry."

She shook her head. "No," she said. "It was just...well, apparent."

"I'll find your father's book, if any copy exists still in this world," he said, "after you solve that equation."

Susan looked at the numbers and symbols and words for a while. She never thought of herself as a numbers woman, though she had a certain skill with them; that's how she'd made so much money so quickly. But, while the mistake was obvious, the correction was less so. She puzzled over it, turned the notepad on its side and upside down to look at it from different vantage points, and consulted the other book as though it might contain answers. In fact, it made a suggestion to her. She picked up the fountain pen. It was a bit thick; she preferred smaller pens, gel pens, neither expensive nor flamboyant. But the ink flowed from this pen with much more subtlety, and she considered, however briefly, that the pen might be guiding her hand.

Which of course, was not true; if the pen could do that, it would've done it for the shopkeeper. No, she'd simply found a path to the solution.

It took some work. This was complicated math. It involved several layers of calculations, and consumed a good hour or two before she reached the bottom of the next page. There were cross-outs, arrows, a few notes of her own in regular everyday English, and, there at the end, a solution. A correct solution.

The whole time, the shopkeeper made almost no noise whatsoever. He wasn't always there, though he did frequently look over her shoulder. Twice, he snorted, though it was hard to tell if that was dismissive or appreciative. She assumed the latter. It would make life easier.

She re-examined her own calculations, double-checking, comparing what she knew and what she didn't know to the things she thought and assumed; there were no assumptions in the formulae. There were givens. There were absolutes. And there was an answer. She put down the notepad and the pen, turned, and called out to the shopkeeper who had gone into his bedroom. "Done."

He grunted. He came out of the bedroom with a leather bound book under his arm. It was not her father's book. He set the book on the couch, came into the kitchen to look at the equations, and nodded twice as he went through it.

"I see," he said.

"What do you see?"

He looked at her. He narrowed his eyes. He said, "Elegance."

Susan smiled.

"You're an alchemist," he said.

"No."

"That wasn't a question."

"I'm good with numbers," Susan said, "but I've never tried to transform lead, or anything else, into gold."

He looked down at the figures again. Ignored, Susan meandered into the living room and picked up the book. The spine and cover were blank, nothing more than a fancy, dappled red leather. The insides, however, were old, faded, crumpled, yellowed in places, torn, and in some places scribbled out. The title page said, simply, *Historia*. She flipped through a few pages, found the entries to be handwritten as if in a diary; the dates started in the 1300's, though the book was not that old, and continued through to the present day. Sometimes, there were gaps of twenty or thirty years between the entries. There were drawings, of varying degrees of competence. She recognized some of the symbols from the notepad. She'd skimmed through the whole thing before the shopkeeper said, "Are you in there?" He'd been staring at her for some time.

"No," she said.

"Your father?"

"Of course not."

"What if I told you your father's book was meant for spellcasting?"

"I wouldn't believe you," Susan said.

"Even after all you've seen?"

"I've seen books," Susan told him, "not spells. I've seen formulas that might, for all I know, reinvent plastic. But I haven't ever seen anything of magic or spells or, for that matter, alchemy."

The shopkeeper regarded her for a while, then said, "You're right. I haven't shown you anything."

"I didn't come here looking for a display," Susan said. She was comfortable with her belief system right where it was. "I came looking for a book. You have it. I will pay you for it, and then I can go back."

"Back where?" the shopkeeper asked. "Back to the city?"

"Home," Susan said.

The shopkeeper regarded her for a moment, shook his head once, and returned his attention to the table. "We'll discuss the book in the morning, after you've eaten. For now, I will show you something, just one thing."

He went to one of the drawers next to the sink and withdrew a paring knife. He found a thick wood cutting board and an apple. He put the knife and apple on the board, stepped back, and said, "If you would, quarter the apple."

Susan hesitated. She wasn't interested in seeing a magic show. Still, she cut the apple in half, and then both halves again.

"It's an ordinary apple," the shopkeeper said. He used the knife to stab and pick up one of the quarters. He bit it, chewed, put the remains on the table. "Take a bite, if you'd like," he said.

"No, thanks."

He shrugged; for him, that was an elaborate inch of movement in his shoulders. He picked up one of the other quarters, carved into its skin until there were a number of flourishes and crevices, until the peeled bits resembled fallen leaves and, in his hand, the red skin and creamy meat seemed to be a slice of flower. "Smell this," he said, offering her the apple slice.

It smelled like apple.

The shopkeeper went through his spices and herbs, gathered a pinch of this and a dash of that, and sprinkled it over the apple in her hand. Then, he closed his hands over hers, so that she held the apple hidden from view. It shifted in her palm. She jumped back, dropped the apple; an orchid flower, instead, drifted to the floor. It drifted slowly, leisurely, a perfect symmetry of reds and pinks and whites; but when it hit the floor, it broke up into dust and was gone.

"The diner serves breakfast from six," the shopkeeper told Susan. "Good night."

"Wait," Susan said, but he didn't. He walked past her, through the living room, into his bedroom. There'd been a light on in there; a moment after he entered, it went out.

He'd left one of the burners on under one of the beakers. She assumed that was intentional. She sat on the edge of the couch, picked up the *Historia* book again, and opened it to it backmost pages, to the present day.

4.

The last few pages of the book were clearly written by the shopkeeper; the handwriting matched what she'd seen in the notepad. He didn't write in it very often, though; over the course of fifty years, there were four entries, none of which were more than a half page.

The first, almost fifty years earlier, was just a name: William Reginald Warren IIII. Susan misread it as third, rather than fourth, the first time. She assumed the name belonged to the shopkeeper.

The second entry was about the lunar landing. It mentioned Apollo and Armstrong, Eagle, Houston, the Sea of Tranquility, and Khrushchev. It seemed to be primarily a list of facts, but it was written in something other than English; Susan couldn't read it. Some of the symbols that accompanied this entry were similar to those in the notepad, or the books on the kitchen table.

The third entry was devoted entirely to what the shopkeeper called a "Theft of Knowledge" by a woman he didn't name. He described her as Italian, beautiful, guileful, clever, and wicked. This, he wrote in English; he said she first stole the impression of his fancy, then his heart, then finally one of his prized books, *The Making of a Shadow*. This was the longest entry, and contained the least amount of alchemical calculations and mathematical acrobatics. It was almost poetic, incredibly Spartan, and unbelievably sad. Other than the title, the entry said nothing else about the book.

The final entry, with today's date, said, *She should be afraid.*

After that, Susan found it difficult to sleep. The couch didn't help; it was less comfortable than advertised, misshapen and sunken. She woke several times, and never really found her way into a deep sleep. One time, she thought she'd been dreaming, but the broken pieces she remembered when she opened her eyes drifted away quite swiftly.

The apartment was incredibly quiet during the night. No sound came from outside, neither cars, sirens, or gunshots, nor crickets, owls, or cats. The only windows were in the shopkeeper's bedroom, which she didn't approach, and the kitchen; but there was nothing to see but darkness. No lampposts lined the street, no headlights indicated any cars, no other houses or buildings had any lights whatsoever. She could make out the vague shapes of clouds in the sky; and the horizon was visible, albeit incompletely. The flame under the beaker remained blue and constant throughout the night; the liquid inside bubbled noiselessly.

Susan looked through the books on the table, and skimmed other sections of the *Historia*, but found nothing engaging. She drifted into a light sleep, once, on the chair in the kitchen, and woke just before falling to the floor.

Finally, night ended, or came close enough to an end for the shopkeeper to wake. He appeared, without warning, in the door-less doorway to his bedroom wearing basically the same type of thing he'd worn the night before. "Get your breakfast," he said. "I'll be downstairs after."

"I have questions," she said.

"They'll wait."

Susan didn't much like waiting, but accepted that she didn't have a choice. She rinsed her face in the bathroom, re-applied the little bit of makeup she wore, and left the apartment. Down the stairs, through the bookshop, she turned the corner and found the diner.

She was not the first person to eat. Two others shared a table in the corner. A thick, happy woman with graying hair led Susan to a table, poured coffee, gave her a menu. She got the corned beef hash and eggs, just as instructed. They were delicious. She got orange juice, too; it was freshly squeezed and a bit pulpier than she preferred.

"You'll want a little something sweet, too," the woman said, "to bring back to the shopkeeper." She left a brown paper bag on the table after Susan had already paid for her meal.

When Susan returned to the bookstore with *Apothecary* etched into its glass, the door was locked. He'd lied.

5.

Susan knocked. She pounded on the door. Flakes of red paint tumbled from the door, and dust, and sawdust. She peered through the window; the lights were out, the bookshop empty, the back door closed. She returned to the door, kicked it, and finally stepped away from the door and cursed.

Until then, she hadn't noticed the shopkeeper leaning against the lamppost, arms folded across his chest, eyes steady and disapproving but lips curved into a slight smirk. "Done?" he asked.

She cursed again.

He shook his head in disappointment.

"I suppose you were out here the whole time," Susan said.

He nodded curtly.

She thrust the bag of *a little something sweet* at him. He looked at it. "Take it," she finally said, thrusting it again, like a weapon, an epee in a fencing match she'd already lost. He took it, opened it, peeked in, then took a big inhalation of it.

"You have a car," he said.

"A rental."

"I don't," he said. "Don't need one. Don't trust them. But you won't leave me alone, will you?"

"No," she admitted.

Following her to the car, he said, "I don't have your book."

"You know where to get it," she said. It wasn't a question. He didn't feign innocence. "Who was she?" Susan asked.

"The Italian," he said, as though that were an answer, as though that were all he needed to say.

"She stole your heart," Susan said. "How?"

"You mean, how is it a man like me ever had a heart?" the shopkeeper asked.

"Something like that," Susan admitted.

"She came to my shop," the shopkeeper said. "She banged on my door."

They reached the car, an anonymous white sedan from Detroit. She keyed herself in and unlocked the passenger door from inside. She didn't feel like extending excessive courtesies. The shopkeeper didn't seem to notice. Susan started the car, then rested her hands on top of the wheel and looked at the shopkeeper. He hadn't shaved, but he'd definitely showered, and changed into something presentable, although there'd been nothing particularly un-presentable about his wardrobe yesterday. He met her gaze and held it, but offering nothing. Susan asked, "Where am I driving?"

He guided her through a series of smaller, more poorly maintained roads, until they left pavement for gravel and then left gravel for packed dirt. The sun cast sharp tree shadows across the roads and showed no sign of diminishing. As they drove, he said, "You won't find your father in that book."

"I know where my father is," Susan said. "In a lonely grave in a far corner of Valhalla." She meant, of course, the cemetery in Mount Pleasant, New York, not the Norse Hall of the Slain. No Valkyries escorted her father from this earth. She left a single white rose in front of his tombstone every February.

The dirt road finally ended at a barely discernible driveway leading to an old, dying house. It had obviously been abandoned. Windows were boarded up, and weather had wreaked havoc on the plywood. There was no siding to speak of, merely wooden slats, damaged and warped and without paint. The roof bent considerably at the center, and had at least two holes visible from the ground. There was a doorway but no door. The porch sagged; the wood there looked as sturdy as overdone linguini. A rocking chair had given up and become a pile of broken pieces—a transformation of one thing (a chair) into something else (debris).

Here, the shopkeeper got out of the rental car. Susan had to follow. "No one's here," she said, which wasn't entirely true; there was wind, a variety of birds, and a feral tabby lounging on the edge of the porch.

The shopkeeper didn't try his luck on the porch; he didn't even seem to consider it. He walked around the side.

At one time, the house had stood in a clearing; but the woods had been encroaching into that property for a long while, dropping broken limbs that were left to rot, sending seedlings and saplings into the empty space, and overrunning the lawn with vines, shrubs, bushes, and stalk-like flowers that nearly glittered under the bright sun. The shopkeeper walked close to the house, where the growth had only begun to touch. He moved swiftly, and with apparent purpose. At least one small snake—or perhaps a large lizard—felt disturbed enough to slither—or scamper—away into the underbrush.

Behind the house, the shed looked worse. It tilted harshly to one side. The aluminum door hung partly open. Its color had been replaced entirely by rust and rot, leaving holes large enough for small dogs. The shed, about the size of the rental car, which wasn't large, seemed to be waiting for an excuse to fall. One touch, the kiss of a strong breeze, might be the final push it needed.

The shopkeeper ducked around the door, not touching it, and entered the shed.

Susan paused behind him, squinting in the light of day. She took a breath and, careful not to disturb any part of the shed, snuck through the small opening.

The shopkeeper knelt on the ground in the center of the otherwise empty shed.

"You were expecting someone?" Susan asked.

"No," he said.

She moved closer. The shopkeeper knelt in front of a trapdoor in the floor. Rust coated the iron ring, but it was thick and still looked strong. The trapdoor was maybe two foot square, and barely noticeable except that there was nothing else to notice. The shopkeeper stared at it, hands on his knees, knees on the ground. The muscles in his arms were tense, the veins more visible than was usual. He clenched his jaw. He stared at the rusting iron ring in the floor as though he expected to move it by sheer will alone. Dirt and dust covered it. He'd made no attempt to open it.

"I forget, sometimes," the shopkeeper said.

"I don't believe you've ever forgotten one thing in your life," Susan told him.

He looked at her. He even smiled. It took her off guard. "I forget the ravages of time," he said. "I suffer them slowly, in due course, but it's something else entirely to see the results of seven hidden years."

Time ticked. The silence grew oppressive, but also deceptive. There was birdcall, and the wind through the rushes, and creeks from both the house and shed. But not even the echo of a distant auto reached them, nor the noise of sirens or footfalls or subways or beeping of any kind, not even the breath of anything human reached them here. They might have stepped off the map, except that there were, in fact, roads, and a house, and not so far away a small town with antique shops, a house museum, a gas station, and a bookshop with *Apothecary* engraved into its window.

Eventually, the shopkeeper said, "Help me with this, won't you?"

He moved aside, actually, to let Susan pull open the trapdoor herself. It was heavy, and wedged in tightly, so it took some effort. It budged, then shifted, then finally opened. She almost didn't get it all the way open; it wasn't just the wood that had warped and decayed, but the hinges had rusted. She disturbed insects and spiders, all of which scattered.

The door didn't lead to a cellar or basement. There was no room, no cave, barely even a depression in the dirt. It was a hole big enough for a cigar box, which was all it contained, a moldy wood cigar box that had seen better days decades earlier, back when you could import cigars direct from Cuba.

The shopkeeper mumbled something, a curse of some sort, not in English, and took the box carefully.

"Take me back to the shop," the shopkeeper said.

"Open it," Susan said.

He shook his head. "This box will never close again. It will break apart when I open it, if not sooner. Most the items in here...are personal, and do not involve you, your father, or your father's book." When he stood, he loomed over her. "Take me back to the shop."

He slept in the car. At least, he closed his eyes. He held the cigar box with both hands. Whatever words or colors had been on its surface had eroded. The remnants of a few rectangular stickers hung in flakes.

The roads back seemed somehow different. Shadows stretched in different directions. There were few landmarks, except perhaps a remarkable Live Oak on the side of the road, or a field of pecan trees, which could easily have echoed other such trees for hundreds of miles in any direction. The roads shifted from dirt to gravel, then from gravel to pavement, and eventually led to a two-lane highway headed east. After a few miles, they reached the road that cut through town, albeit a ways north; she turned right and, before sunset, parked outside the bookshop.

"We're here," she announced, but his eyes were open now. He climbed out of the car, keyed into the bookshop, and didn't seem to care if she followed or not. Upstairs, he cleared a section at the end of the kitchen table and retrieved a relatively new shoebox. He opened the cigar box over this, and dumped its contents into it. Susan saw a leather wallet, a ring, a deck of cards (or a pack of cigarettes; she wasn't sure), papers, clear envelopes filled with herbs or seeds or dust, a few rocks, and a pocket watch, among other things that she didn't notice. He withdrew one or two things and closed the shoebox.

He'd been right. The cigar box had broken into a half dozen pieces.

He dropped these into the trash, then set the retrieved items—a pair of brass dice—on the table.

"Take them," he said. "Roll them around in your palms. Get ready to throw them. It's a crapshoot, much like dice, so tell the dice you want a seven, you need a seven, you can't have anything but a seven. Tell them you need a new pair of shoes. Whatever you think will make you lucky. Roll them around in your palms until they've got the oil from your flesh in them. They're dry now, and dusty, and no longer mine." He paused; Susan had made no move to pick them up. "Do it *now*," the shopkeeper said.

She picked them up. They were heavy.

"Roll them round and round," the shopkeeper said, "until they're a part of you, an extension, something more than just a set of throwing bones."

"They're brass," Susan told him.

"They're metal," the shopkeeper said. "They're bone. They're luck and fortune and fate. But they're not brass."

No, they were softer than brass. "Gold?"

"What does the alchemist seek?" the shopkeeper asked.

"The transformation of base metals into gold," she told him.

He was shaking his head. "No," the shopkeeper said. "We've been through this."

"The transformation of one thing to another," she recited.

He didn't smile, except maybe a little in his eyes. "Tell the dice what you want, what you seek, what you need to roll. Tell them, roll them through your sweat and oils, make them a part of you, and when you're ready, when you think you know what you want and the dice know what you want, *roll*."

Susan was ready. She rolled. The dice bounced on the table, knocking against the shoebox, and dropped. Each landed with a single pip facing up.

"Snake eyes," the shopkeeper said, smiling now.

"Did I just lose?" Susan asked.

"Don't be absurd," the shopkeeper told her. "We aren't playing craps. We aren't playing anything. We're making contact."

"Making contact?" Susan asked.

"Making a connection," the shopkeeper said. "The Italian, she has a copy of your father's book, she may have the only copy in existence. Once upon a time, these dice were hers. She fashioned them out of lead." Susan almost said something, but didn't interrupt. "She left them with me for her own purposes, but now, I think, it's time to use them for ours."

Susan didn't think she believed any of that. "Are they safe?" she asked.

"Not for me," the shopkeeper told her. "Are you hungry?"

"Actually, yes."

"Go get us something to eat, then," the shopkeeper said. "Don't touch the dice again until after."

"After what?"

"After she's responded."

6.

Susan brought back a bag of food from the diner, basics burgers and fries, and two large sodas. They ate in the living room, on the coffee table; she sat on the couch and he turned the chair. They ate in silence. It tasted exceptionally good; but Susan hadn't eaten anything since breakfast some twelve hours earlier, so anything would've been delicious.

She gathered the trash and took it to the bin in the kitchen. He seemed disinclined to do much more than sit back and, presumably, think, or maybe reminisce; she didn't know if he dreaded or looked forward to what would come next.

She had some ideas about that, too, but she didn't entirely believe any of them.

She washed her hands, used the toilet and washed again, then stopped in the kitchen to stare a while at the gold dice that had fallen on snake eyes. She held a hand over them, but didn't touch them. She didn't really know what they were waiting for.

The phone rang.

It was an old-fashioned phone, the type that was old when Susan was young, a black thing with a dial and a resonant ring that pierced the whole apartment and probably the bookshop downstairs, too. The shopkeeper picked up the receiver, unconscious of the cord in a way Susan never could be, and said into the receiver, curtly, "Yes?"

The person on the other end spoke.

The shopkeeper nodded twice during what was, for Susan, silence. Finally, he said, again, "Yes." Then he hung up.

He didn't offer up any details, so Susan asked, "Was that her?"

"The Italian," the shopkeeper said. "Yes."

"So she's responded?" Susan asked.

"Yes."

He still wasn't forthcoming. "How?"

"She'll be here. She's willing to trade for the book."

"She knows what I want?" Susan asked.

"Of course she does," the shopkeeper said. "It's the only physical thing she stole from me."

"How much?" Susan asked. Money didn't matter. She had plenty.

The shopkeeper shook his head. "Terms won't be discussed except in person," he said.

"When?" Susan asked.

"You can't stop asking questions," the shopkeeper said.

"No," Susan admitted. "When will she be here?"

The shopkeeper looked at his wrist, but found no watch there. He shrugged. "Damned if I know."

Susan sat on the couch. She kept her eyes on the shopkeeper. Drilled into his soul. She found nothing but shadow and ice and red brick walls. She took a breath, took inventory of herself, found calm and serenity and peace, things in which she didn't necessarily believe, then said, "Tell me about her."

The shopkeeper grunted. "She's from Italy."

Susan shook her head. "Not enough," she said. "I'm to do business with this woman, I need to know everything."

"She's from Italy," the shopkeeper said. "She's a liar and a thief, and she has no heart."

"She has your heart," Susan said, leaning forward. "Tell me something real. Something substantive. Something I can use."

"There's nothing to tell," the shopkeeper said.

Susan nodded once and counted to three in her head. She never released the shopkeeper's eyes. This time, she was in control. She said, "Tell me anyway."

The shopkeeper growled It came from deep within, but it was necessary. It petered out and became a sigh, and finally the tension in his shoulders and face deflated. "She was the most beautiful woman I've ever seen. Bedazzling and beguiling and, as I said, incredibly gorgeous. Raven hair and deep blue eyes. And she has a name, but I haven't said it aloud in forty years."

Susan resisted the urge to ask. He paused, but he'd get to it. Finally, he said, "Her name is Elisabetta. Elisa."

When it seemed that he'd finished, though he hadn't actually started, Susan said, "Thank you."

"I was resigned to the end," the shopkeeper said, "before you arrived."

"The end?"

"My books, my experiments," the shopkeeper said. "Till my last breath. And now, I'm remembering Elisa, I'm remembering the wine and the song, the summer breezes, the scent of her perfume, everything."

"You don't want to remember?" Susan asked.

The shopkeeper closed his eyes and leaned back. "I shouldn't have to. I've lived long enough to have earned forgetfulness." Susan saw moisture in the corner of one dusty eye.

Susan put her hand on the shopkeeper's. She said, "You're remembering regrets, errors, and misdeeds. You're remembering the things you wish you'd done differently, whatever you tell me. You're not remembering the things you loved about Elisa. You're remembering that she's not here now."

"Alchemy," the shopkeeper said. "You think it's about changing lead to gold. Lengthening life. Discovering the mysteries that give you wealth and health. You know of the failures because scientific types, pseudo-scientific types, would extract themselves from society and devote their lives to formulae and calculations. I, too, am destined to be a grand failure. But you forget the successes, the moments of brilliance, the epiphanies and euphoria. You don't know that medicine is made possible because of the efforts of alchemists. Chemistry and physics rely on alchemical foundations. You, and I mean the world, well beyond you, fail to recognize the alchemists that are our teachers, guiding the transformation of children into adults. But we all forget the ultimate purpose, the original intention. I *had* forgotten, dammit, and I preferred it that way."

It was probably the most words he'd put together in a decade. Susan let them settle and waited for the shopkeeper to go on at his own pace.

Finally, he said, "Love."

"Love?"

The shopkeeper shook his head. "There is no calculation that can prove, disprove, or create love. Love is the question. Philosophers, poets, magicians, musicians...alchemists unable to answer the question."

She was out of her depth. Susan said, "Love isn't a question."

"Then explain it," the shopkeeper said.

Susan shook her head.

"You know nothing of love," the shopkeeper said, opening accusatory eyes. He didn't wait for her to object. "You may have played at it, you may have tinkered with the motions, you may have scratched the surface of emotions, but you have never truly given yourself to it, have you? You don't even seek your father's book out of love for the man you never met. You're the same as the Italian."

"Elisa," Susan told him.

He scowled.

"You're right," she told him. "I don't know love. I'm not seeking love."

"Then don't ask me about it," the shopkeeper said. "And don't ask me about *her*. I've told you everything."

"No," Susan said. "You haven't."

"I've told you enough."

Susan shook her head. "I don't believe a heart can be stolen."

The shopkeeper sighed. "Believe what you will."

Downstairs, so distant it was barely discernible, someone knocked on the bookstore door.

7.

There was gray in her hair and wrinkles around her eyes, but Elisa looked exactly as Susan expected. There was a lot of hair; her make-up was flawless and elegant. Her eyes were vivid and vivacious. She carried only a tiny clutch bag. Susan saw hints of what the shopkeeper might once have seen.

The shopkeeper had gone down to open the door, leaving Susan waiting in the kitchen, but they came up immediately and, apparently, without words. Elisa looked around the room, purposefully avoiding Susan for the moment, and said to the shopkeeper, "You haven't changed a thing."

The shopkeeper grunted, but it was a softer grunt than he'd ever given Susan.

"Still working, I see," Elisa said.

"You aren't?"

"Of course I am. But others...not so much."

"There aren't any others," the shopkeeper said, but it had no ring of truth and Elisa didn't respond to it.

Instead, she finally settled her gaze on Susan, looked her up and down, examined her like a piece of meat, and said, "You must be the daughter."

Susan said nothing.

"Show me something."

The shopkeeper said, "The notepad on the table."

Elisa took it, with Susan's calculations right on top, and examined them. She carried herself like royalty. She examined the scribbles in the path with apparent distrust and intrigue, twice arched an eyebrow in surprise, and near the end squinted and screwed up her lips. "You did this?" she asked.

"Yes," Susan said.

"You've not been trained?" Elisa asked.

"She's a nonbeliever," the shopkeeper said.

Elisa handed the book to Susan. "Do you know what you resolved there?"

"An equation," Susan said.

"Not a simple equation, by any means," Elisa said. "Would you like to see it in action?"

Susan glanced at the shopkeeper, but he saw nothing and no one but the woman who had stolen his heart. Susan said, "No."

"No?"

"I'm looking for a copy of my father's book," Susan said. "*The Making of a Shadow*. I understand you have one."

"I do."

"His copy." The shopkeeper.

"Mine," Elisa corrected.

"I want to buy it," Susan said. "I have money."

"I have money," Elisa told her.

"It's my father's book."

"Ah," Elisa said, "but my copy of it."

"It's important to me."

"No, it's not," Elisa said, "or you would already have one of your own. Why do you not?"

"I never knew my father," Susan admitted. "I only just learned he had written a book. And I know there's something in it about me. I want to see it."

369

"You want to see it, or own it?" Elisa asked. "English may not be my first language, but I know the difference between those two words."

"Own," Susan said.

Elisa nodded. "Now I know what you want. Would you like to know what I want?"

Susan didn't like the wording of that question. "What?"

"I want you," Elisa said. "I want you to work for me. For a year. Then, we'll discuss whether or not I'll sell you your father's book."

Susan shook her head. "I'm not available."

"Whatever appointments you have, whatever plans you've made, cancel them all. You have a job? Resign. Hopes? Dreams? Aspirations? Put all those things on hold. There's nothing more important than my work."

"I'm not going to indenture myself," Susan said.

"You will learn things," Elisa said.

"I know things."

"Tell me one thing you know," Elisa said.

"She knew to find me," the shopkeeper pointed out.

"Quiet," Elisa snapped. "You and I will talk only after my business here is concluded." She didn't even look at the shopkeeper when she said it. She leaned toward Susan in a way meant to show dominance. "How badly do you want your father's book?"

"My time is not negotiable," Susan said.

"Everything is negotiable."

Susan shook her head.

"Then our business together ends without satisfaction for either," Elisa said.

"I'll find another copy," Susan said.

"There are no other copies," Elisa said. "I have the seven that remain."

Susan didn't like the way that sounded, either, because it sounded true.

"Six months," Elisa said. "After six months, we'll discuss whether you should stay on as my apprentice."

"Apprentice?"

"You will learn alchemy," Elisa said.

"I don't believe in alchemy," Susan said.

Elisa swiped the gold dice off the table and held them in front of Susan's face. "Once upon a time," she said, "these were pieces of lead.

Do you not crave the power of such transformation?"

"No," Susan said.

Elisa smiled. She took Susan's hand, placed the dice in them, and closed Susan's fingers over them. "When you wish to discuss our options, you know how to find me. Snake eyes."

Elisa turned, fetched a ceramic bowl from the open cabinets behind her, and set it on the table. "In the meantime," she said, "I will leave you with an alchemical lesson. There are certain degrees of transmutation. Some are more final than others. Fire, for instance, creates something called ash." She ripped Susan's formula out of the notepad, crumped it into a ball, and dropped it in the bowl. She then set a match to it.

The fire spread unevenly but unstoppably. The small flame consumed the calculations. Susan glanced at the shopkeeper; he glared, emitting all his emotion through only his eyes.

When Susan turned back, Elisa had retrieved a book from her clutch and placed it on top of the burning paper. It was a small book, no larger than a tablet. The cover was a rather plain textured gray with black lettering. It said *The Making of a Shadow.*

The book, dry and dusty as it was, embraced the tine flames. The flame spread quickly, devouring the book, turning its pages into ash. The edges burned first, and the cover, then the pages beneath, revealing snippets of words for so short a time it was impossible to read. The paper blackened and curled and fell in flakes.

Susan moved to snatch the book from the bowl, but Elisa stepped in her way and forced Susan back. She was a strong woman, this *Italian.*

The book, though it seemed to burn quickly, also took its time. Susan bit her lip. It took an extraordinary amount of effort not to punch her way through Elisa to get at it. But it would have been pointless; the damage was already done.

"What was wood," Elisa said, "becomes ash, and it can never be made back into the wood from which it came, or into paper, and the ink is gone. Fire is a cleansing force. It chars down to the bone. It changes everything. In nature, it leaves a place for things to reclaim and grow once again. It's necessary and important and inevitable. In a bowl, however, fire is simply a means to an end." She paused. "I now have the six remaining copies of your father's book. I require six months, at least, but I do not expect a decision tonight. Sleep on it, if you must. Consider. Make your arrangements, and get in touch. I will burn one copy of the book every night until you've agreed to my terms. Six nights from now, when I destroy the final copy, my offer is rescinded."

She waited until nothing remained of the book but ash. She sifted the ashes with one of the shopkeeper's forks. She then took the bowl to the sink, rinsed out the ashes, and let them disappear down the drain. She cleaned the bowl, dried it, and returned it to its shelf.

She looked at the shopkeeper, smiled sadly, then looked at Susan. "I expect to hear from you soon."

Susan couldn't move. She couldn't think. She watched Elisa walk out the door, listened to her descend the stairs. The Italian left the bookstore quietly enough that Susan barely heard the door close.

Finding that she'd been holding her breath, she left it go all at once and turned on the shopkeeper. "You knew she was going to do that."

The shopkeeper shook his head. "I only knew she was wicked."

"I don't have a choice, do I?" Susan asked.

The shopkeeper said nothing; there was nothing to say.

"You don't have a copy?" Susan asked. "I'll pay you ten thousand dollars. Cash, tomorrow, if you wish."

"That," he said, "was my copy."

"Then you can't help me anymore," Susan said. She took the dice with her and left. She followed Elisa's path down the stairs and out the door. She went to her rental car without looking back. More than anything else, she felt anger and frustration. She gripped the steering wheel as though it might save her life and guided the car back toward the airport, over a hundred miles away. It was an unpleasant drive. Thunderclouds stained the night sky. Eventually, it would rain. Semis drove too closely to her. The shoulder was tight, the woods close. Cars sharing the highway moved either as though fleeing demonic realms or trying to delay arriving at one. The night felt magical, but in all the worst ways. Susan's skin didn't fit. Her jaw ached from gritting her teeth. Eventually, she stopped a dozen miles shy of the airport and checked into a cheap motel. She slept fitfully.

Susan was not a woman of leisure, but she was a woman of means. On the phone over the course of the next day, she made arrangements to be absent from her businesses and absent from her life. She hired someone to live in her apartment and water the plants. She bought the rental car outright; she didn't want to spend time searching for something else.

Near dinner, she took the dice and sat at the cheap desk that was about the only piece of furniture in her cheap room. She squeezed the dice tightly in one hand. She thought of the Italian, Elisabetta, Elisa, strong and firm and gray-haired, beautiful but frigid, wicked just as the shopkeeper had said. She rolled the dice.

For a moment, Susan was sure they'd land in something other than snake eyes: maybe a two and a three, or a total of seven, or some other doubles. The gold dice danced a moment longer than perhaps they should have, and each fell showing one pip.

Susan sighed. She sat back in the motel chair, leaving only the dice and her cell phone on the desk. She closed her eyes and waited.

8.

Susan waited. She didn't think of anything. She didn't imagine what the next six months might be like. She held on to only one thing: obtaining her father's book. She already didn't like Elisa. She understood why the shopkeeper referred to her as *The Italian*; ignoring her name meant you could possibly avoid thinking of her as human, as someone you might once have loved.

Susan did not have that problem. She had no memory of good feelings for the woman. She had only the burning of a book.

She ate no dinner. Twilight came and went without incident. Midnight followed. The hours between midnight and dawn stretched longer that regular hours. Odd noises filled the night: the cheap motel *settling*, cicadas or other insects outside, the occasional car driving past. When thousands of vehicles drove by every hour, you didn't notice; but you couldn't help but glance out the window when there was only one.

Finally, dawn broke palely in the east. The light seemed overexposed, washing out all colors, leaving nothing but tree silhouettes and birds and a barren parking lot.

Susan checked her cell phone. It was charged, but there'd been no calls. The parking lot was empty except for her car; no one else had bothered staying overnight. Tired and hungry, she took the die and left the motel. She breakfasted at Denny's; it wasn't as good as the corned beef hash. Then, feeling that she had no other choice, she got on the highway and headed back.

Eventually, she found herself in front of the same wood door with the peeling red paint and the glass with *Apothecary* etched into it. The door resisted, but opened, and let her into the bookstore.

The shopkeeper sat behind the counter reading a book. It wasn't the same book he'd been reading the first time she walked in, and it wasn't anything like the books he kept upstairs. It was a pulp detective novel. The spine had been cracked so many times, the title and author were illegible. The front cover was stained. He looked at her over the book, only his eyes visible, then went back to reading.

"Is she here?" Susan asked.

"She burned another book last night," the shopkeeper said.

"I rolled the dice."

"You weren't here," he said.

"They're not very effective, for something magical," Susan said. She didn't really believe they were magical. Magical applied to things like circuses and candlelit dinners and movies. She gave it no thought.

The shopkeeper dog eared the book and laid it, face down, on the counter. He appeared, somehow, more defeated than before. "She came," he said.

"And left?" Susan asked.

"She'll be back, if you roll again."

Susan considered that. "Tell me about the book," she said.

"You don't want to know *about* the book," the shopkeeper said, "or we wouldn't have come this far."

"What happened last night?" Susan asked.

"Told you. She came."

Susan decided to accept a double meaning there. "She left at dawn?"

The shopkeeper narrowed his eyes. Then he leaned back and sighed. "Precisely."

"What else do I need to know?" Susan asked.

"You already know," the shopkeeper said. "You teased me with knowledge, tantalized me with talent, then opened up decades-old wounds. You tore through my past and my mission and reminded me of the things I haven't been doing. My real work, neglected for too long. There's nothing left for me now. I gave the Italian *Historia*. I have no right to it anymore. She's the last, until the next. My part is done."

"Your part?" When he didn't answer, Susan asked, "What was your real work?"

"The formula you solved," the shopkeeper said. "The solution the Italian burnt to ash. That would've been my work. But I cannot start it again, not from the beginning. I'm too old."

Susan took the shopkeeper's hand. It wasn't something she normally did. She wasn't good with people that way. She didn't believe in making those kinds of connections. She said, "You're a fool."

"I know."

"No," Susan said. "You're a *fool*." She squeezed his hand gently. "What was that formula meant to do?"

"You don't care," the shopkeeper said. "You want only your father's book. *The Making of a Shadow*. You don't even care what it's about."

"It's about magic," Susan said. "Alchemy."

"Those are not the same things."

"Apparently, I'm meant to learn it," Susan said.

"Belief is often a hindrance to knowledge," the shopkeeper said. "You'll survive."

Susan almost said, *Was that ever in question*, but of course it was. She'd stumbled into something she didn't quite understand. Where was her father leading her? She wanted to blame her mother. It was easy to blame the dead. You gave their final words far too much weight.

Instead, she said, "Get me some paper."

She remembered the formulae from yesterday, every strange symbol and every integer and every calculation mark. It took a while to regurgitate it, maybe an hour, but not as much time as it had taken to correct it the other day. She wrote it more neatly this time, with only a few scratch-outs. She only needed one sheet of paper.

While she scribbled, the shopkeeper read his book. He didn't seem to have the heart to watch.

When she finished, she clicked shut the pen and presented the page to the shopkeeper. "Now, what is it meant to show?" she asked. She didn't know the symbols or their meanings. She didn't know the intents. She almost didn't release the paper when the shopkeeper moved to take it.

He examined the work again, just as he'd done previously. He nodded once or twice, harrumphed, and finally sighed. "You did this by memory?"

"Mostly," Susan replied. "Remember, I'm good with numbers."

"Not just with numbers," the shopkeeper said.

Now," Sue said, "and I don't want to ask again. What is it?"

The shopkeeper didn't answer right away. He was seeking words. He didn't know how to describe it. Finally, he said, "A miracle."

"I don't believe in miracles."

The shopkeeper folded the paper and put it in his pocket. He wore the slightest of smiles. It completely changed his face, as though he'd become someone else. The smile even reached his eyes. But he moved with deliberate, steady motion. His bones might crumble to dust if he moved too swiftly. His grace was damaged.

"You're not going to tell me, are you?" Susan asked.

"No," he said.

"I can write it again for her."

"You will," he said. The smile disintegrated under the thought. "I can't expect otherwise. But you're the Italian's apprentice now. I must accept that, and therefore I can give you no lessons."

Susan, unencumbered by age and fragility, reached over the counter so quickly, the shopkeeper had no time to react. She reached into his pocket, unafraid of hurting or exciting him, and snatched the folded paper. "This," she said, stepping back as he made a swipe for it, "is my work now."

The shopkeeper settled in his chair. His fighting days were behind him. He glowered now, all traces of the smile wiped away. He barely moved his lips as he spoke. "You're just like her."

Susan opened the paper to verify she'd gotten the right one. He might have pulled some bit of trickery, faster-than-the-eye stuff. Satisfied, she pocketed the paper. "It's a simple trade," she said. "Don't you know how to barter?"

He didn't answer, only looked at her, wearing a mask of civility over a thick layer of malice.

"You're not much of a shopkeeper," she told him.

"I would've happily sold you a copy of *The Book of Lost Fates* and sent you on your way," the shopkeeper said.

It was Susan's turn not to say anything. In fact, she didn't just say nothing; she left the bookshop. She went through the back door and up the stairs to the shopkeeper's apartment. None of the doors were locked; the shopkeeper made no move to stop her. In the kitchen, she noticed the burner under the glass cylinder had been turned off. There was new scribbling in the notepad where the shopkeeper had tried to recreate the formulae from his own memory. He'd gotten half as far as he'd gotten without her. There was a new book on the coffee table in the living room, something innocuous about Jean Eugène Robert-Houdin. The picture on the cover, a faded silver oval, depicted an old man with a severe countenance, not unlike the shopkeeper's. It was a biography.

Susan didn't bother to pick it up.

She sat on the couch and rolled the gold dice around in her hands. She didn't think she needed to roll them. She didn't believe they had conjured the Italian; the woman, Elisa, had come regardless, fully expecting to find Susan waiting.

Under her breath, Susan cursed. It was a simple word, but it eased her soul; so, sitting back, she said it again, this time with less effect. She couldn't blame her dead mother for this.

After a few wasted minutes, Susan leaned forward again and threw the dice. They bounced, twirled, and danced, and almost flew off the table; but they hung on, and they landed with that single pip facing the ceiling. Snake eyes. The dice would roll nothing but snake eyes; they'd been loaded, or shaved, or otherwise tampered with. These dice had no freewill, no hope for personal destiny, no pretense to randomness whatsoever.

Susan almost scooped up the dice again. Instead, she marched into the kitchen. She pulled down a glass, filled it with water, drank it down in a single gulp, and refrained from throwing the glass at the wall behind the kitchen table. She wanted to see the shards rain down on the chemicals and powders and beakers and books. She wanted to hear the violent tinkling. She suspected she'd see the glass break in slow motion; she could follow every individual piece from beginning to end.

She didn't throw the glass. But she didn't let it go, either. Susan simply stood there, frustrated and angry and annoyed, not knowing what to do or what she'd done. She was unaccustomed to uncertainty. She didn't like it.

Eventually, she left the glass, unshattered, in the kitchen sink. She sat at the table, pushed the pen over the pad and corrected the shopkeeper's most apparent errors. She didn't complete the calculations; she'd already done that twice. But she gave him enough to push him in the right direction. Call it an act of charity; Susan preferred to call it a way of passing time.

Time passed. When she looked up again, through the kitchen window, light had left the sky. The shopkeeper stood in his doorway, arms crossed, leaning against the jamb. When he saw that he'd been seen, he cleared his throat and said, "I hope you're ready."

The Italian stood behind him.

"I'm glad you've accepted my offer," she said, her voice tinged by a hint of amusement. "But I feel a certain need for punishment."

Susan narrowed her eyes and stood, but said nothing.

"You should have been here last night," Elisa said.

"I threw the dice last night."

"Oh, I know," Elisa said. "And again today. *I know.* You couldn't help yourself. That's why you're here. But still." She pushed past the shopkeeper and handed a small manila envelope to Susan. "This is yours. It is a warning, not a gift."

Susan didn't need to open the envelope. It contained the remains of a book, *The Making of a Shadow*; it had, like two copies previously, been burnt to ash.

Elisa gave Susan time to open it, but didn't mention it again. She turned to the shopkeeper. "I should thank you," she said to the shopkeeper.

"You've done enough harm," the shopkeeper said.

Still, Elisa leaned in and kissed the shopkeeper on the lips. It was chaste and quick; neither seemed to enjoy it. She whispered something Susan couldn't hear, then turned her head and said, "Let's go, apprentice."

9.

Elisa drove a shiny new Maserati. Susan followed in the former rental car, but Elisa didn't make it difficult. They drove at or near the speed limit for several hours before getting off the highway, then through a series of winding, deserted roads, alongside rows of pine trees and farms and the occasional gas station or convenience store. They drove through the heart of two or three small towns, only one big enough to have a traffic light and a McDonalds. They passed churches and barns and, finally, a sign saying they'd crossed into the next time zone.

Eventually, Elisa's red Maserati turned into a driveway, and even then it was a good five minutes along the packed dirt before a clearing broke and her house became visible.

It was completely unlike anything the shopkeeper had shown Susan. The house was spindly and spidery, a lot of glass separated by narrow strips of wall. It stood at least three stories, and was as deep as it was wide—which was to say, it was huge, huger even than Susan's home, or the home of CEO's and financiers she knew. There were at least three chimneys and, in the far back corner, a turret raised above the rest of the house.

Two of the three doors in the detached garage slid silently open. This was connected to the house by a long, open breezeway. Out of the cars, they walked along the breezeway and entered the main house through a side door.

They came immediately into a great living room. It was spacious and spartanly furnished, with only an undersized white couch, chair, and glass coffee table. Everything was very modern, sleek and chic and without comfort or warmth. There were a couple of bookshelves, but these were mostly occupied by glass sculptures, vases, and candles. The white tiles underfoot echoed loudly as they walked.

Arriving at the kitchen, Elisa stopped at the island counter and said, "This is where you'll be living the next six months."

Susan didn't respond.

"You'll have duties, to earn your keep, and to pay for your lessons," Elisa continued. "It's late enough now, you can prepare our dinner and then I'll show you to your room. You won't be leaving again until your six months have been served, and then you'll be leaving with one of the remaining four copies of your father's book. However, each time you displease me, or do me or my work any damage, I will burn one in punishment. Do you understand that?"

Susan said nothing, but Elisa waited for a response. Finally, Susan nodded.

"Good. At the end of six months, if any copies remain, I shall give you one, and you can drive down that driveway and never return. Now, dinner."

"I'm not much of a chef," Susan told her.

"I'm not apprenticing a chef," Elisa told her. "But we do have to eat." She glanced at the clock. "Be ready to serve in one hour. We'll eat in the dining room."

Left alone, Susan explored the kitchen. It was fully and completely stocked with every kind of cooking utensil she'd ever seen, a variety of pots, pans, knives, cutters, choppers, mixers, bowls, and a great many things she didn't know how to use. The pantry held an immense collection of spices and boxed items, huge bags of rice and flour and sugar, dried fruits, canned meats; it overflowed with all sorts of nonperishable items. The fridge, however, was as Spartan as the living room. There was milk and cheese and yogurt and eggs, a few apples and oranges, tomatoes, some vegetables, a pint of cream, and two small pieces of filet mignon.

Considering the options, Susan chose the filet. It wasn't hard. She added some spices, used the broiler on one of the two ovens, and quartered one of the apples. It made her think of the shopkeeper. It made her consider things in which she did not believe.

At the end of the hour, Susan had two plates on the table, hers at an angle from Elisa's. The table would seat ten; she gave Elisa the head and sat to her immediate right. The cutlery and plates shined and glittered. Elisa, seeing the meal, smiled broadly and retrieved a bottle of chianti and two glasses.

"I believe," Elisa said, "we may become good friends."

Susan believed no such thing.

Elisa cut the meat, examined and sniffed it, then put it in her mouth. Susan waited. "Decent," Elisa said. "Though I prefer my steak a little more rare."

"I'm not a chef," Susan reminded her.

"No," Elisa said, "but you're not an alchemist, either. With time, things change."

Partway through the meal, during which Elisa spoke of the weather and the stars and the remoteness of her estate, Susan asked, "Why do you want me here?"

Elisa paused in her eating. She laid down her knife and fork, wiped her lips with a napkin, and gave all her attention to Susan. "You display an aptitude," Elisa said. "You have talent. You have an eye for numbers and symbols, even when you don't understand. I could see it in your calculations."

Susan waited for Elisa to continue, which she eventually did. "Talent is rare. The alchemists have died out. There are no more guilds, and no more teachers. I will admit, now, I'll be a poor teacher, quick to anger and slow to forgive. You could have learned from someone far better than I. But there is no one."

"You told the shopkeeper there were others," Susan said.

"Oh, there are others," Elisa admitted. "But there are none of my skill, and few of your talent." She returned to her meal, finishing in silence, barely even seeming to remember she didn't dine alone. They finished two bottles of wine.

"Your room," Elisa said, bringing Susan to a guest bedroom on the first floor. The bed looked comfortable enough, and large. There was a desk and a chair, a wardrobe, and windows overlooking the fields and forest behind the house. "Rise with the sun. After breakfast, I will give you the tour, and your first lesson."

10.

Susan slept. Her dreams were dramatic, high contrast, over-exposed affairs through which rivers of mercury flowed and balls of lightning bounced and randomly turned ninety degrees to go after some figure from her past or imagination. They disturbed her, but she didn't believe they were in any way portents of the future, omens, warnings, or anything more than misfiring synapses struggling to get through the night in a strange, overly soft bed.

Susan rose with the sun, which was already her habit, but she didn't feel rested. She showered briefly in her private bathroom. You could still call it dawn when she made it downstairs.

Elisa was already seated at the table. She smiled. "You're late."

"But I'm clean," Susan told her.

Elisa shook her head once. "There are no points for cleanliness."

The dining room table was empty except for one glass of orange juice. Susan said, "I suppose I'm to make breakfast."

"Every meal," Elisa told her.

Susan nodded. "I thought I was meant to learn something."

"You pay for knowledge with service," Elisa said, "or you steal it. I do not think you are prepared to steal from me."

"I'm not a thief," Susan told her.

"You are not," Elisa said, "on trial. Now, breakfast."

In the kitchen, Susan found the fridge had gained a few items overnight, including an open carton of orange juice, spinach and mushrooms. She made omelets, which were a bit messy and cheesy. They came out a bit closer to scrambled eggs, but that was okay. Elisa said nothing about it.

The eastern light came straight through the back windows and lit the dining room brilliantly. When rays hit the chandelier, they broke off into dozens of prismatic displays, reflecting light and throwing rainbows in every direction. Where she sat, the morning blinded Susan, but she didn't get up and move. She could've had any other seat at the table, but she wasn't about to show any sign of weakness to the Italian.

The tour followed. Elisa showed only parts of the house, which included a movie theatre in the basement with maybe twenty seats, several other bedrooms, a large pantry with an immense freezer. On the

JOHN URBANCIK

second floor, there were the rooms Elisa said would be most important
in Susan's studies and work. The laboratory had cabinets full of beakers
and vials, various chemicals in gallon containers, assortments of spices
and herbs and flowers, boxes of rocks, drawers filled with tweezers and
knives and petri dishes. There were microscopes and a telescope, but no
windows here. There were almost as many shelves filled with specimens
and jars and bowls as there had been shelves in the bookshop. Elisa's
library, however, had even more shelves. The collection of books
reminded Susan immediately of the *Apothecary*, all magic and history
and art.

"You won't find your father's books here," Elisa said. "You can, at
your leisure, read anything you find here, but I suspect you'll find little
time for leisure, and a great many assigned readings as it is. Your eyes
will burn, sometimes, from the words."

Elisa referred to another room as the classroom. "We'll do a lot of
work here," she said. "Calculations and equations, research,
assignments, papers."

"You intend for me to write?" Susan asked.

"I intend for you to study and learn more in the next six months
than you have in your entire life," Elisa said. "You will work from dawn
till dusk. You will take books back to your bedroom and read well past
midnight. You will not sleep nearly enough, and you may very well die
of exhaustion. That's the risk. We could have had more time, twelve
months instead of six, but in a moment of weakness I thought you might
be more acquiescent with the shorter time frame." She shrugged. "We'll
both suffer for it, of course, but you more so than I."

The classroom was a teacher's desk and a student's desk. One
towered over the other. There was barely room to write on the student's
desk, while the teacher's desk was well larger than average. Under the
student's, which had its table attached to the chair, was a basket for
books, just as there had been one in Susan's first years of elementary
school. There was a blackboard, a cork board, and a white board on the
walls, and the windows could be completely covered by opaque white
blinds.

"That's enough of the inside," Elisa said. "There's little else you
need to see."

Susan didn't believe that. She knew the tower in the northeast
corner would be important. She wondered if that's where Elisa kept her
father's book. Not even here a day, she was already considering thievery.

Outside, there were additional rooms over the garage, though these were not currently used and wouldn't be used by Susan for any reason. A huge porch circled the whole house; on one side, it was only wide enough for two people to walk side by side. In the back, there was a bench and a barbeque pit and a fire pit. A shed held garden tools and a lawn mower, things Elisa said would not be required during the next six months, though of course this wasn't entirely true. Elisa kept a garden, in which she grew a variety of herbs, several types of lettuce, potatoes, and tomatoes, and also a circular rose garden. At the center, a marble statue of a bow-woman aimed her arrow toward the sky. She might shoot down the moon. She was bare breasted and gleaming, and surrounded by roses of white, orange, violet, yellow, and red.

"We raised roses when I was a child," Elisa said, "so I continue now. There are nineteen varieties currently, but there were once thirty. I'm older now than I was, and they're harder to keep, especially when the weather turns so cold as it has the past few winters."

"They're beautiful," Susan admitted.

"I often have roses in the house," Elisa said, though Susan hadn't seen any. Indeed, the house had seemed nearly completely anesthetic, leaning toward modern and ultramodern, sleek and sparse, every chance it got.

"It's almost noon," Elisa announced as they entered the house again. "If you don't mind, we'll skip lunch and jump right into your first lesson."

Susan thought this was a test. She said, "Let's get started."

They started.

11.

The first lesson, or lessons, stretched for hours. Susan sat at the student's desk, which was too small for her and rather uncomfortable, but didn't complain. Elisa provided a spiral notebook and gel pens, and told Susan she'd use them a lot.

"History," Elisa announced once Susan had settled into her seat. They talked about history, from the dawn of humanity over 200,000 years ago in Africa to the Agricultural Revolution, though there were no names or dates. They talked about Mesopotamia and Egypt and China. When they *talked*, primarily it was Elisa who talked, but she asked questions and expected answers, and she paused often to allow Susan to scribble in her notebook. Susan wrote a lot because she didn't know what would be important. They went through Antiquity and into the Middle Ages, wherein they touched upon witch hunts and medicine and religion. They covered a great many events, natural and otherwise, naming artists and politicians and philosophers and generals, and finally stopped at the dawn of the Industrial Revolution. By then, the sun had set, and Susan was starving.

"Dinner in an hour," Elisa said. "We'll discuss the importance of steam."

Susan made chicken cutlets and asparagus and broccoli, as those seemed to be the freshest items in the fridge. The chicken was dry, the asparagus bitter, but the broccoli, in Susan's opinion, was perfect. Elisa ate without commenting on the food, but they did talk about steam.

"Some might say the Bronze Age, or the Iron Age, was most important in the history of mankind," Elisa said, "but you'll understand that the single most impactful change on society was the harnessing of steam."

Steam, she said, changed the way man worked. It allowed for the creation of machinery well beyond what had ever been imagined before. The steam locomotive was more powerful than oxen. The steamboat was stronger than wind. And steam is still in use today; thirty billion tons of it helps keep a city like New York operating.

"We harness electricity by steam, we move people and cargo by steam, we cook with it, we clean with it," Elisa said. "There's nothing so powerful, and so easy to obtain, as steam. Alchemists, of course, have known this for centuries."

It was the first time Elisa mentioned alchemy.

Steam, according to Elisa, allowed the Industrial Revolution to happen. Steam was natural, and powerful, and deadly. Steam, as far as Susan could tell, was the start and finish of everything.

"We've forgotten the usefulness of steam," Elisa said before popping the last bit of dinner into her mouth. "We've forgotten, and as a society, we suffer for it. You should consider the creation of steam an alchemical reaction. The transmutation of water into vapor, and then that vapor into water—it's a flawed, inconsistent, and ephemeral reaction, but it is at the basis of everything."

Also at the basis of everything, Susan learned later that night, was fire, which was not at all a fleeting change. "Fire burns and consumes and leaves something else in place of what it feeds upon: char, ash, smoke, fumes." According to Elisa, mankind's learning to control fire had been as substantial a contribution to our growth as a species, and a society, as the ability to capture and use the power of steam. "Indeed, it's not impossible, but it is impractical, to create steam without fire."

The lesson went deep into the night, after which Elisa gave Susan three hefty biographies. "Read these," she said.

But Susan returned to her room tired and achy. The student's desk was not good for her. She fell asleep, still clothed, on top of the covers, and didn't wake until sunlight snuck in through the window and teased her.

They spent most of that day in the classroom. When they broke for lunch, Elisa suggested taking some time in the library for independent study—she suggested reading biographies of people she'd never heard of—and to have dinner ready at 6. Left alone in the library, Susan searched for her father's book, though it seemed far more likely that the remaining copies of *The Making of a Shadow* were kept in Elisa's bedroom, or that turret in the back corner. Dinner was simple, though at the start Elisa said, "Tomorrow, I'll show you how to make pasta."

Lessons that night focused on basic arithmetic; they moved swiftly into algebraic equations, geology, logic, and probabilities. The next morning continued with probabilities and led directly into statistics. Over the next days, they covered basic chemistry and physics, and one night stayed outside till midnight with the telescope, charts, maps of the constellations, and books on Greek mythology and history.

"It's all interconnected," Elisa said. "Alchemy isn't purely the study of one thing, it's a relational study of all things."

She taught Susan how to make pasta—the way her grandmother made it—but that lesson spanned several days of failed attempts.

They touched on the biographies of a variety of once-famous people who, today, were unknown, and they worked from books still sticky with spider webs. "How other people live," Elisa said, "is one of the most important things you can know. But the perception of how someone lives, that's far more revealing, not of the subject, but of the biographer." After three or four by the same biographer, Susan started to recognize patterns, just as she recognized patterns in the sky and patterns in the pasta and patterns in the tiles on the bathroom floor.

She never wondered about her ability to learn. She'd agreed to this price to get her hands on *The Making of a Shadow*, and she meant to pay it. The diversion from real life, from the vagaries of micro- and macro-economics, from the imaginary pressures of markets and commodities and boardrooms and the petty people with whom she'd surrounded herself, was palpable and, quite frankly, tempting. Susan thought she could live out her life here; despite the too-small student desk, she enjoyed the studying, though she couldn't fathom how the lessons were, ultimately, related, or the purpose of it all. So on the sixth night, during a dinner of stuffed shells with marinara sauce, Susan asked, "Why teach me at all?"

"We've discussed this," Elisa said.

"My potential, my talent, I understand," Susan said. "But why teach anyone? Why ask this price instead of money?"

"Obviously, I have no need of your money," Elisa said.

That wasn't the answer Susan sought, so Elisa added, "There are perhaps a dozen practicing alchemists in the world, and just as many who have studied it and walked away. You may, in fact, walk away after we're done. You may take the knowledge I give you, the reasoning skills we exercise, and apply them to the worlds of business and finance. I won't stop you. But there is, to my knowledge, only one other active apprentice in all the world, only one person learning the skills necessary to bring alchemy into the twenty-first century. You think I can conscientiously permit all the things I know to evaporate when I die?"

"You can't possibly teach me everything you know," Susan said, "and I can't possibly learn it. Not in six months."

"Perhaps not," Elisa said. "Are you quitting?"

"No," Susan said.

"Good," Elisa said. "I'd hate to have to burn another book. It feels so...final."

After dinner, they went outside again and walked. Trails led from the house through the woods. They felt haphazardly designed, turning this way and that without apparent reason, leading to various little clearings at which there might be small statues or sun catchers hanging from the trees—catching nothing of moonlight or starlight. There were two chairs and a café table at one little clearing, a boulder at another, a wood panel with calligraphy etched into it at yet another. Eventually, the trail forked. Here, Elisa paused and looked at Susan. "Which way shall we go?" she asked.

"I don't care," Susan said.

Elisa frowned, but the frown shifted into a scowl. "You must make your own decisions. I cannot always point the way."

"Is there anything waiting for us down either path?" Susan asked.

"You cannot know that," Elisa said.

"So how would I decide?"

"Decisions don't require facts or knowledge. Sometimes, it's as simple as picking the one that feels right, or looks right, or seems right. Sometimes, it's picking the one that looks more challenging or easier, the safer or more adventurous. Decisions can be based on the angle of moonlight, the direction of the wind, the scent of jasmine on the air." She shook her head. "It doesn't matter to me how you decide. It doesn't matter to me the criteria that affect your choice. What matters to me is that you make the correct choice."

Correct, however, remained undefined. Susan considered a great many things, quite quickly; which direction did Elisa's body position appear to indicate, and was her position meant to misdirect? These, ultimately, seemed superfluous; one path led into the woods and the other path led into the woods. Both would pass trees and clearings and other statues. They might cross paths with owls, spiders, or raccoons down either—or both. This wasn't a question of sell or hold; this wasn't an in-depth study of the mitigating and aggravating factors involved in a merger or spinoff. This wasn't life or death. It wasn't even vanilla or chocolate. This was a trick question. There was no correct answer, and therefore no wrong answer. It didn't matter which path they took.

So, without a word, Susan walked past Elisa and took the left path. Elisa followed.

The trail meandered past a small, artificial waterfall, then an ornately sculpted bench, then a small statue of some random saint, before finally depositing them into the backyard of Elisa's house.

"Tomorrow is your seventh day," Elisa told her. "There's much still to learn, but I'll give you tomorrow to rest, and to study what you will. I'll be away most the day. Use your time wisely. Eat well, and rest well, and prepare. The next day will be your first test. If you fail, I will be forced to burn a copy of *The Making of a Shadow*, and only three will remain."

Susan slept uneasily that night. At dawn, she watched the Maserati leave the garage and silently slip down the driveway.

She didn't bother showering, and didn't go to the kitchen for breakfast. Instead, she explored. There were doors she'd never seen open, a master bedroom suite somewhere, a turret, and copies of her father's book. She didn't like secrets. She didn't like being made to dance for her supper. She was no marionette; nor was she a servant.

The first door she tried was locked. So was the second. She went to the library. There was no card catalog, and the arrangement was nothing like the Dewey Decimal System, but it didn't take long to find books about the craft of magic and illusion, stage tricks, card play, and escape artists. There, she found a book on lock picking.

The lock proved flimsy and simple to open; Susan wondered why she'd needed the book. This opened up parts of the house she hadn't seen. She discovered Elisa's bedroom, dressing room, and closet, a suite that was easily twice the size of some New York City apartments. The four poster bed was an overstatement in luxury. All the furniture was white and soft, or draped with soft, white blankets and throws. Paintings on the wall might have been original Caravaggio's or Titian's. A series of mirrors in the dressing room reminded Susan of an actress's studio, complete with an envious assortment of makeup and jewelry. All the jewels were real, whether diamond or opal or emerald. There was plenty of gold, but also silver and platinum and a few metals Susan didn't recognize. The tub in the bathroom was jetted marble, not unlike what you'd build for an ancient goddess of Rome. Fresh roses filled several vases.

Susan also found another, smaller library, with maybe five hundred books, a long couch, another vase full of roses, and one ornate chandelier. She spent a long time examining every title, though a great many were in Italian, French, or Spanish. They were fictions, all of them, primarily Romance, mixed with some Fantasy and Crime Noir, a few old French Gothics, fairy tales, Jane Austen, and Oscar Wilde. They were arranged in a particular order, but Susan couldn't decipher the system; some authors appeared on several shelves next to disconnected titles.

She'd thought the library might hide her father's book, but she found no sign of it. She had never seen her father except in a few old pictures, but she had finally seen the book so she knew what to look for. She didn't find it. She even checked behind books, in case the remaining copies were hidden, but was rewarded with nothing, not even dust.

Susan found other rooms, the purposes of which were vague; maybe some were guest rooms, or reading rooms, or just to ease the boredom of sleeping every night in the same room. By the time twilight gave the outside sky a deep, brilliant tint of yellow, she still hadn't found her way to the turret. She hadn't realized the house was a maze. Some rooms connected only to other rooms. There were halls, lined with huge black and white photographs or more paintings. There was no lock Susan couldn't pick; now that she knew the secrets, Susan no longer believed in locks.

She never heard the Maserati, but she did hear the garage door opening—barely. It wasn't much of a warning. She went back the way she came, making some wrong turns and going through rooms she hadn't even noticed. She found the little library, but had trouble finding her way out. The garage door closed; she didn't hear it so much as feel its vibrations, but that wasn't exactly true, either. She just knew. She was running out of time.

Growing frantic, heart pounding and out of breath, Susan finally found the first door. She locked it. She escaped the hidden wing of the Italian's house. She got to her room without seeing Elisa and closed her door as quietly as she could.

She waited.

She sat on the end of her unmade bed. She wiped the sheen of sweat from her forehead. She concentrated on controlling her breathing.

Elisa opened her bedroom door while Susan's eyes were closed. She didn't hear it, and started when she opened her eyes to find the Italian staring down at her and frowning. "Was it a restful day?"

Susan said, "Yes."

"You took no lunch," Elisa said.

"No, I didn't."

Elisa looked at her a moment, allowing the silence to stretch awkwardly, then said, "Come downstairs for dinner in twenty minutes."

12.

Precisely twenty minutes later, freshly showered and dressed, Susan came to the dining room and found a copy of *The Making of a Shadow* on a platter in front of a seated Elisa. A three candle candelabra provided just a little light. Elisa wore the same frown she'd had twenty minutes ago.

"I had some travelling to do today," Elisa said. "I had some work, and to gather supplies, things like flour and sugar and potassium chloride."

If that molecule indicated anything, Susan didn't know what; she'd have to look it up later, though she was sure it would come up in her lessons. She couldn't keep her eyes off the book. "Is that for me?"

"No," Elisa said. She removed one of the candles from the candelabra and touched the flame to the book. Fire took to it instantly, flashing through the cover and burning through the pages, obviously accelerated by something. "No," Elisa said again, "and now there are only three copies. Two, if you fail tomorrow's test."

She rose, replaced the candle, and left without a word.

Susan sat there and stared at the book and the fire and the ash. More than half the book had already burned away; the rest disappeared quite quickly. She thought to stop it somehow, but never really had time to do so. Her father's book burned and died, just as her father had before she was born.

Susan slept poorly; when she did manage to slip out of consciousness, dreams plagued her, dreams so vague she didn't remember much more than impressions upon waking. She thought maybe she'd been chased, or she'd been doing the chasing; or instead there'd been a race in an arena, or a bullfight, or a lion taming. It was difficult to say. She was tired when she woke, still angry and frustrated, annoyed, and both a little bit defeated and defiant.

She drank orange juice for breakfast, and chocolate milk, but ate nothing. Elisa did not join her. She went upstairs, to the classroom, and stood near the windows rather than sit in the undersized chair. She expected she'd spend the whole day there and felt no need to rush it.

But Elisa did not join her in the classroom, either.

Susan went to the laboratory, though they'd done no work there yet, but did not find Elisa. She went downstairs again, to the kitchen and dining room, then the big living room, and finally out onto the back porch. Elisa sat on the porch swing, not swinging, reading a book and frowning. She finished the paragraph, or the chapter, and lowered the book to look at Susan. "Do you think you're ready?"

Susan said, "I don't know what to expect."

"You will never know what to expect," Elisa told her. "Are you ready?"

"You can never be ready," Susan told her, spouting some version of some philosophy she might have heard once. "You can only be prepared."

"Are you, then, prepared?" Elisa asked.

"It doesn't matter," Susan told her. "Whether I'm prepared or not, it's time."

Elisa smiled. It was a slick, self-satisfied expression. "You're right. Please, find a red rose, bring it here, and try not to cut yourself."

The rose garden displayed a variety of different colors, including red; this was not a difficult task. Susan picked one that smelled fragrant and had fully opened; its thorns did not bite her flesh. She returned to the porch, where Elisa had put down the book and was watching her.

"Good," Elisa said. "Now, tell me about it."

"What do you want to know?" Susan asked.

"Everything."

Susan hesitated, but then began. She started with the scientific name, the color, the way the rose reflected only the color red from the visible spectrum. She veered into poetry, into Shakespeare, into Valentine's Day and how the actual Saint Valentine likely had nothing to do with it. She did not go off into the territory of religion; she stayed only one generation away from the rose itself.

She gleaned over the War of the Roses, and people named Rose, and the town in New York, though she knew little about it specifically. She described its symbolic meanings, including love and romance, and again brushed against religion when she spoke of rose windows, though those were as related to architecture as anything else.

She said it was the national flower of England, where you would always find ravens at the Tower of London, and how one day they would be gone and King Arthur was supposed to return. She mentioned the Tournament of Roses and the parade and the stadium.

She spoke well into the day, which was warmer than typical and humid; she found herself sweating by the time she reached what she thought might be the end. Elisa rose from the swing and said, "You know more than that. After lunch, tell me what I'm actually interested in knowing."

Lunch consisted of salad, lettuce and other greens, feta cheese, apples, walnuts, spiral pasta and pesto sauce.

Susan knew about The Rose, the theater, and the rose cut used on diamonds; she added that she preferred opals and sapphires, but that was extraneous and didn't help her position much. She wasn't finding what Elisa sought.

She knew a few songs in which roses appeared in the title or at least prominently. She knew a few movies, too, and the story of Beauty and the Beast, though she admitted she didn't know if the rose was important in any other version but Disney's. She mentioned another fairy tale involving Rose Red, who may have been sister to Snow White, who may have originally been called Snowdrop, but she'd ventured into uncertain territory and she was sure she'd made up facts to cover lapses of actual knowledge.

She knew there were hundreds of public and private rose gardens around the world, but she couldn't think of a specific example other than Elisa's.

Susan fumbled through half-memories and uncertainties. She talked about a Renoir painting she was certain she'd seen at a museum, but she couldn't remember which one. She knew many varieties of roses were edible, and that rose hips have been used in jams and jellies, makeup, and medicine. Here, Elisa leaned forward and said, "Go on."

"But that's all I know," Susan admitted, "and possibly more than I actually know."

"Make something up," Elisa said.

But Susan didn't really believe in making things up. "Out of thin air?"

"Is there any other kind of air?" Elisa asked.

Susan thought about that for a moment and made an educated guess. "Yes."

Elisa smiled. "Then yes," she said. "Out of thin air. Tell me what you can do with this rose."

Susan didn't answer immediately, but when she finally did, it was dissatisfying. She said, "I can make a love potion with the petals."

Elisa, too, seemed unimpressed. "A love potion?"

"A love potion," Susan continued, "but also a poison. A poison that acts, first, as a love potion, and makes one believe they're in love, with all the poetic leanings and delirium that entails, but progresses to paranoia and hallucinations and, finally, death, if given in strong enough a dosage."

Elisa took the rose, then flung it off the porch. "That would be, indeed, a dangerous plant. Are you ready for dinner?"

Elisa cooked. It was an extravagant meal, though it took less than an hour to prepare, with sautéed vegetables and wine and bread and seared scallops and Alfredo sauce she made from scratch. They didn't talk much over dinner, except when Elisa explained the how's and why's of what she was doing, the importance of simmering the cream at just the right temperature, the advantages of olive oil over any other, the necessity of freshly baked bread.

At some point during the meal, Susan asked, "Did I pass the test?" Elisa grinned. "Do you think it's over?"

Susan said, "Yes."

"And I haven't burned another *The Making of a Shadow*," Elisa said; that's all the answer she offered. After dinner, she gave Susan more books to read, and said they would start again the next day after lunch.

The second week, and the third, were much like the first, though the particulars of the lessons differed. They focused more on mathematics and chemistry and physics and the history of medicine, but the topics they covered include cocoa and cocaine in South America; diamond mines in South Africa; the silk roads and the opium wars; music and musical instruments and musicians of all sorts; constellations and mythology; astronomy; and poetry.

Susan found herself more and more exhausted, and more and more alone; she was left in the lab to experiment for hours on end, and in the library to read, though Elisa rarely left the house for more than an hour at a time. Sometimes, the Italian wandered her garden, or the paths in the woods; sometimes she read on her porch swing or sat in the living room drinking wine; other times, she locked herself up in the forbidden wing of the house. At least once, while outside, Susan saw the Italian's silhouette in the windows of the turret that, in the back, rose above the rest of the house and had windows facing every point of the compass.

It was obvious Susan had changed the ways of her thinking, but after three weeks she had not turned lead into gold, or seen another copy of *The Making of a Shadow*, or learned one thing about alchemy. She didn't think of the shopkeeper often, the apothecary, or the small bookstore in the small town in Florida, but she rarely thought of anyone she'd known before. She never checked on her business operations; and, as she'd instructed, no one made any effort to contact her. She could disappear—she could easily die—and no one would know for another five months—no one except the Italian.

The lectures transformed into discussions, but the lessons became more pointed and unrelenting. Susan wasn't allowed much time for anything else, though she was able to work a particular experiment on her own. On the twenty-first day, she learns, without warning, it's time for another test.

13.

In the morning, Susan and Elisa met in the yard. Clouds hung low, thick, and dark, but they hadn't yet opened up. A chill touched the air, teased out goose bumps, made everything that much more stark and brisk.

"Today's test," Elisa said, "is practical."

Susan waited. She said nothing. She had no questions. She only wanted her book, and her chance to escape. She'd learned a lot. She knew a lot. She didn't believe she was the same person who entered a bookshop through a peeling red door almost a month ago. Some of that learning, she felt, was despite—or in spite of—Elisa's lessons.

"Make gold."

Susan blinked. "Make gold?"

"Out of lead, if you must," Elisa said, "or any other metal, if you wish. Make it from the gases around us, or the dirt, or the rain when it comes. But I want gold."

"You have gold."

"It's a basic tenant of alchemy," Elisa said.

"It's not," Susan said. "I mean, the gold out of lead thing is a myth. It's smoke and mirrors. It was designed to obscure an alchemist's true intentions."

Elisa raised an eyebrow. "Is that so?"

"You've given me a lot to read," Susan admitted, "and a lot to do, that seem to have nothing whatsoever to do with what you profess to be teaching me."

Elisa frowned. "Go on."

"You're trying to sneak knowledge into me from angles," Susan said. "Showing me a biography, not because I'll ever need to know anything about that person or the things she did, but because I might learn to read between the lines and learn, not about the subject, but about the author."

When Elisa didn't object, when her expression didn't change at all, Susan continued. "You don't show me, directly, anything. You want me to somehow glean it from the things we haven't done. The negative space. You're telling me to make gold, now, not because we ever covered it, but because you believe I should have learned how on my own."

Elisa smiled. "Do you believe you have?"

Susan knelt. She touched the dirt at her feet, ran her fingers over it like over the body of a lover. She closed her fist on a handful of dirt, stood, and said to Elisa, "Belief doesn't matter. Neither does confidence."

"What, then?" Elisa asked.

"Intention."

"You intend to pull gold from dirt?"

"No," Susan said, opening her palm to reveal dust and gravel of gold. "That's simple enough."

"What else, then?" Elisa asked.

"Mercury," Susan said, "to drive a man half mad. Oxygen, for breath. Iron, for strength. Gold, because it glitters, because it distracts." Without any additional warning, she drove her other fist into Elisa's gut.

For a moment, Elisa looked shocked. She gasped for air, but found her breath easily. She nearly double over, but didn't. She did, however, fall half a step back. She looked mad, a good deal more than halfway so, and glared at Susan for a long while.

Susan, too, stepped back. There had been no knife in her hand, or the blade would've slid through the Italian's belly and up, under her ribs, into vital organs.

A tremendous boom of thunder, flash of lightning, and torrent of rain came all at once. They stood there, facing each other in the wet, for far longer than was absolutely necessary. Finally, after the rain had soaked through their clothes and the cold had seeped into their bones, Elisa said, "We'll call that passing."

They went inside, each to their own rooms, to shower and dry off and change clothes, and met on the porch with three bottles of wine and an assortment of cheeses, grapes, olives, and nuts.

"You've learned more than I realized," Elisa said, sipping her wine and watching the storm. It was solid out there, and terrible, but there wasn't much wind so the porch was perfectly comfortable. "But you're still an uncontrolled talent."

Susan didn't believe either word: *uncontrolled* or *talent.* She said, "It's not magic."

"No, it's not."

"It's not simple chemistry, either," Susan said.

"No."

The wine was good; they emptied the first bottle quite quickly, Elisa staring out at the storm while Susan kept her eyes mostly on the Italian.

"You were right, this morning," Elisa said, "in that gold is a deception."

"It's the greatest deception," Susan admitted. "I have more than I need already."

Elisa smiled. "There are some who believe enough is never enough."

"I don't believe that."

"You wouldn't. You don't believe anything."

"That's not entirely true."

Elisa shrugged and didn't pursue it. "You hate me."

"I don't."

"You do," Elisa said.

She did, but Susan wouldn't admit it, not until she'd gotten what she'd come for.

"I don't see a lot of people," Elisa admitted. "I'm alone here for months at a time, leaving only for supplies."

"And wine," Susan said, finishing another glass.

"And food, yes," Elisa said. "I know the girl at the grocery. She's young and unfocused and self-pitying, but she has strength inside her. Someday, she'll learn to tap it. But she's not like us. She can count out change, but I could expect nothing more of her."

"You expect more of me," Susan said.

Elisa shook her head. "No. No, for the first time, today, I realize these six months will be much more like a year than not." She turned away from the storm, leaned toward Susan, and added, "But I should warn you, there are now only two copies of *The Making of a Shadow*."

"What?"

"I burned one this morning," Elisa said. "While you were in the shower."

Susan felt her fists tightening, and her jaw clenching; she tried to prevent both these things and failed.

"There may come a day," Elisa continued, "when you and I face each other on a field of battle, though there are few such fields in the modern world. It may well come to physicalities. But I doubt that. You struck me today, and I concede you succeeded with distraction, intent, and surprise. But I, too, have surprises, and I can also create distractions. Only two books remain." She poured another glass of wine for the both of them as she spoke. "And almost another five months. My anger, my love, burns intensely and swiftly, and leaves nothing but ash." Susan

THE MAKING OF A SHADOW

closed her eyes so she wouldn't have to see the Italian's lips move as she spoke, or her eyes. "I tore out a page at a time and fed it to the flame, until the fire itself demanded more. I truly hated to do it. I hate to be the cause of so much pain for you. But, today, even in testing, you've learned the lesson of Reciprocity."

"You are an evil woman," Susan said, rising quickly and unsteadily. She gulped down the remainder of her drink and left the porch.

Elisa did not follow.

Susan went to her room, shut and locked the door, sat on the edge of the bed, and let the initial anger burn itself out. Even as it cooled, still it simmered. She took one of her books, one of the many Elisa had given her to read, and opened it quickly to a page near the middle. There, dry now and pressed flat, was a petal of the rose. *Another.* It wanted water and air and attention, but it would never be what it was. It wasn't the last of the petals; nor was it the first. She tucked it carefully into her pocket, then let a certain amount of time pass before going downstairs again, to the kitchen, to prepare dinner.

She made soup.

14.

The next day, Elisa gave Susan a stack of books. "These," she said, "are from my private library." No longer biographies of generals, musicians, stage magicians, and scientists, these were alchemical books, filled with theory and practical exercises. They didn't entirely abandon the classroom, but they spent the next several days primarily in the lab. There were methods of inducing catharsis, catalysts meant to slow down reactions, plenty of distraction and show—smoke and mirrors, as Susan had said. There were books on healing, medicine, and philosophy as applied to transformation. They were older, often hand-written, sometimes in other languages; Susan spent the better part of a week brushing up on her Latin.

Elisa decided the thirty-first day deserved a celebration, so she hired a string quartet and had several cases of wine delivered. She had the event catered, hiring a team of chefs and servers, as well as a bar tender; and Elisa called the shopkeeper and invited him.

"You must be doing well," he said to Susan when they had a moment alone.

"I am."

"I mean with your lessons."

"I know."

"I admit," the shopkeeper said, "that frightens me a bit."

"Me, too."

He smiled. It looked no better on him now than it ever had. He said, "I suppose you're exploring a few things on your own."

Susan hesitated, then said, "I am."

Later, he admitted, "I've never been here."

"She still have your heart?" Susan asked.

The Italian heard this. She smiled. She touched the shopkeeper's shoulder. She lowered her voice to a whisper. "Why should I ever let such a thing go?"

"And the impression of your fancy?" Susan asked.

"Only ever an illusion," he told her, but it was a lie. They all knew it.

The food was good, and quite a bit of leftovers were stored in the fridge. The wine was good, but they'd given it up quickly for whiskey, bourbon, and scotch. It was that kind of night.

At midnight, the caterers packed up to leave. The bartender arranged more drinks, and the musicians shifted from the beautiful classical to the fantastically romantic.

Throughout the night, Susan caught Elisa looking at her, with an expression resembling a starved tiger. Elisa stole these looks through her periphery, or when she thought Susan wouldn't see her. Certainly, she got away with most unespied. It made her bold. When she touched the shopkeeper's shoulder or arm, she often touched Susan as well, in a similar manner, but there was a heat to the contact now that had not been there before.

After the musicians finally packed up to leave and the bartender distributed a last round of drinks, Elisa said, "That was wonderful."

Susan had never seen her so drunk. She brought Elisa one last drink, which she personally mixed since the bartender had already gone.

Elisa finished the drink and licked her lips. Susan went to her room to sleep. The shopkeeper stayed the night. Susan heard them. She tried her best not to imagine what they were doing. It was not easy, but it made her smile. If pressed, Susan would admit it was probably more of a grin—a wicked one, at that.

The next day was wasted.

On the thirty-sixth day, Susan spent her time outside. Though the sun shone brightly, it was chilly; she wandered the rose garden and the paths in the woods; Elisa had given her this chance to think on the things she'd already learned, to absorb, to read if she felt so inclined, and to get a breath of fresh air before winter.

On the forty-second day, at dinner, Elisa said, "I think I love you."

Susan smiled. "I know."

"I shouldn't."

"I know that too."

On the forty-ninth day, Elisa left the house. She didn't come back for three days. During that time, Susan picked the locks and explored the unexplored sections of the house. It was, in fact, a labyrinth; she'd really only seen the slightest bit. She discovered a basement, though there was nothing in it but boxes full of memories, dolls five or six decades old, black and white photographs from the Old Country, handmade blankets, old shoes, and a beautiful, elegant violin. Susan didn't try to play it. She didn't know how. But she wanted to, and one day would. When she left this house, she would take it with her.

Through the basement, she finally found an entry into the turret. A spiral stair led up into its center. It was bright, with windows on all sides. It was high, and gave her a strategic view of the property in front of and behind the house. Cushioned seats circled windows, at which a person might sit or sleep or anything else. But the room contained no copies of *The Making of a Shadow*. There were a half dozen books, but they were things Susan had either already read or didn't care to try.

She had been certain this room would hold secrets.

She tried to find hidden cubbyholes or hollow spots in the walls or floor, but in the end there was really nothing to find here. The turret was merely a distraction. Look here, if you can, but you wont't see what my other hand is doing.

Susan never expected to be left alone for so long. She actually studied, read, practiced, and experimented. She made her own meals and slept her own hours. She filled pages in her notepad. She formulated her own theories. She tested them, or at the very least prodded at them. Things that had never made any sense to her before were now obvious and even blatant.

When Elisa returned, she said nothing. She'd gotten groceries, but nothing more than if she'd gone for an hour. She gave Susan another book, and a fresh notepad, and promised to prepare a feast for breakfast.

The next morning, breakfast included sausage and bacon and potatoes and bread and cheese. It was, indeed, a feast. Elisa said, "You confound me."

Susan merely smiled.

Lessons continued. On the fifty-ninth day, over lunch, Susan said, "I cannot remember the calculations I did for the shopkeeper."

"Why would you?" Elisa asked. "You've done so much more since then."

"They seemed important," Susan said.

"They were. To him."

"Not to you?" Susan asked.

Elisa smiled. "That wasn't *my* life's work. Nor yours."

On the sixty-fourth day, Elisa said, "You confound me."

Susan smiled and said, "You've said so."

Elisa shook her head. "I can't have that."

On the sixty-fifth day, Elisa burned another copy of *The Making of a Shadow*. She built a bonfire in the yard before sunrise. It was cold this morning, and the sky threatened rain, but it never delivered. A single tear made its way down Elisa's cheek as Susan approached the fire. The Italian lifted the book, showed her the title, and said, "You've given me no choice."

"I've been perfect," Susan protested.

"Too much so," the Italian said. She tossed the book onto the flames. They watched together as it burned. They shared tears. Only one copy remained. It was the thing that bound Susan to this house and to Elisa. It was the thing she'd come for.

"You're an evil woman," Susan said again, but her voice betrayed no emotion.

"What would you have me do?" Elisa asked. But she didn't wait for an answer.

On the seventy-third day, Elisa said, "I love you."

"I know."

"You confound me."

"I know."

"I want you. I want to keep you. What can I do to make you stay?"

"I want my father's book," Susan said.

"You'll stay until I give it to you," Elisa said.

Susan shook her head. "I'll stay until I've earned it."

"You'll leave if I give it to you."

"We struck a bargain," Susan said. "Do you not intend to keep it?" But Elisa never answered that.

On the eightieth day, they discussed poetry. Words, according to Elisa, were more important than numbers, and just as useful. Letters and numbers were merely symbols, and like any other symbol could be made to mean different things. Language was a tool and a divider; there were over three thousand currently in use and at least as many dead. Words carried denotative and connotative meanings. They were duplicitous. Anyone who used words used them to lie, even when without intention; but words also revealed things that were meant to be hidden. The simple existence of words meant secrets could not be kept.

"They have a way of sneaking out to the world," Elisa said. "They penetrate when they should be deflected. They retreat when they should be embraced. There is nothing so powerful as a word in the hands of a wordsmith."

"I do not believe I am a wordsmith," Susan admitted.

They went through various poets. "Samuel Taylor Coleridge," Elisa said, "has always been a favorite. He dreamt a dream he couldn't remember and gave us *Kubla Khan*."

"I prefer Frost," Susan said. "*Fire and Ice*."

Elisa smiled and brought up Poe as another favorite.

"No Shakespeare?" Susan asked after a while.

"Oh, there is nothing more dangerous than the words of the Bard," Elisa said.

"He spoke for another generation," Susan said.

"He spoke for all generations." Then Elisa said, "I think Eliot summed everything up when he said, *This is the way the world ends, not with a bang but a whimper.*"

"I've heard that before," Susan told her.

"Everyone's heard that."

Then, without warning, Elisa leaned across the table and kissed Susan on the lips. It was gentle and quick, but Susan pulled back. Elisa held her gaze. "Remember," she said, "I love you."

"Maybe it's time to call it a night," Susan said. Every night thereafter, she slept with her door locked and the heavy chair propped against it.

On the eighty-third day, Elisa tried to open it.

15.

After midnight, whilst Susan read a history of French alchemists, which was painfully brief about alchemists and instead focused on their relationships with Napoleon, various King Louis's, and Madame de Pompadour, as well as their extensive, and ultimately self-destructive, travels in Acadia, Senegal, and with the French East India Company, the doorknob wriggled. Susan marked her place in the book and set it down.

The doorknob wriggled again, then opened; apparently, and not unexpectedly, the Italian had a key. She pushed, but the chair, in which Susan sat, did not budge.

"It's me, *mio amore*," Elisa whispered from the hall.

Susan said nothing. She rose, smoothed down her nightgown, and turned to face the door.

"Let me in," Elisa said.

"I'm reading."

"It's too dark to read," Elisa said.

Susan stared at the door but said nothing.

"*Per favore.*" She sounded like she was pleading, like she was desperate, like she was checking over her shoulder to make sure someone—someone in particular, though Susan had no idea who—didn't see her. She kept her voice low, too, in case she might be overheard. There were no servants, no other residents, no live-in lovers, no laborers, no renters, no relatives, and no visitors, but that didn't matter; there were always ghosts.

"It's late."

"It's a test," Elisa said.

"It's not a test."

"Yes, of course it's a test," Elisa insisted. "Why else would I be here at the very center of night?"

It wasn't a test. Susan moved the chair aside, which allowed Elisa to push the door open just enough to slip in. She closed it behind her, pressed her back to the door. She breathed in gulps.

"What's wrong?" Susan asked.

Elisa narrowed her eyes and sneered. "You."

"Me?"

"You did this to me," Elisa said.

Susan did not deny it, though Elisa did not immediately elaborate on *this*. She said, "You're sweating."

"Perspiring," Elisa said.

Susan smiled. "You know that doesn't matter."

"What matters, then?" Elisa asked. "What do you think matters?"

"I think the shopkeeper got it wrong," Susan told her. "He thought love was a question, a problem that needed solving, a quest to be overcome."

"He's wrong," Elisa said.

"Of course he's wrong. Love's the *answer*."

"Yes," Elisa said. "Yes, of course, you're right."

"Am I?"

"You pass the test."

Susan said nothing. They were barely more than arm's length apart. This was the moment, she thought; this was when she might finally obtain her father's book.

"You pass every test," Elisa said. "You are lovely and smart and as talented as the devil himself."

"I don't believe in the devil," Susan told her.

Elisa smiled sadly. "You must believe in something."

Susan thought about it. "I'm sure I do."

"You believe in money."

"Money is transient and temporary and, ultimately, a lie." Susan smiled. She was enjoying this.

"You believe in yourself."

"I accept myself," Susan said, "my strengths and limitations. There's no belief involved. I'm here."

"You haven't always been here."

"And I won't always be here."

"You've poisoned me," Elisa said. "You've tricked and betrayed me. You're as evil...as evil as I am evil."

Susan shook her head. "No."

"You are."

"You're nervous," Susan said. "I've never seen you nervous before."

Elisa grinned. "I've been made to be nervous. Do you know how many shadows there are in this house? In the yard? They used to believe fairies slid through your windows on moonbeams. Do you believe that?"

"You know I don't."

"I didn't," Elisa said. "But they're in the house."

"There are no fairies," Susan told her.

"You must believe in magic," Elisa said.

"Why?"

"You perform it."

"I perform experiments and calculations and chemistry," Susan said. "Not magic."

"You've seen magic."

"I have," Susan admitted. "I know better than to believe what I see."

There was a sound, or what might've been a sound, from elsewhere in the house. It could easily have been natural settling, or perhaps a precariously set book finally falling onto a rug. It might've been the wind, or the lack of wind, or an entirely aural shadow that didn't really exist at all. It shoved Elisa away from the door, straight into Susan. They fell. Tangled, on the floor, precariously placed, they took a moment to examine each other. The Italian looked nothing like she had that first day in the shopkeeper's kitchen. Her eyes were bloodshot. Her skin was cold, except where it burned. Her makeup had been marred by tears, and by sweat—*perspiration*. Her hair was unbound and unkempt. She looked like a vulnerable predator. She looked angry. She looked vicious.

She asked, "Do you think you can protect me?"

Susan said, simply, "No."

Elisa looked away, repeated, "No" under her breath.

"I cannot protect you," Susan said. "I cannot even protect myself."

"Of course I can."

"You've burned all but one copy of my father's book," Susan told her.

"That was always the plan."

"No," Susan said. "It wasn't."

"You think you know things," Elisa said.

"You think I know nothing."

"Come, then," Elisa said. "Let's get you your damned book. That's all you want, anyway. You don't want my knowledge, my wisdom, my experience. You don't want me." She pushed off the floor. "You don't love me."

"No," Susan admitted. "I don't."

"And I don't love you," Elisa said. She grinned. "Your poisons have affected me thoroughly. I didn't suspect...why should I?" She took a deep breath. "Is it the very rose?"

"The very one."

Elisa fled the room. Susan followed. They moved through the labyrinth of the house, through the halls and secret rooms, down one set of stairs and up another, until they came to a room Susan had never seen before. She'd searched the house as thoroughly as she could.

It wasn't a very large room, but it had a fireplace, which was dark and cold, and one small window. It had a table, a chair, a wine cabinet and, on the mantle, a half dozen books. Elisa plucked one off the shelf. *The Making of a Shadow.*

"I think," Elisa said, "you may have earned this." But she didn't hand it over. Instead, she picked up a lighter off the table, an old Zippo, which lit with amazing speed and gave off a brilliant, solid flame. Susan felt unable to move, unable to react, and certainly unable to prevent Elisa from introducing the flame to the book. It jumped. It wavered. It spread cautiously.

When Susan managed to open her mouth, no sound came out. She lifted a hand, stretched it toward the burning book, but came nowhere near it. The Italian flipped the book so the flame could grow up the front of it more quickly. Burnt pages fell, little more than ash now, maybe retaining a bit of burnt umber at its center, but there was nothing of the ink to be seen, no sign of the words or illustrations her father had put to paper.

"You may have earned this, too," the Italian said. "You think you have talent. Gather the ashes. They're yours. They're what I give you, my end of the bargain. This is the last copy of your father's book." She dropped what remained on the table. Nothing remained. It continued to burn. The fire ate each page in turn, teasing little hints of each layer before moving on to the next, showing perhaps a phrase or a symbol or an illustration. She looked at Susan from beneath angled brows and grinned wickedly. "Of course, *I* know every word by heart."

She swept out of the room. She slammed the door shut, leaving Susan to watch the last of the book burn, to watch tiny embers flutter to the ground, to watch her father's book become a pile of burnt cinders and ashen dust.

Susan sat on the floor and cried.

Eventually, she pushed herself to the door, the only door, and slept against it. The Italian could not enter without disturbing her. In this way, Susan slept in the presence of her father. She slept fitfully. Night terrors disturbed her. She remembered nothing, but trembled or shook or cried again every time she woke.

It was a long, long time before dawn.

16.

When dawn came, it came slowly. The sun's light touched the edge of the horizon long before the sun itself rose over the tree line. Susan awakened, and stayed awake, during that moment of washed out, indistinct light that started the day. She watched the sun struggle against a translucent layer of bleary clouds and soft fog. The ugly morning promised an ugly day.

Susan gathered the ashes of the last copy of her father's book. She collected every scrap, every slightest bit, though there wasn't much. The rug was a light, muted color, so the blackened remnants were easy to find; but most were on the table. Though they felt warm to her hand, they weren't; they were cold. The room was cold. Susan's bones were cold, and for the first time ever, brittle. She had almost not survived the night. She collected *The Making of a Shadow* onto the little table, with the Zippo lighter. At the wine cabinet, she found a brandy snifter large enough for all the ashes. She pocketed the lighter.

She barely recalled the path on which Elisa had led her last night, but Susan found a way back to her own room, where the door was still ajar and the chair exactly where it had been left. She laid the book she'd been reading over the top of the snifter so that nothing more would be lost. She withdrew the last bits of dried rose, a substantial amount compared to the daily dosages she'd been feeding Elisa since working out the poisonous love potion, and went to the kitchen.

She prepared coffee, bacon, and eggs. She acted as though nothing had happened the night before. When Elisa arrived, her eyes still bloodshot and swollen from lack of sleep, she said nothing. She took her plate, her coffee, and ate and drank without sparing an extra glance for Susan.

In that way, they ate breakfast. Without a word, Elisa took some cheese from the fridge and retreated to her rooms, to her private, locked wing of the house. Susan went to the lab.

She worked through the day and deep into the night. She consulted books, scribbled in her notepad, crossed out a lot of calculations and passages, and even wrote a haiku. It was the most effective way to vent her frustration. The next day started with an identical dawn, and she took a break to make breakfast. Bread, cheese, and orange juice for herself, coffee for the Italian.

Partway through the meal, Elisa asked, "What did you do yesterday?"

THE MAKING OF A SHADOW

"I worked in the lab," Susan said.

"Did you accomplish anything?"

"No," Susan said. "But I made progress."

"Good."

"Not good enough," Susan admitted. She spent the next three days in the lab. Elisa never visited; they saw each other only at breakfast, which Susan made every day. The days themselves were carbon copies, lifeless and listless, bland and blanched. Near dawn, Susan made a realization; it was actually a leap in logic, close to an epiphany, though it relied heavily upon supposition and possibility. She needed blood to complete her ingredients.

She found a knife in the kitchen that would suit her needs.

She found fresh bread, spinach and feta cheese to include in an omelet, and a fresh supply of juices. She also laid out an antipasto platter, with olives and cheese and meats vegetables. It was the most elaborate meal she'd had in days. It was also the end of her supply of rose dust.

"Are we celebrating?" Elisa asked.

"No," Susan said.

"I'm surprised you're still here. Your father's books are gone."

"You retain the knowledge," Susan told her.

"I've taught you nothing in days."

"Why is that?" Susan asked.

"What might I teach you? You're locked up within your own head now, dealing with your own experiments. I don't even know what you're trying to accomplish in the lab. I'd check in on you, but I doubt I have anything to offer."

"But you do," Susan said. She set a shot glass next to Elisa's plate and the paring knife she'd found. "I need your blood."

"Mine?"

"Mine won't do," Susan said.

Elisa raised an eyebrow. "That's quite specific."

"Yes," Susan said. "No one else in the world would do."

"You're attempting to pull the knowledge out of me against my will?" Elisa asked. "You know I'll give it freely."

"No," Susan said. "I don't know that."

Elisa nodded. She looked like she'd spent her nights hiding from something, her days running. She looked a mess. She looked tired and near defeat. She picked up the knife, gritted her teeth, and ran the blade across her palm. She held her hand over the glass, squeezed into a fist, so that the blood dripped slowly into the glass. "How much do you need?"

"I'm not sure," Susan said.

"You will protect me, right?" Elisa asked.

"There's nothing to protect you from," Susan said.

"From you."

"It's too late for that."

Elisa filled a quarter of the shot glass. It would be enough. Susan took it, returned to the lab, and worked.

Near dinnertime, she thought she'd finished. She'd double checked her figures, crossed all the T's, acknowledged the dead, bleary light outside, and went down for one final meal.

Elisa sat at the dining room table. Her hands were on the table, palms up. Her skin was pale, her head tilted, her eyes sightless. Susan went to her side, felt for a pulse, listened for breath, but there was nothing. The Italian, the alchemist, was dead; her knowledge died with her.

Susan closed Elisa's eyes and kissed her on the lips and whispered, "I'm sorry." It was close enough to truth. "But I believe you have succeeded," she added. "You've transformed me into an alchemist."

She went to the basement to retrieve the violin. She picked fresh roses from the garden in the dying gasps of twilight. She opened and finished a bottle of wine in the hours leading to midnight. The time chose itself by inadvertence; her work required no adherence to any hour of the day.

In the lab, with the ashes of her father's book, Elisa's blood, a series of other ingredients, and the small flame of a Zippo lighter, all of which she'd assembled and prepared ahead of time, she set her work into motion. It was a long, arduous experiment. It would either fail or succeed; there were no other options, and would be no opportunity for a second attempt. She monitored everything closely. She added liquids where and when necessary, and mercury, which must surely have affected her mind as well. She wondered, briefly, about the hallucinations that must have plagued the Italian in her last days and hours.

When dawn arrived, it came in full brilliance, an explosion of color against the horizon. Susan had pieced together the ashes as best she could and reassembled the book. It smoldered back into existence, drawing the pages from the ashes like a Phoenix. But it was not a living thing she'd recreated.

She'd reversed the effects of combustion.

Susan touched the cover of her father's book. It was cold to the touch, though actually quite warm. She understood the differences, and the lack thereof. She didn't understand everything, but she'd succeeded. Carefully, as a test, she opened the book. The words inside were complete, the illustrations vibrant, the symbols nearly whole. In some places, a thing was missing, the result of having an incomplete collection of ashes and soot. Who knew what she'd lost, what she'd absorbed into her own fingers as she'd picked through the ashes?

She took the book downstairs. She nodded her thanks to the Italian, still dead at the table, and went out onto the porch. The warm air embraced her. She hadn't been outside in days; the fresh air reinvigorated her. She opened a bottle of champagne, made a plate of cheese and bread, and dined on the porch swing. When she'd eaten her full, she opened the last remaining copy of her father's *The Making of a Shadow*. She started on page one, the dedication, which said: *For my unborn daughter, so that she may know the things I know, including her origin; these are the answers, my love, to all your questions. This is how you were made.*

AFTERWORD

This started with the door.

Really, that's all I had. And maybe a window with the word *Apothecary* etched into it. A door and a window. Amazing where such things can lead, eh?

Okay, so I also had a woman on a quest. An unusual quest. Not a traditional kind of quest with orcs and magic swords and vanquished enemies and copious amounts of lamentation. This was more of a vision quest, if she didn't know it at first. What she really wanted was a book.

Ah, and the book, of course, is the center of this story, which makes a lot of sense for me. I see books and stories and words at the center of a lot of things. The mistranslation of words, I think, or at least the misuse and/or misunderstanding of words, has caused a great deal of grief throughout human history. But I wanted to approach this on a more personal level.

I knew there'd be magic, but not of the earth-shaking type born of fire and lightning, but also not of the illusionary type. I knew there'd be mathematics involved, despite that I included not a single calculation. Numbers are just as important as words. Ultimately, they're all just symbols, aren't they? The letters on the page aren't a true thing themselves; they represent abstract thoughts and ideas that are coarsely crafted into words and phrases, in an alchemical sort of way; but without knowledge of what those symbols mean, without an understanding of the denotative and connotative implications therein, it's just a bunch of ink stains, don't you think?

snow sparrow

snow sparrow

In the dead of winter, a lone sparrow flies through the falling snow. No place for such a bird, nearby spirits watch carefully as she flies from tree to skeletal tree. This is not the world she knows. Where have the greens gone, the warm sunlight, the gentle breezes?

Two spirits place a bet. "Not through the day," says the wind spirit.

"Always the pessimist," his sister, the snow spirit, says, agreeing to the wager.

They watch as the sparrow alights at the top of an evergreen. Below, a polar bear dines on salmon it had caught in the stream.

She is a hungry sparrow, so the big white bear offers a bite. She declines and continues her northerly flight. By now, many spirits have joined the voyeuristic bettors, cheering for the bird—or nature around her—to overcome the other.

"It's not her time," says one spirit. "What's she doing here?" No answer comes.

There are many mysterious reasons for birds to fly. Crows assist the souls of the recently dead. Owls aid the lost. Falcons help with the hunt. But what is it that sparrows do, and in the very heart of winter?

"Nothing to interfere," the snow spirit reminds the others. "She lives or dies of her own accord."

The sparrow's flight brings her near the ocean, where she pauses to watch seals at play. They ask her to join their games, but she declines.

"No one recognizes her color," says the snow spirit.

"I do," one of the sun spirits says, beaming.

The bird flies close to the ground as she crosses great plains of ice. Further and further north she flies, and now she sings as she travels.

Hers is a pretty song, very unnatural to the howling weather around her. The snows calm, but the wind spirit says, "Nothing to interfere, neither for nor against."

"I only want to hear her song."

"Go south, then, where the ice isn't so constant and the snow not eternal. There, perhaps, you can hear the song of a thousand birds like her."

The sparrow lands on an jagged ledge of ice. This far north, there are no trees at all. She looks quickly one way, then the other. A snow hawk circles above. He offers shelter from the coming storms. She declines.

There are greater forces than the spirits, and soon enough even they express an interest in the strange flight. One among them must know her mission, but none share that knowledge.

The further north she flies, the longer the day drags. The snow spirit argues that the day has already ended where they'd placed their bet, but the other spirits chide her for not playing fair.

Gales howl around the poor little bird. This far north, the wind spirit has free reign. He tosses the bird this way and that as she continues, ever northward, demonstrating a strength and stamina not often found in birds twice her size.

Even this far to the north, day nears an end, even by spirit standards — sparrows lives by shorter frames of time.

She arcs to the east, bringing her away from the setting sun and closer to winning the snow spirit's bet. Over freezing waters, where chunks of ice frequently break away from icebergs, the sparrow settles on a natural ice perch carved into the side of a glacier.

There are few other animals this far north. Beneath the ocean surface, where the water is slightly warmer, a whale sees the bird and surfaces. He asks it the bird would like a warm place to settle, even if temporarily, and offers the protection of his blowhole to shed some of the chill. She declines.

But this time, she does not fly away. She lays one egg as the bottom of the sun dips below the western horizon. It is almost as small as a snowflake, and just as white.

"She will shortly die," declares the wind spirit. Others agree. Some lose interest and return to their various realms and duties. The bet has been neither won nor lost, so the wind and snow spirits remain.

The sparrow comforts her egg. She keeps it warm beneath her wing. She sings to it, even as the winds howl around her and ice crumbles from the glacier and crashes into the ocean with thunderous splashes.

Northern lights spread across the sky, streams of color unfamiliar to the winter skyline. The two spirits step aside as Aurora comes forward in a ray of warm light. Some of the nearest ice melts when she bends over the sparrow. "You won't survive here," she says to the bird, "but I shall protect your child."

The sparrow surrenders her egg to Aurora. In a swirl of brilliance, the lights and goddess disappears.

The sun completes its descent then, and it is at that moment the sparrow exhales its last breath. The two spirits, unsure of who had won, call it a draw.

In a nest of colors, a white sparrow breaks out of her egg. She looks up at the radiant goddess, who relays the story of her mother's tragic flight. "To bring you to the world," says the goddess, "a snow sparrow. Who would have ever thought?"

The baby snow sparrow thanks Aurora for all she's done. She flies easily, expertly, even through the wintry winds and snow, to her mother's perch in the glacier. She snuggles under the red wing and weeps.

ZOMBIES

VS aliens

VS ROBOTS

VS cowboys

VS NINJA

VS investment bankers

VS green berets

ZOMBIES

vs

aliens

vs

ROBOTS

vs

cowboys

vs

NINJA

vs

investment bankers

vs

green berets

1. Tuesday 8:17pm

An angel walked up to the bar, set down his trumpet, and asked the bartender for a double shot of her finest scotch. He wore white and gold. He glowed, ever so slightly, but enough so you knew, without doubt, that he was exactly what he looked like. Looking at the trumpet, you could see, though you couldn't explain how, that it had been recently used.

The angel finished his drink, wiped his mouth with the back of his hand, and said to the bartender, "Another, please. And one for my friend here." He hung an arm on my shoulder, leaned close to whisper, and said, "It's begun. Might as well enjoy the end, don't you think?"

"The end of the world?" I asked.

"You, sir," the angel said, "sound like a man who does not believe."

"I believe in a great many things," I admitted. "Right now, I believe I've started drinking too early."

The angel shook his head and smiled. "No, my friend, you've started just in time."

The bartender served us our scotch. She hesitated a moment, gave me a questioning look, then went on about her bartending business. The end of the world, I suppose, was too much for her to deal with right now. The night hadn't actually begun.

The angel drank his drink and waited for me to finish mine. I didn't tend to swallow scotch like that. Good scotch was meant for savoring. The angel nodded, as if agreeing, though I hadn't said a thing, and said, "Savor what you can while you're still able."

"You're an angel," I said.

He grinned. He wriggled his eyebrows. He shot me with his pointer finger and winked and said, "You got me."

"You've signaled Armageddon?" I said.

He shrugged. "I signaled some of them, yes."

"There's more than one?"

He still had his hand on my shoulder. He turned me toward him. I didn't resist. I still had the scotch in my hands. "Drink up, friend," the angel said, "and I'll show you."

2. Tuesday 6:03pm

The zombie apocalypse began precisely at 6:03pm in the Rookwood Necropolis outside of Sydney, Australia—which was actually about 8 tomorrow morning there. The birds made bird noise. The sun shone starkly on the grass. A girl sat crying silently by a fresh grave. There were, in fact, nothing but tombstones in every direction, and trees intermingled between them—and in some places growing through the graves. I'd never seen such a place. It was a real city of the dead, stretching beyond the horizon in all directions.

"You see that girl?" the angel asked me.

"Can she see us?"

"No," the angel said. "This has already happened."

"Who is she?" I asked.

"You really want to know?"

"You brought me here for a reason," I reminded the angel. As to bringing me here, I had no idea how he'd done it, and I really didn't know why. I didn't know why me. I didn't ask those types of questions. I asked the ones I imagined the angel really wanted me to ask.

"Her name's Jessica," he said. "That's her brother's grave. He died six days ago. She arrives every morning with the sun and leaves with the sun. She thinks she's safe in daylight."

"She's not?"

"As you said," the angel reminded me, "I brought you here for a reason."

I waited. My watch ticked over to the appointed time. In the distance, I heard the trumpet. It sounded like the starting gate at a racetrack.

"That," the angel said, "was me."

A nearby granite stone shifted. Another, further away, trembled. A hole opened up in the earth behind the girl. She didn't see it. Tears shone on her cheeks, but she sat so still she might have been a statue. She was pretty, young, and dressed all in black. She didn't hear the rumblings around her. The sounds were subtle, and distant, and disconnected. Her brother's grave remained undisturbed, even as a hand broke the surface behind her.

"Move," I told her.

"She won't," the angel told me.

I tried to move, to make her listen to me, to somehow make her aware, but the angel still held me by the shoulder. When he tightened his grip, a shock of pain burst like sunbeams into my flesh. My legs, in response, refused to work.

"This has already happened," he told me. "You're too late."

The hand caught a piece of earth and pulled itself up. It was attached to a corpse, recently deceased, so that most of the body seemed intact. Its face was the wrong shade of bruised. Its mouth hung open. Its eyes were vacant. Others rose in other places, from other graves, but not all of them.

"Some," the angel said, "are too weak to rise, too devastated by time. It's okay. If their bones are dry, if there's still muscle attached to them, they will rise."

"It's okay?" I asked.

"What I mean," the angel said, "is that none will be punished for not rising."

"I feel so much better," I told him.

He nodded toward the scene before us. He said, "Watch the girl."

The corpse had managed to pull itself halfway out of the grave before the girl turned her head. She moved like a machine. I thought I was watching some Japanese animated film about cybernetic girls with big eyes and gears instead of bones. She looked at the corpse, she narrowed her eyes, then said, "Keep away from me, dead man. I'm not meant for you."

"Can she know such a thing?" I asked the angel.

He shrugged.

The corpse reached for her. She didn't move, merely glared at it.

The angel said, "She doesn't speak the language of zombies."

"They have a language?" I asked.

"They have a word," the angel said.

On cue, the corpse said, "Brains." It sounded like a question. It still reached for the girl, and still pulled itself from the earth. Others, I could see, had already freed themselves from what was meant to be their eternal resting places. They moved toward the girl. They moved deliberately, without excessive slowness and with no sign of urgency. One moaned. Another giggled softly but incessantly, barely pausing to draw breath.

One shuffled past me and the angel. It paused, turned its rotten head toward us. It was deader than the first corpse, fetid, putrefying, overly liquid. It wore a permanent grin, as the flesh around its mouth had sloughed away. Instinctively, I backed up, into the angel, which was a lot like backing into a concrete pillar.

"He doesn't see you," the angel said. But the angel lied.

"The girl," the angel said again.

They surrounded her. They closed in. Her brother did not rise from his grave. She said, more loudly this time, "I am not meant for you."

The zombies paused. Elsewhere in the necropolis, a woman screamed. I heard running. I heard a car crash. I stepped closer to Jessica to see what became of her.

One of zombies growled. Then it turned away and left. Others left. The fresh one directly behind her, standing now, held out his hand, fingers splayed. He turned it slowly. He tilted his head as he looked at her. He said, again, "Brains." It was barely a whisper. From her seated position, Jessica stared him down.

The zombies retreated.

Her brother's grave remained still.

3. Tuesday 6:05pm

The alien apocalypse began precisely at 6:05 Eastern Standard Time above the White House, where the first alien ship descended and hovered. It was as large as city. It blocked out the sun, casting its shadow across all of Washington.

"Not just Washington," the angel told me.

A swarm of small alien ships launched from the big one. No giant laser blew apart the city, or the building, or the helicopters and buses as people fled. Instead, they threw out iridescent yellow nets, tied to their ships, and lassoed small groups of people, five or ten at a time. They carried the nets back to the mothership, dropped their cargo, and returned. It was all so very efficient.

"Is there a girl this time?" I asked.

The angel shook his head. "No."

The aliens scooped up those buses and helicopters, when they tried to flee. When police or armed citizens tried to fight back, firing all types of handheld weapons at their leisurely fishing vessels—what else could I call them?—they blasted the people with lasers or phasers or ray guns or disintegration beams. When the air force scrambled F-15s, they were blown out of the sky. When battalions of heavily armed marines attempted to board the motherships, they, too, were blown out of the sky. When a child let go of his red balloon and it floated up innocently toward the alien mothership, it was blown out of the sky.

"That's just overkill," I said to the angel.

He nodded. "They're harvesting about a million people an hour."

"Harvesting?"

"They believe they planted you here," the angel said.

"Did they?"

He didn't answer. Instead, he pointed at one of the little ships. It had tried to lasso a tank, and managed to get it only partway into the air before a rocket propelled grenade hit its wing. The ship spiraled and crashed into Pennsylvania Avenue, where a hundred angry frightened people descended upon it. The gray ship was small, and they tore open the cockpit easily. The two aliens inside, pilot and fisherman I suppose, came out of the ship with weapons blasting. People were flash burnt; sometimes, not even charred bones remained to fall to the ground. They took out five, ten at a time. But these two were incapable of defending themselves against the overwhelming number of earthlings that seemed to emerge from every alley and building and manhole and vehicle. Their weapons were wrested from their hands.

The aliens themselves were lizard-like, in many ways, apparently naked, with green scales as skin. They stood upright, and their snouts were extended like an iguana's. When they opened their mouths, their tongues launched like spears a distance of at least two yards. They spit acidic venom that melted human skin. Their big yellow eyes never blinked. Their hands were clawed, as were their feet, and their tails were like giant pythons, pure undulating muscle. Even still, they were overcome. They collapsed under the weight of resistance. People pounded on them with their fists, with Louisville Sluggers, with tire irons and thick branches, with chunks of brick and asphalt and metal. They shot them with .22s and 9mms and .45s, even at point blank range, and tore uncountable holes into the alien bodies. And finally, one of the people who had gotten hold of an alien weapon figured out how to fire it. He slaughtered a dozen people and evaporated one of the aliens in a single shot.

"Little victories," the angel said to me.

A pair of alien ships swooped low, dropping nets, and took more than half of everyone there in an instant. I didn't see where the weapon went. Another pair of alien ships came in behind them.

"Some people ran underground," the angel told me. "That, unfortunately, was a mistake."

4. Tuesday 6:12pm

The robot apocalypse was launched at precisely 6:12pm on a Tuesday from a manmade island in the north Atlantic, where the icebergs were numerous and the storm surges high. A single man, a madman in a white lab coat and black glasses, was pounding his fist on his big mahogany desk and shouting, "No! It's my turn, not theirs."

He was looking at a little television screen, which displayed pictures of New Delhi, Tokyo, Shanghai, Paris, and Mexico City, all sorts of places from which the aliens were taking people, or where the zombies were threatening news crews. He swept everything off his desk, television included, and tried to overturn it like some gamma radiation-filled rage machine, but he only pushed it an inch and a half before giving up. He was not a man of muscle. He was a man of devious intellect.

He stormed out of his office, slamming the flimsy door because that obviously gave him some degree of pleasure, and stormed down the hall.

The angel and I followed. No one else moved out of any of the various offices. No doors opened. No faces peeked through the little office windows. When we passed a conference room, it was empty except for a huge oval table and an old pizza box.

"He's alone," the angel told me. "He's been alone since his assistant died."

"When was that?"

The angel looked at his wrist, where he wore no watch, and shrugged. "About three years ago."

"He's been alone for three years?"

"He had television." It lay on the ground in the office behind us, popping and crackling and emitting a thin stream of gray smoke.

The row of offices led to an elevator shaft. We stepped in, though I presume we didn't have to. The mad scientist waited for us to enter before pushing the UP button. There were only two buttons, UP and DOWN. The cage slid shut, though it didn't obstruct our view of the hall.

"How many people were here before the assistant died?" I asked.

"Her name," the mad scientist said without looking at me, "was Carmen."

"You can hear me?" I asked him.

The angel shook his head.

"Her name was Carmen," the mad scientist repeated. The elevator

shaft closed in around us, a dead gray ascent, and soon opened up into a
long glass cylinder that enclosed the whole elevator. The entire floor was
occupied by legions of robots—not too dissimilar from the one who had
once screamed "Danger! Danger!" They had wiry arms and bulbous
glass heads revealing visible clockworks. They were armed. The wiry
limbs ended with laser pointers that probably did more than torment
cats.

For the record, I saw no cats.

The elevator brought us to the top of a tower, the control room,
which overlooked countless robots. They were idle, but you could sense
the potential energy just waiting to go kinetic on the world.

"Friends!" the mad scientist called. "Robots!"

They responded in a single, thunderous movement, turning if
necessary, raising their glassy heads. There were, I realized, a number of
other styles of robots, becoming more sophisticated the further they were
from the elevator shaft. In the back, they looked almost human, but
sleek and chrome and aerodynamic. I heard machines stop moving.
There were, in fact, machines building other machines, an endless
supply of robots building robots, and there were levels and levels and
levels filled with them. The artificial island fortress descended deep into
the depths.

"The time has come, my machines!" the mad scientist cried.

I sensed malevolence in the minds of the machines. "Why?" I asked
the angel.

"He lost his love."

"Carmen?"

"Worse than that," the alien said. "He lost his capacity for it. He's a
machine fueled by rage and torment."

"Why did he stay here?"

"Where would he go?" the angel asked.

"The time has come!" the mad scientist repeated. "Rise! Awaken the
sleeping robots! The insects and the giants! Find all that live, all of them
and everyone, and destroy them!"

The robots, as one, turned. They marched. They hovered in the air
by means I couldn't comprehend. Giant hangar doors rolled open on all
sides of the fortress, letting in the harsh north Atlantic winds and ice and
blinding sun. They moved. They boarded ships that were, in fact, robots.
They flew on planes that were also robots. Some flew on their own
power. Some dropped into the ocean like divers. Hundreds, thousands,

tens of thousands of robots poured from every level of the fortress. Their cacophony was deafening. Despite the overreaching, overzealous, overly arrogant, utterly ambiguous instructions, none of the robots, big or small, turned on the mad scientist. None crushed him or shot him or even looked at him again.

"All for Carmen," he said, slumping into the single black chair from which he controlled this mechanical army.

When the robots were gone, the North Atlantic weather pummeled the fortress. For a long while, the mad scientist seemed neither to care nor even notice. Seemingly at a whim, he pushed a button, a single big button easily accessible from his control chair, and the great big hangar doors rumbled shut.

When they clamped down, the last sound echoed through the vast, empty fortress. You could no longer hear the North Atlantic. He had no view screens, monitors, televisions, or computers from which to watch the devastation he'd just launched. They were no readouts, nor printers, nor displays of any type. There was only silence.

"Is that all we see?" I asked the angel.

"Quiet," said the mad scientist. Again, he did not look at me. He could easily have been describing the current circumstance. The quiet was, in fact, complete, except for my own breathing, and the distant sound of a single footstep.

The mad scientist heard it too.

We both looked down the gangway. It was on the other side of the control room, visible only because the elevator was surrounded by glass walls. A woman. She walked slowly. Her arms hung limply. She stared blankly at the mad scientist.

He and I said the name simultaneously. "Carmen."

She moved with deliberation and patience. The mad scientist swiveled in his chair but did not rise.

She was not freshly dead. She left a trail of rot behind her. Puss and black fluids oozed from her exposed innards. Her face might once have been beautiful; now, it was a mottled reddish gray, bits of jaw and skull exposed, a series of runny scars and slashes. All color had faded from her eyes.

"How'd she die?" I asked.

"Industrial accident," the angel said.

Reaching the end of the gangway, she lumbered around the elevator shaft. The mad scientist, who might have had time to run, remained still in his chair. "Carmen?" he asked.

She said nothing.

"Everything I did," he said, "I did for you. You understand that, don't you?"

She said nothing.

"I loved you," he told her.

She paused, tilted her head, then continued toward him.

"The world's a cruel place," the mad scientist said. "They give you everything, every possible thing you can want, and then strip it all away. The world kicks you when you're down, steals your joy, destroys the things that kept you honest and sane. I've got nothing, Carmen, nothing anymore. What was I supposed to do?"

She said nothing.

"I won't fight you," he said. "Even when it ends, the world must do so cruelly."

"That," the angel confided to me, "is not strictly true."

Carmen reached the mad scientist. She paused before him, tilted her head the other way, and reached toward him with one hand. Almost under her breath, she said, "Brains."

"Mine," the mad scientist said, "should be more flavorful that most."

She tore into him. She didn't need just his brains. She ripped off his skin and stuffed it into her hungry mouth. He opened his arms to her. She sat on his lap, leaned close to his neck, and savagely tore into his flesh. He held her close. He whispered, "I love you, Carmen. I love you." She ate greedily as he died. She must've had impossible strength, because she broke through his ribcage to shove her arms deep into his chest. She pulled out his heart and licked it. Then she looked over her shoulder, directly at me, still licking her prize.

The mad scientist was dead. But he opened his eyes and looked at Carmen and, almost tenderly, said, "Brains."

"It doesn't mean what you think," the angel told me.

5. Tuesday 6:39pm

Along a dry, dusty road somewhere between Oklahoma City and Muskogee, perhaps closer to Texas—I'm not all that familiar with the geography there—where once, long ago, a ranch had stood, but now there was nothing but highway, electric poles and wires, and lots of dirt, there was nevertheless a stirring.

"Why are we here?"

"Things happened," the angel said.

"What sort of things?"

"Unimaginable things," the angel said. "Now watch."

The summer sun hung low on the horizon. In its stark glimmering light, I saw the silhouette of a ranch house, a big one, with a wraparound porch and a swing and number of horses, which might have been real except that they were translucent. I counted at least a dozen, maybe two, but it was hard to say; they shifted in and out of reality. They were restless, and anxious, and waiting for their riders.

The riders arrived, cowboys, each of them dry and dusty and grim. They wore deputy badges that gleamed in the sunlight. They prepped their horses and spat chewing tobacco and checked their Peacemakers. They filled their saddlebags with supplies brought out by equally dusty women.

"Ghosts," I said.

The angel grinned and corrected me. "Cowboys."

"Dusty ghost cowboys from Oklahoma," I said.

The angel shrugged.

When the sheriff arrived, astride the tallest, broadest, meanest damn horse I've ever seen, a stallion black as the pits of the sheriff's soul, the other cowboys mounted their horses.

"I reckon it's a bit of grim news you bring," one of the deputies said.

The sheriff spoke as though they had all the time in the world. "It's worse than we thought. We cannot win."

"I reckon we lost two centuries back," another deputy said.

"I reckon so," the sheriff said. "But here, through divine provenance the likes of which I ain't never before seen, we have a chance to put ourselves right by history. Would you say I'm overstating that, Father?"

A priest among them, wearing a white collar and a shining deputy's badge, said, "I don't believe history cares for us one whit, sheriff."

"It's true," the angel told me. "You've never heard the names of any of these men, or even the slightest hint of their just and wicked deeds."

"However," the priest continued, "we may still put ourselves right by the eyes of our Lord."

"Amen to that, Father," one of the deputies said.

"Then let's put ourselves as right as the Lord will allow," the sheriff said.

Before they rode off, however, the earth cracked beneath them. Holes opened up and zombies emerged. They were dry, dusty bones covered with tattered remnants of the very clothes worn by the sheriff and his deputies. Some wore skin; many did not.

I shook my head. "That's not right," I told the angel. "Their bodies would be completely decomposed by now. There should be nothing left."

"The laws, as you know them, need not apply," the angel said. "The Lord made breath to enter these dry bones, and gave them sinew and flesh, so that they may strike the very souls that once inhabited them."

"The Lord," I said, "is a harsh master."

The angel shrugged and said, "Old Testament."

The horses whinnied nervously. The women shut themselves inside the ranch. The ghost sheriff hopped off his horse and approached the shambling zombie sheriff. He said, "This earth ain't big enough for the both of us."

The zombie sheriff said, "Brains."

The ghost sheriff drew his Colt and fired, once, catching the zombie between the eyes. It went down.

"Head shots," he called to the others. The engagement had already begun. One man, younger than most of the cowboys, with hardly a shade of whisker on his face, couldn't shoot himself. The zombie grabbed the ghost and, amazingly, bit into the ghost's throat.

"No," I said. "They're ghosts."

"But they're not wholly insubstantial," the angel told me.

Others faltered. But each stood and faced his own flesh made undead. Each either fired or did not. When they pulled the trigger, their aim was true, the bullets found a home between the eyes—or eye sockets—and the zombies fell.

Five of the ghost cowboys failed. Their ghost brethren turned and took out the remaining zombies with a volley of shots from all directions. They also shot the bitten ghosts, presumably so they wouldn't rise again as zombie cowboy ghosts.

The sheriff mounted his horse. "We ride."

They rode east, though I cannot say to where. They put the setting sun behind them. They were returned for a grand reckoning.

6. Tuesday 6:49pm

By now, the streets of Tokyo were a mess. Neon lights had shattered and rained down on the streets. Alien ships buzzed between buildings like they were canyon divers, and came up with a dozen people at a time. The cemeteries had overspilt all their bloated, decaying corpses into the streets. People ran in every direction and found death in each.

Away from Tokyo, in the woods, a series of people started to appear. They didn't all wear what I'd imagined ninja would wear, those black outfits you always saw in bad movies throughout my life. But they bore katanas and various powders and poisons. A massive force gathered. At first, I thought there were hundreds, but there may have been thousands, tens of thousands, maybe more than a hundred thousand. They came from all directions, from the city and the surrounding towns, some by car, horse, foot, or parachute. They surrounded Tokyo. They waited on the go ahead to attack.

I'm not sure who they meant to attack.

"Why not samurai?" I asked the angel.

He said, "The last of them died out during your second World War."

"That's not how I learned it," I said.

"You learned a lot of things incorrectly," the angel told me.

The ninja were mostly silent. They made no sound when they walked. They drew their weapons with barely a whisper of steel. The few who spoke did so with voices softer than the wind and just as brief.

"I didn't think there were so many ninja," I admitted.

"All warriors, at their heart, are ninja," the angel said.

"Is that true?"

The angel smiled and winked and said, "Maybe not."

"There must be a million of them," I realized. They continued to arrive and arrive and arrive.

"I could count them all," the angel said, "but the number changes every second. You realize, of course, similar groups of warriors, ninja in their hearts, even if they're Chinese, even if they're Argentinian, gather in other places."

"So earth has a chance, then?" I asked.

The angel looked at me quizzically. "What part of the word *Armageddon* don't you understand?"

I wanted to know why he was showing me these things, but I didn't really want to know. I wanted to go back to the bar and finish that bottle of scotch. If this was the end of the world, I wanted to go painlessly.

A hush spread amongst the ninja.

"Ah," the angel said. "I believe, now, it started to get interesting."

"Started?"

"This all has already happened," the angel told me. He glanced at his watchless wrist again. "Almost ninety minutes before I walked into the bar."

"If all this has already happened," I said, "why wasn't I aware of any of it? That bar had a television, and people with cell phones, and Internet, and outside in the city there would have been noise, chaos, pandemonium."

"You watched too much wrestling as a child," the angel told me.

"Why is any of this happening?" I asked.

The angel shrugged. "It's not my design. But if I were a gambler, I'd wager that it had something to do with choosing incorrectly during the last election."

"Seriously?"

The angel smiled. "No. When have I ever been serious?"

As one, the ninja started to move. They marched toward the city. The feet of a million ninja should have roiled like thunder, but instead they were silence epitomized. Had I not seen them moving, I would have heard nothing. Certainly, there had never been a command to move.

"Ah," the angel said again, grinning. "The ninja go to war."

The ninja rolled into the suburbs of Tokyo. With their swords and knives and katanas, they severed the heads of a great many zombies. The zombies didn't resist as a force. They said, "Brains." They said it in Japanese, which I admit I couldn't understand, but it wasn't a bad guess. Here or there, a mass of zombies overwhelmed individual ninja. Once they fell, they rose again as ninja zombies, but were cut down by the advancing army of ninja. They moved like a machine. They charged into skirmishes. They cut and sliced and lunged their way through streets and neighborhoods and houses. They descended upon Tokyo as an unstoppable force.

The aliens responded to this resistance. They sent their little ships into the midst of the ninja. They netted ninja and carried them up to the mothership, though some were able to cut through the electrically yellow nets and drop back to the ground; no matter how far they fell, they seemed to land, tuck, roll, and bounce back to their feet.

The aliens changed tactics immediately. They fired lasers and phasers and ray guns and disintegration beams. They burned ninja and dissolved ninja and mowed them down like stray weeds.

Some of the ninja managed to get onto the flying ships. They leapt into the air, often off the backs of other ninja, or dropped from the roofs of small buildings. They plunged their swords into the cockpits, shattering the glass, slicing through the alien pilots and fishermen.

"You know what would've turned the tide?" the angel asked.

"What?"

"Well, not so much what as who."

"Who?"

"Who killed Chuck Norris in that dragon movie?" the angel asked.

"Bruce Lee?"

"Bruce Lee," the angel said. "If the ghost of Bruce Lee, perhaps, had joined the cowboys, maybe this whole Armageddon thing would've gone down differently."

"You think any one person could've made that much of a difference?" I asked.

"Every single person," the angel said. "Yes."

7 Tuesday 7:00pm

The investment banker apocalyptic force went into action less than an hour after the first apocalypse began. In an office near the top of one of the largest buildings in New York City, from which they could see the alien mothership and its baby ships with their nets, from where they could see the corpses rising from cemeteries not even in Manhattan, they had a variety of monitors tuned to various twenty-four hour news stations and a series of red phones that connected them to particular powerful people peppering the planet. It was a safe bet to say none of these men or women had a net worth of less than a billion dollars. It was probable that each had been a CEO two or three times over, each had invented something or invested in something or gotten behind something that had somehow changed the world, even if only in small ways. Some of these men were bitter; they wore permanent scowls, or their jowls flopped on television as they defended themselves from various lawsuits or accusations. Others were *Time* magazine people of the years. Some were pleasant. Some were philanthropic. Some were mischievous. Some were the malignant tumors of the economic structure that made life unbearable for so many others.

Indeed, you could safely say several investment banker apocalypses had already begun and ended under their tenure.

"Movers," the angel said. "Shakers. Game changers."

"Really?"

"They think so," the angel said.

"Again, really?"

The angel shrugged. "Sometimes yes, sometimes no. The answers aren't always easy to come by, as you know."

"In this case," I said, "can they change the game?"

"They will try, yes," the angel said. "Watch."

The man at the head of the table, whose table this probably was, who may or may not have had more money than all the rest of those gathered, said, "Gentlemen, ladies, do I need to elucidate upon our current situation? I'd prefer to get straight to work instead."

The boardroom was, in fact, very quiet, with the exception of the stenographer, a beautiful, leggy woman in horn rimmed glasses. She was older than you would expect.

"Her name's Cynthia," the angel told me.

"Is she the one to watch here?" I asked.

"No," the angel said, "but I noticed you noticing her and thought you might want to know."

"Hearing no objection," the man at the head of the table said, "we'll proceed. Have we launched the satellites?"

One of the women said, "Forty percent were already in orbit. They've been activated. Another thirty percent were successfully launched from various outposts, most noticeable the secret sites in Argentina, South Africa, Australia, and China. Unfortunately, the remainder were either destroyed during launching, or the launch pads, like Kennedy Space Center, were destroyed from orbit before we could act."

Another man spoke up. "That's within the projected success rate."

"Excellent," the man at the head of the table said. He reminded me of Mr. Burns, in that moment, but never in any other moment when I'd seen his face on the news.

"They're not really investment bankers," I told the angel.

"Some are," the angel said. "Or were. We're using it as a catch-all phrase here."

"We can do that?"

"I'm an angel," the angel said. "Do you think there's anything I cannot do?"

The man at the head of the table cleared his throat. He seemed to look straight at the angel. "May I continue?" he asked. No one objected, not even the angel, so he said, "What about our mercenary forces?"

After a brief pause, one of the more nasally of the men said, "The news there is not good. Most of our mercenary forces went into action on their own, or on behalf of their governments, or in self-defense."

Another pause followed. The man at the head of the table broke it. "And?"

"And we're estimating an eighty-three percent loss rate already."

"It's only been an hour," one of the others said.

"That's outside our predicted success rate."

"It is," the nasally man agreed.

"Nothing we can do about it," the man at the head of the table said. "We couldn't anticipate multiple simultaneous apocalyptic situations." He turned his head, ever so slightly, to one of the other men. "The weapon?"

"Untested," the man said. "But it should be ready before midnight, local time."

"Midnight is unacceptable," the man at the head of the table said. No one contradicted him.

"That timetable's been pushed up twice already," the man said. "I'd been told eight tomorrow morning, then five. They've already cut the time."

"Are there further resources we can pool?" the man at the head of the table asked.

One of the women said, "Anyone brought in would be starting from scratch, and would have to be brought up to speed. We have a list of candidates from MIT and the US government. They're the only ones close enough to be useful in time."

"Get them," the man at the head of the table said.

She left the table. Cleanly and efficiently.

The man at the head of the table turned to one of the other men. "And what of our mad scientist?"

"Dead, we believe," the man said. "We lost contact forty minutes ago. After he sent out his army."

"Do we have specifics?"

"No," the man said. "He could have instructed them either way."

"Based on the evidence," one of the other men said, "we should expect the worst."

"Noted," the man at the head of the table said. "Now, on a personal level, I want to thank each of you for your continued efforts for just such a scenario as this. Decades ago, we knew the world militaries would be unable to combine their efforts to defend us from an invasion. There are thirteen battle armor suits prepped and ready in Brooklyn. If any of you should decide to back out, that the reality of the situation is, in fact, too much for you, now is the time. There will be no loss of face. This is immense. We need everyone to put forth their best effort. The world ends tonight, gentlemen, or it does not, and that decision may rest on what we do now."

No one said anything.

"Then this meeting is adjourned." The man at the head of the table rose. The others followed suit, with the exception of Cynthia, the stenographer, though she'd stopped typing into her stenograph.

The room emptied, leaving only the beautiful Cynthia, the glowing angel, and me. "Are we waiting for something?" I asked the angel.

He shrugged. "I thought you might like a last chance to admire a beautiful woman."

"The world's ending out there," I said, "and you think I'd like to spend my final moments as a voyeur?"

"She worked her way through college dancing at one of those clubs," the angel said, raising his eyebrows like Groucho Marx.

I met the angel's eyes. I asked, "Are we done here?"

"So anxious," the angel said. "I believe you're missing a point. But okay."

I glanced at Cynthia. She smiled, almost coyly, then packed up her equipment.

8. Tuesday 7:21pm

It was dark in Baghdad, but fireworks filled the sky. Mostly, they were jet fighters, bombers, drones, and missiles being blasted out of the sky by an alien mothership. Yellow nets streamed across the city, carrying dozens of Iraqis and Americans into the sky. And other nationalities, too. I'm sure the aliens didn't care about the flags to which their prey pledged their allegiance.

Six men, in civilian dress but wearing berets with the black insignia of the 5th Special Forces Group, silently checked their weapons, checked each other's weapons, carried more weapons than any six men should be able to carry, and gave each other imperceptible signs of readiness. The commander, whatever his rank, raised a fist when he saw one of the alien ships trailing its yellow glowing nets in their direction.

The six of them were gotten by one. They went willingly.

"Also in Japan," the angel told me. "Colorado. Alabama. Germany."

"Green berets?" I asked.

"Who better to take the fight to the enemy?"

"SEALS?" I asked.

The angel shrugged.

"SWAT teams," I suggested. He shrugged again. "Marines?"

"Already engaged," he said. "They were the first force to meet the aliens. There's probably not all that much of them left by now."

The little ship carried the special forces soldiers to the mothership.

"Why not the whole army?" I asked.

"This," the angel said, "is about infiltration."

The ship cut its net as it passed over a vast cauldron. The pilot and fisherman had no interest in the ability of their catch to survive the fall. It wasn't necessary. The soldiers tumbled into groups of other people, many of whom were unconscious, either passed out or knocked out or simply overwhelmed. Quickly, and with great efficiency, the soldiers cut themselves free from the nets and moved, even as more people were haphazardly thrown into the midst.

It was a giant cauldron into which humans were deposited. Aliens processed the arriving people like food. There were crates into which humans were stuffed. They were then carried, by conveyor belts, into vast halls in which thousands of humans were already suspended in pods.

"We're food," I said.

The angel said, "There's no other natural resource on this planet so important to them as food."

"What about bacteria?" I asked. "Will that defeat them?"

"Unfortunately, no."

"Water?"

The angel grinned. "Are you serious?"

The Special Forces soldiers moved through the dark, through the shadows, hiding behind massive crates or stacks of people. They spread out in some sort of militaristic flank, three this way, three that, putting a good distance between themselves. Obviously, these particular aliens

ZOMBIES VS. ALIENS VS. ROBOTS VS. COWBOYS VS. NINJA VS.
INVESTMENT BANKERS VS. GREEN BERETS

here, processing the incoming meat, weren't their target. They wanted
to take down the whole ship.

The Special Forces soldiers found stairways that were serviceable, if
not designed for the human anatomy. They descended into the
mothership's depths. The commander, near fifty with buzzed blond
hair, looked more vicious and mean and leathery than any movie had
ever portrayed a soldier. I had faith in this man, and the arsenal he and
his men carried.

9. Tuesday 7:34pm

In a park, far from any church building, somewhere near London, a
thousand people sat in a circle around their leader. There were no
aliens here. No zombies. No robots. They watched no televisions. No
one played with their iPhones to find news. The only bit of any of the
apocalypses they could see was the mothership hovering above London,
and even that was far enough away they could almost pretend it wasn't
real.

They assumed, of course, that the end of the world had arrived.

A man stood on a soap box. The soap box was actually a stage, with a
microphone and amplifiers and a team of bodyguards and devotees all
around him. He wore a bespoken Italian suit, custom shoes, the finest
silk tie you've ever imagined. His hair was perfect, his teeth gleamed,
and the diamond in his tie pin glistened.

He paced the stage, his soap box, microphone in hand, and spoke to
those gathering before him. More arrived every minute. They passed
around bottles of wine, but no one drank.

"We are sinners," the man on the soap box said, "and we have
brought down the wrath of an angry, vengeful god. We deserve to be
punished, to have our sins absolved by fire and sulfur and brimstone."

"I admit," the angel said, "he's a little over the top."

"We have suffered at trials of our own making. But the good Lord,
in his divine perfection, has deemed this world, this experiment of free
will, to be a failure."

"Free will's a failure?" I asked the angel.

The angel said, "No."

"We have walked our various paths through this sinful world, this
prideful world, this demented and delusional world. We have walked,
and suffered, just as our god has told us we would suffer."

"That's not the same god I know, is it?" I asked.

"Everyone sees their gods differently," the angel said.

"Is anyone right?" I asked.

The angel shrugged.

The man on the soap box continued. "Friends, we have reached the end of our journey. We have reached the end of our suffering. The Lord has served us our dead, and the Lord has served us our death. Presently, at this very moment, before the forces of evil overtake us, we have the option to take ourselves out of the path of evil, out of the path of destruction."

"He's wrong," the angel told me. "Also, not indicative of any religion, or even any fundamentalists. He's just one."

"That's good," I said.

The angel shrugged. "There are others."

"Drink the wine," the man on the soap box said. "When you're ready to say goodbye to this world of anger and hatred and fear, drink the wine. When you're ready to join our Lord in Heaven, when you're ready to repent your sins and the sins of your fathers, when you're ready to walk the path of righteousness, drink the wine. When you're ready to escape the evils we have brought upon ourselves, we, this inferior, insufficient human race, when you're ready to cast aside the dictates of a wicked society, drink the wine."

People were drinking the wine.

He wasn't, of course. He kept preaching. His words were vacuous and without sense.

People who drank the wine, of course, died. It was that kind of wine. They fell to one side or the other, they foamed at the mouth, they ceased breathing, and, really quite effortlessly, died. Then they got up and started eating those who had not yet chosen to eschew this wicked path and drink their wine. Those did not die easily. They died painfully, their insides scooped out of them before they ceased breathing, their flesh torn from their bones, their skulls cracked open, the last word they heard being from the language of zombies. "Brains."

It didn't take long for zombies to approach the stage. The bodyguards shot them, and shot them, and kept shooting until they were out of bullets. The man on the soap box kept talking into his microphone, as though anyone cared anymore what he might have to say. The zombies ripped apart the bodyguards and gorged themselves. But there were more and more zombies. They were on the stage. They closed in on the man on the soap box. Finally realizing this, he said,

"Goodbye, friends. I will see you in the Kingdom of Heaven." He laid down the microphone, held out his arms like a martyr, and made no attempt to resist as the zombies fought for the right to tear him apart.

"He didn't drink the wine," I said.

"His type never do," the angel said.

10. Tuesday 7:41pm

Angry robots reached the shores of Norway and Great Britain and Iceland at almost exactly the same time. They stormed the beaches, such as they were. They moved like silver and chrome waves.

"Beautiful, isn't it?" the angel asked.

"Except for all the shooting and explosions," I said.

The robots shattered everything that got in their way. They moved through mailboxes. They shattered police boxes and telephone booths. They crushed people and pets and zombies and zombie pets. They walked through buildings, putting robot-shaped holes into the sides of brick, steel, and glass, until the architectural integrity of those buildings failed and they collapsed with dust and fire and smoke.

The robots had their instructions, and no one to turn them away.

The zombies didn't notice. They were too busy eating. So a great many zombies were overrun by the advancing robots.

Robots reached the shores of Spain and France and Canada and Greenland and the United States. They blasted aliens out of the sky. In turn, aliens blasted the hell out of the robots.

One ship caught a robot in its net. They struggled, a tug of war game unlike any ever seen. This was one of the earlier model robots, with a domed head and visible clockworks and no lasers for blasting alien ships out of the sky. Instead, it pulled the ship closer using hydraulic muscles. The ship wavered, tossed and turned, as though it never expected to be the one lassoed. When the robot finally pulled the ship close enough to stick its metallic hand into the ship's wing, the alien fisherman cut the net loose. They careened to the left, then upwards, where another robot, this one armed with lasers and phasers and ray guns and disintegration beams, blasted it out of the sky.

Another ship caught a robot in its nets, yanked it into the air, and slung it across the sky like a giant silvery Frisbee. It crashed into a series of robots, all of which burst with cogs and gears and diodes and wires. The tossed robot skipped along the ground until it crashed into another robot and ceased functioning.

"How long will this go on?" I asked the angel.

"Until there's nothing left."

"That seems rather fatalistic."

"You expected some other end to Armageddon?"

One of the robots near us stopped shooting at the alien ships. It turned its electronic eyes in our direction. Beeps and buzzes and other electronicized sounds emitted from its mouth-speakers.

"Can they see us?" I asked.

"Of course not," the angel said.

The robot turned its attention back to the sky, to blasting alien ships out of that sky, until an alien ray beam of some sort hit it in the back. It exploded. Robot fragments and shrapnel and innards fell at my feet.

"The apocalypses are colliding," I said.

"They are."

"Did you know that would happen?"

The angel checked his wrist, where still he wore no watch, and said, "This has already happened, remember."

"Do we have a chance?" I asked.

"You and I?" the angel asked.

"The human race."

"Oh, I doubt it," the angel said. "Armageddon, usually, results in the end of an era, not the continuation of one."

In the sky, the mothership warbled.

11 Tuesday 7:49pm

Inside the mothership, down near the engines, another team of green berets were shooting the hell out of aliens. Not protected by armored ships, the aliens were no less able to survive gunfire than the soldiers.

They'd managed to destroy one of the engines.

"They were well-armed," the angel admitted.

"Explosives?"

"Powerful explosives."

The green berets, six of them, were dropping back from their former position. Aliens advanced on them, shooting lasers and phasers and ray guns and disintegration beams, leaving molten slabs of metal where there had been walls. When one of the weapons struck one of the green berets, it blasted a hole in the middle of his chest. He looked down, briefly, at the wound, which was open and gaping and smelled like barbequed pork. He then, quite reluctantly, dropped to the ground.

"Ah, but now it gets exciting," the angel told me.

The five remaining green berets continued to drop back. They were men of action. They said nothing, showed no outward reaction to their fallen brother. They moved like a team, like a machine, not unlike the gears of robots. Another took a glancing shot. It didn't blast a hole in him, which gave him an extra two seconds to stare dumbly at the wound before dropping dead to the ground.

The first of the fallen green berets rose as aliens advanced around him. The zombie green beret grabbed one of the aliens and took a big bite of its neck, coming away with a wash of green blood and gangly green veins and tissue and muscle.

The other dead green beret didn't bother trying to get up. He wrapped his arms around one of the alien's legs and, successfully tackling the alien, swarmed over its flesh and gorged itself.

The other four soldiers neared the end of the hall before additional aliens came from the other direction. Caught in a crossfire, they survived an amazingly long time. They set off additional explosives, which destroyed the hall from which they'd come, burying aliens and one of the zombie green berets. They fought until they ran out of ammo. Then they fought hand-to-hand until they were gutted, slashed, shot, or blasted.

Then they rose as zombies and continued to fight. Even undead, they didn't bother speaking. They didn't seem to speak the language of zombies anymore than they spoke any other language.

Elsewhere in the ship, humans had been stored as future food. They were packed into thousands of pods which seemed to fill more than the entire interior of the mothership. Here, I heard moaning, sighing, laughing, and crying. I heard someone say, "Brains." Not all the earthlings rounded up to serve as dinner had survived the process. They'd risen as zombies. They were feasting on the earthlings that had been rounded up to serve as dinner. There was no way to resist.

They fed, too, on aliens, who also rose in a zombified form. I couldn't comprehend the sounds they used as language, but I knew what they were saying.

12. Tuesday 8:01pm

On the streets of Tokyo, a million ninja slashed their way through zombies. Some failed. Some were not as well trained as others. You could see who had been trained in the ways of ninja from birth and who had, perhaps in the past two hours alone, chosen to take up the sword.

Even those with no skills fought well. The zombies did not fight well; they merely overwhelmed.

And that, they did well. They added to their numbers every minute. Twenty million people had lived in this city. No longer. Half that number were either dead or loaded into the mothership—or both.

Despite the technological disadvantage the ninja had against the superior weaponry of the aliens, they seemed to be holding their own. Where the aliens had lasers and phasers and ray guns and disintegration beams, the ninja had dexterity and acrobatics and invisibility and impressive accuracy. Shuriken, hand-tossed by ninja—on the street, atop neon signs, or clinging to the sides of skyscrapers—typically busted through the cockpit windows and buried themselves in the foreheads of alien pilots; the ships would then shriek, out of control, to a fiery death in the sides of other skyscrapers, or the streets, or other ships.

"Are we looking for anything in particular?" I asked.

"This is the first great victory," the angel said.

"Whose first great victory?"

The mothership listed suddenly to one side. There was an explosion, from the inside, that threw alien metal and alien bodies out of a new hole in the ship.

"Green berets?" I asked the angel.

"Unless you think the shuriken could be successfully launched from the ground and cause that kind of damage," the angel said.

"You're wicked."

"No, in fact, I'm not," the angel said. "I'm divine. My brother, however, is wicked."

"Your brother?"

"You haven't met my brother yet," the angel said.

"Will I?"

"You should wish not."

"But I don't have a choice, do I?" I asked. "It's already happened."

"Well," the angel said, looking at his bare wrist, "you have a funny way of understanding the ebb and flow of time."

Another explosion rocked the mothership. It was spinning now, out

of control, and dropping from the sky. All of Tokyo lay beneath it. The
alien mothership came apart as it plummeted. Pieces were tossed across
miles in every direction. Earthlings, zombies, aliens, green berets, and
ninja dropped from the falling mothership, amid contorted metallic bits
that had once played some vital role in keeping the ship in the sky.

The ship cracked in half as it fell, sending both major chunks in
slightly different directions, the better to spread the damage throughout
Tokyo. I almost turned away when they finally crashed.

The explosions were immense. The twin mushroom clouds knotted
and twisted my stomach until I was forced to my knees. The competing
shockwaves knocked me off my feet. Most of Tokyo was swallowed by
smoke and dust and debris, but not before I saw entire rows of
skyscrapers transformed into skeletons of themselves, and then those
skeletons scatter in all directions.

The angel did not fall. He held out his hand to me. "There's one
more thing to see," he said.

"I don't think I can see anymore," I said.

"I'm sorry," the angel said, "but you haven't got a choice." He
grasped my hand and pulled me to my feet. "Would you like a moment
to savor the victory?"

"You have a strange definition of that word," I said.

But around us, where there had been aliens and zombies and ninja,
there were now only the faces of Japanese men and women emerging
from the rubble. They looked to the heart of the city, which wasn't there
anymore. In the older faces, I saw recognition. In all of them, I
recognized a certain grim determination.

13 Tuesday 8:13pm

From beneath the boardwalk at Coney Island, from a secret hangar
no government or military official ever knew existed, a series of eleven
billionaires in battle armor emerged. They looked like giant versions of
the robots coming out of the water. They were massive, and in the heads
of them, I could see the various investment bankers, men and women
who had made themselves titans of industry and had now made
themselves titans of war.

The man at the head of the table led the charge.

The battle armor suits were easily as tall as the Cyclone, and as
complicated. They were armed, and even their armaments were armed.

Since the robots were blasting apart humans and zombies alike, the man at the head of the table sent forth a volley of laser-guided missiles.

Robots exploded by the dozen.

The robots, communicating by radio or something more sinister, decided as one to ignore the humans and the zombies, to let those fleshy things and flesh-eating things fight it out amongst themselves, and turned all their attention on the investment bankers.

There were a lot more robots than investment bankers.

The first to fall, one of the women, launched everything she had, not just in defense of herself but also to aid her fellow investment bankers, to further thin the ranks of the robots. Still, they damaged something internal, so her suit would no longer fly. Then they took out the legs. The robots swarmed over her machinery, punching holes, tearing sheets of metal off her battle armor skin, blasting her with lasers and phasers and ray guns and disintegration beams. As a final act, she triggered a self-destruct mechanism. When her battle suit exploded, it took out a city block, half a hundred robots, countless zombies, and a scattering of war-weary Brooklynites.

From space, the satellites began raining missiles upon the motherships. These were satellites that had been used to track weather patterns, or facilitate cellular communications, to make the Internet viable and practical. These were satellites that had served foreign and domestic governments and militaries. These were satellites that had seemed to be abandoned for years as space junk. They formed something of a net, albeit an incomplete one, over the earth, and they turned all their attention on the motherships.

Some of the motherships moved, leaving New York City for Newark, leaving Madrid for Barcelona, leaving Sydney for Melbourne. Some of the motherships took the missiles and seemed unaffected. Some of the motherships rose into orbit and launched a thousand small alien ships to blast the satellites out of the sky. Some of the motherships fell, destroying Paris and Cairo and Johannesburg just as one had destroyed Tokyo.

The investment bankers chased the mothership from New York City to Newark. They led a trail of robots that still meant to take them down. They met squadrons of small alien ships. The aliens fired lasers and phasers and ray guns and disintegration beams, forcing investment banker after investment banker to self-destruct. As heavily armed as they were, there were only eleven of them. The aliens and robots, together, cut them to shreds.

Then the aliens and robots cut each other to shreds.

"You said this was a victory?" I asked the angel.

"Someone won," the angel said.

"Who?" I asked.

"Watch the mothership."

Though it had survived a rain of missiles from space, though it had
not been threatened by the billionaires in battle armor, it suddenly
ascended at a dizzying speed.

"The green berets," I said.

"They couldn't get to the engines," the angel admitted, "so they got
to navigation instead."

"Where are they headed?"

"Into the sun."

It would be a long trip, almost forty minutes, and the green berets
would be dead, risen as zombies, and beheaded or disintegrated or
otherwise destroyed before they reached the sun. But that mothership,
in the end, once its course was set, was unable to change it. A swarm of
aliens escaped in the smaller ships, but there weren't enough ships to
save them all. No food remained alive by the time they felt the heat of
the sun; they'd all been made into zombies, who shortly made zombies
of all the aliens, leaving a ship full of aimlessly wandering zombies with
nothing to eat.

When the sun consumed the mothership, there was no indication
that it mattered. Compared to the sun, the mothership was miniscule. It
did not alter the chemical reactions of the sun in any way.

14 Tuesday 8:17pm

The angel walked up to the bar, set down his trumpet, and asked the
bartender for a double shot of her finest scotch. He wore white and gold.
He glowed, ever so slightly, but enough so you knew, without doubt,
that he was exactly what he looked like. Looking at the trumpet, you
could see, though you couldn't explain how, that it had been put to
good use lately.

A minute later, we were gone. But we were there, the angel and I.
He'd left his trumpet before. Now, he walked up to the bar, picked up
the trumpet, and said to the bartender, "Another, please. And one for my
friend here."

"I don't understand," I said. "I don't hear anything."

"No?"

"Did all that really happen?"

"What do you think?"

I met the angel's gaze and didn't waver. "I think no."

"I think you're a fool," the angel said. He turned to the bartender. "Cindy," he said, since that was her name, "what can you tell me about the end of the world?"

"What do you want to know?" she asked.

"How's it progressing?"

"Horribly," she said, "if you were against the idea."

"Are you against the idea?" the angel asked.

"Can't shill drinks to an extinct race," she said.

"Are you an angel?" I asked Cindy.

She looked at me. "That's not a very original pick-up line."

"I'm not trying to pick you up," I said. "I'm asking a question."

"No," she said. "I'm not an angel. Feel better?"

We were alone in the bar, the three of us. Had we been alone the first time we were there? I said, "Actually, I don't feel well at all."

"I've shown you things," the angel said, "that have already happened. But you've been so lost in yourself, in your drink here at the bar, you didn't even realize it."

"You kept it hidden," I said. I wasn't sure who I was talking to.

Cindy shrugged. "I expect you may be my last customer."

"May be?"

"Well, they're still out there, all of them," Cindy said. "The aliens, the robots, the zombies, they're all trying to destroy this world. But I'm not sure you'll let them."

"Ah, see, now we're talking about the present," the angel said. "These are the things that are happening right now."

"What things?"

"The cowboys," the angel said.

"Damn cowboys," Cindy muttered.

15. Tuesday 8:17pm

The dusty ghosts of Oklahoma cowboys arrived in Little Rock after sunset. They arrived upon the backs of ghostly horses. Their ghostly supply of ammunition never ran dry. They shot and shot and shot, and every piece of lead they sent flying hit a zombie between the eyes or went in one ear and out the other. Every time the sheriff or his deputies shot a zombie, it fell, it twitched, it stopped twitching, and it stayed dead, just as corpses were meant to stay.

"How are ghost bullets able to kill fleshy zombies?" I asked.

"Zombies are already dead," the angel said.

"Presumably," I said, "but they're solid and substantial, whereas the ghosts...ghosts are insubstantial, aren't they?"

"Not precisely. Look"

It wasn't a zombie, which had already defeated some of the ghosts back in Oklahoma, but a robot, the first of the robots to reach Little Rock, one of the most advanced robots I'd seen, which used its lasers or phasers or ray guns or disintegration beams and blasted one of the ghosts into a phantasmagoric mess of oozing slime and dissipating smoke.

The bullets, meanwhile, had no effect on the robot. The ghosts scattered. They kept plugging at the zombies. One was overcome by the undead horde, dragged off his shimmering steed, and pulled apart ghostly limb by ghostly limb. The zombies, meanwhile, moaned and sighed and repeated their mantra: "Brains."

The ghostly cowboy deputy, even as the zombies ripped him apart, remained grim but also sad. He took out as many as he could on the way.

"The cowboys are splitting up," the angel told me. "They will fall, all of them, but they will fall as men, as the men they meant to be in life. Look, even now, they spread in every direction but the west. The west is reserved for sunsets, for endings. This is an ending, but it's only the beginning of the end."

"What do you mean by beginning?"

"Oh, it'll get worse," the angel told me. "Would you like to see Hawaii?"

16. Tuesday 8:17pm

There was nothing left of Hawaii. The islands had been overrun by aliens and zombies and robots and ninja. Corpses floated where there should have been land. There were canoes here and there, maneuvering through the floating debris that had once been Waikiki.

The angel and I stood on an unrecognizable piece of something floating in the heavy swell of the Pacific.

"The storms have already come through," the angel said.

"Storms?"

"Cyclone," the angel said. "Tsunami. Earthquake. Volcanic

eruptions. Hawaii, as it turns out, was not a safe place to be."

"There are survivors."

The angel checked his bare wrist, cocked his head, and said, "I wouldn't bet on them reaching sunset. There are still the behemoths and leviathans and elder things under the ocean."

"You're kidding," I said.

The angel shook his head. "They're rising even now. They're preceded by armies of killer whales, stingrays the size of mobile homes, giant squid, all manner of marine life you've never seen on the surface. Crabs as big as Mack trucks."

"Seriously?"

"Have I been anything but serious?" the angel asked.

He'd been all sorts of things, but I bit back my response.

"The earthquake was actually between Hawaii and New Zealand. The tsunami spread in all directions. Another earthquake took California off your map, and most of the western half of Mexico."

"Why?" I asked.

The angel shrugged. "That's what earthquakes do."

"How are we supposed to survive?" I asked.

"Why do you think you're meant to survive?"

"Haven't we survived other cataclysms?" I asked. "Haven't we survived floods, and ice ages, and wars?"

"Oh, you want to know about the wars?"

"No." I shook my head. "I don't want to know about wars. With all this, are we also killing ourselves?"

"It's hard to say who launched the first nuclear missile," the angel said. "You might say they were simultaneous. You might be pleased to know, however, that neither Russia nor the United States launched any."

"Really?"

The angel grinned. "Small miracles, eh?"

"How many were launched?"

"Only forty-two," the angel said.

17. Tuesday 8:17pm

Over Baghdad, the commander and his green berets had locked zombies and aliens together in a huge section of the mothership, and they had control. They fired a directional electromagnetic pulse that wiped out every alien ship employed in netting earthlings. They all lost power. They spiraled, dropped, careened to one side or the other, exploded in midair, cracked, fractured, and splintered. Zombies tore the aliens to shreds. Soldiers and insurgents and terrorists and citizens and militia and criminals and cops, on the ground, working together, swept through the broken city and took care of the aliens that survived, and the zombies. They set fires behind them. They worked like machines.

When the first of the robots arrived, many people were slaughtered, but some found weaknesses in the machines.

In the sky, the commander and his green berets guided the mothership northwest. There were only four of them now; I don't know what became of the other two and I didn't ask. They had rigged the doors with enough explosives to take out the entire mothership, including alien explosives they'd probably never seen before. Three of the men, including the commander, kept their weapons aimed at the two most likely points of ingress. One struggled with the controls. They weren't meant for human hands, but he managed. He had a holographic targeting map in front of him displaying the location of each of the hundred and twenty-nine other motherships across the globe. The nearest, apparently, floated over Istanbul; that was his target.

"Impressive," I said.

"Well, they didn't become green berets because of their lazy attitudes and inability to adapt to a hostile environment," the angel said.

The sounds from elsewhere in the ship were horrifying. When an alien screamed, its voice reached higher decibels and higher pitches than human screams. The zombies moaned and shifted and let out their string of curses: "Brains." I was beginning to understand them, or so I thought.

"If this goes as they plan," the angel said, "they'll be superstars amongst the green berets, amongst all the earthlings. Their names will become anathema to the alien forces."

"They have names?" I asked.

The angel grinned.

The mothership moved with amazing swiftness, skimming low over the surface of the earth, until they saw Istanbul's lights—not the usual lights of the skyline, I'm sure, but the lights of the new skyline, in which there were still minarets scattered amidst the few skyscrapers that hadn't been felled, complete with unnatural fireworks and alien ships and barrages of missiles, lasers and phasers and ray guns and disintegration beams.

The commander, grimacing more grimly than ever in his life, calmly gave the command. "Fire." The acting pilot set off the directional electromagnetic pulse, this time aimed at the whole of the Turkish city still on the horizon. For a moment, nothing happened, then most of the lights went out. There were still fireworks, and shoulder-launched missiles flying through the air. But the alien ships started falling. The mothership faltered, limped sideways, and dropped.

It spared the center of Istanbul, though other cities had not been spared. The explosion was still immense. The shockwaves ripped apart much of the city that still stood, and doubtlessly tore through the fleshy bodies of aliens, earthlings, and zombies still on the streets. A moment later, the shockwave reached us. The mothership listed. Things that had been attached on the exterior of the ship came suddenly unattached. From elsewhere in the ship, beyond this control room, the screams of alien metal joined the screams of aliens.

There wasn't energy enough to fire another such blast. But another mothership had moved to Athens. The pilot set a course. This time, when they approached, they had no weapons with which to announce themselves. Instead, in the Grecian skies, they rammed the second mothership. The resulting explosion was more spectacular than any display of thunderbolts from the fists of Zeus.

18. Tuesday 8:17pm

Thousands of miles above the earth, hurtling toward us at amazing speed, from an angle not in line with the other planets or asteroids or known comets, was a rock the size of Madagascar.

I shouldn't be able to breathe. Shouldn't I be exploding in the vacuum of space? I don't ask the angel these things. I asked, "Is it inevitable?"

"Actually, no," the angel said.

"No?"

"It depends," the angel said.

"On what?"

"The actions of one man."

"Anyone in particular?"

"Yes."

"Me?"

"Yes."

"You're putting a lot of pressure on me," I told the angel.

"It's spinning pretty wildly," the angel pointed out. The rock was. Despite its size, it was fast and unstable and frightening, especially since it seemed to be bringing yet another apocalypse to earth.

"Will it be the final apocalypse?" I asked.

"Probably not," the angel said.

"How many more can we suffer?"

"How many have you already suffered?" the angel asked.

"I've lost count."

The angel shrugged. "So have I."

"How do I stop it?" I asked.

"I don't know. That's not my department."

"Angels have departments?"

"Sure, why not?"

"It seems somehow less than omnipotent."

"Angels," the angel said, "are not omnipotent. We're omniscient. There's a difference."

"What are humans?" I asked.

The angel grinned. "Omnivores."

The rock continued to hurtle recklessly toward our insignificant little earth. I didn't know how far we were from it, but it appeared to be the size of a marble from here, while the sun was immensely larger. I couldn't see other planets. I couldn't even see the moon. It felt almost like this little bit of space was designed specifically for me to see only what I was meant to see: the sun, the earth, and the rock hurtling toward the earth.

"How long?" I asked.

"Midnight in New York," the angel said.

"That sounds like a movie," I said.

"Or a poem."

"Is it?"

"I don't know," the angel said.

"You said you were omniscient."

"Yeah, but I didn't mean it," the angel said.

19. Tuesday 8:17pm

Off the coast of Somalia, pirates, modern pirates, without the parrots and peg legs but armed with a wide assortment of automatic weapons and heavy ordinance, moved away from harbor, away from other pirate ships and fishing vessels and commercial freighters. A trail of zombies floated behind them, most in pieces, food now for the sharks and whatever else might wait beneath the surface.

I didn't ask.

The crew cheered, raising their weapons, firing joyful volleys into the sky. The deck was a mess of blood and gore and body parts, as well as corpses, which they were hauling over the side as swiftly as they could.

They'd rid the ship of zombies. They were afloat, now, on the sea, with stockpiles of food and plenty of clean water, and a ship—a ship that hadn't belonged to pirates an hour earlier.

They spoke, they sang, they passed around rough bottles of rum. I didn't understand a word of it.

They didn't know about the robots.

A half dozen robots breached the hull and entered through the floor of the ship. The ship started taking on water. The ship started listing to one side. Other things seemed to crawl out of the water, but they were too far behind the robots to matter.

The robots ignored the convention of stairs and corridors; instead, they ripped through the ship's guts, gleefully spreading damage and destruction as they made their way to the deck.

When the first reached air, it met one swaying pirate who, an hour earlier, might not have been a pirate at all. He was unwashed, unsavory, unclean, and just a little drunk. He narrowed his eyes at the robot, leaned back and forward at the same time, pointed accusingly, and said something vicious in a language I didn't speak.

The angel translated. "You were supposed to help us."

"Does he really think that?" I asked.

"He won't for long."

The robot reached for him with calculated coldness, wrenched him off his feet by his throat, crushed his windpipe, cracked his spine, then dropped him down the hole the robot had just created. The pirate, not dead, crashed harshly against unevenly torn metals, rolled unintentionally to one side, and dropped further, into water from the Indian Ocean. He couldn't move, couldn't even turn his head so as not to drown in water only inches deep.

The robots devastated the ship. With their lasers and phasers and ray guns and disintegration beams, they created windows where ships should never have windows. They made pretty holes. When they crossed paths with pirates, they shredded flesh and bone in much the same way.

One pirate was sober enough to aim and fire his weapon, and unleashed all his fury in a concentrated blast of automatic fire that knocked the robot's head off its robotic shoulders. The dying robot emitted some sort of radio signal, right at the end. Three others, newer models, sleeker and deadlier, converged on the spot. They each grabbed a limb of the pirate. They struggled amongst themselves for a while, tearing him this way and that, until he stopped whimpering and stopped breathing and stopped bleeding.

By then, the ship was already three-quarters sunk.

"So, the pirates didn't do much, eh?" I asked.

"I know how you once liked pirates," the angel said.

"When I was a boy."

"We're all just a boy inside," the angel said.

"Anyhow, these aren't the kind of pirates I liked."

"Good thing," the angel said. "They didn't amount to much."

20. Tuesday 8:17pm

In the ice of Antarctica, in the endless night of winter, McMurdo Station lay dormant, quiet, and dark. If anyone still lived there, which was doubtful, they hunkered in their quarters and remained hidden. The wind blew harshly. A layer of ice had formed over everything, the structures and the buildings and the roads. There were bodies, but only a few, caught in the ice flow, frozen in fear or horror or agony, frozen forever.

Liquid ice—which I couldn't quite describe as water—flowed like lava from the ice mountains I couldn't see through the dark. The cold, even in the presence of an angel, was numbing.

"Why are we here?" I asked. "There's no one left. What are you showing me?"

One of the structures creaked loudly enough to be heard over the wind. It shuddered, and shifted, but another building, a little more distant, cracked first and crumbled.

"Desolation," the angel said.

"Don't think I don't appreciate it," I said. Surely angels knew sarcasm.

In the distance, one of the giant ice mountains cracked. The thunderous sound rolled across the continent and rumbled through my bones. Cracks raced through the icy ground. In some places this far south, the ice ran a mile deep, and much of that ice had been

453

undisturbed for thousands of years. The newly formed ice crevasses, which continued to form, were in some places a mile deep.

"No matter how remote, no matter how far removed, there was really no escape," the angel said. "No aliens, no ninja, no ghost cowboys came to the southern pole, but still the zombie plague came, and still the ice flows, and still the computer viruses and the electrical problems."

"Do you have a point?" I asked.

"No matter how remote," the angel said again, "there was no escape. Humanity's final hour has arrived."

I shook my head. "I still don't think that's fair."

"Why do you think it has to be fair?" the angel asked.

"We were doing good."

"You were doing poorly."

"Not everyone."

"No," the angel admitted. "Not everyone. Ever hear the saying, kill them all and let God sort it out?"

"I never subscribed to that," I told the angel.

"It's almost 8:20," the angel said, looking at his bare wrist in the blisteringly cold dark. "We have an appointment."

21. Tuesday 8:20pm

We arrived precisely on time for our appointment. So did the others.

Our appointment was in the Red Centre of Australia, amid the rocks of Kata Tjuta. The sand was reddish orange. The rocks, presumably part of a great snake king, were an orangey red. White wisps of clouds raced across the blue sky. The spinifex was maybe slightly yellower than green and grew in individual bunches all around us.

There was another angel. He wore black and gold, just as my angel wore white and gold, and glowed ever so slightly. He smiled more broadly, like a stereotypical used car salesman or maybe a game show host. His black hair was longer and shaggier, and he hadn't shaven in a day or two. The girl beside him did not smile. She'd forgotten what a smile was. She wore black, her hair was black, her eyes were black. It was Jessica, who had stared down the zombies at the start of my journey. She recognized me. She stared at me. Her black eyes were rimmed with red, though dry.

There was another angel. He wore silver and gold, just as my angel wore white and gold, but glowed much more brightly. He smiled more honestly. Freckles had been tossed about his face, and his hair was a coppery red. The woman beside him did smile. She wore horn rimmed glasses, and had legs longer than legs were meant to be. It was Cynthia, who had been a stenographer for billionaires. She recognized me. She stared at me. Her blue eyes were bright and large.

"This is the End of Days," said the black and gold angel.

"The End of Time," said my angel.

"The End of a Cycle," said the silver and gold angel.

"Has it gone as well as planned?" asked the black and gold angel.

"I didn't notice a plague of locusts," said the silver and gold angel, "nor frogs."

"Nor oceans of blood," my angel added, "but you can't discredit the architect of such a finale."

"There is no precision," the silver and gold angel said. He turned to the black and gold angel. "There is merely chaos and destruction."

"Ah, but such a beautiful chaos," the black and gold angel said. "And such a beautiful destruction."

"It gets worse," Jessica said.

"No," Cynthia said, "it gets better."

"It gets both," my angel said, holding out his hands as though to say we were all brothers here. The familial resemblance between the angels, in fact, was uncanny, once you got past the coloration and how they wore their hair.

There were four other angels, also of the same line, perfect facsimiles of each other. They walked as though a single machine controlled all their muscles at once. They wore gold, and more gold, with some trim in black, white, or silver. They were crossing the red sands of the Australian Outback, but their feet didn't touch the ground. As they approached, the six of us moved to let them join us. By chance or design, my angel and I ended up between the other two pairs.

"No more bickering," they said. It was impossible to tell which spoke. Their voice seemed to be a single voice, or the voice of many compressed into a single voice. It was hard to look at them. But the four of them, as one, turned all their eyes upon me. "Choose."

"Choose what?" I asked.

"Choose your path," the four-in-one angel(s) said.

"Sorrow," said the black and gold angel.

The silver and gold angel said, "Or hope."

My angel held up a hand. "Please," he said. "The choice is not his alone to make, as you well know." He turned to me. "Jessica and Cynthia will each show you a thing, and talk with you, and tell you something important." He turned back to the four-in-one angel(s). "Only then can he choose."

"Me first," the black and gold angel said.

22. Tuesday 8:20pm

The sun hadn't quite set over the Amazon. From the top of an ancient step pyramid, where blood sacrifices had been made hundreds of steps over the rest of a ruined city, I could see a long way in every direction. I saw the mighty river of myth, and the rainforest, and distant cities that were too far to really be seen. The overgrowth of forest had only recently peeled back from this ruin, and had left its mark. I don't know whose pyramid or city it had been, but I knew it had never belonged to the Mayans.

Of the distant cities, there wasn't much left but ruin there, either. Fires raged uncontrollably. The earth still shook in places, though not beneath us. The ocean pummeled the shores on both sides of South America. Everything seemed closer to us than it should be, so that we could see zombies still staggering on the beaches of Rio, and the alien mothership laying waste to Lima. All that remained of Buenos Aires was a memory; the earth had swallowed the city whole, and most of the peninsula south of it. The Caribbean had pulled Caracas off the shore. I saw no sign of Trinidad or Tobago.

"Look closer," the black and gold angel said. "You're missing so much."

The rainforest swayed. The treetops danced in the wind, swirled, moved, advanced upon villages whose names I'd never known. Jaguars led the processional of trees into the streets. The big cats were proud and beautiful and sated; the trees, however, hungered. When they found a person who had somehow evaded the zombies and the aliens and the robots, who had somehow survived the weather and the earthquakes, the upended roots of the trees would snake around their limbs, crush them like a python crushing its prey, and draw them closer to the carnivorous trunks of ancient rainforest trees that had never even been seen by modern man.

"It's alive," I said.

"It was always alive," the black and gold angel said.

"The vampire infestation of Berlin and Prague and Warsaw was worse," Jessica said. "They were almost unstoppable, until the cyborgs stopped them."

"I saw no vampires," I said. "I saw no cyborgs."

"The ants were even worse," Jessica said. "Have you ever seen a colony of red warrior ants swarm a man? They're like piranha. Bones, dry bones, clatter and crack when they drop. The ants leave nothing else."

"An ant apocalypse?" I asked.

The black and gold angel shook his head. "Originally, they were mean to win this."

"I can't imagine there'll be any winner," I said.

"There can't be," Jessica told me. She put a hand on my shoulder. She looked me in the eye. A single tear hung at the edge of hers but did not fall. "You know, we buried my brother this week. For me, that was the start of it, this heartache."

I didn't know what else to say, so I said, "I'm sorry."

She smiled. It was brief, and not robust. "When the earth moves on from this, when fields blossom again, there will be only the shattered remains of humanity. There will be traces, in the ruins of cities, in the fragments of streets, in the massive graveyard that the earth will become. There'll be you and me, alone, to mourn a whole race. We weren't just a single civilization, we were a multitude of civilizations, some stronger than others, some more beautiful. We will, if we're given enough time, light a candle for every soul lost today. We can honor them, and keep them in our hearts, and remember all that they suffered, so we don't simply dissipate into mist. You and I, together, can retain all that."

"That's beautiful," I said.

She closed her eyes. That burgeoning tear finally slipped out of her eye and rolled, unmolested, down her cheek.

23. Tuesday 8:22pm

A very still Dove Lake perfectly reflected Cradle Mountain and the blue skies above it. Off to the right, a boathouse remained undisturbed, coated by a soft, white layer of snow. There was snow on the mountain, snow on the trails circling the Tasmanian lake, and snow under our feet, but none fell from the sky.

"It's beautiful, isn't it?" Cynthia asked. She stood beside me, looking out over the lake. The angel in silver and gold waited behind us. He seemed extraordinarily impatient, which is probably why I was took my time responding.

"It is," I said.

"Have you ever seen a Tasmanian Tiger?" she asked.

"Anything like the devil?"

She shook her head. "No. The devil is a scavenger, and leaves nothing behind. That's why no one's seen a Tassie Tiger in decades. They believe it's extinct."

"They're wrong?" I asked.

"Oh, yes," she said. "I saw one before our appointment. You know, when they captured what they believed to be the last, they killed it, or allowed it to die."

"That's sad."

"I don't believe we'd do that today."

"I don't believe we have any say in the matter anymore," I said.

She looked at me, with eyes bluer than the sky and the water, eyes frosted as if by a layer of snow, yet still filled with passion and intensity. "None of the apocalypses reached this place," she said. 'There are others, too, where there are so few people, the juggernauts and the snakes didn't bother, where you would find no fashion models with scimitars, no giant bears, no killer bees."

"I didn't see any of that," I told her.

She shook her head. "Doesn't matter. Look, there, now."

There, now, was a baby, crying, in a cradle, twenty steps away on the water, where no cradle should be. It was an old, rocking thing made of wood, but the infant was bundled in pristine white blankets.

"She wants her mother," Cynthia said. "And look, there she is."

The mother appeared out of nowhere. She ran, hunched, and stopped long enough to scoop up the child in her blankets. She didn't seem to notice the water or her audience.

"She's not here," the angel in silver and gold said. "But still waters, like these, can be quite reflective. We can only take you to one place, but other rules...we can bend."

"Where is she?" I asked.

"Not far," the angel in silver and gold said. "Perth."

"Robots stormed the Indian Ocean coast of Australia," Cynthia said.

"I saw robots," I said.

Cynthia took both my hands in hers, leaned close, close enough to kiss, close enough that her horn rimmed glasses brushed my cheek, and whispered, "The baby and her mother survived."

"Is that a good thing?" I asked.

"Of course it's a good thing," Cynthia said.

"In fact," the angel in silver and gold added, "there may be several thousand survivors."

"So only about seven billion dead?" I asked.

The angel shrugged. "I think our time here is done."

"Wait," Cynthia said, shaking her head. She still stood too close. "There may be fewer than a hundred if..." She stepped away. "There may, in fact, be only four, and even from four we can start again, try again, maybe get it right this time."

"Were we that wrong?" I asked.

She averted her eyes. "I don't know."

24. Tuesday 8:30pm

At the bar again, the bartender, Cindy, already had seven champagne glasses out. Upon our arrival, she popped the cork. She looked at each of the us in turn as she poured, and maybe, in her mind, she said something to everyone, or gave some indication of things she'd known and seen. She winked at me, as though I were meant to correctly interpret her meaning. I couldn't. The four-in-one angel(s) stood off to the side, staring at us, waiting, but not partaking. The other angels each picked up two glasses, and each gave one to their human charge. I accepted mine from my angel in white and gold.

"I propose a toast," Cindy, the bartender, said. She lifted her own glass. "To the future, whatever it may hold."

"The future," the angels said.

But Cynthia said, "To hope," before she drank.

Jessica said, "For sorrow."

I said nothing, but lifted my glass anyhow, and closed my eyes, and drank. It was the sweetest, bubbliest, most intoxicating champagne I'd ever had.

When he finished, the angel in black and gold threw the glass against the wall, shattering it. The angel in gold and silver set his gently on the bar. My angel held his out to Cindy and said, "If I might indulge once more."

"You might," Cindy said, refilling his glass, and then her own. She glanced at the four-in-one angel(s). "Have all the conditions been met?" she asked.

"They have," the angel(s) said, in their single multiplied voice.

"Excellent." Cindy smiled, and I realized quite suddenly that all eyes, more eyes than I cared to count or calculate, were turned toward me. Other eyes, too, in other places, may have been watching, waiting, anticipating the next words I might say. I felt the weight of them, seven billion pairs of eyes, twice that many, all who lived and all who died, all who ever were or might have been.

My voice cracked. "I have questions."

"Your time for questions has passed," my angel told me.

I glanced at the four-in-one angel(s), who had taken one step closer when I spoke. "I don't care."

For a moment, time froze. It had been crooked and cockeyed and bent and misshapen for all the days of my life, it seemed, so there was nothing strange about it here, at the very edge of the end of it.

The four-in-one angel(s) turned to face each other. It was hard to look at. They seemed to be breaking physics laws, or bending light, or twisting space itself to look at each other, but theirs was a short palaver. They said, in their multiplied, single voice, "You may ask one question, which we may choose not to answer, but if you don't make your choice, we will find someone else to make it."

"You can't," Jessica said.

"You shouldn't," Cynthia said.

But the four-in-one angel(s) had spoken, and no argument could be made against them. I cleared my throat. It was a delaying tactic. I had a number of questions I should have been asking all along. Now it came to one. "Why us?" I asked.

The four-in-one angel(s) seemed to smile. "The angels are angels, and therefore beyond your understanding of reason, and very unlike you imagine. Cindy was chosen because she was the best bartender who ever served a drink in the Four Great Cities, of which you know nothing."

Cindy smiled and curtseyed briefly.

"The humans," the four-in-one angel(s) continued, "because they are representative of their conditions. Other humans might have been selected. It was arbitrary."

"So, it was luck?" I asked.

The four-in-one angel(s) said, "We have answered your question. Now you must choose."

I held up a finger, to indicate that I needed a moment, and turned to Jessica and Cynthia, neither of whom would meet my eye. They were both beautiful, in their way, but they weren't asking me to pick a mate or a partner. This wasn't a dating game. I closed my eyes, so that I might not be swayed by appearances. I said, "This seems so unceremonious."

I opened my eyes again and looked at my angel. He nodded. He smiled. I said, "The rock?"

"The size of Madagascar," he reminded me.

I nodded. Did I believe we, as a society, could rise from the ashes of this, or would we better off cremating what little remained? I turned to Jessica, who I'd first seen telling off zombies outside of Sydney. "Jessica," I said, giving her my saddest smile, "I'm sorry, but I have to choose Cynthia."

"Excellent," the angel in silver and gold said. He turned to Cindy. "More champagne."

As she popped open another bottle, my angel put a hand on my shoulder, tilted his head, and said, "Now, you must follow through."

I didn't ask what that was supposed to mean. I knew. "You'll leave us in Brooklyn, then?" I asked.

"If that's what you wish."

"What remains?" I asked.

He shook his head. "Not much."

The angel in black and gold grinned at me. He put a hand on Jessica's shoulder. She leaned her cheek into it. Her eyes were closed. She was crying.

"Wait," I said.

"You chose," the angel in black and gold said.

"Yeah, but she stays."

"She can't."

I shook my head. "I think my choice was clear. Whether she wants to hold onto her sorrow, that's for her to decide. But she doesn't die. I chose hope."

"That, you did," the angel said. "But you'll never see her again. You're going to New York, what's left of it. Jessica, however, will be returning to Sydney. There's a small group of survivors under the Opera House even now."

Just before they disappeared, Jessica opened her eyes and said, in barely a whisper, "I'm sorry."

Cynthia took my hand. She grinned. She said, "We have work to do."

25. Wednesday 6:21am

On the boardwalk of Coney Island, as the sun peeked over the horizon's edge, zombies shuffled aimlessly, the Cyclone shuddered as the roller coaster spun round and round without any riders. The Wonder Wheel circled lazily. Over a hundred years ago, there'd been a golden age of carousel production here in Brooklyn, but the sole survivor of that time remained quiet and still. The alien ships had begun ascending into space. They'd gotten what they'd come for, and more, and were uninterested in fighting for what little remained. They were damaged, though, and left earth with only half their fleet.

An army of robots gathered across the Long Island Sound in Connecticut. There were other apocalypses to end, as well, but Cynthia and I had our weapons. The investment bankers had left two fully armed, completely hidden battle armor suits in a secret laboratory several floors beneath what most believed was the bottommost floor of the aquarium.

The aquarium housed no creatures of the sea or the land; it had been completely leveled.

In the new light of a new day, we rose from the depths, ascending a huge, unknown shaft for just such a purpose, in two identical suits. Nothing remained of the eleven investment bankers or their suits. They might never have existed.

We went north.

We went with gritted teeth and barely contained fury.

We went with a vengeance.

As we reached the Connecticut shore, robots came to meet us. They outnumbered us a hundred to one, but there were far fewer than had faced the investment bankers. We used our lasers and phasers and ray guns and disintegration beams and blasted the robots out of the sky. We didn't worry, yet, about the remaining zombies; in time, we'd get to them, too. We cut down the robots. We evaded their weapons. We destroyed their sense of well-being and their equilibrium. We kicked robot ass.

High above the atmosphere, beyond the range of earth's orbit, the last of the green berets and those ninja that had boarded the alien motherships, or maybe the zombies that had infected their harvest of human food, got the best of the aliens. They flew, perhaps intentionally but perhaps not, into the path of a rock the size of Madagascar, and the series of explosions lit up the sky more brightly than the sun. The rock broke up into a billion smaller pieces that scattered, so that most of it would not rain down on the earth. Those bits that did burned up in the atmosphere. For two days straight, it rained fire. For two days, Cynthia and I, in our investment banker battle armor suits, hunted down the robots. We crushed the zombies. We found pockets of people, a family here or there, up and down the east coast of the United States. Others, in other hiding places, began to emerge.

That first night, with fire raining from the sky, a field of broken and dead robots behind us, the sun set over the Appalachian Mountains and it was beautiful. It was a thing of wonder. It was a thing of hope.

AFTERWORD

Zombies versus this. Zombies versus that. Pirates and ninja. Cowboys and aliens. Don't you think there's been enough of this? Apparently not, because they keep coming. One day, in jest, I suggested online I would write "Zombies versus Aliens versus Robots versus Cowboys versus Ninja versus Investment Bankers versus Green Berets." I soon realize even that wasn't enough. I had to throw in more. And I knew, right from the start, the ants would emerge victorious.

After the title, you'd think the rest would come together easily. But what I didn't know about, before the beginning, was the angels, and how their presence would shape the story. It didn't go where I expected, though I did toss in a comment about the now non-victorious ants. The first scene in my head, in fact, was the very first scene in the story: an angel walks up to a bar (stop me if you've heard this one), sets down his freshly blown trumpet, and orders a double shot of the finest scotch.

The rest just happened.

Pocketful of Smoke

Fistful of Glass

Pocketful
of Smoke

Fistful
of Glass

1.

The illusionist steps calmly onto the stage, acknowledges the crowd on his right, then his left, winks at someone in the audience, and stretches out his hands.

His assistants, in pasties and g-strings, step forward from the dark, each grabbing a hand and tying it to the ropes hanging from the ceiling.

One finishes first. The illusionist twists his hand, yanking the rope tight. If you look, you can see where the ropes have burned the flesh of his wrists.

The other girl finishes her knots, and he shows that this hand, too, is secure.

The lights die, and the darkness is absolute, impenetrable. A violin breaks the silence with a song that is more race than sonata, pure driving adrenaline, quick and high-pitched and dangerous.

Light returns. The girls are gone. The illusionist, still bound to hanging ropes, leans to one side, draped by his arms, muscles taught. If the knots slip loose, he'd fall into the audience.

And he's wearing a mask, bright red, eyes painted over so he cannot see.

The lights drop, for but a second, and when they return the illusionist drips in the opposite direction and the mask is green.

Another flash, he's slumped forward and the mask is blue.

Another flash. His knees are lifted, so he hangs suspended over the stage. Unmoving. The mask is again red.

Flash, green, still straining against the ropes, the violin racing faster and faster, the notes more and more frantic.

Flash, blue, draped to the left.

Flash, red, right.

Flash, forward, and the violin pauses. The mask is black now, with silver stars for eyes and mouth. The light lingers. Indeed, it brightens. Every spot hits the illusionist, every house light comes up, the violinist races between notes more quickly than should be mortally possible.

Then the lights vanish. One final, elongated note fills the air. A heartbeat. Two. Three.

The lights return. The mask is unchanged, still black and silver, but the illusionist is gone. In his place: the girl, silver stars concealing her nipples, bare feet, the tiniest black panties.

The illusionist, seated in the audience, is the first to rise, leading a standing ovation–though of course, it's his own applause he conducts, and not everyone in the audience has yet realized what has happened, how fast the change was, how tightly those ropes are tied.

He climbs onto the stage, puts a hand up to the girl's cheek–she seems to melt into him, though the cheek is a black mask and he can't actually touch her. He unties one knot, then the other, swoops his beautiful assistant into his arms–she kicks her legs playfully and waves–and after three or four bows to various corners of the theatre, carries her offstage.

"Bravo," says a man in the shadows backstage.

The illusionist lets down the girl. She rushes away to change for her next part.

"What are you doing back here?" the illusionist asks. Then, "Who are you?"

"An admirer," the man says, bowing his head slightly, but ignoring the first question entirely. "We've met before, you and I. Once."

"No," the illusionist says. "I'd remember such a face." And certainly, he doesn't, as he can't even see the man clearly. And the audience is cheering one of the girls, who by now should be wearing nothing but feathers.

"You shouldn't be back here," the illusionist says. He has another bit in five minutes, and though he needs half that time to prepare he feels suddenly rushed, uneasy, unsure of himself. "If you can wait until after the show."

"I have waited this long," says the man, still in shadows. "What's another few minutes?" When he smiles, his teeth catch a glimmer of dim lights. He recedes deeper into the dark, though he seems not to move at all, and even his eyes, cat-like, reflect a stray bit of something.

The illusionist hesitates. Does he remember? No, he cannot remember, does not remember, there's nothing there to see.

2.

He is not merely an illusionist. He is an escape artist. A master. Locks, chains, doors, walls, ropes, tanks, sacks, blankets, and the occasional jealous husband. There's an escape piece toward the end of the show. Naked girls are the best distraction. Stage illusionists always have the most beautiful assistants. It's part of the show, part of the magic, a necessary ingredient and an oftentimes wonderful, more personal, distraction.

He once escaped the real world. Ended up here, in Midnight, City of Night, where the sun never shines and the show must go on, and he truly belongs here. He feels it in his bones. Once, he lived in New York City. Once, he worked dives in London, Paris, and Berlin. Once, he did silly card tricks and pulled flowers from hats and spent a good portion of his income on rabbit feed.

No rabbits at the Palais Royal, though he was never far from a good deck of cards.

3.

She arrives on stage with a flutter of feathers and a flash of skin, accentuated and hidden by the tiny points lights and the expert, seamless motion from one shadow to the next. It is a dance, even when only the lights move, even when her every muscle is still and her eyes have fallen upon a specific, random man who suddenly finds himself sweating, fidgeting, uncomfortable in the grip of her gaze.

The next beat of music erupts in movement, and you'd swear you just saw more than she meant for you to see, a flicker, a taste, though you can't be sure it wasn't your imagination.

She makes no mistakes.

Beads of sweat become visible on her neck, her waist, the back of her thigh. It's hot under those lights. Hot, even if she wears nothing but a fan of feathers in either hand, even if the air conditioning--is it really only the chill?--raises goosebumps on your arms.

She moves slowly, languidly, and then in a frenetic fury, either driven by or driving the violin which accompanies her. The violinist moves also in the dark, never visible, never seen, never revealed but in one perfect note followed by the next.

Tonight, her name is Stephanie, and she's a Russian runaway, having left her parents at fourteen and coming to this great City of Night, where she survives by seizing all the things she most desires.

She's the exhibitionist. Last night, she was someone else, someone older but less jaded, someone less dark. But tonight, she risks her past, fluid though it may be. She dares that past to step up, to claim her, to whisk her back to Leningrad, where winter comes too coldly and night ends too early and her parents suffocate their single, lonely child.

She wants to cry.

She focuses that energy, instead, on the dance.

But the man in the audience, whose eyes she had so greedily and contemptuously locked, surely he saw the depths of her sorrow, the blurred edges of her history, the desperate promises and faux declarations.

The violin slows. The dance draws to a close. The exhibitionist, Stephanie tonight because that's who she's chosen to be, steps backwards toward the curtains, the fans held in front of her like a second, trembling skin. She looks left, right, toward the parts of the audience that glimpse more of the tease, the shadows of her breasts and the curves of her hips.

Then she looks straight out to the back of the theatre, so deep into the darkness she sees not shapes but a smoky, undulating mass of black beneath the glare of the spotlight.

With a twist of her wrists, she flings the fans off stage, revealing all of herself to all of her audience, her captives, her worshippers. There's a gasp or two, and a whistle, and general applause as she bows low. Deep.

It was a flash. Only a flash. She likes it that way. She likes to give them what they want, and immediately take it away.

From the curtains, the gentleman emerges in all his splendor. Tails and white bowtie and shiny shoes and waistcoat, and those wonderful white cotton gloves. He bows behind her, cups a breast in one gloved hand (his forearm crushing the other close), slides another between her legs and covers the razor sliver of hair there.

He hides everything, but takes no pleasure in it.

He rises when she rises, his gloves her new bikini, hands cooling her skin beneath the cotton, hiding bits of her from the lights and the audience's eyes. He holds her tight, tight enough that she could spread her legs and hang in his grasp, which she does some nights but not tonight. That's not Stephanie. That's not who she's chosen to be.

He steps back, pulling her behind the curtain, the pair of them vanishing before the spotlight goes dark.

She snuggles back into his arms. He whispers, "No time, my child," though he is certainly no older than she. He says the same words every night. And though his lips touch her ear and he gently squeezes her breast, his other hand never reaches deeper, never explores, never even slides across her most vulnerable, swollen, exposed part; and his own vulnerable parts betray neither excitement nor interest, nor even life.

He slips through the curtain, on stage and into a new spotlight. A flute replaces the violin.

The exhibitionist shudders, having felt the gentleman's hands as Stephanie, as the Russian runaway all grown up, as the girl she herself might have become. She retreats toward the dressing room, to prepare for her next bit. She offers the illusionist a smile, notices but does not acknowledge the stranger so well hidden in the shadows. Let him think he's as stealthy as he is. She has the eyes of a hawk, an owl at night, a cat, a sharpshooter. She sees the things the rest of us hide. She sees, even, the pallor of the illusionist's skin. She hopes the stranger has no words for her. But if he does, she wants his voice to be velvety thick and slow, his accent to be European--but neither French, nor Italian, nor British. She wants the sound of him to ease the cut of his words.

4.

The stranger is not of her past. He has no words for her, and therefore offers none. He doesn't doubt she sees him, and is comfortable with that.

5.

She used to be someone else, but in her search to become somebody, she'd shed persona after persona; the exhibitionist doesn't remember her earliest names. They don't matter anymore.

But sometimes, like tonight as she stares into the mirror, she wonders who she was supposed to be. It's a momentary, fleeting thought, but it passes through her mind nonetheless and it impacts her. Stephanie, the Russian runaway, melts by the merest notion of identity. She doesn't want to know. Doesn't want to care. Seize life. Grab it by the horn, by the balls, by whatever cliché you want, she has only an eye for the future.

Her eyes, however, are powerful, more so than even she knows, and in the audience there's a man, Bob, becoming more and more uncomfortable, squirming in his seat, in the memory of those perfect green seas. Green like jade, translucent, letting light shine through--but not without its tint.

Bob's afraid, because the woman he came with knows more than he does, recognizes the symptoms of his infection. Ann's okay with it. He never became important to her, hadn't had time to burrow into her heart. She's lost more than one in just the same way, by another's passing gaze.

Ann doesn't realize, of course, that she never gives her men a chance to burrow, she builds barriers and hazards no mere mortal can surpass; if she were to glimpse into her future, she'd see a solitary but content aged woman on a rocking chair recounting stories of her conquests, of the fish she'd carelessly tossed back into the ocean.

Ann puts a hand on Bob's arm, leans close to whisper, "It's okay."

"It's nothing," he protests.

"It's not nothing," she tells him. "Follow your path."

6.

The gentleman has only just reappeared on stage. He steps to its center, casting his gaze about the room like a fisherman's net but seeing nothing and no one.

Every man has a story to tell.

His just happens to not be his own.

It involves a cowboy or a ninja or an astronaut, and there's of course a woman scantily clad, a femme fatale or a damsel in distress. It's the same story every night, with minor variations, so that one day it begins in Amsterdam and another day it ends in Hanoi. Sometimes, the villain is the hero, and sometimes the hero is the villain, and sometimes there's only girls giggling about the men they've enchanted and discarded.

He'd been discarded once, not by a woman but a man, a gorgeous and rare specimen, worthy of Greek marble, an Olympian if ever there had been.

That was long ago. Before the theatre.

The gentleman is kind enough to exclude his personal reflections from the story he tells. His voice is perfect, honed and polished until it is smooth, soft, and enthralling.

He spreads bawdy jokes throughout his story, throws out words like boobies and Johnson because who expects them to come from the mouth of so finely dressed a gentleman? Perhaps, in a burlesque show, that is exactly what the audience expects; yet such silly nonsense terms never fail to elicit a response.

Sometimes, when he speaks, the flute drops to near silence. The musician wonderfully matches his mood, shifting her notes with the melody of his tale.

Tonight, as on other nights, there's a heroic battle at the end, followed by a moral, something about getting what you wish for, and wishing beyond your reach, something feel-good and comforting, a healthy dose of encouragement with a touch of lesson.

It's not only merely words, though; his stories are a breather for the audience, a moment between what was and what will be. They're not half way through the show, and already they need to be brought down, reigned in, pushed back off the edges of their seats.

He enjoys his tale, because though it's always the same it always changes, and he never knows where it will lead him.

Tonight, it leads no where special, no place he hasn't ever seen before. The audience loves it, especially the part about the monkey, probably because of the monkey suddenly leaping around the room like a madman.

For a moment, the gentleman blinks, and the animal is gone. As if it never existed.

He bows low and long, taking extra time for himself. He feels the curtains calling. He feels an end coming. He feels sad, yes, but not in the way the exhibitionist is always sad. Nor does he feel lost.

The monkey is not part of the show, and nobody seems to care.

7.

The illusionist is shaken.

He returns to the stage. The violin returns, accompanies him as he presents one empty hand then the other, reveals the hollow and empty sleeves of his jacket. One trick per bit, that's all he does, but he's nervous now and doesn't know if he can pull it off.

There's a stranger backstage, a stranger who knows him, whom he knows, a stranger he's never ever seen before tonight but almost remembers, very nearly remembers, and it scares him.

The girl joins him on stage. It's the girls they've come to see, of course, though the audience is not made up merely of horny old men and teenagers. It's a performance, after all, not a strip club, not a peep show, not a tug job. You want that, go to Old Possum's, next door; one of the girls will set you up quite nicely, give you what you need or at least what you want.

Don't fuck with them, though; those girls can be nasty when they want to be, and can back it up in ways you simply can't.

The girl bows to the audience. She's in a rabbit outfit, or something like what a bunny might wear in one of those Vegas clubs, a tight sparkling leotard stretched to cover all the essentials. She smiles brightly, dazzlingly, and the illusionist wonders if the audience would care about his tricks if his assistants weren't so damned gorgeous.

The stranger backstage is part of his audience tonight, and the stranger certainly cares more about the illusion than about the props.

Yes, the girls are props. So, too, are his hands. All just tools for illusion.

He passes a hand in front of the girl's face. Her eyes drop, she's asleep, standing, under the influence of his instant hypnosis, so he can make her do anything.

For example, she can climb into a box.

It's pushed out from behind the curtain, a golden box with mirrored sides (a mirror is part of his final illusion). It's on a chrome cart that slides quietly across the stage. He locks the rollers, one at a time and with flourish, so the audience doesn't miss a movement.

Smoke rises from the sides of the stage, thin wisps wafting into the air, maybe nothing more than cigarette puffs, maybe nothing more than a dry ice machine, certainly not enough to obscure anything.

The box is a three foot cube, solid wood with those mirrors, painted gold by its former owner, an illusionist from this City of Night's past, to whom the illusionist owes no debt.

The illusionist sets a stepstool next to the cart with the box. He takes the girl's hand and guides her as she walks, each long leg making an elaborate journey from one step to the next until finally she's in the box.

He waves in front of her face. She waves to the audience. Kneels, then lowers her head and chest into the box, and she's gone from view.

He closes the flaps on all four sides of the box.

The violinist shifts her song into something faster, more violent, as the exhibitionist steps onto the stage with a sword.

He takes it, slaps it hard against the side of the cart so that its metallic sound echoes into the furthest reaches of the theatre, and plunges it through the middle of one side of the box.

The gentleman brings out a second sword.

Then the exhibitionist.

Sword after sword, until the illusionist has driven two in on each side and four through the top. He unlocks the rollers, spins the cart to show the blades sticking out from all sides, then relocks the rollers and draws the swords out, one at a time, with style--as he was taught--and throws each backstage.

The illusionist opens one flap, looks into the top of the box, and shudders.

He closes the flap. Looks about the audience quickly. Gauging their belief in his disbelief. They know it's a trick. If it were real, if he had looked at them in horror with blood dripping from the swords, still they would think it was part of the show.

He refolds the flap into the box. Then another flap. Another and the last. Then he bangs one side. It unhinges, dividing the mirror in half, and folds into the box. Another corner, another side, until the box is now a one foot cube. He picks it up, shows it to the audience, and closes the final hinge so that it seems he holds nothing but a handheld mirror.

He holds it in one hand.

The cart is empty, and offers no place to hide. He unlocks the rollers, pushes the cart behind the curtain. The exhibitionist steps out, a blanket draped in her hands. The illusionist takes it, wraps it around his neck like a cape, and waves it for the audience.

He throws it over the exhibitionist as she drops to her knees. He lifts it off, and she's transformed into the girl, unscarred by the swords, uncrushed by the box, the same leotard and smile she wore at the start of the act.

The audience cheers.

The girl struts across the stage, the violin following her movements now, the illusion already fading into the past. She sways and wriggles and kicks like a Rockette. For all he knows, she was one once. In her life before the City of Night, before the Palais Royal, before the burlesque.

Backstage, it's not just the stranger who watches him, who follows his every move; it's the Grand Madame.

8.

She might not be the blood of the show, but the Grand Madame is certainly the bones, and the heart, and the muscle. When she has an opinion, she makes it yours, and you'd do well to simply agree and pray she turns her attention elsewhere.

She's not big. Indeed, she's a wire, and stands not much taller than a dwarf. (There once was a dwarf in the show, a woman whom everyone called a girl. Some believe she simply got old and left, or died. Others will try to tell you the Grand Madame ate her.)

She runs things next door, too, though presumably she answers to Old Possum himself, whom no one ever sees but everyone has seen at least once.

They say she trains all her girls in the arts. Dance, seduction, martial, paints, poisons.

They say the girls at Old Possums are a formidable army.

They almost never say the girls are two dollar whores. The Grand Madame is mighty talented with her knives.

9.

The contortionist takes the stage.

She twists into a knot, her legs bent back, up, and over her neck, and holds herself up on one hand. She's all of ninety pounds, and at least two ribs shy of the average woman. She bends backwards in ways that make men swoon, though experience has taught her they haven't got the faintest clue as to how to exploit such talents in bed.

(She knows. Oh God does she know.)

She wears only a g-string, but the angles and arcs she forces her body into inspire much (albeit poor) imagining.

The contortionist has other talents. She can throw knives. It's a useful skill around this part of town. She can whistle in seven languages, which is amazingly useless. She can count to ten forwards and backwards, which isn't much of a talent, but apparently amazes a lot of drunks at the bar. She does it standing on one hand wearing a blindfold and tossing back a shot of whiskey with every number.

She's also got an amazing sense of hearing.

Yes, she hears pins drop. She hears beads of sweat fall from the foreheads of the audience. She hears the quickened heartbeat of the illusionist as he leaves the stage, and knows enough about him to make him uncomfortable. She hears the silent footsteps of the stranger, though she has not yet seen him. She has no desire to meet him. He's got two of their troupe twisted up already, and she does a decent job of that on herself.

She does one-armed push-ups with her ass facing the audience, wrapped in a ball, and she knows some of them out there are now thinking of holding her like a bowling ball. As if that would satisfy her. Or, ultimately, them.

She stretches one leg out to her side, bends her body to touch it, raises the other leg high into the air. Her breasts are tiny, child-like things, exposed, cold despite the hot lights, and she hears so much.

The contortionist also swallows swords and breathes fire and bathes in cream, but no one will see that tonight.

She pushes herself up to stand on one leg, the other still aimed heavenward. Her arms curl unnaturally behind her back. She's skinny enough to fit through the tiny windows in the dressing room, and limber enough to slip between the Palais and Old Possum's, all of twelve, ten inches. Because of this, there are men who think, even now in the audience, that they'd break her.

She can lift twice her body weight easily.

No one has broken her yet. Indeed, the score is well in her favor on that count.

The musician favors her with the flute tonight, so she feels whimsical and mischievous. She winks at a woman at one of the front tables, making her blush and avert her eyes.

The contortionist turns slowly on one foot, aware that some of these people are here just to see the view she's giving them now. She doesn't care. She's comfortable with that. She's already got their money lining her pockets--well, the pockets of her civvies.

She bends her leg down to her other side, her body hanging between them like a pendulum. Her leg moves slowly, deliberately, and touches the stage without a sound.

Not quite without a sound; the contortionist hears it.

She hears something else, too. The stranger, popping open a pocket watch, or something similarly mechanical and small, following this with a little, impatient sigh. He'd told the illusionist he would wait. She doesn't think he will.

The contortionist bends her knees, lowers her elbows (hanging just below her head) to the stage, and tries to decide if either the stranger or the illusionist matter to her.

10.

The illusionist returns reluctantly to his dressing area, where the man in the shadows is looking at his pocket watch. It's nice, old-fashioned, brass or even gold, connected to his belt by a thin chain. It looks old, but well-weathered, and it somehow connects the man to reality. Shadows, apparently, hadn't been enough.

"You do remember me, don't you?" the man asks.

"No," the illusionist says. He's no longer sure this is true. Not entirely. But he's not lying to the man in the shadows; he's lying to himself, and that scares him. He is not, by nature, a liar--despite the apparent contradiction of his trade in illusion.

"No," the illusionist says again, turning away and staring instead at himself in the mirror. His next bit isn't a trick. He has to change. He has to get ready. The clock, even if it's merely in the shadow man's pocket (but it's not, it's held out, open, vulnerable), is ever ticking, and the Grand Madame certainly watches it.

Where is she? What would compel her to allow a stranger, any stranger, into the backstage area? She keeps her girls safe, and by extension all her performers. The illusionist feels a great many things right now, but safe is not one of them.

"Do you believe in magic?" the man asks from the shadows.

"What a strange question to ask an illusionist."

"Ah, but pertinent," the man insists.

It surprises the illusionist. No one has ever asked him this. He can make balloon birds seem to become actual ravens. Force the jack of spades to dance out of the deck and bow to the audience. Drink an entire jug of water whilst a little wooden dummy talks. He can read minds, or seem to read minds. He has mastered the balls and cups so well, he can direct an audience member to maneuver the pieces and never touch them himself. He has levitated women, and sawed them in half, and blindfolded them both on stage and in bed. He can find dollar coins tucked in a woman's cleavage, or behind a child's ear. His ropes cut and retie themselves, stand up straight, and slither like snakes.

All tricks and misdirection. Smoke and mirrors. Deception, if not outright lies. Performance. But real magic, the kind that changes base metals to gold, the kind that transport unwilling participants to faraway beaches or alleys or bunkers...that's something entirely different, isn't it? Hypnotism, yes. Enchantment? Maybe not. Lightning from your fingertips? Sure. With props.

"It's a show," the illusionist says. "You'd enjoy it better from the loge."

"I rather doubt that," the man says, flipping his watch closed and returning it to his pocket. "What would you say is your greatest trick, illusionist?" He coats this last word with sarcasm, perhaps a touch of irony, and a hint of contempt.

"I have many," the illusionist says.

"Perhaps a memory trick?" the man asks. "No? No, of course not. You fancy yourself an artist, not just of illusion but of escape, do you not?"

"The escape was my first act," the illusionist says.

"And your finale?"

The credo of illusion does not allow him to reveal his secrets; though this isn't really a secret, the illusionist is hesitant to answer. He glances at the prop, a mere flick of the eyes in the direction of the mirror. The man seems to smile, though it may be a trick of the shadows.

11.

The gentleman and the girl dance. A piano, hidden in the darkness, draws out a waltz, and the dancers glide effortlessly, in perfect step, as the exhibitionist narrates.

Sometimes, she dances, but she's Stephanie tonight, and Stephanie never learned to dance. She never learned music at all, though she fits comfortably into the patterns it creates.

"Once, they were lovers," she says, loudly enough that everyone in the audience hears. "Once, they were even friends. But a storm came." The piano strikes a discordant chord and the dancers suddenly stagger to a halt. The contortionist slips out from behind the curtain, twirling her extraordinarily petite body in little pirouettes, her red shoes sparkling, and her red lips, her red fingernails, and the long red dress that flows like streamers around her legs.

"Always," the exhibitionist says, suddenly wondering why she isn't the one dancing, why she isn't the one about to be swept away into the story. "Always," she says again, "there comes another woman."

The contortionist laughs.

The piano plays a crooked and shifting piece, maintaining bits of the waltz, interjecting modest melodies and inappropriate accents. The dancers struggle. The contortionist spins around them, neatly, perfectly, her fingers sliding across the gentleman's shoulders, then the girl's back, his waist and then hers, until finally she wedges between their arms.

"Temptress. Seductress. You might call her witch, or evil incarnate. You can call her Jezebel." The dancers are all still, except the contortionist, who lifts one leg up between the dancers' arms. She hooks it over the gentleman's forearm. The slit of her dress allows a full range of motion, even for a person with her talents.

"But she doesn't need a name, does she?" the exhibitionist asks. "You've met her, too, haven't you? The other woman?"

The leg cuts down, pulling the dancers apart. They each step back.

The contortionist looks first to the gentleman with a wicked, evil grin, and then to the girl. She holds out her hands for a dance. The girl falls into them. The gentleman drops his head and turns to go as the piano returns to its waltz and the girls dance.

"You know where this ends," the exhibitionist says. The gentleman nods, his eyes cast backstage. He sees nothing and no one, remembering a scene from his own past, a boy with whom he was once in love.

"Then you should stay," the exhibitionist says. "See all you can see."

The waltz turns into a tango. The girls take to it like professionals, which of course they are, and the exhibitionist flashes skin as she sashays across the stage and slips an arm into the gentleman's. She says again, "See all you can see, that's my message to all of you. Take what is offered. There are no second chances."

Together, they leave the stage, and the girls are left to conclude their dance.

12.

Bob's seat in the theatre is empty. Ann sits back, arms folded across her chest, a mixture of satisfaction and disappointment playing across her face. She understands all too well the idea of the other woman. She's even been that woman, on occasion, though that has also never worked out well.

She's beginning to wonder if love, itself, isn't meant to work. Perhaps it's a fleeting thing, which you can sometimes grab hold of and sometimes keep for extended lengths of time. Maybe it's not supposed to be the glorified romantic lifestyle in her head. What if love is more a state of mind? What if it cannot be taken, but only given?

Was it an act of love, then, to send Bob to follow his path, whatever path that might be? Or would it have been more correct to tell him it's okay to resist those urges, to be the person he thinks he should be rather than the person he wants to be.

To be honest, it's too much for Ann's head. She waits for the next act, certain that the seat beside her will remain empty for the night.

13.

Bob rinses his face in the bathroom. It's marble and tile and dark, somber wood paneling and scarlet sconces on the lights. It's so plush and fancy and comfortable, you can almost forget there's a toilet.

He suffers no crisis. No loss of faith, no wandering eye. Sure, the merest glance from the exhibitionist set his heart aflutter and dropped lead weights into his stomach, but there's no man–and only a few women–in that audience who wouldn't feel the same way. It's a lot like when a god steps out of the clouds and shares a secret. You've been acknowledged by something higher than you, something greater.

He knows better than to think such a woman would have any interest in him. He almost lost his life once because of a stripper, because of his obsession in this Russian girl who could barely speak English and never wanted anything more than his money.

Sorrow has a firm grip on Bob, however. He's years, and miles, away from that tiny stripper. He's given himself completely to this other city, this other world, and he thought he had given himself completely to Ann.

Her rejection, subtle as it may have been, hurts.

14.

The audience is made up of anonymous strangers, just as the night before, and the night before that, all with their varied reasons and expectations, hopes, dreams, beliefs and fears.

Bill used to work in burlesque and stand-up, and though he's pushing seventy, he still knows he would shine in the spotlight.

Sue wants to see the naked girls. Not because she's into naked girls, but because she can't imagine the courage it must take to stand on a stage and expose yourself like that. She wants courage, and strength, and she wants to expose herself to the guy in the mailroom at work, but she can't even manage to say hello when they're in line together for coffee.

Tom also wants to see the naked girls, and that's really all there is to that.

Mike just wants to enjoy the show, and maybe impress his date. (For the record, Jess is, indeed, impressed.)

Ed is here for the magic, Kim for the music, Liz for the wine, Ben because he thinks he might find a girl, Tim because he thinks he might find a guy.

Eighty-six souls in the audience–almost a full house. Thirteen cast and crew. The man in the shadows makes one hundred.

15.

Between acts, the gentleman has a chance to rest. He sits on his chair, which is plush and purple and frilly and comfy, his own chair from home. He lives further from the theatre than any of the cast, and he loves the long walk every evening.

He catches his breath, which shouldn't be so difficult, and glances at the girl. She's changing. None of them have a shred of modesty, though he's fairly certain of their moral strength. Despite appearances, they are strong girls, all of them. That brings him comfort. He knows he lacks the moral fiber, the strength and courage, even the confidence, to match any of these girls. He loves them for it. He needs them for it. He's weak, and growing weaker.

He's not sure, but he thinks there is a monkey somewhere in the rafters.

That's his mind, then. Cracking. Showing its edges. Abandoning him to Fate.

There's a man, too, in the shadows, watching everyone and everything. Without moving, the gentleman says, "You shouldn't be here."

"No," the man says. "I shouldn't."

That's not exactly how the gentleman expected the confrontation to end, yet it's over. He's deflated. He'll go on, only because the show must. Otherwise, he would rather melt into the baseboards, seep beneath the damp concrete of the basement, dissolve into the night and into the city.

Despair. The gentleman faces a beast with a name. Its form is the monkey. Its voice is his own.

"You shouldn't, either," the man in the shadows says.

The gentleman turns his head, slightly, though it droops and he has to look over the top of his shoulder.

"Whatever you left behind," the man says, "is gone. It's time to forget about it."

The gentleman shakes his head. Images pour through his mind: Sunday mornings, the two of them eating pancakes in bed; the lights of Broadway, under which they shared so many kisses; kicking puddles in the rain; holding hands.

"There is no forgetting," the gentleman says.

The man in the shadows smiles. It's a cruel smile. Vicious. Wicked. It's the smile of a killer monkey–part snarl, part mischief, part euphoria. It's enough to scare the gentleman off his chair.

"There is always," the stranger in the shadows says, moving his fingers as if weaving the words, "forgetting."

16.

The girl doesn't think of herself as a girl. It's a label, applied by all the others. Cast, crew, audience, lovers, it matters not. They think of her as girl, they call her that, they imagine her limits and they build up their expectations.

She doesn't mind. She enjoys shattering expectations. Shredding the persona. Tearing and clawing and biting her way through the bits and pieces of a life everyone else thinks she should live.

She lives her own way.

She keeps mementos, fragments of what they believe her to be, on a shelf in her room. Yes, there's a pressed lily in her Bible, dry and fragile. There's a porcelain ballet dancer, an inch and a half tall, forever balanced on a single foot. She especially loves the foot-shaped pendant, gold, tiny and delicate. It's from Hawaii, she thinks, though she's never been there. A gift from the dad who thought she'd forever be his little girl.

When she's on stage, she's never naked. Though she may remove every stitch of cloth, there's always the thin, frost-like chain around her waist. Also a gift, from an admirer who wanted her not to be just a girl but a dirty little girl.

Sure, she plays the role. She eats their hearts. Devours their souls.

The illusionist, he thinks of them all as girls, mere props for his performance. He's not that good, and he's not that smart. She sometimes thinks about breaking him, but she'll do nothing to damage the show. She won't let the Grand Madame down. No other person in all the world who has ever scared the girl with quite the same verve as the Grand Madame.

Since she's tiny, and she's quiet, and since no one ever guesses what kind of cat waits beneath her skin, she's often ignored. Or not even seen.

Thus is the case this very moment.

Indeed, she tries to hide, tries to take one deep breath and suck all of herself into her tiny lungs. She remains silent, and still--except for her eyes. She looks from one to the other, stranger to gentleman, all too aware of what's happened.

The gentleman is a rarity. He lives up to his title. He talks kindly to everyone. He even knows the girl's name, her real name. He's the only one. Probably knows everything about everyone, and never will tell. He's the kind of man you can kiss and know there's nothing more to it, just that moment, that embrace of lips. No promises, no demands, no hopes, no fears. She would never break him. Indeed, she protects him when she can, though there's never been any need.

Never before, anyhow.

The girl suddenly feels all those things she's supposed to, as a girl, be feeling: small, frightened, vulnerable.

The stranger in the shadows remains obscured, though less patient than before.

The gentleman steps toward the stage to spin his second tale.

There's a power in his words. The girl's always felt it. It's not just his voice, which is a power itself. He adjusts his white gloves, rolls his head left to right, right to left, then enters the hall behind the curtains.

The girl glances at the stranger. But the stranger is watching, instead, as the gentleman approaches the stage.

17.

The illusionist juggles flaming knives. It's the end of this bit, the finale, with seven long, burning blades. He catches one, tosses it back up, catches another. A bead of sweat rolls down the side of his face, where never such a thing happens. His level of discomfort has risen with the tempo of the harpsichord.

It's a huge instrument, and the furthest from the shadows the musician ever seems to be. She's a silhouette, sitting there, her back to the audience. She can't possibly see the stage. Yet every note is perfect, and not because of the performers.

The contortionist, on the receiving end of the knives, throws them back. They have worked this act together for sixteen months, and both had worked it before the Palais Royal. Just another part of the show. Another oo for the audience, another ah, another chance to perhaps see something they aren't meant to see.

That's why they come, isn't it? To see that forbidden flash of flesh. Or the flaming knife caught by its blade instead of the hilt. The anticipation is enough, else they wouldn't keep coming back.

The act nears its end. He'll catch three, she'll catch three, the seventh will clatter at the center of the stage. The audience can't generally see the scars the blade has already left. Unlike stories, or illusions, there's not much room for adlibbing in fire acts.

One, two, three, they're caught. The last bangs dully, and the flame goes out. The illusionist (all illusionists, once, were called jugglers; he never forgets this) bows to the audience, and then points to the contortionist.

She does the finale in this act.

The blades still aflame, she lifts one over her head and slides it down her throat.

It's a trick, yes, but not like you might think.

She puts out each of her daggers in the same manner, then smiles broadly and faces the audience.

There's something wrong.

The illusionist knows this at once, but you can't betray such knowledge on stage.

The musician, too, knows, as the song rushes to an end.

The contortionist's smile is forced. Her eyes are watering. One tear spills evaporates. In the heavy lights, her trouble's not visible from the audience.

The illusionist rushes her off stage as the audience applauds. He drags her past the gentleman, who offers only a brief look of concern before pushing through the curtains.

The musician starts again.

The Grand Madame comes rushing out of the dark.

18.

The Grand Madame takes over.

She's directing her cast like a colonel yelling at soldiers. To the illusionist: "Get her over here." To the girl, she names three of the girls from Old Possum's. "I want them here now." To the exhibitionist: "I need damp rags."

The contortionist's eyes are red, beyond bloodshot, with tracks of white where it should all be white. She sweating, and crying, the tears falling like regular tears in streams down her cheeks.

"She's burning up."

The Grand Madame takes a damp rag from the exhibitionist, presses it to the contortionist's forehead, whispers words like, "It's going to be alright, stay with me, fight it, you're the strong one here."

With the suddenness of a tiger, and the intensity, she snaps her head toward the man in the shadows. He hasn't moved anything but his head, to better watch. "Who the fuck are you?"

This surprises everyone. No one gets backstage without the Grand Madame knowing. No one stands here and waits, or acts, or draws curtains, or stitches torn costumes, or delivers pizza without the Grand

Madame's permission.

The man's smile is all teeth, beast to beast, an answer to the unvoiced snarl in the Grand Madame's voice. He can't possibly see her as a threat. She's small, and she's tending one of her fallen. "Just trying to stay out of the way," he says.

The contortionist reaches up, touches the cloth, guides it toward the sides of her face. Her eyes are whiter now, approaching normalcy. She coughs, once, and says, "Water."

The exhibitionist shoots off to fill a glass.

The Grand Madame locks her eyes on the illusionist. She plays the role of mother, yes, but also detective, and she's not very happy in either. "What happened?"

"Nothing," the illusionist says.

The Grand Madame's eyes glare. She doesn't accept the answer.

"Just the usual," the illusionist adds. "The bit was going just fine. We tossed the knives, she doused them in her throat, just as she does every night. Nothing went wrong."

"Not nothing," the Grand Madame says.

"It's...not his fault," the contortionist says, accepting the glass of water and allowing the Grand Madame to help her sit up. She swallows most of the glass in a single, extended draught, and hands the glass back to the exhibitionist. "More, please."

Please is not a word you often hear backstage at the Palais Royal. There's never time. One bits leads directly into another, ten or twelve acts in total, and when the curtains close, the cast members scatter to their various holes and hovels. Perhaps the gentleman says it, but he's busy now, his part in this the most important: he's keeping the show going.

Backstage, they don't hear him. He's telling one of his stories. The musician's accompaniment is, as always, perfect, though this isn't a regular part of the show. There should be dancers with him, girls twirling about wearing next to nothing. It's a story about cowgirls, or Indians, or perhaps trans-Atlantic travelers aboard a doomed cruise ship. There's something uneasy about his story. It lacks playfulness, and depth. It meanders when it should jab a point. It staggers where it should swagger. It falters.

The gentleman pushes on. There's noise backstage, the kind that barely makes a sound. It tickles his ears and the back of his throat. He doesn't feel right. He feels abandoned. It's a familiar feeling, but he doesn't remember why. He has no experience to match it.

There should be girls twirling drunkenly across the stage, hanging on his arms, tottering over the audience. The exhibitionist should be showing her ass to the men at that table there. She should be shaking it the way no one else can. She should be infecting the fancy of their dreams.

He can't hold the audience on his own.

He's just a storyteller, but he remembers no stories. He reaches into the nothingness around him, pulls random characters and situations from the faces he sees, but he can't put them together.

The audience is uneasy.

The harpsichord is discordant.

He wishes it was a piano. He remembers pianos. He knows how to speak to their sweet notes.

The harpsichord, instead, stifles him. He glances at the musician, sees only her back swaying. She's struggling to keep him in check, to control the ebb and flow of their rhythm. She's failing.

The gentleman doesn't know why he's on this stage. Doesn't know what he's supposed to do. He falls silent, staring from table to table, then up to the rows of faces in the loge, the balconies on either side. He clears his throat.

To her credit, the musician forges on.

The gentleman clears his throat, lowers his head, and apologizes.

The audience, uneasy though they may be, doesn't know if this is part of the act.

19.

The contortionist feels fine, if parched. She doesn't need all the attention. Everyone's around her like she's a freak show. In a way, perhaps, she is, but these are the freaks around her, the bearded ladies and illustrated men and goat boys.

She looks to the exhibitionist. "Shouldn't you be on stage?"

"Go," the Grand Madame tells the exhibitionist.

"I think I need to rest," the contortionist tells the Grand Madame.

"Of course," she says. "Your last act is cancelled."

"You don't have to..."

"Already done," the Grand Madame says. "I can't have my girls exhausting themselves. I'll have no injuries, you hear me?"

The contortionist lowers her head. Her throat aches, and her eyes still burn. There's a ball of iron tacks in her stomach weighing her down. "Yes, Madame," she says.

"Now." The Grand Madame turns again to the man in the shadows, who might've until that moment believed he'd been forgotten.

"Yes, Madame?" he says, bowing his head in proper deference.

"Leave."

"I'd rather wait here," he says.

For some reason, the contortionist would rather he wait here, too, in sight even if in the shadows.

The Grand Madame's voice drops in volume, soft as ever. "And I'd rather not see your blood spilt down my drains."

"Excellent argument," the man admits. He turns to the illusionist and says, "I'll wait."

The Grand Madame lowers her voice even further and tells the contortionist, "We'll talk later." There's as much threat in those words as the ones she gave the stranger.

20.

You should know something about the building itself. There's a lot more to the Palais Royal than you can generally see. The stage, an orchestra section (albeit, for no more than a string quartet, a piano, and a harpsichord), tables on the floor, rows of seats on the loge, and two balconies that hold eight each. That's what you see. The auditorium, restrooms, coat check, a few offices. The usual stuff.

There's another two levels above, with apartments and storage, where you can find costumes from shows past and empty medicine bottles in wooden crates. With five basement levels, it reaches deeper than Old Possum's Kitty Supplies; it's older, too, and its history is more unusual.

They say the Wandering Reverend settled here at one time, but you shouldn't believe everything they say.

A theatre more than once, and a pharmacy, a refuge for runaways, a brothel, a speakeasy, a stop on the underground railroad. If you believe all the stories. It's been in the musician's family for over a hundred years. Yes, the musician. Did you think the Grand Madame owned it?

There are a few secret passageways, some of which the musician knows, some of which are known to others. The complete blueprints are probably buried somewhere within the Historical Society.

At least two ghosts have been witnessed with some regularity, though there's no reason to think the sightings were anything less than whiskey-fueled delusions. There's the fat lady, wandering around the stage after the audience has gone and the lights are dowsed. Which, interestingly enough, infuriates the fat lady who sings there now. And there's the old man in a rocking a chair who has apparently taken residence in the men's toilet just off the auditorium. He offers toiletries and cologne, and has a ceramic bowl for tips. If you see him, it's best to leave a dollar or two.

Currently, four of the apartments are occupied. The musician resides in the main suite, which is complete with a private kitchen and bath. The others rooms share amenities. That's where you'll find the illusionist, the contortionist, and Julia.

Julia used to sing on the Palais Royal stage, back when it was an opera house in the 30s. She's ancient, creaks when she walks, and feeds the stray cats in the alley behind the theatre. She also talks to the girls from Old Possum's when they need someone for talking.

The Palais Royal is dark, except in the spotlights, because it's old and angular and none of the lights seem to stretch deeply enough into the shadows, even in the auditorium where the hundred-bulb chandeliers replaced the hundred-candle models. Still grand, still elegant.

The man in the shadows sticks to shadows as he walks through the auditorium. At the last minute, he doesn't push out the doors, but slips through one on the side, one that's always locked because no one has a key (except, perhaps, the musician). There, engulfed in darkness, he descends to the basements. The metal spiral stairs squeal as he walks, and seem to sway, but lead him where he wants to go.

21.

You might expect ghost stories in one or more of the basement levels. The atmosphere begs for them. There's not enough light. The deeper levels are not just darker, but stonier and narrower and shorter, a warren of corridors and passageways--and even a few staircases--that seem to lead nowhere.

Several doors are locked, and several rooms are empty. They say there are tunnels under the city, connecting many of the aboveground buildings with those that exist beneath; but they also say beasts live under there--spiders the size of Volkswagons, train-men who haven't seen the surface in generations. Perhaps there's some truth to what they say.

But they say nothing about ghosts in the basements of the Palais Royal. Indeed, they say little, because people rarely disturb the air. As the man walks the corridors, whirling dervishes form in the dust and follow him, dying as quickly as they are made.

In one room, there's an old footlocker labeled, in uneven script, 1902. Although it's locked, the man could easily open it. He doesn't.

Rooms are filled with old wardrobes, stuff that could be worn in the burlesque, ribbons of silk and satin and sequins, feathers and lace. There are stacks of old shoes and batons and dingy carnival masks that once sparkled and dazzled.

Memories fill these rooms, though it's tough to say to whom those memories belong. In one room, there's a model of the stage and the seats around it. Under the dust, it's all vibrant colors. There's even a liquor cellar. Although not empty, it does appear to be forgotten.

The man brushes the dust off a bottle. The scotch is older than he is, and older than his father. He opens it with reverence and savors the aroma.

"Lovely," he says. His may be the first voice that's spoken at this low level in a decade or more. As there are no glasses, he drinks from the bottle. He wants just a taste, but it is incredibly satisfying, and he cannot resist a second swallow.

Then he closes the bottle and slips it into one of his larger pockets. It's a souvenir he can properly enjoy later.

He finally finds what he's been seeking, a room in which dancing girls once polished their shiny bits and tied whatever bows they wore. There's a big mirror, large enough for a man to walk through should he be so daring (or foolish). He withdraws a lighter, a shiny butane job he picked up as a souvenir of his time in Matanzas. Though it was long ago, it gives him the briefest flicker of a smile. He spends a moment preparing a cigar, lights in, and takes two or three deep inhalations before exhaling on the mirror. He touches as much of the surface as possible with the smoke; although there's no chance of covering the mirror, still he manages to obscure it. His own features fade through shadows. An image wavers into view.

The stage. This very moment, as the exhibitionist dances and the befuddled gentleman stares.

This, too, sparks the tiniest sputtering grin on the man's face.

22.

The mirror is flawed and smudged, and therefore the image upon its surface is flawed and smudged, and no sound comes forth, but the man in the basement sees the show clearly enough.

23.

The exhibitionist dances around the gentleman. He stands there. He watches her. He looks silently out to the audience and makes no move to either tell one of his stories or leave.

He's the storyteller, and he's brilliant at it, but now he looks half dead and entirely amazed.

There's a part of her that wants to take advantage of his confusion. To press her dance closer to him, and maybe remove bits of his clothes. But he's the gentleman, and throughout the show he never even loses a glove. She's close to naked, getting closer every three or four measures, winking to the darkness but unable to focus on any particular person.

The exhibitionist is confused, as well--by the gentleman.

She takes his hand and guides it above her head, then twirls like a ballerina. She lowers his gloved hand to her waist and spins in tight. Though she knows she could guide his hand to her breasts and he wouldn't resist, she finds herself unwilling.

Yes, she's a little surprised. But she's more concerned. Maybe that's what stops her.

Hers is a relatively slow dance, solo--albeit, she's using the gentleman as a stripper might use a pole. Ask what differentiates her burlesque acts from stripping, and she might feed you some bullshit about intention and class, but in her mind the Palais Royal merely offers a safer variation.

It's not safe because of the theatre; it's safe because of Old Possum's Kitty Supplies--well, because of the kitties they supply, anyhow.

Truth is, the exhibitionist loves doing what she does, and it doesn't matter if it's a strip joint or a burlesque theatre or a nightclub. It's a matter of presentation, and then basking in the adulation and shock and awe and lust it inspires. She's almost a virgin, though she's never admit it. She doesn't do this for sex (though she'll accept anything the gentleman offers). It's arousing enough for her without the partner. Indeed, a single person might fail to satisfy her. She needs the spotlight. The attention. The glory.

Yet on stage now, moving around a mystified and mystifying gentleman, she feels lost and alone and scared. But more than anything else, she feels exposed.

Exposed.

Not in a good way.

It's as if she feels the extra set of eyes upon her, and they're a violation. An abomination. She tries to whip the audience into something of a frenzy just so she can feel them in her own chest, but she knows she's failing and there's nothing she can do to change that. The tide is being sucked out of her. A palpable sense of uneasiness spreads like wildfire through the audience, bouncing and reflecting off the stage.

Even the musician feels it–you can tell through the music–and she never feels anything.

Several people have left. There are a few empty tables, a few missing bodies in the loge. The exhibitionist never saw anyone leave, doesn't see anyone moving now, but she feels their absence and it makes her nauseous.

She needs to get off stage.

The next bit belong to the illusionist, but he's not at the side of the stage, he's not ready, he's not coming at all. Panic races through her. The music shifts. The music becomes what she is, frenetic and uncertain. Good. Fantastic. Gives her a chance to work it out, to move from one type of dance to another, to not just whip up the audience but to whip herself up and about and around and across the stage. Work up a sweat. Burn through the fear. She's still Stephanie, still the lost Russian runaway, but she's a later version, one with confidence, and experience behind her, a Stephanie willing and able–and also determined–to seize all that life offers.

She rips off the last bit of cloth, revealing everything, and throws herself dangerously into the rhythm. She moves and moves, dances as if she's wearing red shoes (she's barefoot, actually, which is only a touch uncomfortable on the wood stage). She barely sees through the perspiration stinging her eyes, but now she's got the audience. No one's even thinking about leaving. The gentleman still stares, his mouth hanging open, his eyes wide and boyish. He's nothing but an obstacle now, center stage but out of the spotlight, a prop to be used. When she gets close again, she whispers, "Take me backstage, my dear gentleman, and do what you will." She doesn't wait for an answer, doesn't even care.

It's more automatic now, routine, a tease perhaps for the audience but, this time, not for herself. And never for the gentleman.

This one time, he doesn't know how to respond.

24.

Memory is a tricky thing. Scents can trigger long dormant images; so can snippets of songs, or even a turn of phrase. As the gentleman's memories sieve mercilessly and completely, so much so that he doesn't remember who he is or why, the illusionist struggles to resurrect a deceased memory.

It's not easy. He had buried that memory deeply, beyond the standard six feet. Then, he'd erected an iron fence, spiked at the top, the bars chipped and rusted to better cut up your hands if you tried to climb. There's not only the blank headstone set above this memory, but also a footstone, and a granite covering. Underneath, the memory itself is not just encased in a coffin, but a cement burial vault designed to stand against the worst ravages of time and nature.

The illusionist is ill-suited to defeat his own defenses.

Yet there are attached memories, including the very idea that he escaped something. How does his arrival in this city translate into an evasion of fate? What pursued him so terribly? Until tonight, until he saw the man in the shadows, he hadn't even given it a thought.

The thought's there now. And he hasn't got time for it. His final act is next. Then, since they're skipping the contortionist's finale, the fat lady sings and it's all over.

(The fat lady also opens the show; her voice is that of a diva, her range covering a full eight octaves, which seems impossible and is at least improbable, but her lows are lower than the illusionist could ever manage and her highs reach into a realm heard only by canines and birds.)

The illusionist rolls his mirror toward the stage. The exhibitionist is out there, not strutting or sashaying as usual, but completely wild. Whipping her hair, thrusting her hips like weapons, her nipples like razors. The gentleman shrinks into himself, either unable or unwilling to move. She hangs off him, uses his body like grips and handholds to pull and push herself around. Whatever she's doing, it's rapturous, and infectious. You can hear it in the music. See it in the audience. Feel it on the air.

It increases the illusionist's anxiety, and weakens his efforts to revive dead memories.

The exhibitionist pauses, catching sight of him. She wears nothing but a mischievous grin. Reminds the illusionist of a predator about to strike. She returns immediately to the performance, but it's different now. In no time at all, the music's crescendo has built to an incredible height. It crashes to an end, leaving the exhibitionist perfectly posed, as if some Greek artisan discovered her shape in marble. Her body glistens with sweat. Only her panting breaths reveal life. Then the lights die.

She drags the gentleman behind her as she rushes off stage. She pauses at the illusionist's side, whispers, "I am so hot tonight."

"I saw."

Her hands crawl all over the illusionist, despite that he has a mirror to roll onstage. "I want you," she says. "Tonight. In that very same way you've always wanted me. Don't think I never noticed. Don't think I never cared. Tonight, tonight, I want you to perform your greatest tricks for me, illusionist. I want you fucking me tonight, all night, till you're sore and exhausted and unable to think, and even then I won't be done. Do you hear me, illusionist? Do you feel me?"

It's impossible not to feel her. She's pressed against him now, the gentleman discarded to the shadows. She gropes his face, his chest, his crotch, she leaves no part of him untouched that she can possibly reach in the moments between acts. His music's already started, but he's been derailed.

He hasn't dated anyone in years. He's slept with most of the cast (even the gentleman, once, as an exploration), but never the exhibitionist. She's a see-don't-touch kind of girl, always has been, yet she's now not merely offering but demanding. He can't help but react. As if her dance hadn't been arousing enough.

She's already gone off into the shadows. The show, being all important, trumps her desires–whatever brought them on. The illusionist recognizes this, sees the Grand Madame's face in his mind and hears the disappointment in her voice.

By the time light returns to the stage, the illusionist stands bedside his mirror with arms outstretched and a forced grin.

25.

The man in the shadows of the basement, watching the stage in his own mirror, also grins. But the image wavers; it doesn't respond well to reflective surfaces. No, he'll need to see this act from the audience.

26.

Bob has spent much of the show in the bathroom. When he finally emerges, he doesn't know what to do. The object of his infatuation has just finished her extraordinary dance; he missed the whole thing. His date, Ann, has basically dismissed him; they had seemed to be doing so well, too. He figures that's life in the big city, or even the small city. There'll be someone else. Somewhere. Still, he's sad, and doesn't wish to see any more.

So instead of returning to the theatre, he goes the other way down the hall, past the grand brass columns and huge paintings, over thick red carpet beyond the coat check and bathrooms and refreshment stand, past alcoves and locked doors, and very possibly into the heart of the Palais Royal. Very possibly into the heart of darkness. The heart of nowhere. He passes another man without a second glance, and wonders what he'll find.

27.

He didn't notice her backstage, and he certainly doesn't see her now. The girl sits to the side of the stage, at a table with a single small candle and a glass of whiskey over ice. Every night, she slips into the audience to watch the final acts—or more precisely, to watch the audience watching those final acts.

She tries to reclaim some of the familiar by following her routine, but already she's out of it. She's not watching random faces. She's not sizing anyone up, wondering who might or might not be a challenge, what she's interested in tasting tonight. Her eyes cannot leave the stranger, the man in the shadows, whom the Grand Madame surely had removed.

He's back.

No one else notices as he joins the audience. He sits at an abandoned table halfway between the doors and stage. He moves so fluidly, it's like he's part of the atmosphere.

There are some challenges the girl isn't willing to take on.

But at the same time, she realizes he'll change everything if she doesn't accept the challenge. But he'd done something to the contortionist, without touching her, without even seeing her, from the comfort of the shadows backstage. The girl isn't stupid; the girl fears him. She doesn't know much about fear. She's discovering that it impacts your motor control, prevents you from standing when you should stand, locks up your vocal chords when you should speak, staggers your movements and yet somehow sharpens your senses.

Fight or flight. She's got plenty of room for the latter, plenty of time, but she can't do it. It's not in her nature. Sure, she's felt fear, albeit rarely; but she's never been much of a runner. She's not about to start.

The illusionist has begun his act. First, he chooses a victim from the audience, oftentimes someone pretty, someone he might talk to after the show, someone with whom he might share a bottle of wine in his apartment upstairs.

Tonight, it's a woman sitting alone at a table for two.

"And who are you?" he asks.

Her voice betrays her nerves. "Ann."

"Please, everyone, a round of applause for Ann."

His voice is smoother than his words. Another man couldn't pull off such overused and tawdry language. They're show business lines, translated from the original tongues of his illusionist ancestors.

The man from the shadows does not applaud, gives not even a polite hint of encouragement. He's glancing again at his pocket watch.

The girl is not alone. Three kitties are in the theatre, other girls from Old Possum's Kitty Supplies, loyal to the Grand Madame—not mere courtesans (or harlots, if you prefer), but soldiers. Though there's no war, they are prepared. A day may come.

She doesn't see any of them, but that doesn't mean they can't see her. They're strong, and skilled, and stealthy. And surely they know who to watch. The girl is part of that army. She doesn't just dance at the Palais Royal. Her own arts are not limited to those of tantric and kama sutran origin.

The girl draws strength from her knowledge, her self-confidence, and her trust in her comrades. She rises from her chair. Finishes the whiskey in a gulp so as to further fortify herself, and steps toward the man from the shadows.

He rises, too, but not in answer to the girl's motion. He doesn't see her, doesn't look in her direction. His eyes are on the stage, where the illusionist has just transported Ann from the audience into the mirror and back onto the stage again.

28.

The man from the shadows is applauding more loudly than anyone else in the audience; indeed, after everyone else has fallen silent, the staccato of his successive, singular claps drowns even the violin.

The musician falls silent, perhaps for the first time throughout the performance. Ann has already returned to her seat. The illusionist stands there, staring, his eyes unsteady and uncertain.

"Bravo," the man says with his final clap. "Could you do it again, good man? Could you transport anyone from this audience?"

"Anyone," the illusionist says. Any other night, he would be certain.

"Amazing," the man says. "Absolutely stunning. One would think you studied with masters."

In fact, the illusionist has studied with masters.

"I wonder, however," the man says, "what you might do faced with, say, real magic? Not mere parlor tricks, not sleight of hand or other trickery, but honest, solid magic. Ah, but you don't even believe such magic exists, do you?"

"Magic," the illusionist says, pulling random words from the air because he doesn't trust himself to put together his own sentences, "is in the eye of the beholder."

"No," the man says. He's at the edge of the stage now, looking up. "That's beauty."

"I'm sorry," the girl says, suddenly beside him. "I'm going to have to ask you to leave."

29.

The illusionist watches from the stage. He's right up at the edge, looking down, not much further than arm's reach from the magician.

No mere man in the shadows, he is a magician. That much, the illusionist remembers. He also knows, now, the memory is buried too well to ever fully surface. Unless the magician chooses to tell, the illusionist will never know when or where they'd met, or why he had to flee off the map into a city so dark, so hidden, so lost as Midnight.

The magician turns to the girl, who is standing taller than she stands, showing more muscle than she has, and more courage than the illusionist would've imagined. She's always been gorgeous, in that mysterious, elicit, perilous way all the girls at Old Possum's have, a girl from whom you must ever protect your heart lest she decide it looks good on her mantle.

He's been in her room. He's seen the keepsakes from her conquests. He's seen the staggering remains of men who fell too deeply, gave up too much of themselves.

(Which is not to say she took anything from them. They gave willingly; they merely gave too much. The girl only accepts.)

She probably doesn't know she's protecting him–a stroke of fortune for the illusionist. The girl is protecting her theatre, her home, her family, and her way of life.

The magician only wants one person here.

Apparently, his patience doesn't stretch the length of a single show.

Quickly, the illusionist calculates; he's done at least three Halloween shows in this theatre, which means he's been here a while; as the magician said up front, what's another few minutes?

30.

Half the audience thinks this is still part of the show, and some have even seen the show before. Ever changing, is this burlesque. Some remember the soprano, or the clown, or the tango couple and the roses they tossed out into the audience. Some saw the illusionist's first tricks, which involved ropes and rings now stored in the basement. Some remember the costumer (a girl called Velvet) who had made the most elaborate outfits before stealing away one midsummer night.

Half the audience knows something's wrong. They recognize the magician, if only from nightmares. They sense the illusionist's fear, or the magician's malice, or the girl's claws. There are whispers: "We should go." "C'mon." "I think it's over."

They should know, no show ends at the Palais Royal without the fat lady, who even now stands off stage awaiting her shiny moment.

Rustling sweeps through the theatre. The musician sits at the harpsichord, violin resting on her knee. Twice, she almost picks up the instrument to add the proper soundtrack, but she doesn't want to calm an audience in danger, doesn't want to validate the magician's role.

The magician turns slowly to the girl, surprised to see her there, surprised to see her at all. "You?"

The girl's claws are real, and sharp, tiny blades she keeps in her belt. She holds one in each hand. She knows how to swipe, slice, and lunge–

and throw. They're not traditional weapons, but they are unforgiving.

The magician looks at her, and smiles, and shakes his head slowly. "I feel so unwanted," he says. He leans closer to the girl, whispers so no one else hears. "Do you like spiders?"

It's a loaded question. Because the knives in her hands aren't knives anymore, but spiders, thick hairy bodies and eight long legs and venom-dripping fangs which sink into her palms.

Intense burning pain is followed by a numbing cold. The girl staggers back, unable to lift her arms. The knives in her belt, also spiders, crawl under her clothes, down the flesh of her thighs and across her belly and the small of her back. Each fang digs into her skin like a knife. The venom is as potent as any poison she's ever mixed. She cannot speak, cannot move, can barely see her flesh charring around the bites.

The magician stands upright again. It's only been a moment. The spiders are knives again. Most clatter to the floor. A few are stuck in her skin. The poison spreads through the girl so quickly, she almost doesn't suffer.

"Now," the magician says, turning back to the illusionist. "Where were we? Ah, yes. Magic. Do you still claim to disbelieve, illusionist? Do you feel safe when you crawl beneath your covers at night?"

The illusionist's voice shakes and breaks. "I believe."

"Of course you do," the magician says. "Of course. Now. You cannot deny the evidence of your eyes, even eyes like yours that lie and cheat and steal."

"I don't..."

"You don't," the magician says. His grin has grown. "You stole something, illusionist. Something of mine."

The illusionist shakes his head, takes a step back. He doesn't know if he's telling the truth. "I've never stolen anything."

"Come now," the magician says. "When you were a child in Budapest, you mean to say you never stole a loaf of bread or an apple to stave off hunger?"

"I was never a child in Budapest," the illusionist says.

The magician shrugs. "My mistake. Bucharest. Tel Aviv. Cairo. I fail to see how it matters. I can see the things of which you are made, illusionist. Weak things, flimsy things, trickery and thievery. You know nothing else."

"I have nothing of yours," the illusionist says.

"No," the magician agrees. "You do not."

"Then what do you want?" the illusionist asks.

"Ah. Finally, to the point. I want to see what you've got in you. Behind the facades, underneath the deceit. You are an escape artist, are you not? No lock holds you, no cell, no chain or rope." The magician hops onto the stage with catlike grace. "What if I broke your thumbs, illusionist? Could you still escape?"

"If you mean to kill me," the illusionist says, "then kill me."

The magician's smile is as honest and broad as can be, because the illusionist still knows nothing. Less than nothing. If not for fear, the illusionist would crumble to the stage, would've dissolved long ago. He's held together by the barest of threads, and this saddens the magician. He's not a teacher, but sometimes he has to spell it out anyhow. "I do not mean to kill you, illusionist."

31.

The contortionist hears everything.

She's backstage, alone because everyone's running this way or that, and though the gentleman stands nearby staring out at the stage he doesn't count anymore.

She's lying on the couch beneath the window. It's not much of a window, but it allows air to pass, and the idea was to give the contortionist a chance to catch her breath.

She hasn't quite caught it.

She hears, but unlike the illusionist, she also understands.

The window's not large enough for a person to sneak in or out--not any normal person, anyhow. Her missing ribs now prove to be more than worth the sacrifice.

She slips out, feet first, slowly because she's got to bend with the narrowness of the alley. Alley is an overstatement, as there's only about a foot, maybe a foot and a half, between the Palais Royal and Old Possum's Kitty Supplies. Would've made more sense to share a wall, or to create an actual alley. Would've made more sense, too, not to let the magician back into the theatre.

She leaves much behind. Her diaries. Her clothes. She's in costume now, and will be quite the spectacle running through the city streets. So she'll slip into Old Possum's and wait it out there.

She bends inhumanly to get through the window. She shuffles up, climbing, hoping the walls don't lean any closer. She's already in danger of getting wedged between the two buildings. Bare bricks scrape her skin. Dust flutters about her. Night animals and birds and insects scuttle aside. She tries to ignore them. Concentrates instead on the heavens, which of course she cannot see. Focuses on ascending. She moves slowly. She has to go around bits of concrete and brick that jut too far from either building. She can rest, when she needs to, because she's in no danger of sliding back down. There's nothing smooth, and it's an effort to move in any direction.

She can't turn her head well enough to see how much further she has to climb. Doesn't matter. Eventually, she'll reach the top.

She still hears them, the magician and illusionist on stage, the restlessness in the audience, the breathless panting of the exhibitionist, the unfathomable depths of silence emanating from the gentleman.

32.

The exhibitionist bursts out of the backstage area and into the hall. Far back, away from the auditorium and coat check and ticket takers, away from the public eye but in a harsher light and a softer carpet. She's still naked, unable to catch her breath, reeling from something--a drug?-- that's infected her. She wants, needs, desires, requires, but insatiably. Unstoppably.

There's a man in the hall. Bob. From the audience. Earlier, she'd winked at him, captured a part of his heart though she hadn't realized it. She grips him by the shoulders, leans close and whispers, "What's wrong with me?"

Fever roils through her blood--not the good kind. Not the kind you dream of when imagining the woman of your dreams accosting you in some unfamiliar hallway.

"There's nothing wrong," he tells her. "You're wonderful the way you are."

"You don't know," she says, pushing him aside.

He merely looks at her. She goes nowhere, aware his eyes aren't crawling up and down her body but locked on her own eyes, the green irises and black pupils. Soul windows, they say.

"Not enough," she tells him, whispering still, afraid to raise her voice and attract unwanted attention. "If the eyes are the window, you can help me. You can help me, but you have to go through the door."

He blinks his confusion.

"If the eyes are the windows," she says, "then the door is the kiss."

She throws herself at him and kisses him, hard, deep, with all the power and fury and need she can muster, all the pain and longing and joy, every shred of her being. It's not enough to be seen; she needs to be known. There's no other way.

For her, the kiss lasts half of forever.

For Bob, the kiss lasts all of forever.

If you were to sculpt passion, capture it in marble, in its purest form, you would choose this moment. All their energy is on the lips and mouths and tongues. Everything else hangs loosely, haphazardly, moving part out of instinct but mostly by reflex.

When the exhibitionist pulls away, they're both breathless.

She wipes her mouth on the back of her hand. "Amazing."

Bob's mouth hangs open, the muscles of his jaw overworked and nearly useless.

"Now tell me," the exhibitionist says, though she feels calmer, more in control, "what's wrong with me?"

He shakes his head. For a moment, it seems he can't regain speech, but finally he says, "Don't lose track of who you are."

She grins. "No problem. Today, I'm Stephanie."

33.

Around the Palais Royal, there are three girls who, not part of the burlesque, have blades and poisons. They move through shadows in ways that would make the shadows themselves jealous. Unseen by anyone else, the Grand Madame, with a signal, orders their attack.

As far as the Grand Madame is concerned, the magician has declared war. He defies her, just by being in the theatre. He has killed one of her dear children. And he's unraveling every string that holds the burlesque together. The damage is irreparable. The theatre may not close permanently, but this particular show is at the end of its final performance.

The girls, kitties from Old Possum's, loyal not just to Old Possum himself but their Grand Madame, throw from three angles. Blades blur the air, cut through the spotlight, and strike the magician's back as feathers. They float gently to the stage.

The magician doesn't bother to turn. He sees all three in the illusionist's mirror. He decides to broaden his plan.

"You're this great escape artist," he says to the illusionist. "Escape."

Light flashes. The Grand Madame covers her eyes. Her kitties surge forward, toward the source, not an ounce of fear to share between them. The illusionist flinches, nothing more. The audience, as one, gasps.

(Except for Bob, still in the back hall with the exhibitionist.)

Outside, the contortionist shudders, the entire theatre wavers, but she's only just reached Old Possum's rooftop with her fingers. (The theatre stands taller.)

The kitties converge on the magician, but he's no longer there. Or he's only partly there, translucent, shimmering. They step back, confused, their knives slicing impotently through a mirage.

The illusionist appears in the mirror first, and the magician, then the stage and the kitties and the audience. The entire Palais Royal slips into the mirror, which is not actually another world, just a momentary place with the life expectancy of a thought and the substance of smoke.

The magician casts the kitties out before they can touch him.

"Escape," he says again to the illusionist.

And the illusionist does. He finds himself standing on the bare foundation of what was once the Palais Royal. Three kitties stand beside him. The contortionist dangles from the roof of the next building. The illusionist exhales, then closes his eyes and kneels beside the mirror. The magician remains inside, with the theatre.

Unseeing, the illusionist smiles.

The Grand Madame plunges one of her own blades into the magician's back. He was so surprised, he never heard her coming, never saw her, never knew the threat. He reaches out to the mirror as he folds to his knees, the blade buried deep between vertebrae, his spinal cord unraveling, his eyes glazing. His fingernails scratch the surface on both sides.

The musician strikes the harpsichord, starting a frantic, furious arrangement, calling on every musical talent she's ever had. "There's magic in music," she announces, though not everyone hears. "Hold on to the notes."

Those who are able, grasp what they can.

The cracks spread like spider webs. The magician spits a spell at the illusionist, but it bounces back, it explodes in his face, it shatters the mirror.

Shards rain to the ground in a torrent.

The basements remain. Otherwise, the theatre is gone. The harpsichord remains, and the musician, but the instrument's notes have soured and stretched and broke. Maybe half the people in the audience are scattered about in an irrational tangle.

Bob is gone, and the exhibitionist (Stephanie). The gentleman is gone, and also the Grand Madame, and the fat lady, and even Julia in her upstairs apartment.

The illusionist's eyes are closed, because he remembers what he stole from the magician. It didn't seem like much at the time. A mistake. One wrong door, and he sees—well, he's still not quite sure what he saw. Spellwork. The magician drawing calligraphy in the air with red hot charcoal over the bruised body of a girl.

The illusionist stole merely a glimpse.

The magician pursued him until he escaped to this city. Even Midnight was not far enough.

34.

The fat lady will not be robbed. She sings.

AFTERWORD

Pocketful of Smoke, Fistful of Glass was an opportunity to step back into the City of Night and explore parts only hinted at previously. It also creates connections. For instance, you'll find the Palais Royal next to Old Possum's Kitty Supplies, which had been seen, briefly and underground, in *Beneath Midnight* almost ten years earlier (next to *The Poppery*, where they make popcorn).

We get a taste of what the city offers, and what can happen here, and establish quite firmly that, while there may be a difference between magic and illusion, both are alive and at play in the City of Night.

The title is a play on smoke and mirrors, and a direct allusion to the magic contained within.

While the rest of this collection has already existed in a limited electronic way, I thought the printed version ought to have something extra, and this is it. One of my favorites. Yes, *Pocketful* also exists as a standalone novella in certain electronic markets, but it's seeing print for the first time here.

Did you note who had names and who were known only by titles? I had fun with that. No one's ever mentioned it. So now I mention it to you. I sometimes have reasons for the things I do, and sometimes those reasons are more whimsical than anything else.

I hope you found much whimsy, a touch of terror and delight, in this tale and in this collection. Thank you for joining me on this journey.

MIDNIGHT POETICS

There's a bar underground where all the poets hang. At midnight, a procession of eight or ten will get on stage to read their latest. It's a small stage, but no place for the timid. If you read something old, they'll throw coffee mugs until you retreat in a shower of ceramic. But they applaud magnificence, and celebrate even failed experiments.

They say Poe read "Eldorado" here before it saw print. They lie as often as he did.

This is not just a place for true poets, but also people suffering word disorders. Roger always speaks in iambic pentameter. Lillian rhymes. Marisol sits and watches and drinks shot after shot of cheap whiskey, but never says a word except when she's on stage. Harold works on his courage, and scribbles tiny phrases in the margins of well-worn notepads, but never seems to find the strength.

Maybe that's because, until tonight, no one's ever challenged him. "Go on," the girl says, the girl with kohl in her eyes and honey in her throat. "I dare you." A dare is never just a dare. It's a promise, a covenant, an unmistakable invitation.

Harold signs up for his chance to poeticize in front of friends and strangers and wordsmiths and cutthroats and one intoxicating beauty with smoky sapphire dust eyes.

Twelve others go before him. Tammy is chased off stage trying to mix words on her feet. Maria leaves half a dozen men in tears. So does Reginald. As usual, Christopher's words are brilliant and quickly forgotten. Tristan falters in a treatise on love. Andrea opens her heart. Mikhail recites something utterly incomprehensible, which does not make him clever. Janice reminds everyone of their last sunset. Nick cries—with rhythm and cadence. Martin loses his nerve. Kevin offends—not in a good way—and leaves the stage with ceramic-induced scratches. Claire steals everybody's breath for most of a minute.

On stage, the lights don't blind Harold. He had hoped not to see. The bar goes quiet, so that ice cubes clinking against glass is the only sound. He had hoped not to hear. No nervous whisperings ripple through the patrons, no fits of laughter or giggling or hiccups. No one coughs.

Harold starts.

> *Poetry is useless.*
> *Words cannot describe*
> *that which defies description.*
> *Images cannot be painted*
> *without your eyes.*
> *Love cannot be won*
> *by words you scribble.*
> *Take my hand,*
> *walk with me,*
> *and let's forget*
> *these silly metrics.*

It may not be stellar poetics, but the girl loves it. Hand in hand, she and Harold abandon the bar, the poets, and silly words with their rhythms and metrics.

MIDNIGHT STORMS

When rain falls on Midnight, it never stops. It comes in torrents, and rushes down the mountainsides in normally dry waterfalls. Lightning dances between the mountaintops, a dark, electric ballet. Thunder rumbles and roils until it's one ceaseless note so deep it hurts your teeth.

When rain falls on Midnight, it flows into storm water runoffs underground, weaving beneath subway tracks, through residential districts, around sewage lines and access tunnels and forgotten catacombs and dusty basements and subbasements and vaults.

Rain sluices off the rooftops, washing them clean, displacing secrets, upsetting crows' nests, disturbing an entire culture of roof dwellers. They hide in air conditioning ducts and canvas tents and, sometimes—sacrilege—seek shelter indoors.

Storms awaken emotions in even the stoniest of hearts. They encourage fear and inspire; they weaken the weak and embolden the strong. And storms—when perhaps the stars are improperly aligned, an incantation has been inadvertently or unadvisedly uttered—sometimes, under those kinds of circumstances, the sheer power of storm unleashes something.

Day and night, the City of Night burns with a million lights, tiny diamonds on the streets and in the windows. Streetlamps and headlights and urban Will-o-the-wisps, neon and fluorescent and halogen, and—except for during storms like this—the constellations. Sometimes the moon. Never the sun. The City of Night glows and sparkles and twinkles and burns. Ominously. Dreadfully. Beautifully.

The city between two mountains opens onto forest in the north, dense and ancient woodland filled with ghosts and gypsies and godlings. The storm clears dead limbs from the treetops, adds nobility to the streams, and feeds the monsters.

In the forest, something awakens.

It is old and huge and hungry. A million hearts beat within the city. A million voices entice and implore and invite. The creature has a million reasons to pull itself from the ground, from the depths, from the abysmal nightmares of wretches and sinners. When the beast breathes, Midnight trembles.

At the gate, which cannot properly be called a gate, a man alone stands and looks to the north. He feels the chill wind. Falling rain like ice picks pummel him. The city lights are at his back; he peers into the gloom. He sees what has awakened. He knows what it is. He has read books of prophecy, of apocalypse, of sulfuric deluges and demonic gales. He dares the old, huge, and hungry to come nearer to *his* city.

He breathes calmly.

When the storm finally subsides, the creature, the beast, the otherworldly behemoth, retreats back to its slumber.

At the gate, satisfied, the Wandering Reverend returns to Midnight.

MOTORCYCLE RACE

There's a ramp that leads straight out of Midnight, but it doesn't go far. It's four lanes wide and stops abruptly between two massive pillars. A brief bit of asphalt balances precariously on the next pillar, but it's not a jump for the weak of heart. Beyond that...well, they say if you can get that far, the road will open up before you.

At the base of those pillars, you'll find the twisted, shattered, burnt-out remnants of a dozen failed attempts.

The girl says, "You can't do it. No one can do it. Just come back with me, we'll drink whiskey, we'll make love. We can have a good, good life here."

The boy on the motorcycle grins wickedly and says, "The sun shines bright in Miami."

She's young, her hair is wild, the wind is fierce at the edge of the precipice.

He's young, he's brave, he's recklessly optimistic, and though he loves her with all his heart and soul, the Midnight Madness has got him in its grip.

Theirs is the type of love that inspires sonnets and tragic plays.

The boy revs the engine. It's a solid, sleek, crazy fast machine, it's excessively loud, it's sexy and dangerous—just like him.

"You only get one shot," she says.

"I only need one shot," he says.

Wind whips maniacally through the streets of Midnight. A raven lands on the very edge of the balanced bit. It caws once, either in challenge or warning.

The boy doesn't believe in omens.

The girl does.

He kisses her, one last time before he jumps, a hot, fierce, desperate kiss that ends abruptly. He revs the engine one more time.

"There's no turning back," he tells her.

"There's no turning back," she tells him.

She climbs onto the back of the bike, presses herself tight against him, thrills at the vibration of the machine as he guides it to the bottom of the ramp. She peers over his shoulder. You don't close your eyes for a trip like this.

He guns the engine. They climb the ramp, ripping through the wind, able to hear nothing over the roar of their hearts.

They leap. They hit the balanced bit—but uneasily, without balance. They are swallowed by Destiny.

ONE FOR SORROW

Seven!

Larry grins. That's a rare thing. He dangles his feet over the side of the roof, lets his eyes stray over the Fairgrounds, where there are no rooftops, and even through the Mirage, despite that the garden's also got a metro station.

Larry's not comfortable underground, and so much of Midnight, too much of Midnight, is made up of caverns and crevices and cracks and holes. On the rooftops, he can breathe. He can drink the rain when it comes.

And he can count birds.

That magpie, there, on the fire escape, proud of its black feathers and its white feathers, makes seven so far for the night, and the red light of dawn shall soon grace the mountaintops. Seven's wonderful. Mystical and magical. The number for releasing secrets.

Larry knows so many counting rhymes, he's lost count. Some involve fingers or thumbs, eggs, marbles, or aces. Many of the rhymes, maybe even most, agree with the Bible: seven is important. Many end at seven.

He has to be careful. When the new day starts, he must begin counting anew. It's always sad, starting with one, but since Larry cannot remember a night that ended with one, it's a brief bit of sad and he can handle it.

Larry he likes secrets. He loves mystery. If he ends the night at seven, that's the best kind of omen. He'd go down to the surface, to the streets, amid the cars and the noise and the chaos of all those damn people, to discover his secret. He'd go into the womb of the city, the tomb, the catacombs with their skulls and the sewers with their shit. He'd ask questions.

He practices, now, using a voice that scratches his throat. He says, "Hello," slow and uneasy, and then again with emphasis on the last syllable. He tries, "Hi," but it sounds like he's clearing his throat. He tries again. Still dusty and rough, like charcoal. He opens a canteen, the water canteen not the whiskey, wets his lips and his tongue, then takes a swallow. He says it again: "Hi." It sounds almost human, or at least a reasonable facsimile of what he thinks human sounds like. He's still grinning. He says, "My name is...Larry."

He's happy being Larry. He's always been Larry. He sometimes tries to imagine being someone else, but it never works right and often ends in panic.

Maybe this time—with his seven magpie omen guiding him to the asphalt and pavement—maybe this time the secret he'll uncover is the name of the woman who first called him Larry. It counts as a secret if you knew once but no longer.

Larry turns to the magpie perched beside to him, nearly delirious with joy and wonder and hope and fear, and says, "Hi." He says it before realizing dawn has yet to redden the mountaintops. He says it before realizing his count has changed.

Eight. No secrets for eight. He's not ready for eight. Larry's grin retreats, though he's not sad, not really. Maybe tomorrow he'll count only as high as seven.

ISABELLA

There's a hot young artist in Midnight named Isabella. She does these wild, nearly abstract things on huge canvasses. While painting, she wears a red dress and heels and a modest bit of gold jewelry, maybe earrings, maybe a necklace or a bracelet.

It's not the art so much as the spectacle. Her paintings are a performance. She sashays and struts and sways; she dances as she paints. She doesn't even see the audience. Sometimes she sings, too softly for anyone to make out the words, but her notes are precise and organic, and more than one man—more than one woman—has fallen either hopelessly or helplessly in love.

But Isabella doesn't care. She's all about the art. She's all about the moment. She was born in Barcelona, but you'll never hear her speak of that city or its wonders. The past is lost, abandoned and ignored, and with it all her sins, her lessons, her failings and her glories. She's twenty-two. She's got time for more of everything.

She inspires devotion and respect. When she's done with a piece, which may take days to complete, the people crowd around her; they want to touch her red hair, perhaps her hand for the briefest moment; they want to praise and please her and fulfill her every desire.

Isabella thanks them all, and always has time for everyone no matter how young or old or foolish. Worse still, she remembers you, and calls you by name the next time, and maybe that's why many Midnighters are so enamored with her.

On no particular Thursday night, after she has finished a blue and green canvas she calls "Mediterranean", she accepts the adulation and accolades, kisses the cheek of an old man, squeezes the hand of a young boy, and throws a wink at the girl too shy to approach her. The crowd disperses slowly, but inevitably, leaving Isabella a moment to see the fullness of her painting for the first time.

"Beautifully rendered," one last onlooker says. It's the mad preacher, the wise stranger, the freak who always wears black and stands outside the Fairgrounds judging you with his eyes; it's the Wandering

Reverend, and Isabella suddenly finds herself nervous. "It reminds me," the Wandering Reverend says, "of the flood." Then he wanders off to do whatever it is reverends do.

Isabella goes home. It's a nice place, spacious, bright—incredibly vibrant, in fact, for this City of Night. She keeps a friend there, a boy her own age, with his own definitions and expressions of art, but as yet nobody knows his name. She lingers in his embrace, and steals extra kisses, and then insists on bourbon.

"Tonight," Isabella says between glasses, "I received a visitation."

"Was it glorious?" the boy asks.

Isabella finishes another glass of bourbon and, in her heart, misses the *cava* of home, misses it though she has never missed it before. She says, "No, it was not glorious. It was far from glorious." And for the first time in a very long time, she wishes she could leave Midnight and go home.

THE DREAMER

Under the streets of Midnight, beneath the subways and sewers, hidden from the mapped apartments and known hovels and illicit meeting places, deeper still than any of that, a woman wears chains.

Though thin, the chains are strong. They bind her wrists together and, with little leeway, bind her to the floor. She has a bed, if you would call it that, more of a cot, the canvas of which is hard, aged, and unforgiving. The walls are brick, old, the mortar crumbling, but though not one day goes by in which she doesn't pick at the pieces—which by some alchemical reaction transmute into dust and thereby fill her lungs—the pins that hold the chains refuse to come loose, no door or window lets itself be known, no light penetrates the dark.

Pipes run across the roof, too high for her to touch; she hears water move through them, and drinks the copper-tinged condensation or drippings or leaks.

She is bone thin and angelic pale, she has never spoken a word and, if she has ever heard any spoken, didn't know them. The pipes knock, distant rumblings echo in her chamber; she hears hints and suggestions of all manner of incomprehensible noises.

She doesn't remember who imprisoned her here or why. She doesn't know that he's dead, or even that there's anyone anywhere in the world besides herself. She doesn't know if her eyes would work, or what they are, as she only sees clouds of black wafting through smoky darkness. She's weak and fragile—like porcelain, like crystal, though she doesn't know these things. She might not be real, nothing more than a ghost, a lingering phantom, the briefest of memories. Her essence may belong to someone long since gone.

Ah, but her dreams. Shall I tell you of her dreams?

She dreams of sunlight so bright it washes everything out, it nearly blinds you, it makes every color seem simultaneously pale and vibrant.

She dreams of music, notes and chords strung together with such complexity they require mathematical geniuses to comprehend.

She dreams of sand between her toes, between her fingers, cinnamon in tint and so incredibly soft, on dunes the size of mountains stretching infinitely to every horizon.

She dreams of snow, delicate and cold and temporary, always drifting easily, sleepily, effortlessly. Flakes touch her skin, kiss her flesh, then melt away.

She dreams of waterfalls, gentle streams, raindrops on puddles, icicles melting off the needles of gigantic pine trees.

She dreams of sapphires and whiskey and sharp city edges.

She dreams of you, you, breaking into her brick cell, releasing her from chains that are in fact jewels, releasing her from the darkness and the false silence and the ceaseless waiting. She dreams of your fingers touching her hair, your breath on her throat, your nonsensical words whispered delicately into her ears.

Oh, but how she dreams.

AFTERWORD

6 Nights of Midnight was an event originally appearing at DarkFluidity in October, 2009, in which I wrote six micro-stories in six days to introduce readers to the depths, the mysteries, and the characters of Midnight.

Leading up to the 2011 publication of my novel, *Once Upon a Time in Midnight*, I did another series.

The six here are selected from both. You can find the rest at my website, www.darkfluidity.com.

profile:

john urbancik

profile:

John
Kirkpatrick

I'm sitting with John Urbancik at a Panera's where he's sopping up clam chowder with a piece of warm bread. He tells me he didn't eat soup until a woman in Maine made him a bowl of clam chowder. I tell him I don't care.

It's going to be that kind of interview.

"I started writing young," he says. "I made up stories about the Peanut Butter Planet and the Jelly Planet, and their enemies, the Bread Planets."

"Were you abused as a child?" I ask.

He looks puzzled. He says no. I can't imagine how else to explain Bread Planets.

He grew up in New York, in the borough of Queens until he was seven, then the middle of Long Island. His father, who was at one point a bread man, and who also drove black cabs through New York City nights, also worked at an off-set printer and sometimes brought home vast amounts of unusual paper. John once traded Hulk paper for Superman pens with another kid at school.

"So you've always had a bit of an obsession with paper and ink?" I ask.

He glances wistfully out the window and says, "You'd think that, wouldn't you?"

He can be frustrating to talk with. He can be evasive and sarcastic, and you can never be sure if there's any truth in his words.

"I haven't lied to you yet," he tells me before flashing one of those famous wicked grins. You wouldn't expect that sort of thing to carry so well into real life.

He reminds me he's a writer, so he should drink more whiskey than he does. He doesn't drink coffee. Or tea. Or much of anything, really, except water and wine. I tell him that sounds boring. He grins again. "I guess you could say that."

But you can't. Not if you're honest. John Urbancik may be quiet and unassuming, he may watch more than he is watched, he may consciously shun a spotlight he consciously craves, but you cannot call him boring.

It's true, he never served in the military, never ran messages for the mob, and never spent a night in jail or prison or as a hostage during a bank heist gone wrong. But it's also true that he's lived 10,000 miles from the place of his birth; he's been in the ocean with dolphins, sharks, and barracuda; and he makes the world's best baked potato.

"I've never wrestled alligators," he tells me. But he lived in Australia. They have crocodiles.

"My first novel was *Star Wars*," he tells me. He pauses. "A bad version of *Star Wars*, anyway." He wrote it in seventh grade. He was encouraged by a science teacher. "Actually," he adds, "I had a few good teachers." In fourth grade, Mr. Hogan introduce him to Charlie's chocolate factory, James' giant peach, and a fourth grade nothing. In fifth grade, Mr. Schwab was one of the first teachers on earth to bring a computer into the classroom. This was the 70's.

"In college, one professor told me if I kept writing like this, I'd make a shitload of money." He pauses again. "She lied."

I caught up with John a few days later at his home. His office is a mess of papers, books, pens, discs, more books, framed photographs, maps of seemingly random cities, a litter of Moleskines and other notepads, and a few more books. He's proud and embarrassed at the same time. That's the kind of grin he's flashing.

"My first published novel," he tells me, "was about a gargoyle."

I tell him to tell me something I don't know.

"There's a sequel planned," he says. "I may write it." He glances at his wrist. He wears no watch (just like an angel he wrote about). "I may write it in eight years."

Eight years?

He shrugs.

I ask about childhood influences and literary influences. He gets a little cocky. He says, "I thought you were planning to challenge me."

I remind him he's a photographer as well as a writer. "I think visually," he says. "I write visually. I see every scene as a great big movie in my head." His visuals have included gothic cathedrals, dark mountains, an underground Paris, the Amazon, Sydney, and the surface of the moon.

"I learned description from Anne Rice," he says. "But also over-description. I learned color from Tanith Lee."

Color?

He assures me it's important.

"I think too much, so sometimes I write too much. But sometimes I move too fast. Sometimes I leave out things I think are obvious because, well…they seem rather obvious to me. But I bring a specific set of knowledge and experience and bias to the words I write, and I have to remember not everyone's going to share in that knowledge and experience."

I remind him I do. He's not impressed.

John Urbancik is a man who likes to challenge himself. When no deadlines are imposed externally, he creates them. His first attempt at a Novel Dare — writing a novel in one month, years before NaNoWriMo was a thing — was eventually completely rewritten and published as his second novel, *Breath of the Moon*. What does he think of that book today? "A beautiful failure. I wasn't ready to write that one the first time, and I'm not sure I was ready the second time." It was too fantasy-based for a horror crowd, too much horror for a fantasy audience, but John's never been good at coloring inside the lines.

"Genres are great," he says, "except that they're limiting, they're short-sighted, and more often than not, they're wrong."

I ask what he prefers to write. "A woman once told me, after reading an unpublished story, that I wrote New-Age Gothic Erotica, and I loved that label. It worked for me. The next time I sat down, I tried to write a New-Age Gothic Erotica tale." He grins again, dammit. "I wrote nothing."

I tell him I don't think that's a real genre. He ignores me. "I wrote a story once I thought of as High-Key Noir. I'm not sure I could've done that on purpose." I ask how many genres he writes in.

"All of them."

When we talk about his work ethic, John admits he doesn't write as much as he should. There are always other things that need to be done, friends and bars and concerts and adventures, and he feels guilty when he misses them. Yet when he's out there in the real world, doing those very things, he feels like he should be writing. It's a catch-22. What do you write about if you haven't lived? If you're so busy living, when do you make time to write? "Balance," he says.

I'm not sure he's answered my question. At this point, I'm not exactly sure what I asked.

He's always working, even when he's not. Everything if fodder for story. He has books planned that aren't fiction. He has ideas and visions he doesn't yet know how to make real. "Life," he says, "is a learning process." I thank him for that and suggest he get a job writing for fortune cookies.

"I'm always trying to push beyond what I've done. I look at things differently, even the normal and expected things. Especially the expected things." Like in his story about the ghost of a woman living downstairs, or his belief no vampires live in his city of Midnight where they would never have to fear the sun.

He's held a variety of jobs in the past, everything from newspaper delivery to maintenance at a publishing company, real estate appraisal, customer service, gas station attendant, burger flipper, and vacuum cleaner salesman. What do all these things have in common? "Day jobs," he says. "Fodder."

We're back to that. Everything ends up in a book. He goes out to eat fondue, and the next day he's writing a scene in which vampires are having their own version of fondue. He moves to Australia, and suddenly all his stories take place in Sydney. He rides in a subway, he writes a scene set under a city. He snorkels off the coast of some Caribbean island, and a week later he's writing a tale set in Atlantis.

Somehow, despite a lengthy interview process, despite the most in-depth research a person can do on a subject, despite conversations with members of his family, former lovers, victims, and fans, I'm not sure I learned anything. His imagination is absurd and expansive, his ambition is high and his drive is strong. He listens to music when he writes prose but not when he writes poetry, and his tastes are eclectic yet typical of him. Indeed, he's not typical of anything except himself. He's not a typical man, not a typical adventurer, not a typical photographer, and not a typical writer. He's quiet, but if you do manage to get him talking, good luck shutting him up. He wants to drive a faster car and visit eight continents (ask him yourself) and climb Kilimanjaro before the glaciers are gone. He wants to write more stories and create more books, and those things aren't necessarily the same. He wants to do things he's never done. It's all fodder for story. Everything he does makes up who he is, and everything he is ends up in his words.

My conclusion: you only learn about the real John Urbancik by reading him.

ALSO BY JOHN URBANCIK

NOVELS
Sins of Blood and Stone
Breath of the Moon
Once Upon a Time in Midnight
DarkWalker

NOVELLAS
A Game of Colors
The Rise and Fall of Babylon (with Brian Keene)
Wings of the Butterfly
House of Shadow and Ash
Necropolis
Quicksilver
Beneath Midnight
Zombies vs. Aliens vs. Robots vs. Cowboys vs. Ninja vs. Investment
Bankers vs. Green Berets
Colette and the Tiger

COLLECTIONS
Shadows, Legends & Secrets
Sound and Vision

INKSTAINS

www.ingramcontent.com/pod-product-compliance
Lightning Source LLC
Chambersburg PA
CBHW072010020726
47501CB00006B/1752